RIVERS

Center Point
Large Print

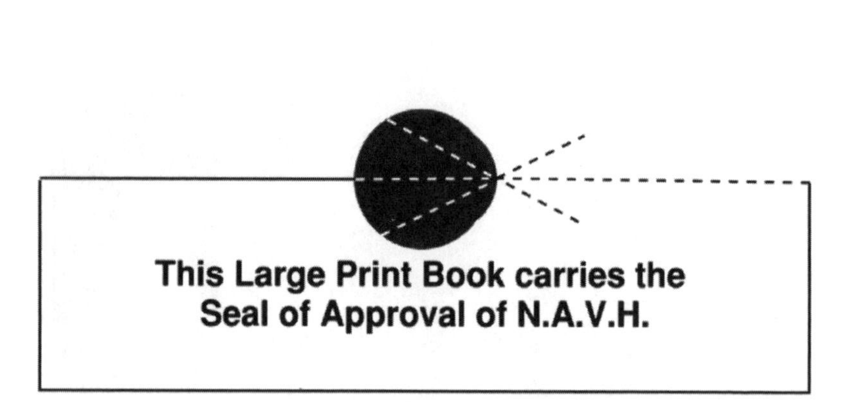
This Large Print Book carries the
Seal of Approval of N.A.V.H.

RIVERS

Michael
Farris Smith

CENTER POINT LARGE PRINT
THORNDIKE, MAINE

This Center Point Large Print edition is published in the year 2014 by arrangement with Simon & Schuster, Inc.

The text of this Large Print edition is unabridged.
In other aspects, this book may vary
from the original edition.
Printed in the United States of America
on permanent paper.
Set in 16-point Times New Roman type.

ISBN: 978-1-62899-001-0

Library of Congress Cataloging-in-Publication Data

Smith, Michael F. (Fiction writer)
Rivers / Michael Farris Smith. — Center Point Large Print edition.
pages ; cm.
ISBN 978-1-62899-001-0 (library binding : alk. paper)
1. Wilderness survival—Fiction. 2. Mississippi—Fiction.
3. Large type books. I. Title.
PS3619.M592234R58 2014
813′.6—dc23

2013038568

In memory of my grandfather,
the Keeper of the Place

When neither sun nor stars appeared for many days and the storm continued raging, we finally gave up all hope of being saved.

—Acts 27:20

Solitude produces originality, bold and astonishing beauty, poetry. But solitude also produces perverseness, the disproportionate, the absurd and the forbidden.

—Thomas Mann, *Death in Venice*

1

1

It had been raining for weeks. Maybe months. He had forgotten the last day that it hadn't rained, when the storms gave way to the pale blue of the Gulf sky, when the birds flew and the clouds were white and the sunshine glistened across the drenched land. It rained now, a straight rain, not the diagonal, attacking rain, and it seemed that the last of the gusts had moved on sometime during the night and he wanted to get out. Had to get out of the house, away from the wobbling light of the kerosene lamp, away from the worn deck of cards, away from the paperbacks, away from the radio that hardly ever picked up a signal anymore, away from her voice that he heard in his sleep and heard through the storms and heard whispering from all corners of the short brick house. It rained hard and the early, early morning was black but he had to get out.

He stood from the cot and stretched his arms over his head and felt his way across the room in the faint lamplight. He slept in the front room of the house. The same room of the house where he cooked and read and changed clothes and did everything but relieve himself, which he did outside next to where two pines had fallen in a cross. He wore long johns and a sweatshirt and he put on jeans and a flannel shirt over them. When he was dressed, he walked into the kitchen and took a bottle of water from a cooler that sat where the refrigerator used to be and he drank half in one take and then put the bottle back into the cooler. He picked up a flashlight from the kitchen counter and he walked back into the front room and went to a closet in the corner. He shined the light first on the .22 rifle and then on the sawed-off double-barrel shotgun and he chose the shotgun. On the floor was a box of shells and he opened it up and there were only two left and he loaded them.

He turned and looked at the dog, curled up on a filthy towel in the corner of the kitchen.

"Don't worry," he said. "I ain't even asking you."

The rubber boots were next to the cot and he pulled them on, picked up a sock hat and the heavy-duty raincoat from the floor and put them on, and then he walked to the front door, opened it, and was greeted by the roar of the rain. The cool air rushed on him and the anxiety of the walls inside disappeared into the wet, dark night. He stepped out under the porch and then went around the side of the house, hundreds of tap tap taps on his hood and water to his ankles and the flash-light pointed out in front, the silver streaks racing across the yellow beam.

Around the back of the house, Habana

whinnied. He opened the door to what had once been a family room and was barely able to avoid the horse as she raced out into the back field. She ran small circles, Cohen holding the light on her and her steps high in the moist land and her neck and head shaking off the rain but her own anxiety being set free in the downpour. He let her be and he stepped inside and took the saddle from the ceramic-tiled floor and once she had run it out, he whistled and she came over to him and he saddled her.

With the sawed-off shotgun under his arm, he led the horse down the sloppy driveway to the sloppy road and they rode half a mile west. He rode Habana carefully in the storm, the single beam out before them, but he knew the route. They moved around trees that had fallen years ago and trees that had fallen months ago and trees that had fallen weeks ago. Back off the road, abandoned houses sat quietly, lined by barbed-wire fences brought down by the fallen trees or the wild ivy or both. After an hour or more, they came to the fence row that at one time had been cleared all the way to the sand in order to lay pipe or cable or something that was supposed to help lift them from their knees but that had been abandoned like everything else.

The rain came stronger as he turned the horse south and they splashed through the brush and mud. There had once stood an electrical pole every hundred yards but only half of them remained upright and the lines that linked them together had been rolled up onto giant spools and taken away. Habana buckled several times in softer spots but fought on and in a few miles they came to the clearing and there was only ocean in front of them and beach to the east and to the west. He shined the light down on her front legs and they were thick with mud and he told her she did good and he stroked the side of her wet neck. They stood still in the rain and it washed them clean.

He turned off the light. Blended with the sound of the storm was the sound of the wash against the shore, the tumble of the whitecaps. A cold wind blew in off the water and he pushed the hood from his head and felt the wind and rain on his face and leaned his head back and felt it around his neck and ears and it was in those moments that he could feel her still there. Still there when there was only the dark and the sounds of what she had loved. He closed his eyes and let the rain soak into him and she was there at the edge of the water, the salty foam rushing around her ankles and her hair across her face and her shoulders red from the sun. He let himself fall back and he lay stretched across the horse, his arms flailing to the sides, the barrel of the shotgun pointing down toward the wet sand and the flashlight dangling from his fingertips. The rhythm of the waves and the crash of the rain and the solitude and the big black world around him and it was in these moments that he felt her there.

"Elisa," he said.

He sat back up in the saddle and pulled on his hood. He looked out across the dark ocean and listened and he thought that he heard her. Always thought he heard her no matter how hard the wind blew or how hard the rain fell.

He listened, tried to feel her in the push of the waves.

Thunder roared out across the Gulf and then far off to the west a string of lightning turned the black to gray for an instant. And the rain came on. Twice what it had been when they left the house. Habana reared her head and snorted the water from her nostrils. The ocean pushed high across what was left of the beach and the thunder bellowed again and Cohen raised the shotgun and fired out into the Gulf as if this world around him were something that could be held at bay by the threat of a bright orange blast. Habana reared with the sound of the shotgun and Cohen dropped the flashlight and got hold of her mane and she leaped forward a little but then steadied. He patted her. Talked to her. Told her, "It's okay. It's okay."

When she was still, he got down and felt around for the flashlight, and then he mounted again. He turned the flashlight on, then off, and he turned Habana and they started back.

“It’s getting worse,” he said to Habana, but the words were lost under it all.

Cohen stood at the kitchen window with a cup of coffee. The dog, a shaggy black-and-white shepherd-looking thing, stood beside him and chewed beef jerky. Cohen stared at the pile of lumber, switching the coffee cup from hand to hand, trying to bring himself into the day. The morning was a heavy gray and the rain had eased some. Maybe enough for Charlie, he thought. The pile of two-by-fours and two-by-sixes was so wet that he figured he could pick one up and simply fold it end over end. The grass and weeds grew high around the lumber as it had been sitting there for years. He sipped the coffee, looked away from the lumber pile and over to the concrete slab that stretched out from the back of the house. The last frame he had built, months ago, was in a splintered mess in the back field. Almost got to the last wall before another one came and lifted and carried it away. Twice he had gotten two walls done. Twice more he had gotten to the third. He had never gotten to the fourth before it was destroyed.

It wasn’t going to be a big room. She won’t need a big one for a while, Elisa said. Then you can build us a big house with rooms like concert halls. With whose money, he had wanted to know. She shrugged and said we’ll worry about that then. So it was going to be an average room, built onto an average house, protected by the same blond brick as the rest of the low-ceilinged ranch-style house. An average room for what they expected to be a much more than average little girl. Her place to sleep, and play, and grow. Four years ago the foundation had been poured, before it was impossible to pour a foundation, before it was impossible to imagine such things as building a room onto your house.

Now all it did was rain. Before the storm. During the storm. After the storm. Difficult to tell when one hurricane ended and the next one began.

He sipped the coffee and then lit a cigarette.

Goshdamn wood will never dry out, he thought. And he had thought and thought of ways to frame a room with wet wood, onto a wet slab, that would stand against hurricane-force winds, but he hadn't made it there yet. Unless God changed His laws, he wasn't going to ever get there. He scratched at his beard. Drank the last of the coffee. Watched out the window and smoked the cigarette. Then he decided to go and see if Charlie was around.

He climbed on a chair in the kitchen and moved away a water-stained ceiling tile, reached his hand up into the hole, and took down a cigar box. He opened the box and there was a stack of cash and he took out four hundred-dollar bills and he folded and stuck them in the front pocket of his jeans. After he put the box away and set the ceiling tile back in place, he picked up the radio from the kitchen counter, turned it on, and listened with his ear close to the speaker, the distant voice of a man overrun by clouds of static. He turned it off, and then he walked over to the cot and picked up the raincoat and sock hat and put them on and then he walked over to the closet. He chose the sawed-off shotgun over the .22, kicked at the empty box of shotgun shells, and then made sure the one and only shell was still in the chamber. The dog crossed the room and stood at his side and followed him to the door but stopped there.

"I'll leave the door open for you," Cohen said and the dog looked up at him, out at the rain, then went back inside.

He went out to the Jeep and sat down behind the wheel and set the shotgun on the passenger seat. He had drilled holes in the floorboard to keep the water from puddling, and an overflowing rain gauge was tied to the roll bar. The Jeep cranked and then he drove across the front yard toward the muddy gravel road, leaving tire tracks in the earth.

At the end of the road, he turned onto the two-lane highway that connected him to the busted interstate running parallel to the water. The sky was a lighter gray to the west, but far off in the southeast was a gathering of pillow-like clouds.

He turned onto the highway and drove along with cold rain against him. At a lower stretch of road, he slowed because of the water and drove on with his eyes far ahead to where the road showed itself again and he aimed for the higher ground, hoping he would remain on the asphalt that he couldn't see beneath the muddy water. He made it through the water and then after several miles he came to a crossroads with an old gas station where he used to buy boiled peanuts from an old man who sat on the tailgate of his truck in the parking lot. Past the crossroads he came to a small community and he slowed and looked at the remaining houses and stores lining the highway, wondered if there were people somewhere back in there, back in the faceless gray buildings that seemed to be disappearing, as if they were slowly flaking away and sinking into the earth. Even so, he felt like somebody was watching him. Always felt like somebody was watching him when he made his way through one of these ghost towns.

There was a beautiful sadness to it all that he couldn't explain. It was a sentiment he had tried to ignore, but it had seeped into him and remained, some kind of grave nostalgia for the catastrophes and the way of life that once had been. As a boy he had ridden with his father, and his father would point out the buildings and houses he had framed. Seemed like he had worked on the entire coast-line. Gulfport, Biloxi, Ocean

Springs, Moss Point. Didn't matter where they were, what road they were on, his father was always pointing and saying put that one up. Put that one up. Worked on that one there. Put that one up. And Cohen sensed the pride in his father's voice. Felt his own pride in his old man and his rough hands and what he did with them. His father seemed magical. During the day erecting houses and buildings along the coast and in the evenings feeding cows and bush-hogging the place and in the night sitting in his chair and sipping a drink and walking outside to smoke and talking to Cohen like he was a little man and not a little boy and Cohen wanting to be like him. He had always believed that one day he would ride around with his own children and then grandchildren and he would point out of the window and say put that one up. Did that one over there. Put that one up. And he had been like his father. He had put some of them up. But there were no children to show them to, and even if there were, what he had put up was now down and all he could say was that's where one used to be. Put one up over there that's gone. Used to be one right over there. Whenever he went out in the Jeep, he looked around at the concrete foundations, at the splintered remains, at the heaps of debris, at the places where his work once stood, and there was sadness, and despair, and awe. And he wondered what his father would say if he had lived to see his work stripped bare. He wondered how his father would feel now to have his work gone. Simply not there. Removed by the wind and the rain. Removed with violence. Removed without prejudice.

As if it had never been.

2

It had been 613 days since the declaration of the Line, a geographical boundary drawn ninety miles north of the coastline from the Texas-Louisiana border across the Mississippi coast to Alabama. A geographical boundary that said, We give up. The storms can have it. No more rebuilding and no more reconstruction. The declaration came after several years of catastrophic hurricanes and a climate shift suggested that there was an infinite trail of storms to come and the Line said we give up. During those 613 days, there had been no letup in the consistency and ferocity of the storms. Recent months had seen a turn for the worse, something few thought possible.

Those that decided to stay had decided to stay at their own risk. There was no law. No service. No offering. No protection. Residents had been given a month's notice that the Line was coming and a mandatory evacuation order had been decreed and help was offered until the deadline and then you were on your own if you stayed behind. The

Line had been drawn and everything below was considered primitive until the hurricanes stopped and no one knew if that day was ever coming.

Left to itself, the region below the Line had become like some untamed natural world of an undiscovered land. The animals roamed without fear. Armies of red and gray squirrels and choruses of birds. Deer grazing in the interstate medians and packs of raccoons and possums living in garages until they were blown away, then moving on to another dwelling that was now welcome to them. Honeysuckle vines bunched together and azaleas bloomed like pink jungles with the warmer temperatures of the spring. The lemony scent of the sprawling magnolias wafted in the air like perfume.

The kudzu had begun to creep like some green, smothering carpet, taking over roads and bridges. Finding its way up and around chimneys and covering rail lines. Swallowing barns and houses. Sneaking across parking lots and wrapping itself around the trunks of trees and covering road signs. The constant flooding and drying out and temperature swings had split the asphalt of parking lots and roadways, the separations becoming the refuge of rats and skinny dogs. Chunks of beach had disappeared as if scooped out by a giant spoon, leaving the flat waters of a lagoon where people used to sit with their feet in the sand and drink beer from cold glasses and eat shrimp from a bed of ice served in a silver bowl.

This was Cohen's world as he navigated the Jeep carefully through the rain and the debris.

He came to where the highway met the interstate, and standing on the side of the road were a teenage boy and girl. A thin white boy, his hair wet and stuck to his head, and a dark-skinned girl with long black hair under a baseball hat. The boy wore a letter jacket with an LB on the chest and the girl wore a tan overcoat much too long and dragging the ground. They were soaked. She had her arm around the back of his neck and she limped along with his support. Cohen moved over to the side of the road opposite them and he watched them as he passed but he didn't slow down as the boy called out to him. Hey or Help or Stop. He didn't make it out and he looked in the mirror and they turned and watched him driving away and the boy raised his hand and motioned for Cohen to come back.

He drove along the ragged remains of Highway 90. Keeping it slow. A sign read Gulfport 5. The once busy highway now littered with sand and driftwood and much closer to the water than it used to be. Along the highway, the antebellum homes were long gone, the first to go in the earliest and most violent of the storms, and splintered marinas floated in the water like broken toys. A pier where he had stood in a black suit with Elisa in her white dress, holding her white flowers, was nothing but a random cluster of stumps sticking out of the water. Some lampposts stood and some leaned and some lay across the interstate and he bounced over these as if they were dead logs. He looked out onto the beach and noticed tire tracks in the wet sand and he reached over and took the shotgun and held it in his lap.

A few miles on and he saw what he had hoped for. Despite the rain, the U-Haul truck was there, off the interstate and in the parking lot next to the charred remains of the Grand Casino that was still standing, though crippled. Black streaks stretched out of the window frames and stained the orange stucco. The roof gone and the floors caved in. A small gathering of people stood at the back end of the truck, half with their shoulders slumped and jackets pulled over their heads. The other half simply took it.

Cohen drove up and stopped the Jeep and the back of the U-Haul was open and Charlie was standing in the back pointing out something to a heavyset man wearing a flannel shirt that was too small and revealed the beginnings of his belly. Outside of the truck stood Charlie's muscle—four broad-shouldered guys in black hats and black pants and black jackets with automatic weapons slung over their shoulders. If they knew it was raining, they didn't acknowledge it as they stood like watchdogs. While Charlie bartered with the man in the back of the U-Haul, the muscle watched those who were waiting their turn as if they were capable of an overthrow. But of the twenty or so gathered, none of them appeared capable of much more than hopefully getting back to wherever it was they came from. All men. Unshaved and dirty and with sunken faces but not the menacing faces of power. Some stood with bicycles. One had a warped guitar on his back. A few more stood in a circle and tried to light cigarettes while pointing at an old Chevrolet truck that must have belonged to one of them. A couple of other trucks off to the side. Another man, an older, hunched man, stood a few feet away from the back of the U-Haul, next in line, and he wore a sign draped around his neck made of plywood that read THE END IS NEAR. But NEAR had been crossed out, and written underneath was HERE and all the words were streaked.

Cohen put the shotgun back underneath the seat as it wasn't allowed. He then got out of the Jeep and pushed back his hood, took off his sock hat and left it on the seat. He rubbed at the hair stuck down on his head and then took the empty gas cans from the backseat and he walked over to where the other men stood in a staggered line.

He watched Charlie. The same old Charlie. Much had changed but not him. He was the cow trader, the horse trader, the guy who sold used cars and used tractors or whatever else he could scare up right out in his front yard. No wife to complain about killing the grass. Just Charlie and his land and his barn and his storage shed and his knack for hustling a dollar. Cohen had sat between his father and Charlie on the bench seat of the truck. Both windows cracked. His father driving and smoking with his left hand. Charlie's arm propped on the door and smoking with his right hand. This was how they rode up to Wiggins to the sale, the trailer hitched to the pickup, sometimes getting rid of cows, sometimes buying. Sometimes bringing home a horse. Always looking for something better than what they already had, the haggle the most anticipated moment of the day. They would ride up to Wiggins and pull into the big gravel parking lot filled with more trucks and more trailers, and his father and Charlie would toss their cigarettes and tuck their pants in their boots and tug at their belts and light another cigarette. Let me have one, Cohen would say each time. Hell no, his father would say. Let him have one, Charlie would argue. He ain't but ten, Charlie. And the next year his father's answer would be, He ain't but eleven, Charlie. And so on until Cohen was big enough to find his own cigarettes elsewhere but it was still fun to ask. He would walk with the men across the parking lot toward the giant metal-roof building, his father and Charlie waving and making small talk to the other men who all seemed to walk at the same lethargic pace, as if they were in slow motion or maybe some type of pain. They walked slowly and kinda crooked, smoked slowly, spoke to one another in half sentences. Cohen watched and listened and sometimes felt like he was in one of those black-and-white westerns his father used to watch as he mingled with the rough-faced cow traders of southeast Mississippi.

He watched Charlie now. His pants still tucked in his boots. Still hustling for a dollar. Still the man you needed to see.

"I told you, I ain't got no power cords today. You gonna have to wait till next time," Charlie was saying to the heavyset man, who looked at him dumbfounded. Charlie wore his glasses on top of his head, and his face had the wear of a man who had worked outside his entire life.

"What about right back there in that box?" the large man asked and pointed.

"Are you goddamn deaf?"

"Naw I ain't deaf but I know you got some. You got some every time."

"I got some every time when I leave out, but this ain't the only place I stop. I had em when I left out this time but sold em all before I got here. Hell, it's a wonder I got anything by the time I get way down here. You understand that?"

The man shook his head. Tugged at the bottom of his shirt.

"You want something else?" Charlie asked, poking his head toward the man.

“Gimme some of them lanterns and some of them batteries.”

“What is some?”

“Three.”

“Three lanterns or three batteries?”

“Three lanterns and enough batteries for all of them and then some more. Come on, Charlie.”

“Don’t come on me. It ain’t that hard to tell me exactly what you want the first time. I ain’t got all day.”

Charlie reached over into a box filled with camping lanterns and he lifted out three and handed them to the man. Then he took a plastic bag from his back pocket and reached into another box and filled the bag with D batteries. He gave the man the bag and then he counted on his fingers and mumbled to himself. “Fifty dollars,” he said.

“Jesus,” said the man.

“I meant eighty.”

“Fifty’s fine. Don’t piss on me.”

The man set down the plastic bag and unbuttoned his shirt pocket and took out two poker chips and held them out.

“What in God’s lovin name is that?” Charlie said and he shook his head in frustration. “You think the damn counter is open over there for me to cash in?”

“These here are hundred dollars apiece.”

“Hundred dollars apiece in what world? Where the hell are they a hundred dollars apiece?”

The men with guns and the other men waiting began to laugh as they watched and listened.

"Take em on up to Tunica," the man said. "You can use em there, I'm guessing."

"Tunica? Tunica floats."

"Vegas, then. Or somewhere."

"Yeah. Vegas. Hell yeah, let's go to Vegas, like they're gonna give me two hundred dollars for two dirty old chips from the shithole casino in Gulfport, Mississippi. Not to mention it'd cost me how much to get to Vegas? Spend three grand to cash in two hundred damn dollars. Hell, maybe I'll just mail em to them and they can mail me back my money."

The man put the chips back in his pocket and looked at his feet. He bit at the inside of his cheek. "I ain't got no money this time," he said. "I ain't got nothing."

Charlie propped his hands on his hips and walked a circle and then turned back and said, "I ain't the Red Cross and I ain't running no credit applications. You want something, you got to have money or something mighty fine to trade up. You got neither. Gimme them lanterns." He didn't wait for the man to hold them out but reached over and took them out of his hand. Then he scooped up the bag of batteries at his feet. Charlie set two of the lanterns back in the box and he gave one back to the large man. Then he took two packs of batteries out of the plastic bag and handed them over.

"Take this shit and go on and you owe me next time. You got it?"

The man nodded and said I got it and then he turned and walked down the metal ramp that led in and out of the truck.

Charlie stepped to the edge and said, "Anybody else out there got anything other than money or trade needs to go on. I thought that was common knowledge."

Two of the men in line stepped out and walked away.

Charlie looked to the back of the men and saw Cohen and waved at him. "Come on up here, Cohen. You ain't got to wait."

"Hell naw," said the old man with the sign. "You know how far I had to walk to get here?"

"Take that stupid sign off and shut up. How long you gonna wear that thing?"

"I'm gonna wear it till I want to."

"That don't even make no sense."

"Well, that don't matter. I'm sick of standing in this rain."

"Then dance around."

Cohen walked past the line and set the empty gas cans down at the back of the truck. He walked up the ramp and shook hands with Charlie. Charlie looked at him sideways and said, "I see you still cuttin your own hair."

Cohen nodded. "My beauty parlor is on vacation."

"Same ol shit. I try harder and harder to get down here, though. Don't never stop. Your house still standing?"

"Still standing."

"I knew when your daddy built it that it'd take the damn apocalypse to knock it down. Me and ol Jimmy Smith stood there and made fun of him triple-stacking the frame, but he was like that third little pig, just kept on how he wanted."

"I know it. Mom wanted it tall but he wouldn't have that either."

"Nope. You and that dog and that house are about like cockroaches."

"Don't jinx me."

They stepped up into the back of the truck and Cohen looked around at the open boxes stretched across the floor, a small pathway made down the middle. At the front end of the truck was a small backhoe.

"What the hell's that?" Cohen asked.

Charlie shrugged. "Don't never know what you might need. Got a deal, anyways."

"Don't tell me you're one of them now."

"One of them what?"

"You know what. Treasure hunter. Tomb raider. Whatever you wanna call it."

"I ain't no tomb raider 'cause there ain't nothing but dead shit buried in a tomb. What I'm after is alive and kickin."

"Come on, Charlie. You don't believe that."

"May or may not believe it but I'm gonna find out and that backhoe is the thing to do it."

"Well, if it turns up, I want fifty percent off what's in the back of this truck."

"If it turns up, you can have this truck."

Cohen shook his head and moved in between the boxes and said, "First off, I need some water and some liquor."

"Got that," Charlie said. "Back left."

Cohen found a stack of cases of bottled water and he lifted two and brought them to the end of the truck. Charlie grabbed a fifth of Jim Beam from a box up front. "You need a bag?" he asked. Cohen nodded and Charlie gave him one and Cohen walked back down the middle. He picked up boxes of macaroni and cheese and packs of dried fruit and a carton of cigarettes. He asked Charlie if he had any chain-saw blades and Charlie pointed and Cohen found the box. He took two and then he asked about gas.

"Got a couple of full tanks in the truck cab. They only three gallons, though."

"That's fine. It'll hold till next time."

While Charlie got the gas, Cohen got two boxes of shells for the shotgun and a box for the .22 and he took two bags of beef jerky. Charlie came back with the gas cans and told one of the gunmen to put them in the back of Cohen's Jeep. Then he climbed back up into the truck and looked at all Cohen had gathered.

"This ain't as much as usual," Charlie said.

Cohen shrugged. "I don't guess I need as much."

Charlie frowned at him and said, "Why don't you just come on and work for me. I told you a thousand times. Ain't no reason to stay down here."

Cohen didn't answer. Shook his head with his lips together.

"You been hearing anything?" Charlie asked.

Cohen thought a second. Heard himself talking to Elisa. "No. About what? Who am I supposed to hear anything from?"

Charlie looked out of the back of the truck. Rubbed his hands together. "Nothing, really. Just wondered. You got a radio still?"

"Yeah, but it don't pick up like it used to. Am I supposed to be hearing something, Charlie? About what you're after maybe?"

Charlie turned back to him. "Not about that, Cohen. You know me and your daddy was friends for a long time. And he'd want me to tell you to get on out of here. When's the last time the damn sun shined down here? Hell, anywhere?"

"I know what he'd say."

"I know you got that place and all and I know it goes way on back with the family. I know you got them ghosts out there. But I don't know about the rest."

Cohen wiped the dampness from his face, then said, "It doesn't matter."

"There ain't nothing to do down here but die,

Cohen," Charlie said, turning his back to the line of men and lowering his voice. "And it's just gonna keep on."

"From what I hear there ain't nothing but hell at the Line anyway."

"Wouldn't nobody blame you for leaving," Charlie said.

"Guess not. Ain't nobody here."

"You might think about moving on, Cohen. That's all I'm saying."

"Why?"

Charlie didn't answer. He looked past Cohen out of the back of the truck.

Cohen reached into his pocket and pulled out some money. "How much I owe you?" he asked.

Charlie huffed. "Gimme forty," he said.

"I know it's more than that."

Charlie reached down and picked up a couple of four-packs of the Ds and dropped them in Cohen's bag. "No charge for these," he said.

Cohen reached into his pocket and took out a hundred-dollar bill and gave it to Charlie. "I don't need no change," he said.

"Why the hell you do that?"

Cohen shrugged. "What else am I gonna do with it? Put whatever's left toward one of them."

Charlie took the bill and shook his head. "At least listen to the damn radio. You got a radio?"

"I got a radio," Cohen said and he set the bags on top of the cases of water and picked it all up.

Charlie slapped him on the back as he headed down the ramp.

"Come on up, old fellow," Charlie said to the man with the sign.

" 'Bout time," he answered.

"Really? You want to move to the back?"

Cohen nodded to the muscle as he walked over to the Jeep. He set the water and bags in the backseat next to the two gas tanks and then he put his sock hat on. One more look back at the ocean and then he got in the Jeep and turned around and headed back in the other direction. The rain, for now, was tolerable, soft and steady, but the southeastern clouds seemed to be turning into great black mountains. When it was time to turn off the highway, he stopped and opened a bag of the beef jerky and drove on with it between his legs. A couple of miles along the highway, before he got back to where the water covered the road, he saw the boy and the girl again. Her arm draped around his neck like before. Her limping along and him helping. The sound of the Jeep stopped them and they turned around to see what was coming and Cohen stopped again. He put the jerky on the floorboard and he took the shotgun from beneath the seat and then he drove on toward them. He knew they would wave him down and he knew better than to stop. As he approached, the boy moved the girl's arm from around his neck and began waving and the girl doubled over.

Keep on going, he thought. Keep on going. Then the look on the face of the big man in the flannel shirt crossed his mind. *I ain't got no money this time. I ain't got nothing.*

He slowed down. Rolled to a stop several car lengths from them. "Stay right there," he called out.

The boy reached back out to the girl and she leaned on him. Her baseball hat was gone and her long black hair fell across her face and shoulders in a wet, tangled mess.

Cohen raised himself up to where he could talk to them over the windshield. Before he spoke, he gave them a careful look and they didn't appear to have anything other than what they were wearing. The wind blew cold and the girl folded her arms and held herself.

"What you doing out here?"

"Walking," said the boy.

"Where to? I don't see nowhere you could be going."

"We're going to Louisiana," the girl said, throwing her hair back off her face with a toss of her head.

"You got a good long ways to go," Cohen said. He pointed out toward the water covering the road ahead and the land on either side of the road for as far as they could see. "That right there is good as a swamp."

"We know it," the boy said.

Cohen leaned over and spit on the ground. Then he sat back up and said, "You got something in Louisiana?"

"They got power over there, we heard," the boy said. He couldn't have been more than sixteen, and his shoulders were narrow even in the bulky letterman jacket.

"So," Cohen said.

"So what do you care?" the girl snapped and she stood up straight.

"Hush," the boy told her.

"You hush."

"Y'all both hush. What's wrong with her?"

"What you mean?" the boy asked.

"Why you dragging her along?"

"She got snakebit on her leg."

Cohen rubbed at his rough beard. Watched their faces for any kind of strange look or movement. "Too cold for snakes. Has been for a while," he said.

"It's been a while. Back before it got cold. Look," the boy said and he bent down and pushed the overcoat away from her leg and raised her pant leg. She was wearing tennis shoes with no socks and the area around her ankle looked like it had been poked with the tip of a knife.

"That ain't a snakebite," Cohen said.

"Hell it ain't," she answered and she pushed her pant leg back down. "It swelled up and won't quit."

"It ain't swelled. And if it was, walking don't help it," Cohen said.

"Don't nothing help it," said the boy. "Nothing but a doctor. You seen one?"

Cohen shook his head. The three of them stared at each other. Cohen looked behind him to the east and those deep clouds were beginning to creep across the late-afternoon sky. Lightning flashed beneath them, a crooked sharp line that touched the horizon. There was maybe an hour of daylight left and it was getting colder.

Let them be, he thought.

Then the boy said, "I don't guess you'd take us over the water."

"If I take you over the water, I'll have to keep on taking you."

"No you won't. Swear it."

"Don't beg him," the girl said.

"I ain't begging. I'm asking. What the hell."

Cohen raised the sawed-off shotgun and showed it to them. "You see this?"

They nodded.

"You understand?"

"Yes sir," the boy said. The girl didn't answer.

"What about you, snakebite?" Cohen asked. "You understand?"

"I get it."

"Across the water," he said. "Across the water and then you get out."

"That's fine," said the boy. "That's all I'm

asking. We just got to get to Louisiana."

"Stop saying that," Cohen said. "Don't know who you been talking to. That water over there you're wanting to get across is about half as deep as the same water all of Louisiana is under. Now wait right there."

He climbed down out of the Jeep and rearranged the gas cans and plastic bags and cases of water so that one of them could sit in back. He then took the boxes of shells and the chain-saw blades out of the bag and slid them way up under the driver's seat. When he was done, he waved them over and the girl limped alongside the boy without his help. Cohen pointed at the boy and told him to sit up front and put her in the backseat. The boy helped her up over the side of the Jeep and she shifted around in the seat to unwind the coat and then he got in the passenger seat. When Cohen was happy with the way they were sitting, he climbed behind the wheel. He now had to shift gears with the same hand that held the shotgun and he didn't like the loose grip but the decision had been made and they moved on.

He turned his head and told the girl to get them some water and she tore the plastic wrapping off the bottles and handed one up to the boy. They drank like thirsty animals and had each killed a bottle before they got to the water's edge. Cohen told her to take a couple out and put them in the pockets of that coat and she did.

The Jeep crept through the pondlike water. He had to watch the road ahead and maintain a grip on the shotgun and keep an eye on them. The boy reached down and took the bag of jerky off the floorboard and asked if he could have some and Cohen told him to take it. The boy handed a few strips to the girl and they chewed and chewed as the Jeep made small waves across the flooded land. Halfway across, the boy turned and seemed to say something to the girl and Cohen told him to face the front and don't look back there no more. He then told the girl to keep her eyes ahead, too. The gearshift shook some in the steady low gear and knocked against the barrel of the gun and he had to squeeze his thumb and forefinger tightly to keep from dropping it. They moved on, the deepest part behind them, and they were beginning to climb when the boy turned and looked at the girl again and Cohen slammed on the brakes and the jerk caused the water to splash into the floor of the Jeep. He stuck the shotgun under the boy's chin.

"You hear me?" he said. "You hear me now? Do you goddamn hear me?"

The boy's chin was toward the sky. Without moving his mouth, he said, "Yeah."

"Face forward or get out."

"Yeah."

Cohen lowered the shotgun and shifted into first gear and moved on.

"I was just checking on her," the boy said.

"Don't say nothing else," Cohen said.

"You know she got snakebit."

"I said hush."

"I swear to God she got snakebit."

"I said shut the fuck up."

"She can't halfway walk," the boy said and he turned again to the girl and this time the girl came forward and Cohen felt the cord around his neck and his head snapped back and the shotgun fired off and blasted out the windshield. He dropped the gun and tried to get his fingers between the cord and his neck and the boy punched him in the face and he fought with one hand and tried to pull at one of the girl's hands with the other and his air was running out in a hurry. His eyes bulged and the girl's hair fell over his face as she choked him with everything she had and the boy kept punching at him, hitting her as much as him. Cohen tried to twist and get around the seat but the boy held him down and the blood turned his face red and in desperation he let go of her wrist that he was trying to pry away from his throat and he snatched her by the hair and snatched him by the hair and yanked as fiercely as he could before he was choked to death. The girl screamed and came forward enough to ease the pressure from the rope cord that had been yanked out of a lawn mower and the boy clawed at Cohen's arm to get free. As he got his air he got strong again and they saw they couldn't handle him. The girl jumped out of the backseat and into the water, the cord still tight around Cohen's neck, and it brought him down headfirst and he splashed into the water. She yelled at the boy to get the gun, get the gun, and the boy picked up the shotgun and was holding it on Cohen as she let go of the cord and hurried back away from him. She climbed into the back of the Jeep and they waited for him to come up. He'd hit his head on the asphalt bottom on the way down and his body was lifeless in the dark water. They watched. The boy with the gun on him and the girl breathing heavy from the fight.

"You think he's dead?" the boy said.

"I don't know."

"Go poke him."

"I ain't going to poke him."

Suddenly Cohen shot up, gasping for air and falling back again. He fought to get to his feet and he flailed his arms like a child learning to swim and then he was on his feet but staggering, a red line around his neck and red down his face and he choked for air and spit out the dirty water. The boy gripped the shotgun tightly and the girl moved behind him and she was yelling shoot him. Shoot him shoot him now.

Cohen got straight up and he wiped at his eyes and held his arms out in submission.

"What you waiting on?" she said and she

elbowed the boy in the back of his shoulder.

He cocked back both hammers and pulled the trigger and there was a click. He pulled it again and there was another click. "Holy shit," he said and he sat down quickly behind the wheel and cranked the Jeep and Cohen rushed at them, the girl yelling and the boy fighting the gearshift but he got it in first just as Cohen was diving for him and Cohen's shoulder banged against the crossbar as the Jeep jerked forward. He fell limp into the water and floated there, dizzy and gagging and left in the wake as the Jeep moved on ahead, up out of the water and onto the highway, the girl's wet black hair flapping in the wind as she stood in the seat with her back to the road, watching Cohen as they drove away.

He raised out of the water, his right arm drooping, and he didn't have to look to know that his shoulder was separated. He stood still to get his breath and he grimaced with the pain of his shoulder and water and blood ran down his face and neck, his forehead gashed from the headfirst fall. When he was breathing steady, he began walking out of the thigh-high water, his right side lagging. It was a heavy walk and the line around his throat burned and he wanted to wait until he was out of the water to try and pop his shoulder back in but he couldn't wait. He felt his shoulder socket to figure out where it was supposed to go and then he took a deep breath and with his left hand he lifted his right arm and shoved and it didn't go and he screamed and went down to his knees. Oh goddamn, oh goddamn, he said and then without getting up and in anger he lifted and shoved the arm again and there was a pop and a fiery pain but it was in.

He screamed out again and let his face fall into the water and then he raised up and spewed the water out of his mouth. He stood up and began walking again and it took a few minutes but he came out of the water and he sat down on the asphalt between the wet tracks from the Jeep. He was cold and wet and the blood from his forehead wouldn't stop and the pain ran from his shoulder and down through his back and the red line around his neck was raised. He pushed his hair back from his face and found the gash with his fingertips. Floating out in the water was his sock hat and he got up and walked back out and got it and pressed it against the gash. Then he walked out of the water again, looked back behind him at the gathered clouds and the pops of lightning. Still far away but coming. Out in front of him the sun was nearly down and a red sky stretched the width of the skyline. It was cold but would get colder when the sun fell and he was too far from home.

He looked around. Nothing but land and water in every direction. But he couldn't stay there so he started along the highway, dripping and bleeding and hurting, the clouds moving in his direction.

3

Almost dark and thunder now with the lightning back off to the east. The wind had picked up and he shivered in the wet clothes and the falling temperature. He tried to remember as he walked. Tried to remember anything along the road that was still standing. Even halfway. Anything that he could get into for the night, before whatever was in those clouds got to him. But nothing was left save a small church down one of these side gravel roads and he'd have to guess which one as they all looked the same. Maybe the church was still there. He couldn't be sure but it was the only option. As he walked, he was repeatedly startled by the movements in the brush off the side of the road—rabbits and possums and he hoped that was all. A doe walked out into the road ahead of him, stopped and stared, then went on. Dark now and the sky littered with stars in the low western horizon and he tried to hurry but the fatigue and the pain were wearing on him and he shook with chills and he felt the beginnings of a fever. He came to another gravel road on his right and he looked down it. Some trees remained along the roadside and he thought hard. Knew the church was a mile or two walk down whichever road. There was thunder and he looked back over his shoulder and the lightning danced in the clouds and he didn't have time to think about it anymore.

The road was mud and it gave under his feet and he slipped over and over again as he half-ran. He hoped that the road wouldn't be washed away up ahead, sinking mud and giant potholes, and it wasn't. He hurried on, the wind stronger now and hanging limbs beginning to fall away and the lightning bright behind him and helping to light his way in split-second bursts. He had no idea how far he had gone and it seemed that he had gone far enough but there was still no church and still nothing else and he tripped and fell and tried to land on his good shoulder. Up quickly and wiping mud from his chin and the lightning flashed again and this time he saw up ahead the small brick church. The thunder crashed and felt like it was right on top of him and he took off running, his knees buckling as he hit the puddles and nearly falling but keeping on, and the lightning hit and he saw the front doors of the church missing and then he heard footsteps beside him and he was startled but then there were more and more footsteps surrounding him and he raced into the church doors and collapsed in the aisle as the baseball-sized hail pounded the earth.

It beat against the roof and it beat into the church where pieces of roof were missing above the choir loft and the baptismal. He rolled under a pew, his shoulder throbbing as the hail attacked the earth and what was left of the church, the sound of a hundred hardworking men and their sledgehammers. The lightning snapped and the crack of snapping wood and the scurrying of four-legged creatures sharing the church with him. He rolled over onto his stomach and crossed his good arm and put his head down and his other arm lay limp at his side. More thunder and more lightning and more hail as he lay shivering.

He folded his arms and squeezed, breathing in short bursts and wary of what might be in there with him. The hail beat beat beat against the church and he heard limbs cracking and breaking and thuds to the ground outside. He leaned back, anticipating any moment that the ceiling would give with the hailstorm, but the frequency of thuds became less and less until they stopped and then there was a strange dead calm.

He climbed out from under the pew and sat. Something moved toward the front of the church, the clatter of paws across wooden pews, and then several more to follow and Cohen sat on the edge of the pew as if he might have to make a run for it but then whatever it was moved again and it didn't seem big enough to worry about.

Everything seemed to pause. There was no more hail. No wind. No rain. All was still, dark, quiet, like an empty theater.

He knew what that meant.

He waited and then a soft rain began to fall. He

listened to the trickles of rain coming down into the church and he was reminded of the sound of the spring creek that he played in as a boy. The creek buried in the shade of the trees and the spring-fed water ice-cold and the chatter of his chin as he played in the clear, crisp water. The same chatter of his chin now as he sat there cold and wounded. The rain fell and the thunder echoed and he looked across the shades of black in the broken sanctuary and saw her. Something hazy and gray but he saw her only the way that he saw her now, in undefined, ghostlike images, the clarity of her face and figure beginning to fade some even though she was all he had in his isolation. He watched her move, coming down from the pulpit, moving along the aisle toward him, standing there and waiting for him to say something.

He reached out his hand.

He was shaking and he took heavy breaths to try and stop it but he could not. She hovered there in front of him as if waiting for something and he closed his eyes and it was then that she became more clear as she was lying there with her head in his lap and his hand on her pregnant stomach. On the asphalt of Highway 49, underneath an eighteen-wheeler, surrounded by the screams of those who were running for it as they had all seen them coming, the handful of tornadoes breaking free from the still black clouds, like snakes slithering down from the sky, moving toward the hundreds, maybe thousands of gridlocked cars that were only trying to do what they had been told to do. Get the hell out of here. Don't pack anything. Don't stop. Get your family and get in your car and get the hell out of here and that was what they had done. Like they had all done so many times in the last years but this time there had been no head start. No window. Only get in and get out. And the tornadoes splintered out of the sky and weaved toward them and then exploded through the bodies and the cars and trucks, metal and flesh being lifted and catapulted.

As Cohen and Elisa had run between the rows of cars, she had gone down and when he had bent to help her up, a piece of something shiny was sticking out of the back of her head and her eyes were like the eyes of someone who had seen something from another world. Elisa, Elisa, he said, but she didn't answer and her body was limp and he lifted and carried her and he slipped underneath the eighteen-wheeler and she lay with her head in his lap and the blood puddling underneath their bodies and her eyes open through it all and his hand on her belly that was as big as a volleyball and there was nothing that he could do but scream out against the chaos of the world. Cohen on his knees and her head across them and the rig swaying with the power of the earth and nothing to do but hold her and watch her go with her eyes never closing. Her lost, wandering eyes. As if the dead didn't understand anything more than the living. The life going out of her and Cohen's face on her stomach, talking to the baby, telling the baby things he couldn't remember now, talking to her so that she could hear him and know she was not alone with this terrible thing coming for her. His bloody hands on Elisa's belly, his mouth against it, his child within, his voice begging the child to somehow know she was loved. The rig swaying but holding and the tornadoes breaking away and tearing off in other directions and the sky blue-gray and nothing to do. Nothing to do.

He opened his eyes and the clarity dissipated and there was only her hazy image out before him and then it was gone like a drift of smoke. And he tried to remember, like he always did, if he had even said goodbye to Elisa.

His lips were dry and he licked them and he was so thirsty but he would have to wait. He adjusted himself on the hard wooden pew and shook and tried to figure how far a walk he had ahead of him back to his place but his thoughts would not settle and for the moment he wasn't even certain of the direction. The rain fell and the wind picked up and something nasty was coming on now. He lay down across the pew. His chills staggered his breathing and his thoughts twisted in knots and he thought he might be better off if he took off the wet clothes but he didn't move and then he heard the voice of the black-haired girl.

Shoot him. Shoot him now.

The rain began to crash and the wind roared like an approaching war. It roared and the little church cracked and swayed and held on, the wind whipping around inside, and outside the trees bent and some gave way and he knew it was only the beginning.

He rolled off the pew, underneath again. The vision of Elisa and the child had awakened his mind. She'd be three years old now. No, four. No, three. And Elisa would be how many? He subtracted the five years between them and she would be thirty-four and he made himself stop thinking about it all and then he began to think about the house and how foolish he must have looked with the long flatbed trailer, loaded with enough lumber for several tries, driving down toward the coast while everyone else drove in the other direction. Look at that idiot, he imagined them saying. What the hell does he plan on building? Don't he know what's going on? Don't he know it's over down here? Even if he gets something up it won't belong to him no more. Soon as that Line is drawn, we're all done.

He imagined their conversations. Looks like they were right, he thought. Ain't no way to get anything built. Not enough time in between them. And now the rain that never stopped. But that hadn't kept him from trying to finish the child's room, because he and Elisa had set out to build a child's room, and he had the foundation to build the child's room before she and Elisa went away, and fuck all the storms and fuck the Line and fuck the government and their bullshit offer for my house and my land and I'm building this room for this child no matter how many times I gotta build and rebuild and no matter how long it takes. He realized how ridiculous it all looked but there wasn't anyone around to look anymore and he wasn't going anywhere until it was done, but for the first time, lying under this pew, with this shoulder, with this whelp around his neck, with his Jeep taken away, with this church cracking and swaying, with the water soaked into his bones, with this goddamn rain that wouldn't stop, he wondered if there would ever be a child's room. Wondered if the lumber would ever dry out. Wondered if he would one day be an old man, no longer beaten by the weather but beaten by time.

His mind raced and the storm raged on and lying on his stomach, with his arms folded and his face buried in his arms, he fell asleep. And the dreams began. The anarchy came back to him, the hours after the Line became official. The fires that were set to the looted stores and the crumbling buildings and the empty homes. The coastline going up in flames, bands of those left behind setting fire to whatever would burn and then moving on to something else that would burn. The casinos the most direct targets, the symbol of frustration among the coast dwellers who had watched the casinos always be the first to go back up while everyone and everything else around them suffered. Some of the casinos had been lifted by the roaring tide and turned on their sides and pushed inland. Some of them had sunk. Some of them stood like Roman remains, only structural shells of a more prosperous time. Those that would burn, were burned, like all else, patches of fires burning red in the night, across Gulfport and Biloxi and other small, deserted communities.

He saw the fires in his dreams, heard the gas lines catching and exploding and the glass shattering like pistol shots, and he saw the fire setters celebrating like a ritualistic people who believed that the carnage was somehow serving this way of life. He saw the smoke gathering and forming a far-reaching cloud that sat in the sky and waited for the next hurricane and he saw the next hurricane and how it sucked the smoke into its swirl and gave the already gray sky a deeper, more menacing gray, like some slick, sharp stone. He saw the fires and heard the screams and the explosions and in his dreams there was destruction and swirling around him in his sleep there was destruction and he slept without being startled, desensitized to the orchestra of demolition.

Cohen woke with a jerk and the pain shot through his shoulder. He forgot where he was and he raised up and banged his head on the pew and he lay down again, holding his shoulder with his face twisting in pain. When the pain eased, he rolled out from under the pew and got up and sat on it. The wet chill all over him and the wind and rain bruising the land. He hugged himself, shivered. He closed his eyes and tried to think of somewhere warm. Somewhere safe.

He was standing at the back door of the house watching them. They sat together on a blanket out in the field. Elisa's brown hair in a low ponytail, a sundress baring her shoulders, sunglasses on. The little girl with the same brown hair, wavy and long, sitting next to her mother. The light drawn to them like angels. They played together with something, he couldn't see what. They talked with one another but he couldn't hear their voices, some kind of static drowning them out. He called to them but neither responded and he began walking out to them and the sunshine grew brighter and brighter until the landscape flashed white and blinded him and when he looked again they were gone, and the blanket was gone, but the static was there and he pulled at his ears and rubbed at his eyes as the static filled his brain and he cried out and then he opened his eyes and they disappeared in the dark church.

The wind shoved something through the busted

roof and it landed with a crash and he slid off the pew back onto the floor. He lay with his eyes closed and arms crossed in half an inch of water, and somewhere through it all he heard the sound of the voice, calling, *Shoot him. Shoot him now.*

4

It was like riding in the bed of a truck. Some rocking, some pushing. Enough uncertainty to be wary of letting go. Mariposa sat on a mattress on the floor of the trailer, her arms beside her, hands flat on the floor, the winds jerking at the trailer that was strapped to the earth by an erratic arrangement of ropes wrapped tightly to spikes driven deep into the ground. The ropes were tightest across the middle of the trailer top and the ceiling gave some with the strain and the ropes crisscrossed the trailer like the web of some deranged spider. The small trailer rocked in the big winds and she had sat there many nights before and she had yet to take flight but that didn't keep away the fear. Three lit candles stood in three empty beer bottles in the corner, knocking together but standing up, and the candle-light danced with the rhythm of the storm.

She was wrapped in a sleeping bag and she wore only panties and a flannel shirt. Her clothes lay spread at the foot of the mattress, soaked from the day's work. Her thick, long hair still had not dried and it lay across her shoulders, down across her breasts, and touched her folded legs. She swayed back and forth a little, mumbling to herself, trying to talk herself through the storm, trying not to think about tomorrow, wondering what had happened to the man they left behind. She looked over at the overcoat Aggie had given her to wear and she thought that the lawn-mower cord was in the pocket and she imagined the flakes of skin from the man's neck that must be crusted in the rope.

She was a Creole girl with Creole parents and grandparents and she had grown up on the east edge of the French Quarter in a shotgun house with wood floors and windows painted shut. Anywhere from six to ten other people lived in the house, depending on how many cousins or uncles or sisters settled in at a particular time. Her family owned a convenience store on the corner of Ursuline and Dauphine that sold groceries on the right side of the store and liquor and wine on the left. There was a room at the back of the store that was for the voodoo. Incense and spirit soaps and books on the occult and herbs of the darker arts. And in another room, farther back into the soul of the building, was where her grandmother sat in a cloud of cigarette smoke at a rectangular wooden table and read tarot cards or palms or whatever anybody wanted reading.

The room was no bigger than a closet, no windows, and a single naked blue bulb hung from the ceiling. Three of the walls were draped in dark-colored tapestries, reds and purples and crimsons reaching from ceiling to floor. The fourth wall was made of brick and a strip of wire hung across its width and clothespins held black-and-white photographs to the wire. Most of the photographs were yellowed, some were curled on the edges. Some of them thirty, forty, even fifty years old. The photographs were of family members dead and gone who served as Grandmother's sources, and as she delivered the promises of good fortune or of ill fate, she would call to the photographs by name, trail her hand back over her shoulder as if to reach out and hold them while they spoke, and it was not unusual for a repeat customer who had been delivered a stroke of predicted good luck to ask for a particular family member by name, believing that the stoic face in the weathered photograph was a guardian angel in a drab disguise.

Her grandmother was named Mariposa and the girl had been named after her. She had the same features as her grandmother and mother and aunts. Thick, wavy black hair, deep-set brown eyes, and skin like fine, rich cocoa. As a child she was always close to her grandmother, sitting in the corner as her grandmother called to the spirits to give her the prophecy, walking with her around the streets of the Quarter as she told tales of the old buildings and the ghosts who haunted them. Sitting in Jackson Square feeding the birds and listening to her grandmother speak of Christ and the saints one minute, of the spirits of the dead slaves and dead pirates the next. They would walk along the river and the old Mariposa would tell the young Mariposa of the lovers who had been separated at the river, one leaving on the steamboat, the other standing on the pier, torn apart by things they could not control, star-crossed romantic tales that built up the heart and then tore it down. There was not a street that didn't have a story. Not an alley without a ghost. Not a burning candle without a spirit hovering close by. A carnival of imagination.

She sat Indian-style on the mattress in the trailer, the sleeping bag covering her, and leaned forward with the shoe box she had taken from the house they found—it had to be the house of the man they'd ambushed—and she rummaged through their lives, him and his wife. She plucked the champagne cork, smelled it, held it out in front of her. Heard the piano playing at the reception, saw the women in their long shiny dresses, wearing their long shiny earrings. She put down the cork and picked out a small stuffed frog. Won at a fair or bought at a gas station on a spur-of-the-moment excursion along the panhandle. She took a hard candy bracelet from the box and put it around her wrist and noticed that some of it had been eaten away. She opened up the cards and letters and read the words he had written to her, read the words she had written to him. *A whole year?* she wrote on a first-anniversary card. *One down and how many more to go?* And then an *I love you* and her name with a fancy E and a looping A at the end. *I can't tell if you're getting better or I'm getting worse,* he wrote on a birthday card. *There is the water and the sky and there is you above it all,* he wrote on a Valentine. Their lives seemed to appear before her in the sultry light of the candles, two people loving and laughing and living with ease. She read and paused and watched them.

She went through the cards and letters and then there were more things. A red bow, a shiny rock, half of a shoestring, a pacifier. Two dried roses tied together with a white ribbon, and on the ribbon was written *Sono ubriaco.* She said it aloud, wondered what it meant. She knew it wasn't French and didn't think it was Spanish and guessed it was Italian. *Sono*, she said aloud again, trying to figure out one word in hopes of putting it together with the second. *Sono.* She tried and tried but couldn't place it.

She looked up from the box and stared at the three flames swaying back and forth. She thought of her grandmother and she thought of standing at the river, watching the people get on and off the riverboat. She thought of the stories of the lovers separated by what they could not control and she felt the same rise and fall that she had felt as she walked away from the river, holding her grandmother's hand, filled with sympathy and envy by whatever story she had been told.

At the bottom of the box was a large envelope, sealed, folded in half, with nothing written on the outside. But she didn't open it, wanted to save something for later. She returned everything to the box and put the top on and for a little while she had forgotten about the storm. Forgotten about this place.

Then a massive gust came and the trailer seemed to rise and drop and the bottles fell over and the candles went out and she let go a yelp. She pulled the sleeping bag tight around her. Dark all around her, the storm beating like a thousand hands against the trailer roof and sides. She tried to sing a little song she remembered her grandmother singing to her but the words were gone and only fragments of melody came out of her nervous mouth and all she wanted was for the night to end but that was a long ways away. She wondered if Evan and Brisco were awake, if any of the others were awake, and knew they had to be, it'd be impossible not to have your eyes open, and she wondered if they were holding on to the floor like she was, or if they were praying that the ropes would hold, or maybe praying that the ropes wouldn't hold and that the storm would grant mercy and break them free and lift and carry the trailers away and set them down gently in the thick, twisted arms of the kudzu. She stared into the dark and she listened to it all and she held on and she hated most that during nights like these there was no way to hear Aggie coming in your direction.

5

It was midday before there was a moment of relief. The wind finally gave, and the rocking stopped, and the rain slacked. Mariposa unwrapped herself from the sleeping bag, put on her jeans and sweatshirt, socks and boots, stood, and moved to the window. She wiped the fog from the glass with her shirtsleeve and looked around.

It had the look of a makeshift military compound that you might find in the middle of some forgotten war on the edge of a faraway jungle. A corral of sorts of the trailers that the government had once provided for those who had lost their homes. Short rectangular white things on wheels that symbolized the inadequacy of the effort to provide for the suffering. There were a dozen of them in a loose circle on the high ground of an old plantation where only the chimneys remained from the three-story antebellum. Stretching across the top and down the sides of each trailer were the same wild webs of rope that held her trailer to the ground. All but two of the trailers locked from the outside with deadbolts.

Around the trailers the grass was high but in the circle there was slick red clay and a square fire pit built from cinder blocks taken from the rubble of broken-down country stores. Scattered behind the trailers were old pickups, some that would crank and some that wouldn't, a couple of cattle trailers, refrigerators and freezers, odd pieces of furniture and mattress frames.

She saw Cohen's Jeep behind the old man's trailer. Then she took a step over to her trailer door to see if it was locked. It wasn't. Which she figured was a reward for what she and Evan had done. She walked over and took the shoe box from the floor and set it on the mattress and laid the sleeping bag over it. She then opened the door and hurried next door to Evan's trailer and it was also unlocked so she went in.

Evan and Brisco both rose up, startled.

"What the hell," Evan said. His blond hair was wild and his young brother, Brisco, squeezed a deflated football.

"Nothing. Just don't want Aggie to see me out."

The boys sat up on the mattress. Clothes and empty water bottles strewn about. An overturned chair and a busted Styrofoam cooler across the floor. Brisco lay back down and Evan got up, rubbing at his head and face.

"Where you think he put the keys?" Mariposa whispered.

Evan moved past her. Picked up an empty cup and looked in it as if expecting something to be there. He tossed it aside. "Why you whispering?" he asked.

"I don't know," she said.

"Then stop."

Mariposa moved around the small space, her arms folded. "I wish we wouldn't have told Aggie about that house," she whispered again.

"Me, too," he answered. "Stop whispering. You're making me nervous."

"The keys," she said at a normal volume. "Where you think he put them?"

"Keys to what?"

"To the Jeep."

"I don't know. Same place he keeps the rest of them, I guess."

Mariposa exhaled. She dropped her head in disgust. Brisco picked up two empty water bottles and started playing drums on the wall.

Evan moved to the door, opened it, and sucked in the rainy, cool air, and closed it again.

"I can't take it anymore," she said.

"I know it."

"I ain't joking around. I mean it."

"Just don't do nothing dumb."

"I already did something dumb when we came back here with the Jeep. I told you we shoulda run on."

"Jesus, I can't leave Brisco. What the hell are you talking about? Haul ass if you want to, but I'm with Brisco, don't matter what shit I gotta put up with."

Brisco stopped the drumming and said, "Leave me where."

"Nowhere," said Evan.

She shook her head. "I know. I didn't mean it like that."

"I hope like hell you didn't."

He paused. Eased up. "You could if you want, though."

"I can't do it by myself. Neither can you and him."

They squared off. One waited on the other with an answer. Like they did together most every day. And still neither had one. Brisco tossed aside the water bottles and sat down and crossed his legs. His shoe was untied and he played with the lace.

"We could walk together," she said.

"It's too far. We done decided that."

"Well, maybe we need to decide again."

"We'd starve before we got there. Or get found and end up worse off than this. You heard all the same stories I heard."

"We could walk at night."

The boy shook his head. “Night’s worse. And now it’s raining all the time. We can’t walk in the dark and the rain. And Brisco can’t do it anyway. He’s too little.”

Brisco turned on the mattress and said, “I ain’t too little.”

“Yes, you are,” Evan told him.

“I’m seven, you know.”

“Not yet, you ain’t.”

Brisco flopped back over and Evan turned to Mariposa and said, “We got to hold on. We got to keep doing what he tells us and he’ll keep our doors unlocked and we’ll find a way, I swear it.”

But it didn’t matter what he said because she was already gone, already turned from him, already done with the same conversation they’d had a hundred times. She moved over to the corner of the trailer and sat down on the floor and put her face against her knees. She had come to know desperation but it seemed as if her desperate feelings were beginning to develop into something else. She didn’t know what that was but she felt herself moving degrees past desperation. She didn’t like the thoughts in her head and in her heart when she promised herself that she would do anything to get out of this place. It scared her to imagine what those things might be.

Across the way a trailer door opened and out came Joe. He wore a flannel coat and muddy boots and his hair was long and brushed straight back. He walked over to the fire pit and looked down at the floating ashes, his eyes puffy and red. The smell of whiskey and cigarettes in his breath and on his clothes as he drank all night, through the duration of the storm, sitting on a crate inside his trailer with one hand on a bottle and the other clutching at his knee until it was over. He rubbed his hands together then tugged at his coat and coughed a hacking cough and he leaned over and spit. Around the compound the locks were on all the doors but for the two belonging to the boy and the girl and he had told Aggie it was a bad idea to leave them open, no matter what they'd earned, but Aggie hadn't listened. A dull pain filled his head and he stretched his arms and twisted and when he did he saw Aggie standing out in the field, looking out across the low, flooded countryside. Out above Aggie was a cluster of white birds, circling and diving and circling and diving. A grace in their rise and fall, as if they were high-class performers trained to illustrate beauty in the arc of flight. But Joe paid more attention to Aggie than the birds. His fixation on the landscape, his concrete stature, his apparent adoration for the new morning.

Joe rubbed at his eyes. To him, it was just another morning after another night of big wind and big rain and all he wanted was a cigarette to deliver him to Aggie's level of tranquillity. He reached into his pocket and pulled out an empty pack.

He sighed and walked out toward Aggie.

Aggie smoked and gazed across the flooding. He had never been anything but grateful for the calamity of the storms and the subsequent drawing of the Line, this perfect godforsaken land where a man like him could create his own world, with his own people, with his own rules. The rage of God Almighty. The fractured and forgotten order. In his most selfish moments, he believed that this had all somehow come about explicitly for him.

In his back pocket was a worn, floppy Bible, the size of a small notebook. The books and chapters he didn't like had been ripped out and there was a cigarette marking chapter six in Genesis, where the story of Noah began. On his belt loop was a ring of keys. He turned his head from side to side, as if being careful to record and save this image for some later time when he would need it. His hair was thin and slick and age spots spread across his forehead and over his hands. A revolver that he made sure everyone could see was tucked inside the front of his pants and he wore an army coat that he'd pulled off a dead man floating in the water in a long-gone cul-de-sac down the shoreline.

Aggie didn't turn when he heard the footsteps.

Eyes out across the land. Joe stopped next to him. They stood in silence for several minutes and the rain bothered neither man.

Finally, Joe took a light out of his back pocket and flicked it a couple of times.

Aggie didn't move at first, but then he eased his hand into the front pocket of the army coat and he held out a pack of cigarettes. Joe took one and nodded and then he lit it. The two men stood there with their cigarettes held inside their coats. The rain on them and the waters out before them. Their kingdom behind.

"I don't guess we lost nothing last night," Joe said.

Aggie lifted his hand to his mouth and smoked. Then he shook his head.

"If it didn't get us last night, won't get us," Joe said.

"You say that every time."

"Damn ropes must be tight as hell."

Aggie turned to him. A bend in his eyebrows as he said, "Don't doubt God's muscle. If He wants them trailers, He'll have em."

Joe smoked and let out a frustrated exhale. Some mornings there was no talking to Aggie and this seemed like one of them already. He rubbed at the back of his neck to try and ease the throbbing. He squatted down and picked at the weeds. "You letting them out today?" he asked, his eyes on the ground.

"Later on," Aggie said.

Joe pulled his cigarette out of his coat and smoked. "We going out to work?"

"After we let them two take us to where that house is."

"We ain't spinning wheels, are we?" Joe asked. "Seems like looking for a needle in a haystack."

Aggie shook his head. "No. We ain't spinning wheels. And if we are, it's better than not."

"Yeah. I reckon."

Aggie looked away from the birds and the lowlands and looked at Joe. He grabbed his shoulder. "Don't doubt me, Joe."

Joe nodded.

"Then come on. Go get them two and then come and help me hook up the trailer. That little one stays here. Sooner we get back, sooner we can go out and have a look. I'll go ahead and throw the shovels and pickax in the other truck over there," Aggie said. He looked once more across the flooded fields and then he walked on toward the trailers.

6

Cohen had never known anyone who had gone to Venice. Or Italy. Or Europe. When he asked Elisa what she wanted for their first anniversary, he expected her to say she wanted a necklace. Or a day at the spa. Or a swanky dinner at one of the upscale casino restaurants. Or anything but what she said.

"I wanna go to Venice." They were sitting on the front porch, late in the day, in the falling purple light. He kicked off his work boots and leaned back in the wicker chair and drank from the cold beer. She was barefoot and had her legs crossed in the chair, her legs and arms and everything brown from the summer sun.

"Venice where?" he asked.

"Venice, Texas," she answered and kept her eyes ahead and waited for him to give up.

"Never heard of it," he said and she reached over and slapped his arm.

"You know damn well what I'm talking about."

"I know, I know. What makes you want to go all the way over there?"

She shrugged. "I don't know. Saw it on TV the other day. Looks nice. All the canals and the old buildings and churches and stuff. No cars or nothing. Don't you think it'd be kinda cool?"

He wrinkled his brow. Thought about it. "How much?" he asked, knowing she had already looked.

"A lot."

"A lot a lot, or just a lot?"

"Just a lot."

He drank from the beer. The crickets and tree frogs sang their song and it echoed through the twilight and across the land.

"Well," he said.

"We probably can't save it before our anniversary."

"Probably not."

"But we could probably save it by the spring. That's six months. You think?"

He liked how she sounded. Excited and hopeful and a little nervous. He had never once thought about Venice but the thought of it now, with this woman, made him feel as if he were about to commit to a romantic adventure that you only read about in paperback.

"I think we can. If that's what you want," he said.

She uncrossed her legs and got up from her chair. She pushed his arms back and sat down in his lap and squeezed him around the neck until he coughed.

They arrived in an overcast city and for the first three days of the ten-day trip it rained off and on, but they didn't care. Their hotel room was on the top floor and the window looked out across a courtyard and a canal. In the mornings the man who arranged the small tables in the courtyard sang beneath the light rain in a gentle tenor voice. They crawled all over one another as it rained, then fell back asleep and woke again and listened again and felt as though they had been removed from reality and set free in some other place that existed only to please them.

The hotel was three floors and the rooms were small. The staircase was wide enough for one and its turns were tight. The walls were brick with clumps of mortar hanging from between the bricks and Cohen couldn't go up or down the stairs without commenting on the sloppy job someone did a long time ago. The hotel was run by two sisters and their cluster of indistinguishable teenage children who vacuumed the rugs, watered the plants, attended the small bar and two tables, went out for morning croissants, swept the foyer, changed the towels and the sheets, delivered the morning newspaper, and whatever else. The sisters wore their black hair pinned up and only one showed streaks of gray. They were frumpy and sat with folded arms and talked incessantly and moved only if someone came along and needed something and sometimes not even then, only shouted out a quick instruction to whatever child happened to be in earshot and that child would hurry to it but not without mumbling something in the tone of teenage angst that was discernible in any language.

When it wasn't raining, they walked and walked. Though Elisa had two guidebooks and a detailed list of what she wanted to see and when she wanted to see it, she was taken by the city and its ancient streets and the heartbeat of the language and the quaint bridges and the architecture and all she wanted to do was walk. They avoided the museums and cathedrals except to admire the exteriors—the Gothic arches and the details of the statues of the saints and the complexities of the stained-glass windows. All of which fascinated Cohen, as in the world of efficiency and symmetry that he had learned from his father, he had forgotten or perhaps never realized that buildings could be constructed with such imagination. Instead of following the lines of tourists in and out of the starred spots on the map, they moved across the canal bridges and walked down narrow streets that led to other canal bridges and other narrow streets. They were frequently lost, having to double back, spending an hour or more trying to figure out exactly where they were but finding local cafés and bars along the way and not caring a bit, reveling in the notion that they had discovered some secret part of the city that the sightseers would never know. For three days they clung to one another in the hotel room and then walked with locked arms through the floating city.

7

Cohen got up from the wooden pew and looked at the place where he had found refuge. A tree covered in Spanish moss had fallen through the roof and lay across the pulpit and mold had spread across the choir loft and the baptismal. The stained-glass windows remained only in fragments. A lamb at the feet of someone in a white robe. The bodiless head of Christ bleeding from the crown of thorns. Half of an angel looking over the headless Mary holding the baby. The Bibles and hymnals remained in the slots in the backs of the pews, but their pages were yellowed and wavy. The hardwood floor of the aisle was covered in water and scratched from the nails of the animals that came and went. He rubbed his forehead and it was damp and he ached all over and he walked to the open doors of the sanctuary and looked out. He figured this was about as good as it was going to get. He was weak but knew that he had to begin.

He walked out in the rain to the muddy road with his arms folded and his hands tucked under his arms. His clothes were still damp and he couldn't have spit if he'd wanted to. His mouth was dry and his throat tender, the muscles of his stomach and chest tight as he shook from the fever and he wanted to run but knew better. Things moved in the brush, startling him and startled by him. At the end of the road he knelt and rested for few minutes and then he got up and kept on, the walking easier along the two-lane highway, out of the mud and puddles.

He walked on. An hour behind him and he hoped he was halfway. At a gathering of honeysuckle along the fencerow, he stopped and put his face into it and opened his mouth and shook the bushy vine. The rainwater splattered onto his face and tongue and he lapped like a desperate dog at the cold, refreshing drops. The water from the leaves ran down into his mouth and throat and momentarily relieved the fever and he moved along the fencerow, doing the same thing with anything leafy that would shake, and then he sat down for another few minutes before walking again. Another hour and he could see his road up ahead and his pace quickened as he thought of the bottles of water and the dry clothes and the bottle of aspirin and the dry place to lie down. He moved in some half-walk, half-run, gimpy and awkward with his wet, numbed feet but driven by the thought of home. He came to his road and hurried across the red mud, sloshing along as fast as his worn body would take him, and then there was the house and he almost cried out in relief but as he got to the driveway and saw the tire tracks and the front door open his anticipation quickly turned again to despair.

He stopped in the front yard. Watched and listened.

Then the dog stuck its head out of the front door and he walked on up. The dog met him at the steps and he touched its head as he walked past and into the house.

In the front room, the cot and the blankets were

gone and the closet door was open and the .22 and the black raincoat were gone. The electric heaters that he ran off the generator to keep warm were gone. He limped on into the kitchen and the cooler that had been filled with water bottles was not there and the upper cabinets had been cleaned out. Every can. Every box of anything. He got down on his knees and opened the bottom cabinets and what little there was in them remained, including a dozen or so bottles of water, and he opened one and drank and drank and when it was done he tossed it aside and he opened another and did the same. He found a few ounces of whiskey in a long-forgotten pint bottle and he opened it and took a swallow and it burned and warmed. He took another swallow and it twisted his face and then he sat on the floor and let the whiskey settle all the way through him. He looked again through the lower cabinets and there was nothing to eat as he had put all the food up high to keep it safe. He stood and opened the drawer where he kept medicine and bandages and antibiotic ointment and other pills and creams and it was emptied but for half a bottle of aspirin that had slid to the back. With his hands shaking he managed to get the top off and he shoved a handful of the chalky tablets into his mouth and chased them down with several gulps of water.

The shivering now at its height, he walked back into the front room and took off his clothes while the dog watched him and then he walked naked to the hall closet where he found that some but not all of his clothes were gone. He took out a pair of jeans and socks and two long-sleeve shirts and he put it all on and then he looked down the hallway. The drywall that he had used to cover up the entrances to the bedrooms had been busted and pulled away from the frame. He cussed himself for putting up and puttying the drywall but then not finishing it. What the hell good did it do to make a wall to hide a room if you're not gonna finish the damn wall. No good, that's what. He went back into the front room and put on the wet boots and then he walked down the hallway, stepping across and kicking at the broken drywall, and he stopped in the dark doorway of the bedroom that he and Elisa had shared.

There was a musty smell as the room had been closed up for over two years. He walked in and the drawers to the dresser had been pulled out and her clothes that remained lay scattered across the floor. He knelt in the midst of the clothes, the gray light coming through the sheer curtains and around him like a cloud and holding him like some nameless black-and-white character from an old movie. He picked up one of her gowns, silk and silver, and he felt its softness in his rough fingertips. Touched it against his damp, hot forehead as if it had the power of remedy.

He set the gown on the floor and picked up and

put down her other things—a bra and her T-shirts and black stockings and red panties. He picked them up slowly and held each garment and set it down just as slowly, as if they were dead, dry leaves that could crumble with the slightest force. He got up from his knees and saw their fingerprints and handprints across the top of the dresser in the filthy, almost slick film that had settled over the room during its closure, and then he noticed the cobwebs stretched across the blades of the ceiling fan. He moved across the room, stepping around the bed that had been stripped of its comforter and sheets, and he sat down on the bare mattress and saw on the top of the nightstand more traces of their hands. Her wooden jewelry box had been opened and turned over and there was nothing left. The engagement ring and the wedding band and earrings and necklaces were gone and he pictured them in the hands of strangers. People who thought no more of what belonged to her than they thought about rocks in a gravel road. He picked up the empty jewelry box and closed the lid and held it on his lap and tried to force himself into a good memory but all he could think of were those strangers who had taken what he had left of her and who had taken everything else they could take and who were probably unloading and planning to come back and take the rest.

He held the jewelry box on his lap and he

swung his legs up onto the mattress and he leaned back and stretched out. He wanted to sleep. Needed to sleep. Needed to lie still and let the aspirin help chase the fever. Needed to drink water and eat something and rest until he was strong again but he knew that he didn't have that option. They would be back and there might be more of them and they had his guns and his Jeep and he didn't have anything. The dog wandered into the bedroom and sniffed at the clothes on the floor and then looked around as if to say, I didn't think this woman lived here anymore.

He closed his eyes. Wanted to sleep and one day wake up and this life would be a different life. The dog walked around to his side of the bed and lay down beneath him. They both lay still for several moments as if the day belonged to them. At the edge of sleep, Cohen made himself sit up, and he put the jewelry box back onto the night-stand next to the picture of them waist-deep in a blue ocean. He picked up the frame and opened the back and he took out the picture and held it close to his eyes. Touched his fingertips to the faces of another time. He folded the picture in half and he stood and put it in his back pocket and then he got down on his knees and said, "Be there."

He bent over and looked under the bed and the shoe box was gone and he yelled goddamm it and pounded his fist on the floor. Bent over and pressed his head against the floor and pounded at it and yelled out over and over again. Goddamm it, goddamm it, goddamm it.

He sat doubled over for a minute and then one more pound at the floor and he got up and walked over to the closet. The sliding doors were open and they had taken the things that held warmth. Her coats and her sweatshirts and her jeans. The dresses remained. The summer dresses that once hung delicately on her tanned body. The black thing that she wore with grace when they buried someone they had known. The other thing that she wore that gave away the freckles between her breasts. He looked away from her clothes to his side of the closet and he looked down and noticed an old pair of work boots that he had forgotten. He picked them up. Black and dusty and steel-toed and dry. He tucked them under his arm and he ran his hand along the length of one of her dresses and then he walked out of the room and down the hallway and stepped inside the other room.

It had been an office until the news of the baby and then it had become a shared room for all, a place to keep things until her room was finished. The dresser had been opened up and some of the tiny clothes had spilled out onto the floor. He walked over and put down his boots. He knelt and picked up each small sock or nightshirt and folded it neatly and put it back in the dresser. Two drawers had been filled in anticipation, Elisa unable to go anywhere without picking up some little hat or pair of tiny slippers. Unable to stop thinking about it, smiling as she'd come home with something else, him smiling back and making fun. He closed the dresser drawers and stood. Empty picture frames on top of the dresser. A lamp with a giraffe lampshade. A piggy bank that he raised and shook and the coins rattled. He set it back down and walked over to the closet. The door open and his two suits hanging there, next to them a gathering of tiny pink hangers. Toys in boxes on the floor. A stack of colorful books on the top shelf.

He stepped back. Stood in the middle of the room. It felt as though a great hole might open up beneath him and swallow him into the earth and he wished that such a thing were possible.

He stood there, still and insignificant, with unfocused eyes.

Minutes later, he walked back to the dresser and opened the drawer and took out a pair of the tiny socks and stuck them in the front pocket of his jeans. Then he picked up his boots and left the room.

He sat down on the floor in the front room and took off the wet boots and put on the dry ones and tied double knots. Then he walked outside to look for Habana and the dog followed him.

At the back of the house he expected to find her door open and he was right. He looked inside the converted family room and was surprised to see her saddle and bridle there. He called out and whistled for her as he looked across the back fields. He asked the dog where she was but the dog didn't answer. He walked out into the backyard and stepped across the mangled barbed-wire fence and he stood out in the field with his hands on his hips and turned in a circle, calling for her and looking for her and hoping she would appear from somewhere along the tree line once she knew it was him. "Go look for her," he said to the dog, but the dog stayed at his side. He called for her three times more and then he walked back to the house shaking his head as he looked for what might have been left outside. Below the kitchen window he found the generator and he was certain now that they would be back. That they had put everything they could into the Jeep and were unloading and coming back for the rest. Nobody left a generator.

The dog barked and Cohen turned and looked and Habana was walking across the field toward them. He walked out to meet her and he stroked her neck and then he hugged her. With her mane across his face, he began to cry a tearless cry, short rhythmic pulses of hurt. He held on to her and his body shook and the hacking sound of anger and pleading came from his mouth and the horse stood still for him as if she understood. A passive sunshine bled through the veiled sky and found them and he held on and cried as they stood together in the soft, wet ground and then when he was done he raised up and told her not to ever tell anybody what had just happened. Don't know what somebody might say if they knew about this. Promise me, he said and in her large glassy eyes he saw that he could trust her. He sniffed and then he spit and then they walked back toward the house. The dog had waited in the backyard and watched them and Cohen tried to swear the dog to secrecy as well but the dog turned and twitched its tail as if it were jealous that it hadn't been included.

He put the saddle and bridle on Habana and left her grazing in the backyard and he started walking out across the back field. A hundred yards away was the tree line and he splashed his way there, the ground sucking at his feet. The trees had the look of losing the fight, some splintered, some on the ground with their massive roots reaching out like flailing arms, some sagging from the rain like old men. Scattered around in the trees were two-by-fours from his efforts with the child's room. He walked to the base of a fractured oak to the two tombstones. Only one body but two tombstones.

He knelt in the wet earth.

Around him the blue-gray world. The world that he tried to hold on to, that he tried to keep alive with the old colors. The gray world that he didn't think could win but was winning.

He stared at Elisa's tombstone. Only her name and the dates of her birth and death. He stared at the baby's tombstone. Only her name.

The stones were slick, splashed with dirt and wet leaves. Cohen leaned forward and with his hand he wiped them clean. Once he had walked out to the graves with a hammer and chisel with plans of carving a cross for each of them, but when he got there, he changed his mind. The rain tapped and the sky rumbled.

She was difficult to see now. She had been for a while. Even the photographs seemed to change her image, shifting her eyes and ears and nose slightly, making her out to be a little different than the way she was. She appeared most clearly in his subconscious. In the dreams. As an apparition shifting with the clouds or flashing in the lightning crashes. Her voice in the thunder or the drone of the rain. He leaned over and pushed his fist into the soggy ground and wondered if she were even there. If he started to dig, whether he would hit a casket, whether she would be in it if it was there, or was there only a bottomless, muddy hole where she used to be and a wet earth that would suck at his feet and drag him down, farther and farther from the surface into a never-ending tunnel of mud, an earth soaked to its core and slowly devouring itself.

He pushed his fists into the ground and they sank and the brown water covered his knuckles and he felt there was nothing there, only this wet, sucking ground that had taken everything he had loved. And what had he loved? He had loved the sweet, sticky ocean breeze and swimming in the ocean and the salty taste on his lips and the gritty feel of the sand on his hands and feet. He had loved the pier on Friday nights and the buckets of wings and ribs and bottled beer and the two guys with the guitars who played Buffett and Skynyrd and Steve Earle and whoever else you called out. He had loved the bush hog and its rhythm and cutting in the hot-ass sun in July and sweating until he couldn't sweat anymore and the neat rows he cut and the nameless cows and their calves that had fed off their land. He had loved the girl with the red toenails and their quiet spot along the gravel road and what they had discovered together in the summer nights with the windows down and the mosquitoes at their bare bodies. He had loved baseball practice and the thwack of the ball coming off the bat and sliding headfirst and the ridiculous dugout conversations and winning. He had loved the sting of a sunburn. He had loved the blooming dogwood trees in the sprawling lawns of the antebellum homes in Biloxi. He had loved riding up and down Highway 90 with a cooler of beer and two or three buddies and all the bullshit they fed one another and cranking up the radio to the hair metal. He had loved the excitement of the coast once the casinos started going up and he had loved the jingle-jangle of the slot machines and the free drinks you got while playing blackjack and he had loved the long-legged waitresses in the fishnet stockings who brought them to you. He had loved the first warm day and smell of her suntan lotion and he had loved taking a blanket to the beach at night and her falling asleep with her head on his chest and the way the stars looked as he held his hand on her back and felt her breathing. He had loved marrying her in bare feet, standing on the dock with the ocean out before them. He had loved the buildings that he framed and he had loved going to the cooler he kept in the back of the truck at the end of a long, hot day and the sound the beer can made when he popped it open. He had loved the gleam in her eyes when she came out of the bathroom and nodded and said you're gonna be a daddy and he had loved that she wasn't scared of the storms and he promised her he would stick it out because this is our home and it can't last forever and he had loved sitting on the living room floor and thinking about baby names. He had loved that it was going to be a girl.

He lifted his fists out of the ground. Small imprints where he had been pressing filled with water. He didn't know if she were there or if the earth beneath her tombstone was as vacant as the earth beneath the child's.

His fingers dripped with muddy water and he held out his hand and watched the brown drops fall from his fingertips. He then got up from his knees and walked back to the house, refusing to turn around and look again.

He went inside and in the kitchen he climbed up on a chair and slid over the ceiling tile and took out the cigar box. He took out all the money, a stack of hundred-dollar bills. He then reached up into the ceiling again and felt around once more and his fingers found the knife his grandfather had given him. It was a bowie knife in a leather sheath and he took out the knife and the blade was a smooth and clean silver from the years that the boy and then the man had taken care to shine it. He slid the knife back into the sheath and then snapped the sheath onto his belt loop. He tossed the cigar box back up into the ceiling and moved the tile into place. Then he stepped down from the chair and folded the stack of bills and put them in the front pocket of his jeans.

In the front room the pillow from the cot was on the floor. He picked it up and removed the pillowcase and began rummaging through the kitchen, filling it with whatever he could find. The remain-ing bottles of water and the nearly empty pint of whiskey and the aspirin. Knocked onto the floor in haste were a can of pears and small tins of Vienna sausage and two cans of green beans and a pack of crackers. In the bottom cabinets he had a spare flashlight and a few feet of rope and some duct tape. It all went into the pillowcase and then he walked to the hallway closet, and what clothes were left he put in. Some random socks and faded T-shirts and underwear and a long-sleeve shirt. In the front room he looked again in the closet where the shotgun and .22 had been. A couple of paperbacks were on the floor and a pair of work gloves and half a box of dog biscuits. He took the random items and he tossed the pillow case over his shoulder like a white-bearded man with a sleigh waiting outside. He walked around the side of the house and set the sack on the ground next to the generator, then he pulled the cap off the spark plug and unscrewed the plug and put it in his pocket. He took out his knife and cut the gas line and he unplugged the extension cord and sliced it through.

The dog was in the backyard with Habana and he came over to them and said, “It could be the start of one long day. Longer than it has been. Thought I’d let you know. Especially you, girl.” He scratched at Habana’s ear. Thought of the day she had appeared across the field, wet and muddy and saddled but without a rider, her name engraved across the saddle. He thought of how he had approached her slowly, and she had let him, and he had checked her for cuts or scratches or the blood of whoever had been on her last. How she had helped him survive, taking him places the Jeep couldn’t go, into the swamplands that now extended by miles from the flooding rivers, where pieces of boats and the tin roofs of wooden shacks hung in the clutches of the gray monster-like moss trees. Along the highways obstructed by trees and telephone poles and covered in lower stretches by still, tepid waters. Along the beach-front that had shrunk back and served as the dumping grounds for whatever the storms could drag in or haul away. Half-trailers and metal signs from flattened hotels and gas stations and dead animals. Poker tables and mattresses and steel pieces from crumbled oil rigs and a school bus. He thought of filling garbage bags with canned foods and paperback novels and blankets and batteries and gas cans and whatever else seemed necessary, how for weeks they had moved across the countryside until he felt like he had hoarded all there was to hoard.

And then he thought of how they were back in the same spot, starting all over again, and he hoped Habana knew how much he needed her.

He left the animals and walked inside, once more into the bedroom.

Closing his eyes, Cohen listened for their voices. The voices of the two people who had made a home here. In the house they had built. On the land that had been in his family for generations. The ocean so close. Everything seemingly where it was supposed to be. He listened for those voices. Tried to hear the laughter. Tried to hear what they were talking about as they stood together in the kitchen or sat in the living room with the windows open on a cool night. He couldn't hear them, so he tried harder. Squeezing his eyes shut with his face tense as if fearful of some imaginary, invisible, yet very real monster.

Still he couldn't hear them. He opened his eyes.

He walked to the window and looked out at the concrete slab. Looked at the pile of lumber. In the wildest part of his mind he thought that maybe one day, when all of this was over, he'd be able to come back and finish like he had promised.

He walked over to the nightstand and opened the drawer. He found a pencil and a piece of scrap paper and he wrote a note. At the doorway, he looked around the room once more, and then he felt in his back pocket to make sure he had the photograph and it was there. He stepped across the hallway and looked at the child's clothes and toys and he said good night. And then he walked into the kitchen and left the note on the counter and he walked outside into the damp, chilling world where he picked up his pillowcase and climbed onto Habana and told the dog to come along. They moved lazily down the driveway to the gravel road. At the end of the driveway, Cohen turned Habana and he looked again at the house. He had said goodbye to them a thousand times, but this time felt the most real.

And then he nudged Habana and they moved on.

8

They arrived half an hour after Cohen rode away with Habana and the dog.

The Jeep stopped on the carport slab and the four of them got out. Joe walked over to the generator and noticed the cut gas line and said, "Looks like your boy has been here. Damn cut the gas line. And took the spark plug."

Aggie said grab it anyway and they each took an end and loaded it onto the trailer hitched on to the Jeep. The boy and the girl went inside and searched through what they had left on the first run, taking anything that might matter but mostly happy about the clothes. The girl went into the bedroom and she stood in front of the dresses, looking through them as if spending a leisurely day in a department store. The men came in and began taking the furniture out of the bedrooms and they called for the boy to help them. Piece by piece the nightstands and dressers and mattresses were taken out and loaded onto the trailer.

"I didn't know there was nobody down here still living this good," Aggie said as he carried out a set of bed rails.

"Me neither," said Joe. "He ain't no more, though. What you reckon he's doing?"

"He might be sitting out there behind a tree

somewhere with his sight on the back of your head."

"Evan said they got all the guns. Didn't you?"

"Think so."

"Think? Better goddamn well know."

"Don't worry," said Aggie. "If he was sitting behind a tree with something to shoot we'd be shot."

They went back to work. Around the back of the house, Joe noticed the foundation and the wet, discolored pile of lumber. He called out to Aggie and Aggie came around.

"Looks like we got a winner for most ambitious resident," Aggie said.

They kept on and soon the house was emptied and Evan called out to Mariposa to come on. She was lingering in the bedroom, had picked five dresses, and they were folded and stuck into her overcoat. She came out of the front door and said, "Go see if that horse is still back there."

"That horse is long gone," said Joe. "But there's a cellar back around there, about two feet of water in it. Got some shelves, though. A bunch of saws and nail guns and stuff."

"That's gonna do a lot of good," Aggie said. "Leave that stuff. We know where to find it if we change our minds."

"All right," Joe said. He turned to Mariposa. "You and Evan sit back there on top of the stuff to keep it from bouncing off."

"I ain't sitting back there," she said.

He reached over and slapped her hard across the face and told her to shut her goddamn mouth and get back there. One of the dresses fell out of her coat and onto the ground and the man said, "Where the hell you think you going? To the ball, Cinderella?"

The two men laughed and Evan picked it up for her and looked to see if she was okay but she pushed him back and walked to the trailer and climbed up on top of the mattresses. Evan followed her and sat beside her and Mariposa glared at the two men. Aggie got behind the wheel and Joe said he was gonna walk through one more time. Inside, he passed through each room, checking for anything they had missed that might be of use or value, but the place had been stripped of its offering. In the kitchen he found a note on the counter that none of them had noticed. He picked it up and read. Didn't laugh but smiled an uncomfortable smile. He folded the note and walked out and got in the passenger side of the Jeep.

"This is a good old place," Aggie said as he settled behind the steering wheel. He cranked the Jeep and then Joe handed the note over to him.

"What's that?"

"Looks like their friend left us a little note."

The older man unfolded it, read it, then huffed and gave it back.

"What you think?"

Aggie paused. Pursed his lips and put the Jeep into first gear. "Don't think nothing," he said. "Too much of that'll get you killed down here. You should know that by now."

The gray of day was beginning to fade and thunder that had been far off now rumbled more closely and Aggie said the digging would have to wait until tomorrow. The Jeep moved off the concrete slab and out into the backyard and circled the house, the tires spinning some and the trailer tires sinking some but they made it around to the gravel and moved on, the girl and the boy vibrating with the furniture and generator like mindless wind-up toys. Aggie had shrugged off the note but Joe thought about it as he tucked it into his pocket. They moved along the skinny road and he looked out at the crippled trees and the twisted countryside and thought for the first time in a long time about his mother in her burgundy dress, his hand in hers as they walked through the front door of the little brick church on the dusty road. It seemed like the memory of some other woman and some other child and his thoughts drifted away from what he had become as he considered the mother and child and the tranquillity of the sanctuary. The cream-colored walls and cherrywood pews and slightly out-of-tune piano that played for the slightly out-of-tune choir composed of workingmen in short ties and old ladies with their glasses held around their necks by beaded silver chains. The rough voice of the preacher and the stories that he told about the man who walked from place to place. Touching them and healing them. Speaking to them of forgiveness and tolerance. Feeding them with crumbs and giving them all the chance to live in golden castles on golden streets in golden clouds.

And then how they nailed him up and laughed at him.

They moved off the road and onto the highway and he thought about those stories and he thought about that woman in the burgundy dress and he thought about the place they had just left where they had taken what didn't belong to them. He thought about the man who had written the note and why he had chosen the words that he had chosen. He looked out across the sky, imagined it clear and blue, and imagined the words from the note written in large, looping trails of white.

To whom it may concern—he is not dead he is risen.

9

By the time they made it to the church, he was slumped forward on Habana with his pillowcase of all his possessions dragging the ground and his head resting against her mane. He all but fell off and went down to his knees and the dog licked at his forehead. He reached up and brushed the dog's head and then got to his feet and walked inside the church, dragging the pillowcase along. Night was closing in and the stiff rain had returned and he sat down on the back pew where he had spent the night before. He found a bottle of water and the aspirin and he took a few more and then he opened a can of Vienna sausages, trying to figure out if it was starve a fever, feed a cold, or feed a fever, starve a cold. Either way, he ate half of the thumb-sized sausages and gave the other half to the dog and he tossed the can on the floor. Habana clip-clopped into the church foyer.

Lie down and sleep, his body told him.

Get up and go find them, his mind replied. Find them. The ones who took your Jeep and invaded your home and took the pieces of Elisa that you had left. Find them and give it twice as bad as you took it. Forget the fever and the soreness and the weakness and get up and go. If they're not gone already, they will be, and you don't have long.

Lie down and sleep, his body said again, and he stretched out across the pew.

Just for a minute.

He closed his eyes. The dog pushed the empty can around the floor as it fought for every last taste of food. Habana shuffled, clopping and splashing.

So hot, he thought. So hot so fast. He remembered a fever as something balmy and creeping that eased you gently into bed and let you lie there and watch for a few days until it was gone. Not this sharp, stinging thing that was on him now, burning him in the cold air.

Get up. You don't have time. Get up.

Only a minute, he thought, and he felt himself beginning to go. Still and drifting. Behind his eyes there appeared strange images of life before that seem to roam in the vast caverns of the mind when it perches on the cliffside of unconsciousness. A barrage of images that stretched from life before the storms, through the devastation, and up to the last days of his life. Faces of those he barely remembered and odd remembrances of grocery lists or the scores of games and the voices of those who had hurt him and then it all left him and there was only black and he was asleep with twitching eyelids.

He awoke hours later. He sat up and rubbed himself and shivered. In the pillowcase he found the flashlight and he shined it around. The dog was curled on the end of the pew and he didn't see Habana. The wind blew through the church and there was a rustling in the dead leaves and limbs of the tree lying across the pulpit and a raccoon crawled along the trunk, stopped and looked at him, then climbed on down and out of the church.

Cohen went outside and shined the light around

and Habana was in the field across the road and he called out to her. She saw him and began walking back as he looked around for anything dry enough to burn. Inside the church he filled his arms with small branches scattered about, but anything big enough to last was too wet and mushy. He climbed onto the fallen tree and broke off limbs and dropped them into a pile in the choir loft below. Then he climbed down into the choir loft and took a couple of the straight-back chairs and in the aisle of the church he piled it all together and it seemed like enough to make it through the night. Or at least until he could get a few hours' sleep because tomorrow there could be no more rest. He felt guilty for wasting the afternoon but it had helped him recover some and he knew he had to be ready for a fight.

He started the fire on the concrete slab outside the front doors. The smoke climbed and hovered in the ceiling of the porch and then drifted out into the night. He sat in one of the chairs while the other one burned and he drank water and ate aspirin. Habana's saddle and bridle were on the offering table and the dog lay on the concrete next to him on a purple choir robe that he had found in a back room. The rain was steady and almost stopped once or twice.

He talked to the dog.

"The first one was white. Old as dirt but slow and careful like you like the first one to be. Don't want a bronco to sit your kid up on. Didn't even know we were getting him. Dad pulled up with the trailer, honked the horn. Me and Mom came out and he called me over. Said look at this. We walked to the trailer and her snout was sticking out and he said about time you got up on a horse. Her name was Snowball, I think. Real original."

He drank a little water. The dog stood, walked in a circle, lay back down. Cohen rubbed at his beard. Thought some.

"First car was a VW. Little two-door something. Four gears. Couldn't tear the son of a bitch up. I used to see how fast I could go in third gear. Seventy-two was the record. Damn thing sounded like it was about to blow any second. Crashed it. Or got hit. Or something. It folded up like tinfoil. Me and Elisa went on our first date in that car. Tenth grade. Valentine's dance in that smelly old gym. It coulda been at the prince's palace, though, 'cause I was out of my mind, I was so nervous. I mean nervous like wet hands and armpits and nearly-tripping-and-falling-down nervous."

The dog laid its head down. Whined some.

"She wore a yellow dress. Everybody else had on red or pink. She wore yellow."

He stopped talking and stared out into the night. It seemed as if his words were floating out there somewhere and if he looked closely enough he could see the pictures they described.

He leaned back in the chair and stretched out

his legs. The rain had eased and somewhere out to the side of the church a tree branch cracked and fell. He looked back at the dog. "I don't know," he said.

Cohen had always talked to the dog. It had appeared one day. Just like Habana, and he had never bothered to name it because he knew it already had a name. He fed it once and that was all it took to make them friends and he talked to the dog in the way that one might talk to a child or a stranger on a train. Stating the obvious. Asking questions he already knew the answer to. His voice amicable and safe.

The dog rolled over and Habana walked around the side of the church. Cohen watched her and it was then that he saw the orange eyes back off in the trees behind the building. Two large orange eyes caught in the light of the fire, perfectly still in the dark. Habana kept on walking until she was around in front of them but Cohen didn't move and stayed fixed on those eyes as he knew they were the eyes of something that mattered. The dog, seeming to sense his unease, sat up and looked out to where he was looking and began to growl a low, cautious growl. "Shhhhh," Cohen whispered. The dog continued on and he reached down and rubbed its head and whispered for it to be quiet. Be quiet. Don't move.

He slowly moved his hand to his belt and gripped the knife. "Sit down," he told the dog but the dog stood stiff and its growl had turned into a tempered whine. “It’s okay,” he whispered. “But do not move.”

Habana walked closer to them and snorted and that scared the dog, which tucked itself behind Cohen’s chair.

The eyes remained. Still, like knots in a tree.

His mind raced back to the voices of his grandfather and the other old men that he would listen to at the camp on the edge of the bayou. To the things they had seen and the tall tales they had told and he tried to figure out what those orange eyes belonged to but all the voices of the old men did was conjure images of swamp monsters and nameless bloodthirsty creatures that lifted children from their beds in the middle of the night. The eyes staring at him were real and they were close and they were paying attention with an uncommon patience.

It’s gotta be a panther, he thought. A big-ass panther.

He unbuttoned the sheath and pulled out the knife and tried to figure out the best way to kill a panther or whatever the hell it was and he smiled a dumb smile at the absurdity of the thought.

Cohen shifted his gaze to the horse when she snorted again and when he looked back, the orange eyes were gone. Vanished in the dark as if he might have imagined them. He breathed, unaware that he had been holding his breath. And then he told the dog to relax. For now. He stood slowly and walked around to the side of the church and he called the dog and Habana to follow. There would be no sleeping near the fire tonight, not with that thing so close. So the three of them went through a back door of the church and into the room where he had found the choir robes. There were more piled in a closet, and he felt around in the dark and grabbed several and laid them across the floor. The dog immediately lay down on them but he told it to get up. Cohen picked up one of the robes and wrapped it around himself and then he went back to the door, feeling his way with his hand on the wall, and he closed it. Back in the room, he lay down on the robes and the dog lay next to him and Habana stood at the window with her nostrils against the glass and her breath fogging the window. They would be cold and they would be uncomfortable, but they would be safe. And then he started talking to the dog again.

10

Since the proclamation of the Line, they came down like packs of wild coyotes coming in from the hillsides after smelling the scent of fresh blood. Some like gangbusters, with coolers of beer and good weed and radios blaring through the rainstorms, whooping and hollering like crazed spring breakers certain they were having a good time. They crashed the beach, milled around an upturned casino, and started digging not in unison or with any goal but all heads working independently and the holes they dug weren't large enough to hide a basketball in, much less trunks filled with millions of dollars. The gangbusters didn't last. They drove hours, maybe days, to get down to the coast, unaware of the severity of the life below the Line, and they left almost as quickly as they arrived, once the buzz wore off and the shots were fired over their heads.

Others knew the terrain. Those that remained below. Those that knew the winds, knew the thunder, knew the gaps in the seaside and where the bridges were washed away, and knew the lineup of casinos that once stretched for twenty miles along the shore. They knew which ones were still there, and if they weren't still there, they knew where they had once been.

What separated the others were the tools they worked with. Those with no chance came in bunches of four or five, riding in truck beds, shovels and pickaxes for each man. They knew the landscape, had the heart but no guns and no strength or energy to dig quickly and make any headway before being seen and having to make a run for it back into the soggy hole they had crawled out of.

Those with a chance, if there was actually anything to be found, had the guns, had youth, had the vehicles to get through, or across, or over. Men in army-green jeeps and trucks, four-wheel-drive vehicles made for war, with gadgets that detected metal underneath the ground. Men who possessed the physical strength and training to work hard, dig deep, make haste. Men who had been left behind by their government, stuck in outposts in the region below the Line, for God knows what. To help those who didn't want to be helped. To protect those who didn't want protection. To sit in steel-braced cinder-block outposts, day after day, ducking from the storms, watching the rain, listening to the snap of lightning and the moan of thunder, staring at the walls and staring at the floors, so the same government that had abandoned the region could still maintain authority over it, even though there was no law to be followed. No law to be made other than what seemed right at the time. These were the men who sat there day after day, because they had been ordered to by other men who lived on dry land, and now they had grown restless and anxious and this was their opportunity to get out and go and do something and they came in their jeeps and trucks, their big guns racked on top or showing out of the open windows, to express to whoever might be interested in the same treasure they were looking for—do not fuck with us.

The coast was crawling with them and they all came after the same thing—the buried casino money. A lot of damn buried casino money. In the panic of the evacuations, and later in the panic of the Line becoming official, it had been rumored that casino executives ordered the burying of trunks of cash in an effort to hide it from the taxman. The less money the casinos moved, the less money they had to claim. Rumors swirled of men in the middle of the night, loading the backs of trucks with trunks large enough to hide bodies, filled with stacks of crisp dollar bills, and then disappearing into the dark to deposit them into the earth.

The rumors of the buried money were not dispelled easily. In newspaper articles and magazine exposés that covered the movement of the casinos and banks and other financial institutions from the region, the buried money was consistently part of the conversation. The men in the suits flatly denied it, but there was always some casino services manager or pit boss or cocktail waitress who had been in the right bed, ready to proclaim that it was not some ridiculous rumor, I saw the money being loaded, so-and-so told me about burying the money and then he laughed because he said it was so primitive and brilliant at the same time, not only were the big trunks taken out and buried but the big shots filled up their own bags and stashed them across the coast as a retirement plan. The economy was breaking down and banks were folding and many of the casinos were not reopening elsewhere and cash was what mattered. And it's out there. Somewhere.

So they came looking.

II

11

The next morning, Cohen got up and he decided what to take and not to take. In the corner of the room where they slept, in a small closet, he left his extra clothes, some food, and all but one of the paperbacks. He fed the dog what was left of the dog biscuits and then he gathered the rest of the food and water and went outside. He put the food and water and aspirin in Habana's saddlebag along with the flashlight and some matches and the book. In his back pocket remained the picture of Elisa and in his front the small socks. He then covered himself with one of the purple robes and mounted the horse. He looked down at the dog and told it to stay, I'm coming back here at some point in the next few days. But the dog ignored him and walked and then trotted along with them.

A gold cross decorated the back of the robe and Cohen had the appearance of a medieval crusader scouring a godless land in the name of the Almighty. For the next three days, he suffered the rain, rode Habana, and looked for his Jeep and the two who had taken it but he spent most of his time ducking away from others he came across. More movement than he had seen on the coast since before the Line. There was movement along the beachfront, movement in the wastelands of the casinos and hotels and restaurants. Movement even in the scattered remains of the neighborhoods of Gulfport, where there was usually only the quiet of the world of concrete foundations and chimneys. He hid away and watched them. Groups of men standing in a spot and digging. And then maybe gunfire, and ducking and dodging and driving off fast in any direction. He came upon this a couple of times a day, and he had no choice but to hide, and watch them through the rain, and marvel at their dedication to a legend.

He searched most freely away from the city limits and in the miles surrounding his place, and in the miles surrounding the stretch of flooding where they had abandoned him. He followed dirt roads and jagged highways that he had known all his life but they all led to nothing and there was too much space to search it all. His fever came and went and he was sore all over. More sore in his shoulder than anywhere else and he always slept on the other one.

For a time he had taken refuge in a mostly standing gas station and garage on the outskirts of Gulfport. The doors to the bays remained locked down and he built a fire in the garage at nights and the smoke sneaked away through the gaps in the metal roof. The roof dripped from everywhere, smacking at the concrete. At night he slept under the counter in the station and Habana and the dog stayed in the garage. The wind blew and the sounds of the metal roof bending kept him anxious, so on the second night he put the dog outside in order to differentiate between the real and the imagined. During his searching, he had been able to gather a few items of need—clothes, canned foods, a lighter, a hatchet, and a length of rope. He'd held on to some things, not from necessity but because they interested him—a personalized coffee mug with a picture of twin girls, a Saints football jersey with a faded autograph, a pair of roller skates, and a Merle Haggard CD. He sat around the fire in the garage and held these things and imagined the lives they had belonged to. The names of the twins and which one had been born first. What kind of kid still knew how to roller-skate. The boy standing against the railing with his football under his arm and a hopeful look on his face as the players stopped and began to sign autographs. The roughneck or maybe the old man sitting on the back porch in a still, starry night, with a strong drink in his hand, while Merle played over the stereo. The woman who came out and sat with him and their hands together and no words. Only the song in the air and the quiet that belonged to two people who loved each other. He kept these things on a shelf in the garage next to empty oil drums and forgotten socket wrenches.

As he lay down to sleep at the end of the fifth

day, he decided they were gone. Didn't matter where to. Just that they were gone and the Jeep was gone and he could not believe that he had been separated so easily from the Jeep. On the morning of the sixth day, as he sat eating from a can of peaches, the rain stalled, and then another one blew in.

The hurricane rains came violently and he recognized the menacing tone of gray that had moved in from the south and he knew he wouldn't be going anywhere. It rained relentlessly for two days, and then the winds picked up, shooting the rain diagonally and then horizontally, an infinite array of tiny stinging pellets. Cohen tried to figure out the best way to ride it out but there was only the small office of the gas station and the garage, so he left Habana in the garage and he hid under the counter in the purple robe with her saddle across him and the dog at his feet. With him he kept the flashlight and some water. As he lay hidden several miles inland, at the waterfront the water began to rise and surge and it reached across the beach and slapped against the highways and the ruins of the coastline.

And then the worst came on. The sky turned dark, almost night, and he had no idea of time. A constant roar as if he were trapped inside an engine. He shined the flashlight on the dog and it was wide-eyed and trembling. The rains fell and the wind blew as the storm began to exert her strength. In the next hour, the already strong wind became a force and he heard groans in the steel frame of the gas station and the snaps and crashes of trees falling to the ground. Water began to drip onto the counter and sheets of metal were torn from the roof and once or twice there was an extended moan of metal and he sat up and so did the dog. Habana reared and wailed. Moments later the groan came again and there was a cracking above him. The next thing he heard was glass shattering and the wind and rain invaded the station. On the other side of the wall, Habana reared and whinnied and snorted and bumped into the wall in her frantic pacing. He called out to her but it was no good and the dog stood with its ears perked. Then there was the metal groan again and he realized that the garage was about to go.

The winds bore down and the rain bore down and underneath the door a stream of water ran across the concrete floor and all he could do was lie and wait until the garage gave and as soon as the last piece of roof was twisted off into the storm, the bay doors bent and snapped away like buttons and the aluminum walls were ripped free and that was the last he heard of Habana. There was nothing but a metal frame bending and moaning as if it felt the pain.

The dog jumped up on his chest and he hugged the dog as the roof of the station came off and everything not hammered down and even some things that were began to fly away and the rain whipped. He curled himself up as tightly as a skeleton could curl and he held the saddle on top of his head as the wind tried to take them away and he and the dog held on to each other and Cohen called out to Elisa and he called out to God though there was nothing to do but take it.

Cohen stayed curled with the saddle pulled over him to protect himself from any flying or falling debris. The hurricane sat on top of the coast and punished through the night. By morning, the rain fell straight and the damage had been done. He had been sitting in several inches of water for hours and he was beyond cold. His lips had turned purple and his body cramped with the shivering and the jerkiness of his breath. Around him, everything seemed blurred. He stood and the water was over his ankles and he looked up to where there once was a ceiling and the rain fell on him. He walked out of the station and into the parking lot. His hands and fingers were wrinkled and waterlogged. His entire body soaked and shivering.

He knelt down and cupped his hands and lapped the rainwater. The dog stood beside him and whined. Cohen raised and looked up and down the road. He called for Habana, but his voice was muffled by the rain and she didn't come.

They got back to the station and crawled back

underneath the counter. The rain played a song in the water and he stared out and was overcome with the notion that before night, he was going to die. He wasn't sure how it would happen, only that it would. Something hungry and savage would find its way to him and sniff him out and tear him apart with its claws and jaws. Or his fever would explode something in his head and he would fall face-forward into the standing water. Or he would nod off and never wake again because his body and his mind and his heart didn't want to go through the trouble. Or this goddamn rain would finally erode his brain to the point to where he would simply find a deep hole and stick his head in it and never raise it out. He felt as if he were sitting at the end of the world, in a place that the light had long ago abandoned and undiscovered creatures moved about in the black using their instincts to feed off one another. Somewhere unknown to man and unsafe for man and forgotten by the one who had created it. He was going to die in this place and it wrecked his spirit at first but then this became an apathetic notion. He didn't know what there was to live for. And he didn't know what there was to die for. Only that he would die in this forgotten place and be a part of its unaccounted history.

The water ran down his head and face and arms and legs. Under his skin. In his bones.

He looked at the dog and said, "I don't

understand." He fell over on his side with his arms over his head. Rubbed at the red streak around his neck while the rain fell on him. He was too tired to think. He just lay there, cold and wet, and he fell asleep.

Hours later Cohen woke and sat up. Massaged his shoulder. Wiped at his face with his hands and decided that he was going to get up and walk to that church and get his food. He was going to sit down and eat and drink the bottles of water and maybe the roof was still on the place and he would be able to put on dry clothes. "And when I'm done with all that," he said to the dog, "we are getting the hell out of here."

12

Mariposa hadn't slept and her jaw was sore from holding it clenched through the worst of the storm during the night. She stood and looked out but there was nothing new to see. There was enough light now, at least, and that was what she had been waiting on.

She had been sleeping with the large envelope she'd found in the bottom of the shoe box. Holding it, dreaming about it, imagining what was inside, not wanting to open it because she knew the reality of its contents would be a letdown. But her curiosity had won out and she had only been waiting for enough light so she could open it and see what it held and she discovered that she wasn't disappointed.

There was a deed to a house and to land. A marriage license. His and her passport, each with a single stamp from Italy. There was a letter from the state of Mississippi, making an offer for his house and land. There was another letter, dated three months later, from the U.S. government, making a slightly larger offer for his house and land. There was another letter warning him to take the offer or risk losing full rights to the properties. And there was a final letter explaining that the time to accept an offer had passed but he could retain the rights to his house and land but that those rights would disappear once the Line became official, and in the event that the region ever regained its original status, rights would revert to him.

There was a death certificate. There were bank statements from closed accounts. There were letters from insurance companies claiming that, according to recent legislation, they were no longer responsible. There was a letter from a bank in Gulfport that confirmed a certificate of deposit in the name of the child. She noticed the dates on each of the letters or statements and everything went back three to five years.

She spent time with each document that came from the envelope. She read again and again, trying to put it together, their lives becoming more vivid now, the truth blending with the illusion of the memories in the shoe box. These people had been real, not simply whispers of romance that swirled away and landed safely somewhere else. Outside the rain fell and the wind pushed, but inside she was in another world, lost in Cohen's creation.

13

To whom it may concern—he is not dead he is risen.

Joe read it once. Twice. Three times. He sat up on the mattress, naked with a blanket across his legs. The white paper once clean and pure against the filth of his hands and fingernails but now smudged with the same filth. He had read it a hundred times over during the night as the rain and wind beat against the trailer. As the storm had dragged on and the winds became stronger, he drank harder and clenched his jaw tighter and by the light of the lantern he read that note over and over and over. By the end of the worst, he was no longer reading it but reciting it aloud, pacing across the short, narrow floor and rearing back his head and screaming it upward as if to join with the forces of nature. He is not dead he is risen! He is not dead he is risen! Turning up the bottle and reciting it louder and stripping off his clothes and falling drunkenly against the walls of the trailer as it rocked with the weather. Howling all night until the storm let go a little and the bottle was empty and then he fell face-first on the bed with the note clutched in his hand.

Joe sat on the bed with it now and thought of tearing it into a thousand pieces. But instead he held on to it as he got to his feet, put on his clothes, searched around and found a half bottle of water. He drank the water in one take and wiped his mouth on his shirtsleeve and then he walked outside.

Aggie stood under a tarp, drinking coffee and smoking a cigarette. A coffeepot sat on top of a small gas burner and Aggie poured Joe a cup as he walked over. Joe took it and cast his bloodshot gaze out at the rain. He coughed some and spit and rubbed at his forehead. "I want to go off and look around some."

Aggie leaned over and took the Bible from his back pocket and turned it back and forth in his hands, its cover worn and soft like sheepskin. "Might wait until it lets up some."

"I can't. I can't wait."

Aggie drank the coffee. "You all right?"

"I'm all right. Just a rough night, you know."

"Seemed like it."

"I guess you slept through it."

Aggie shrugged.

“I’m getting out for a while. You might let them out, too,” Joe said and he motioned his coffee cup at the locked doors of the trailers.

Aggie nodded. “Go on, then. Keep your eyes out for stragglers and whatever else. God knows who’s running around down here now. Take that Jeep.”

“All right,” Joe answered. He drank his coffee. Waited for any more instruction from Aggie but it didn’t come. Aggie stuck the Bible back in his pocket and he took the key ring from his belt loop. He picked out the key to the Jeep and he took it off and gave it to Joe. As Joe took it, one of the women began to beat on her trailer door and call out.

“That was a bad one last night. Let em breathe,” Joe said.

“I’ll worry about that.”

Joe shoved his hands down in his pockets. Pushed his boot heel into the ground. “It was a bad one last night and it’s been like one long bad one here lately.” He waited for Aggie to say something, but he didn’t. “Seems like it’s badder all the time. Don’t it?”

“Don’t feel much different to me.”

“I didn’t say it feels different. I said it is different.”

Aggie turned to him. “So?”

“So, all I’m saying is, we got a plan for if it gets too bad?”

"It ain't gonna get too bad."

"You don't know that. I damn near shit the bed last night."

"Then you need to get your shit together," Aggie said. "This is where we are."

Joe took a couple of steps back and forth, then said, "Fine."

"You look stir-crazy. Go on out of here."

Joe nodded, then said, "You got Mariposa and that boy locked?"

"Yep."

"You better keep them that way."

"How come?" Aggie asked, his tone gently patronizing.

"They both got that look here lately. They'll get brave."

"That boy is plenty smart enough to weigh the consequences. He listens when we read."

"He listens but he's got that look. And so does she."

"She," Aggie said and he stopped. Thought about her and her amber skin and her wavy black hair and the look in her eyes. "She is just right." He tossed the cigarette. "See what you can see," he said.

Joe nodded and walked back to the compound and into his trailer. He opened up a beer and drank it fast. Let out a grunt when he was done. Then he picked up a towel off the bed and wiped his face and he put on a pair of work gloves and a black sock hat and a coat with a hood. Before he walked out, he grabbed his newly acquired sawed-off shotgun and he took a fistful of shells and stuck them in his coat pocket. He walked out and across the red mud and saw them beginning to peek out from behind the curtains, like they did every morning. Their doors locked from the outside. The pale, exasperated faces in the dirty windows. The sunken eyes. Wondering if he was making the rounds and unlocking the doors. Wondering if they would be allowed outside. Wondering if this would be one of the days when they were allowed to be human. Wondering why they couldn't have just been blown away.

14

Cohen's mind began to betray him as he walked on. The hunger and the fever and the exhaustion. Things that weren't there dashing in and out of ditches and out from behind trees and calling to him with hollow, singsong voices. He shook continuously now. Stopped every hundred yards and knelt or sat down. Water standing everywhere. He sometimes held the trunk of a tree to keep himself upright. He moved along with pain in his shoulder and down his back but he kept on, fighting off the tricks in his mind, trying to keep toward the church, trying to ignore the rain, thinking about the food and water he would find when he got there. He called out as he walked on, Please God be there. Please God be there. There was no knowing if the church was standing but he believed it would be. He didn't have another choice.

The dog started out with him but would get ahead and turn back and look at Cohen, impatient with the lack of pace. Now and again the dog would wander off, out into a pasture or off into a stretch of woods, and then come back and walk with him again. He found freshly flooded roads and bridges that caused him to detour several times, but he kept going in the right direction and could feel the church road getting closer. He fought on, burning and chilled but encouraged by the familiar landscape. Not fifty yards away from the gravel road that would take him to the church, he sat down in the middle of the road. Then he lay down in the middle of the road. He draped his wet arm across his wet head and closed his eyes and there was only the constant drumming of the rain but as he lay there it seemed quiet to him. The quiet of the forgotten.

And then he heard it coming.

He sat up. Listened. Wasn't sure if he was imagining it.

But the sound remained. Coming from the other direction. Getting a little bit louder. He looked down the road and there was a curve and coming from the direction of the curve was the sound of a vehicle that he knew. A deep, chugging sound that rose with the push of the gas pedal and fell with the ride of the clutch.

He got up and slid off the road and splashed into the ditch, his head just high enough so that he could see it coming from around the curve. He waited, anxious, like some hungry animal. And then there it was.

"Please God, be real," he whispered.

And it was real. The Jeep was coming in his direction and he could see that there was only the driver.

Then it slowed. And then it stopped.

The driver stood in his seat and looked around. It wasn't the boy and it wasn't the girl. Cohen wanted him to come on his way but didn't know what he could do if he did. He looked around for a stick or a big rock or anything but there was nothing except wet, limp grass and weeds. He thought to simply get up and flag the man down. Try to get the Jeep back the way it was taken from him. But he wasn't strong enough to fight. Wasn't strong enough for anything. So he lay there and watched.

The Jeep came on forward a little, and then it turned down the church road.

Cohen hurried out of the ditch and onto the road and he was running. The frail, broken run of a sick and hungry man and he kept it up until he reached the church road and he saw the tracks in the mud. He bent over with his elbows on his knees. Gasping for breath and his head light.

He stayed bent over until he caught his breath and then he began again, the sound of the engine fading away.

He was going to shake this free and then that would be that. The note that was driving him crazy. The note that had stirred the past with the images of the burgundy dress of his mother and the backwoods church. It would all be gone after this. For reasons that he didn't understand, he was drawn back to this road. Back to this place. Back to years long before the barrage and the lawlessness.

He drove and thought about Aggie. How he first saw him standing outside of the liquor store, drinking out of a pint of whiskey and smoking a cigarette. Wearing a heavy jacket with his hood pulled over his head but his eyes sharp even from a distance. Joe had walked past him, exchanged a glare. It seemed like that was all anyone did at that time, glare at each other, the coast quickly becoming the land of desertion, a smattering of liquor stores and strip clubs turned whorehouses and the random gas station all that remained with lights on and doors open. The Line only a few months from being official. The coast rats sleeping in what was left of abandoned houses and businesses. Nobody trusting anybody. Destruction all around.

Joe had gone inside and gotten his own bottle and when he came back out Aggie was still there. Watching him. Joe walked toward his truck with his eyes on the man with the hood.

Aggie tossed his cigarette and said, "You got a hitch on that thing?"

Joe said, "What'd you say?"

"A hitch. You got a hitch on your truck there?"

"Yeah, I got a hitch. So what?"

Aggie drank from his bottle and took a few steps toward Joe. "You wanna make some money?"

Joe laughed. "You ain't got no damn money."

"I got it if you want to make it," Aggie said. He pushed his hood back from his head, reached into his jacket pocket, and pulled out a folded stack of bills.

"I ain't queer," Joe said.

"Me neither. Damn."

"Then what you want?"

"I need a truck with a hitch. I got some things I gotta get towed."

"To where?"

"Not far. I got two trucks already but the hitch is busted on both."

"If you got two trucks, why you standing here without one?"

"Walking don't kill people."

"It might down here."

"My trucks are where I need them to be. You

wanna see, take the money. You wanna help, take the money. If you don't, don't take it."

Joe thought about it. He needed the money. Everybody needed the money. "How much?"

Aggie held the folded bills out to him. "All of it."

"Shit," Joe said, shaking his head. "You must think I'm damn crazy."

Aggie had kept moving toward him, was close now, could reach out and touch him if he wanted. "I don't think you're crazy. I need something. You probably need something, just like everybody else down here. Or why else would you still be here?" Aggie held out the money again. "Take it," he said. "Take it and let's ride and talk a little while. We got drinks. I got a pack of smokes. You smoke?"

"Yeah, I smoke," Joe said and he reached his hand out for the money. He then took a long, cautious look at the man. "Open up that coat."

Aggie opened his coat and he had a pistol tucked in his pants. "I know you got one, too," he said. "So we can call it even."

"You're gonna have to let me hold it while we ride."

"No, I ain't. You got every nickel I have in your hand right there. You won't hold my gun. I won't be dead and broke."

Joe thought about it. The man seemed to stare straight through him and there was something about him that told Joe his side would be a good one to be on in a place like this.

So he had told Aggie to get on in. That was three years ago.

It had been easy to go along with Aggie. He was a man who spoke with conviction, with a straight-ahead honesty. A man who had a plan and a way of making Joe feel like there were only benefits. At times he had felt like Aggie was a brother and at other times he had felt like Aggie might cut his throat before daylight. And Aggie had a way of talking to people, a way of getting them to believe. He had heard the way Aggie spoke to the stragglers, to the people they had found at the rope's end. Come on, we'll get you something to eat, he'd say with the compassion of a grand-father. We got a warm, safe place to sleep. People down here gotta help each other, he'd say. Like the Father takes care of the birds of the sky, He takes care of us. And I'm helping Him. Come on and let's get something to eat and then you can decide what you wanna do. We can even drive you up if you want, he'd tell them. And they would climb in the back of the truck, maybe because they trusted him, maybe because they had no other choice, but they climbed in. And they were grateful for something to eat and for the dry place to sleep and they thought they had come upon a savior. Joe believed Aggie when he said this was for their own good. They would die without this place. And you know that the men are a danger and if you don't want to walk them out in the woods, then I will do that. I will do what we need to be done and you stand up straight. This is yours as much as mine. This is your land. It is ours.

Joe had watched. He had learned. Had participated. And he had finally walked a man out into the woods and returned him to the earth and everything else seemed easier after that. But last night was on him. Or maybe it was the culmination of many nights like that one and their growing consistency. The wind never seemed to cease. The rain never seemed to stop. It was bad and getting worse and sitting in the trailer in the dark with his knees tucked under him while the storm pushed and pulled was a too common event. He had to get drunk to get through the nights and then getting drunk spun him around inside and it was a vicious loop. And now he had this note and he had these memories of his mother and this church and what this world looked like before and he felt a pressure welling up inside.

He drove slowly as he moved along the muddy gravel road, the Jeep sliding some and him uncertain if this were the right place. It was difficult to remember anywhere in this land the way it had been because of the way it was now. It was so much worse and there appeared to be no end in sight. The tree line tight against the road seemed familiar, but there were gaps in it that hadn't been before. Houses that might have reminded him were no longer there. It was only his hunch that led him to where he thought the small church would be.

A careful mile or two and he saw it. Sitting up ahead, to the right, back off the road. He drove on up and stopped and looked. He could see the men standing outside in the Sunday sunshine, in their short-sleeved shirts and ties, smoking their cigarettes with their calloused hands. The kids running between the cars playing chase, their shrieks and laughter breaking into the peaceful Sunday morning. The women and their clean dresses with their Bibles tucked under their arms and their faces a soft pink.

The thought occurred to him that all he had to do was to get in the Jeep and keep going. Maybe his time with Aggie had run its course. Maybe he didn't want to be responsible for all those women and what was to come. Maybe he had found that note for a reason, to shake him loose, to set him free. Maybe it wasn't going to be as simple as coming to this place and clearing his head and going back to the circle of trailers and the faces that occupied them.

The shotgun and the shells sat in the passenger seat and he picked up the shotgun but then set it back down. He got out and pushed the hood from his head. He looked at the place. The beige brick stained and molded. The front doors gone. He walked up closer and saw the wet black ashes from a fire on the concrete porch. He poked at them with his foot and then he walked over and stood in the doorway. The fallen tree splitting the roof of the sanctuary and its moss hanging down across the pews. The stained glass in shards below the windows. He looked for the pew where they had sat. Listened for his mother telling him to sit still. Wondered what she would say if she knew what he had become a part of. He stood in the doorway and smoked. Thought of what he'd say in his own defense.

It's a different world, he thought. And he could think of no more explanation.

He walked back outside and around the side of the church. Thought he'd take a look in the back. See if there was anything worth having. At one of the windows he knelt down and picked through the broken stained glass that sat at the bottom of a puddle. He fished the pieces out. The purples and blues and reds. He held several together in his palm and admired the purity of color. Imagined the sunlight against them. The illusion of something brighter and better.

And this would be the last memory that he would have as he lay dying. The memory of kneeling there, in this place where he had been a boy with a mother, with the pieces of the holy glass in his hands. Not the realizations of what he had done, the flesh and blood that he had claimed along with Aggie, the women he had corralled and made his own, their bodies and their minds and maybe even their hearts and souls, unlocking the doors when he wanted and feeding them when he wanted and doing what he wanted when he felt the urge. For what other reason was there to keep them? He didn't think of them or the men he had separated them from. The blood on his hands and the filth on his fingertips. He didn't think of the man that he was and the power he had grasped and he didn't sing for forgiveness or call out for redemption. In the next hour, as he lay dying, he thought only of that moment of serenity, kneeling next to the church where he had been a boy before he had grown into a man and realized the clarity of strength, his knees damp in the wet ground and in his palm the blue and red and purple glass. As he lay dying, his flesh ripped like fabric, his blood flowing freely like the rain that came so often, he thought only of those beautiful shards of glass and the weight that they carried, and he found it difficult to comprehend that while he held those small holy things, how something so big and so powerful and so violent could have been so silent as it crept up behind him.

Cohen didn't wait for the dog to reappear and he went as quickly as he could along the gravel road because he thought the sound of the Jeep had quit. Not disappeared far down the road and out of distance but quit as if whoever was driving it had stopped and the only place close by to stop was the church. He hurried on, pulling at his pants pockets as if to drag himself. When the church was in sight he saw the Jeep parked in front of it and he stopped running and he moved over to the edge of the road, closer to the tree line, to keep out of sight.

He didn't see the man who had been driving and it occurred to him to make a run for it. The rain would muffle his steps and the keys would be in the ignition and just go, take off, don't slow down. Go as hard as you can.

But then his thoughts were interrupted by the high-pitched howls and screams of he didn't know what. Something awful and horrific and acute slicing through the hazy morning. He kept on, walking faster now, breaking into a light run and then he was at the church and next to the Jeep and then he saw that the terrible sound, the howling and screaming, was coming from a tangle of man and panther at the side of the church and the panther was winning.

Cohen looked over into the Jeep and saw his sawed-off shotgun and some shells on the passenger seat. He took it out and loaded it and put some shells in his pocket, keeping one eye on the panther and the man. He tugged at the backseat as if to lift it but it didn't move. The man shrieked as the panther had him pinned and was tearing at him with its mouth and claws. Cohen walked over very carefully, staying behind them so that the panther wouldn't perhaps turn and rush him, and ten feet away he aimed the shotgun and fired and the panther jumped and twisted and cried out. Cohen fired again and the panther jumped again but there was no more crying and it fell dead next to the ripped, screaming man.

Cohen moved closer and looked down. Half the man's face was red and torn and there were gashes across his throat and on his head and down his chest and arms. A bad tear in his rib cage. He was breathing in a terrified, irregular rhythm and his eyes were wide and sharp against the red surrounding them. He held his arm up to Cohen and tried to say something but only a shaky grunt came out. Cohen didn't reach for him but he knelt a few feet away. The rain washed the blood as quickly as it came out of him.

The man's grunting kept on and Cohen watched him for a minute and then he held the shotgun out toward him. "Where'd you get this?" he asked. Then he turned and pointed at the Jeep and asked the same thing. "All of it's mine. Mine. Where's them two that jumped me out there on the road?"

The man turned on his side and coughed out blood and he acted as if he were trying to get up. Cohen moved back. The man seemed to be trying to say something but Cohen didn't know what, so he asked again. “Where are they? If you want anything else from me, you better speak up.”

The man got over on his belly and began to crawl toward him. Bleeding from everywhere and his face like some horror film and he moved himself forward on the ground inches at a time, reaching for Cohen. He kept coughing and spitting and coughing and spitting, the bloody mess like the trail of a slug across the ground as he inched forward and Cohen kept moving back.

Cohen then lay down on his stomach, eye to eye with the man, and said again, “Where the hell are them little shits? I ain’t asking you again. You want help, speak up.”

The man dropped his head and cleared his throat, then spit up again like a sick baby. Then he tried to say something. “Umrow,” he said.

Cohen leaned in and said, “Huh?”

“Umrow.”

“Calm down. Speak up.”

The man extended his arm and pointed awkwardly as if trying to give directions. Then he said, “Him. Himmel.”

“Himmel?”

He nodded his red head. “Row,” he said.

“Road?”

He nodded again.

“Himmel Road,” Cohen said. “Himmel Road out there past Crawfield. That old plantation?”

The man nodded and grunted and he began to

push himself up from the ground. Cohen stayed back. "You sure?" he asked.

But the man didn't answer and he managed to get himself to his knees. Moaning and crying out but his voice feeble. Cohen got to his feet and stood back and he saw that the man was reaching behind him for something. Cohen raised the gun on him but the man only went into his back pocket and pulled out a scrap of paper. He dropped it on the ground in front of him and then fell on his side. Cohen stepped over and picked it up and he looked at it. He read his own note. And then he said, "I told you."

The man was on his back now and he reached his arm up. Tried to talk again but couldn't, but he formed an imaginary pistol with his thumb and index finger and he held it to his head and pulled the trigger. When Cohen only looked at him, he slapped his hand on the ground and grunted and did it again. Still Cohen only looked at him.

"If you wanted something from me, you should have thought about it before," he said and he tossed the note aside. Then he walked on away from the dying man and the dead panther, toward the back of the church, out of the rain, where he found his food and his water and he sat down and tried to make himself better.

After he ate, he changed into the dry clothes he had left behind and then he fell into an exhausted sleep, lying in the middle of the purple choir robes. He dreamed of a backyard with thick green grass and pinks and whites in the flower boxes and a clothesline. A wooden picnic table in the middle of the yard, surrounded by people he had known. Uncles and high school friends and Mom and strange faces from random moments in his life. On the table were plates of food. Fried chicken and hamburger steaks and mashed potatoes and biscuits and sliced watermelon. Everyone ate and ate but the food from the plates never seemed to diminish, yet every time he tried to fill his own plate, someone pushed him aside to talk or took him out front to show him a new car or something. He kept trying to eat and they kept distracting him and when he had the grease of the fried chicken on his fingertips, he woke with his fingers in his mouth.

He shook free from the dream and sat up. He was sweating and this seemed a good sign. The day was nearly gone and the rain had let up. He got up and walked outside and he dragged the dead man and the dead panther out into the woods, laying them next to each other like ill-fated lovers. He then went to the Jeep and looked under the seats and in the glove box. Under the seat he found a hatchet and a half box of shotgun shells and in the glove box there was a flashlight and a pack of cigarettes and a lighter.

Over the next few days he went through the rest

of the food and water, and the empty tin cans and water bottles were scattered across the floor of the back room of the church. He ate and slept, ate and slept. Between sleeping he would walk up and down the road looking for the dog but he stayed off his feet mostly, knew that he needed to get his strength back as soon as possible because there was a journey ahead.

The rain and wind came and went. At night the wind howled as it whipped through the church roof and windows and the water dripped from everywhere. In the day he sat out by the road and imagined a sun sitting in the sky, the sky open and pale and the chill gone from the air for a little while. In the field across the road, a quarter mile away, he saw two black cows meandering about, seemingly unaffected. Heavy, rippled clouds covered it all. Sometimes when the rain and wind eased, there were birds and armadillos and deer.

His fever remained but he felt it beginning to break. At night he listened to the symphony of Mother Nature and smoked the cigarettes. Possums and raccoons visited the church in the darkness and he wondered if they knew about the panther so he told them about it. Pointed out toward the woods where its body lay if they wanted to see for themselves. Each night they came and went as he sat on the front porch next to a small fire reading one of the left-behind paperbacks and each night he spoke to them about the panther or the weather or the advantages of being nocturnal.

When he slept his dreams were less the nightmare and more the comfort of a life that used to be, but when he woke he never hurt any less from having seen the faces of those he missed.

He had options. He could drive to Gulfport, to the casino parking lot, and hope for Charlie. He could get enough gas and supplies to make it to the Line and go from there. But he couldn't be sure that Charlie would appear, or if he had already come and gone. The last hurricane had seemed stronger and more bitter than the recent ones and there could have been roads and bridges washed away, keeping Charlie from making it to the coastline.

Or he could go out on Himmel Road, find the Crawfield Plantation, and find those two who had jumped him. He believed that where he found them, he would find his gas cans, his .22, probably some food and other supplies. Didn't know what else or who else he'd find. But it seemed worth pursuing because he also knew he'd find the things that belonged to Elisa, that belonged to their life together, that belonged to him.

And then after that, he would go for the Line.

He tried for days to talk himself out of caring about those things and that shoe box. It was only tiny bands of silver or gold, only a small diamond, only dainty things that went in your earlobe or hung around your neck, rhinestones and rubies, and all of it together didn't add up to much. Only pieces of paper that didn't prove anything. Only silly little mementos of years long gone. They're not worth anything, he'd think. They won't do no good. Let it go like you should have already. Let it go.

Even in the moments when he had convinced himself that finding Charlie and getting out was the safest, easiest plan, somewhere beneath it all where there was the truth he knew that he was going to find that girl and that boy and get back those small, precious things. Because it was her and because she didn't belong with them and if he was leaving, he was going to leave the way he wanted to leave. He had his Jeep. He had his shotgun. He was finding his strength, invigorated by hope. On the morning of the fourth day, as a steady, drifting rain crossed the land, he loaded the shotgun, draped a robe across his shoulders and head, lit a cigarette, and sat down in the Jeep. He sat and smoked, talking to himself. Telling himself that he was ready for anything. When he finished the cigarette he flicked it out and then adjusted the rearview mirror and looked at himself. It was the first time he had looked at himself in weeks. He noticed his cheekbones and he put his fingers to them, more round and pronounced than they had been. Then he touched the healing line around his neck. He leaned closer to the mirror and looked at his eyes. Thought they had changed color. Or maybe it was the skin and face around them that was so different and made them strange. He leaned back. Huffed.

Then he cranked the Jeep and turned out of the parking lot.

At the end of the gravel road, the dog was standing there. Wet and ragged. He whistled and the dog jumped up into the passenger seat, and they started down the highway in the direction of Himmel Road.

15

Aggie had always been the kind of man who needed to be watched. A strong, wiry build and a sharp brow and thin lips that held tight when they weren't sucking on a cigarette. Thick gray-black hair down tight on a low forehead and tanned skin that didn't lose its dark shade even in the winter months. He had been fired for stealing, stabbed for sleeping with married women, jailed for taking cars that didn't belong to him. He had seldom slept in the same place for longer than a couple of months and the women that he had known weren't aware until he was gone that the name they called him wasn't really his name. He'd always had a curious ability to make friends, to get people to trust him, that had allowed him to live the life of a renegade and when, on a dare, he had started handling snakes in front of a congregation in the strip-mall church on the east end of Biloxi, his calling had been found.

Energized by the reaction of the worshipers, his adrenaline pumping with the pulse of the snake in his hands, its tail rattling and tongue seething, he had become the man who could heal or cleanse or predict the future before he had hardly even acknowledged to his followers that he was capable of such things. It was as if those who sat in the metal chairs and chanted and sang as he twirled the rattlers made him what he was without his consent. Yet he knew that it was right. That the power he held over them was in the proper hands. And he had been wielding that power for almost twenty years, back and forth across the Gulf Coast, moving his serpent church in a carnival-like caravan that waved the flag of the Holy Spirit until the room was full and then in the dark corners of the night, using his position that had been delivered by God to penetrate both bodies and souls that didn't belong to him.

In this new world, the snakes had been exchanged for guns and the strip-mall church exchanged for a colony.

He had let the women out to go to the bathroom and to eat. They were scattered in the fields around the trailers, pants down and squatting, the high grass the only shroud of modesty. Aggie stood under the tarp next to a low fire with the revolver in his hand, dangling down against his leg. The rain blew in below the tarp and the fire hissed back at it like a threatened snake. He watched them carelessly as he tapped the revolver against his leg, humming an old gospel he remembered his grandmother playing on the living room piano.

Four days now since Joe went off, he thought. He couldn't decide if Joe had run off or if he was dead or dying, but he didn't believe the man would desert. They'd been in it together for too long, gotten in and out of too much, hoodwinked too many people, and Joe had been as much of this new world as he had. Helped him find the place, helped him tow and circle the trailers, helped him loot houses and stores, helped him smile at the stragglers, promise them food and shelter. Helped him keep the women and get rid of the men. And nothing Joe had done or said suggested that he would run off. Aggie had taken one of the trucks and gone where he could, looking for the Jeep. Looking for Joe. But Joe was gone. At least for now. Aggie was finding it more difficult to believe that he'd see him again. So without his enforcer, he'd been more careful with his colonists, keeping the doors locked longer during the day, showing the revolver when they were out.

He thought that without Joe, it was time to start

working on Evan. He would need another man. Someone strong enough to help hold them the way they needed to be held. Someone to increase their numbers.

One by one they came back into the circle of trailers and on a table next to the fire there were paper plates and plastic forks and gallon jugs of water and Coke. Next to the plates were two loaves of sliced bread, a package of bologna, peanut butter, and jelly. A bag of apples sat on the end of the table. They moved about slowly, as if resurrecting from a lengthy, dreamless slumber, unfamiliar with this place and what might have brought them here. Odd, shapeless figures, so draped in layers that it seemed as if the bodies beneath were nothing more than knobby frames of bone and flesh. They formed a line and waited for him to speak. Their coats were too big for their hungry bodies, some with bandanas tied around their heads, some with sock hats, some with gloves. Eight of them. Eight women who did not do anything that they were not supposed to do. Two of them pregnant. One in a big way. At the end of the line stood the blond boy and the dark-haired girl and the child, Brisco. Evan held Brisco's hand and the child pushed the man-sized sock hat up off his eyes so he could see. All of them were damp, like everything else. The smoke gathered against the tarp and made a cloud around them.

Aggie stood in front of them and he tossed away his cigarette. Then he removed the Bible from his back pocket and opened it up to the same place that he read from every day before they ate. His rough fingertips brushed the featherlike pages, then he began.

" 'The earth also was corrupt before God, and the earth was filled with violence. So God looked upon the earth, and indeed it was corrupt, for all flesh had corrupted their way on the earth. And God said to Noah, The end of all flesh has come before Me, for the earth is filled with violence through them, and behold, I will destroy them with the earth. And behold, I Myself am bringing floodwaters on the earth, to destroy from under heaven all flesh in which is the breath of life, everything that is on the earth shall die. But I will establish My covenant with you, and you shall go into the ark—you, your sons, your wife, and your sons' wives with you. And of every living thing of all flesh you shall bring two of every sort into the ark, to keep them alive with you, they shall be male and female. Of the birds after their kind, of animals after their kind, and of every creeping thing of the earth after its kind, two of every kind will come to you to keep them alive.' "

One of the women coughed and Aggie stopped. Looked for the culprit. Then he read again. "'Then the Lord said to Noah, Come into the ark, you and all your household, because I have seen that you are righteous before Me in this generation. So Noah, with his sons, his wife, and his sons' wives, went into the ark because of the waters of the flood. Of clean animals, of animals that are unclean, of birds, and of everything that creeps on the earth, two by two they went into the ark to Noah, male and female, as God had commanded Noah. And it came to pass after seven days that the waters of the flood were on the earth. In the six hundredth year of Noah's life, in the second month, the seventeenth day of the month, on that day all the fountains of the great deep were broken up, and the windows of heaven were opened. And the rain was on the earth forty days and forty nights.' "

Aggie paused. He looked up at them and moved his eyes from one to the next to make certain they listened and watched the man who spoke. He rubbed his hand over his mouth, smacked his lips, turned a page in the Bible and began again.

" 'So He destroyed all living things which were on the face of the ground: both man and cattle, creeping thing and bird of the air. They were destroyed from the earth. Only Noah and those who were with him in the ark remained alive.' "

Aggie closed the Bible. He looked toward the sky, shut his eyes and held out his arms, and repeated the last verse with something akin to vengeance in his voice. " 'Only Noah and those who were with him in the ark remained *alive*.' "

He lowered his arms, opened his eyes, and nodded to them. In unison they spoke a broken amen. One of the women stepped out of line and toward the table.

"Hey," Aggie snapped. "You hold your ass right there."

She took a slow step back.

"You forget how we work?" he asked and pointed the Bible at her. She shook her head. "What did you say?" he yelled.

"No. I ain't forgot," she mumbled.

Aggie put the Bible in his back pocket. "You better not. None of you," he said. Then he clapped his hands together, said a final amen, and told them to eat.

16

It took a while to find it, but he found it. Roads washed over that hadn't been washed over before. Detours off the highway, trailing the back roads, sometimes off into fields or ditches to get around fallen trees or light posts. But he found Himmel Road, a single-lane road that had been patched many times, and at the beginning of the road was a moldy white wooden sign that read CRAWFIELD PLANTATION in Old English lettering. The sign was on a fence post and was amazingly erect though it stood in a pool of water in what was now a ditch.

He remembered Crawfield Plantation from school field trips when he was a boy, and then later looking at cattle and horses with his dad. A few hundred acres of thick forest and grazing pastures. Stables and barns and a white wooden fence stretching the length of its acreage along the road. And what seemed like a sky-high antebellum, with four columns across the front reaching from the porch to the roofline, a balcony that stretched across the length of the front of the house, and on the backside two smaller balconies that reached out from bedrooms. Azaleas circling the house and along both sides of a bricked pathway that led from the front door down to the circular drive-way. Magnolias and oaks in the front and side yards and in the back a courtyard with a bricked patio and walkways, a concrete fountain in the middle, and arches and columns decorating the corners with vines of moonflower and black-eyed Susies and honeysuckle twisting and blooming.

None of this was there now. Cohen moved along the road in low gear, looking ahead to where he remembered the wonderful house that sat up on a hill and seemed to keep watch across the land like a mother might watch her children playing. Nothing now. The house gone and the magnolias and oaks broken and in the place of majesty was a gathering of the once white rectangular boxes that the government had delivered with a hand-shake and a smile. He slowed, then stopped. A half mile away. Then he turned off the ignition. The rain was dying some, falling in random, almost undetectable drops. He pushed the robe back off his head and shoulders and he lit a cigarette. The gas gauge was on empty and he knew he wasn't going much farther. In any direction. It seemed that the dying man may have told him the truth, that the boy and girl were at Crawfield Plantation. But so were others. He watched a group of them mill around the trailers. And he reminded himself that whoever was there, they weren't safe. Nothing was safe and nothing was certain.

He smoked and thought about it some. It was probably midafternoon, hard to tell from the sky, but dark couldn't be more than a few hours away. He'd wait, go take a closer look. Maybe it would rain harder and keep him covered and quiet. The dog sniffed around in the backseat and they discovered the bag of beef jerky still tucked underneath the driver's seat and they sat and chewed while they waited for night.

He took off the robe and knocked the Jeep out of gear and rolled it back some to the side of the road, along the bushy fence line. He took the flashlight and the shotgun and he and the dog started walking up the road, close to the barbed wire wrapped in thick, leafy vines. In the time that he had been watching there had been little movement and he figured from the array of vehicles scattered around the trailers that there had to be gas up there somewhere. He walked hunched over, his knees bent, as small as he could be. His breath out before him. The nightfall bringing the cold. The rain steady. Fifty yards away he told the dog to stop and they knelt down and he watched. Low lights burned from the insides of the trailers. Candlelight, he thought. The solitary man who had been moving about all day sat on the end of a let-down tailgate of a truck, facing their direction, with a hood over his head. It was getting difficult to see.

They edged along. Ten yards or so at a time and then stopping and listening. Then moving some more. He was at the gate that led into the plantation land and he stopped again. Told the dog to stay. The dog looked around, stayed at his heel. Then they moved across the opening of the gate and there was an alarming clap and the dog fell dead as the clap echoed across the land. Cohen jumped, and then froze, and then darted back behind the gatepost as another shot rang out and splintered the post above his head. He sat with his back against the post, breathing hard, trying to decide if he should run for it or fire back and he pointed the shotgun around the post and fired without looking. Another shot splintered above his head and he fired back and then he hurried to reload with the shots from the compound whacking against the post and their echo stretching out into the early night.

He looked over at the motionless dog and said son of a bitch, son of a bitch. The shots kept coming and he felt them coming from closer and closer and he was dead if he ran and dead if he didn't run and all he knew to do was to turn and fire out into the dark in the direction that he thought was right. So he caught his breath, ignoring the shards of wood scattering about his head, and he leaped out and fired twice. Bright blasts in the gray-black world and then he felt the seething-hot pain shoot through his thigh muscle and he hit the ground. Writhing and wrestling with the shotgun, trying to reload, then he heard the voice say, "Don't do it, boy. Don't do it or I swear you'll drink the blood."

17

The man held the rifle on Cohen as he limped through the mud to the circle of trailers. He told him to sit down over there by the red coals covered by a head-high tarp tied off between two trailers. Cohen did and the heat that had shot through his leg was up into his head and he clenched his jaw as he sat down on the wet red ground. He squeezed the gunshot wound with both hands and they were covered in blood and it ran warm down his leg and into his boot.

"Don't move," Aggie told him as he left him at the fire. He went into a trailer and came back with a tackle box and a pint of whiskey. Heads looked out of windows in the trailers surrounding the fire.

Aggie held out the bottle and Cohen let go of his leg and took it and unscrewed the cap and turned it up in one fluid motion. He drank some and spit some out and by then Aggie had opened the tackle box and taken out a roll of gauze and something in a spray can and a heavy bandage.

"Son of a bitch," Cohen said, spit and whiskey running down the sides of his mouth. He turned the bottle up again and then tossed it aside and it spilled out.

"Careful with that," Aggie said. "Shit don't grow on trees." He held the spray can up and sprayed it once and then moved toward Cohen.

"Get the hell away from me with that shit," Cohen said and he slid across the ground.

"Come here and shut up."

"I said get on."

Aggie came forward and Cohen stiff-armed him.

"Ain't no bullet in there," Aggie said. "So we gotta clean it up. Stop it bleeding. Looks like it missed the bone. Hold still."

"I ain't holding still."

"You will if you want it to quit."

"Fuck you. You shot me."

"Shot you. And could have killed you. Still could. So quit squirming and rip them pants. It's that or sit here and bleed."

Cohen shook his head. Breathed frustrated, painful breaths. Shook his head hard, then said, "You rip them and you fix it."

"Then get up," Aggie said.

Cohen struggled to his feet and Aggie stuck his fingers in the bullet hole of the pants and ripped them open. A circle of crimson, fresh and flowing. The leg shook and Aggie sprayed it with a white spray that made a freezing white foam and then he put a thick bandage on top and told Cohen to hold it. Then he moved around to the backside and sprayed the exit wound and put a thick bandage on it and told Cohen to hold it with his other hand. He quickly wrapped the gauze once around the leg, then several more times tightly. Cohen stood straight-legged and his fists were balled and then he fell back down on the ground, grabbing for the pint bottle and taking a big drink. He didn't toss it away this time but held it close to his chest as if someone might try and take it from him.

He finally caught his breath and he sat up straight, his legs out before him. He kept drinking the whiskey in little sips. Aggie stood back from him, facing away from the fire, his features vague. His rifle and the shotgun lay on the ground at the door of his trailer and Cohen looked over at them. Cohen's face was streaked with mud and sweat and rain. Nobody talked for a while and Cohen couldn't figure out why he wasn't dead. "You shot my dog," he said.

Aggie took out a cigarette and offered Cohen one.

"Light it," Cohen said and Aggie lit them both and handed one to him. "You didn't have to do that. Shoot the dog."

"I know it," Aggie said. "But I don't trust animals."

"Shit," Cohen said, shaking his head.

Aggie turned toward the fire, his silhouette sharp and menacing. "Where'd you get that Jeep?" he asked.

"It's mine," Cohen said. And then he looked around and between two of the trailers he saw the generator and some of his furniture. "So is that and that and that," he said and he pointed. He noticed the heads in the windows. "Where's that boy and girl?" he said.

Aggie smoked. Didn't look at him.

"I said where's that boy and girl?"

"Where's Joe?"

"Who's Joe?"

"You know who Joe is."

"Just like you know who the boy and girl are."

Aggie took out another cigarette and lit it with the one in his mouth. Then he tossed the old one in the coals. "Come over here by the fire," he said.

"Where's that boy and girl? She got something

of mine. You all got something of mine, from the looks of it."

"Did you kill him?"

"Naw, I didn't kill him."

"Then where is he?"

"Where's that boy and girl?"

Aggie turned and walked closer. Knelt down. The glow of the fire dancing on their faces in the cold night. Aggie looked at his leg and the wrapping turning red and then he looked up at Cohen. "Only what is alive is strong," he said.

Cohen adjusted himself on the ground. Grimaced and pulled at his leg.

"And what is strong gets the right. You killed him, that's fine. That makes you strong. That makes us strong. That gives us the right."

Cohen took a long drag from his cigarette, tilted back his head and blew the smoke, then he said, "I ain't interested in your rights or my rights or nobody's rights. I want to know where that boy and girl are. I didn't kill your boy. A panther got on his ass and tore him up and he laid there and bled to death. So there."

Aggie sighed. Stood up. He walked back to the fire and said, "That's why I shot your dog. 'Cause there ain't no trusting animals."

"My dog wouldn't rip your balls off. Animals ain't all the same."

"Animals are all the same. They're down here," Aggie said, holding his hand down toward the ground. Then he held the other hand up and said, "We're up here."

"That's good. Real good," Cohen said and he put his hands behind him and leaned back and watched Aggie. He stared down into the fire as if waiting for something to rise from it. Then he looked around again. Heads disappeared behind curtains when he caught them looking. This man in his army coat and his cigarettes and his face like something hardened in the sun. Locks on the doors. Guns leaning against the trailer door. He let his head fall back and the whiskey made him dizzy so he raised his head again to stop the spinning.

"What kind of sight is that on your rifle?" he asked and nodded toward the rifle that had shot him.

"The kind that you can see far with."

"And I'm guessing the kind you can see in the dark with."

Aggie nodded. "You'd be surprised what you can find clutched in the hands of a dead man."

"How many dead men you been around?"

The man held his palms out to the fire. "Enough. Everybody down here's been around enough. If the weather don't get them, something will."

Cohen looked around again when a light flashed in a window. "Who are they?" he asked.

Aggie lifted his head and his eyes went from one trailer to the next, slowly, as if he were trying to remember something about each one. Then he said, "You want something to eat?"

Cohen moved his leg a little and grunted. "I don't want nothing to eat."

"Got plenty."

"Why they locked up?"

"Drink some more whiskey. You need to keep it in you with that leg."

"Why you got people locked up?" Cohen's voice raised as he spoke, no fear of the man. No sense in any fear now. He had been shot and dragged up and his house was done and he was sitting on the wet ground surrounded by a circle of trailers tied down with ropes and it didn't seem to matter. Didn't know if he had been done a favor by being allowed to live but he didn't care and if he was going to die the least he could do was get a straight answer about something before he was shot by this old man who seemed to be the gatekeeper of this prison or slum or whatever it was. He had come for Elisa's keepsakes and he knew that the boy and girl were behind one of these locked doors and that was all he cared about.

Aggie stood still and quiet, turning his hands in the warmth.

"Where's that boy and girl?"

Nothing from the man.

"That girl's got some stuff of mine and I want it and then I need some gas and I'll be on my way. I'm getting to the Line."

Aggie laughed a little. “What Line?”
“You know what Line.”
“You must’ve been way down in a hole somewhere, not laid up in that nice house of yours.”
Cohen adjusted some to sit up straight. “What does that mean?”
Aggie then turned from the coals and walked slowly to a stack of cinder blocks on the other side of the fire and sat down on top. “The Line is our problem.”
“I don’t know what your problem is. It ain’t my problem.”
“The Line is the problem for us all. Those above it. Those below it. Those who drew it. It’s the symbol of hate. Fear. Symbol of disbelief.”
Cohen took a swallow from the bottle.
“The Line don’t do nothing but point fingers,” the man continued. He sat with his legs crossed and his arms folded. “It tells us some people are all right. Some people ain’t.”
“Well. It’s true. Some people ain’t all right. Nobody down here is all right. Except for me. I was all right until about a week ago.”
“You ain’t all right, either,” Aggie said, looking at Cohen. “You think you were, but you weren’t. What makes you all right? Alone. Nobody to talk to. Nobody to pray to. You pray to anybody?”
Cohen took another swallow, ignored the question.
“The Line thought it was taking away, but it

don't. The Line gives. Gives those who believe and who care about something more a place to go and live their own way. With their own kind. It's them above that will wash away. Not those below."

He spoke like a man who had thought for a long time about what he was saying. Either that or he spoke like a man who had rehearsed. His tone was certain and the air of certainty was in his face and eyes.

"So who are they?" Cohen asked again.

The man raised his arm and held out his hand as if reaching for something, and then he began to wave in slow motion. "They are like me. Like us. They belong here. They are who I take care of. Who I am responsible for. They are for me and I'm for them and we are for you. You came to us and we'll make a place for you."

"I didn't come to nobody and I don't need a place. I need that girl and some gas."

"You need a place. We all need a place."

"Why are they locked up?"

Aggie lowered his hand. Got up and walked a circle around the fire and then sat back down. They were quiet for a while. Cohen's leg throbbed and the bleeding slowed and they watched the fire dying out. There was no more use in talking, Cohen thought. Not now. Not tomorrow. Talking wasn't going to get him what he wanted and talking wasn't going to get him out of here.

The whiskey caught up with Cohen and he felt light and numb. Around them the night was black and still like a painting.

But then the quiet was interrupted by a knocking. Cohen seemed to be the only one to hear it as Aggie didn't move. It kept on. A patient, consistent knock coming from the trailer closest to them. Cohen looked over and there was the round beam of a flashlight in the window and the knocking kept on, turning into a banging, and then there were the voices of two women calling out. "Aggie, open up. Aggie, come on. She's ready. It's ready. Open up."

Aggie stood. He reached into his pocket and took out a ring of keys, and he turned himself toward Cohen so he could see the revolver stuck in his pants. Then he walked over to the guns and picked them up and opened his door and set them inside, locked the door and turned, then walked over toward the voices. "Get back," he called out.

"Open the door. She's ready," a woman called back.

"I said get back."

From behind the door, there was a painful moaning.

Cohen got to his feet and stood with his back to the fire. Aggie unlocked and opened the door and one woman held the flashlight on another woman who stepped out. Her face was twisted in pain and she held her hand across her big, round belly and she was wearing two coats, one with a hood pulled over her head. She stepped out of the trailer carefully, as if the ground might crack beneath her. The woman with the flashlight came out behind her and held the pregnant woman by the arm.

Cohen almost didn't believe it but he had learned that in this land you should believe everything. And not believe everything. Some-where in the midst of his thoughts, in the middle of this night, the woman's moaning seemed like the perfect sound. He watched her walk with her back arched and her steps small and her anguished expression, and he momentarily forgot about the pain in his leg as he realized what type of hurt was coming for her. He felt for the knife beneath his coat. In its sheath, tight against his belt. Then he felt for the picture of Elisa folded in his back pocket. And then Aggie reappeared, holding what looked like the medicine bag of an early-century good country doctor.

18

Ava walked with Aggie and the pregnant woman, holding her arm and hand, asking Aggie what they were going to do as if having this baby in this place was an idea that only moments ago had occurred to any of them. While they walked laps around the fire, Aggie moved away from the circle of trailers and off into the field to a cow trailer with two pieces of plywood laid across the top. He opened up the back of the trailer and the iron groaned from rust and he stepped up and in. Cohen stood still as the women passed him around the fire and they acted as if he wasn't there until he asked if he could do anything.

They stopped and the pregnant woman shook her head and the other said, "Why don't you run on down to the hospital and bring back a doctor and a nurse and a grenade to shove up Aggie's ass." They were short women and the one who did the talking wore a faded blue bandana tied around her head and the same kind of army coat as Aggie and mismatched gloves. The pregnant woman's hands were bare and she made fists when she grunted. She pushed her hood back and sweat glistened on her forehead in the dim light of the fire.

Their names were Ava and Lorna. Lorna about to become the mother.

"You need to get some help out here, Aggie," Ava said. She spoke as if she were unafraid of the man with the keys. "And figure out where the hell we gonna do this."

"We don't need any help," he said and he set the worn black leather bag on the ground. He lit a cigarette and sat down on top of the stack of cinder blocks. "Ain't no hurry."

"You don't know that," Ava said.

"Holy Lord," Lorna said, squeezing at Ava's hand.

"Breathe big and let it go. Breathe big."

The contraction lasted a long minute. No one spoke as they watched her breathe. When the pain subsided, they walked over to where Aggie sat and he got up and the pregnant woman eased down.

"That your new boyfriend?" Ava asked without looking at the men.

"How long you think it's gonna be?" Aggie asked.

"Don't know. Before the night is over."

Another contraction came on and the woman clenched her jaw and threw back her head.

"This ain't a good idea," Cohen said.

Aggie cleared his throat, spit. Took a drag off the cigarette and looked at Cohen and said, "At times I am afraid, I will trust in the Lord."

"Go tell her that," Cohen answered.

"Holy Lord, holy Lord," Lorna cried out. "Holy Lord, here it comes again. Goshdamn it hurts. Holy Lord, holy Lord, holy Lord." She talked through it, her voice rising and falling with the rise and fall of the contractions, and almost as if summoned by the gods, the sound of her voice and the promise of a new life into this land brought on the spirit of the winds and the sound of thunder.

Cohen looked at her and at all the other women

pacing about and then he thought of Elisa. When I'm big and fat people are gonna open doors for me and give up their places in line, she had said. They already do that, he told her. Because you're so damn pretty. I'm gonna eat and eat some more and you know some women eat dirt and he didn't believe that but she explained that it was true and then she stuck a pillow under her shirt and patted her belly and said she was gonna get fat and not worry about it and he'd better not, either. And enough with all the sweet talk 'cause you already knocked me up. The work is done. She took the pillow from under her shirt and threw it at him and he said if the work is all done then I'm getting a beer and she didn't like that, either. Didn't like that he could drink beer and coffee and smoke a cigarette and she couldn't and she didn't like that he didn't mind doing any of these things right in front of her. Drove her crazy. Made him laugh.

"Okay, okay, okay," Lorna said, breathing hard as the contraction eased.

Cohen walked around. He remembered being right, though she was certain it was going to be a boy. Told him every day for three weeks before they found out. It's a boy. I know it's a boy. Nope, he told her. And I'll bet you twenty bucks. She laughed and said you don't have twenty bucks and you'd better hope like hell it's not a girl anyway. Because you won't be worth a damn if it is.

"Oh hell, it's coming again," Lorna groaned and the intensity returned.

He thought of the twenty dollars she had given him when they got back to the house after the doctor visit and the piggy bank he stuck it in. He thought of his hand on her belly. Her stomach was round now and it all seemed more real than it had before they knew it was a girl. As he walked around the compound and listened to the woman cry out, he held out his hand and tried to feel that round belly again, tried to feel the baby in the only way that he had ever felt her. But his open hand didn't feel anything but the cold air and his memories of Elisa were chased away by the sounds of the pleading woman and the notion of what Aggie had done to her.

Nearly dawn but nearly impossible to tell beneath the cover of thick clouds. The women had gone back into the trailer, where Lorna could lie back and spread her legs. The labor had lasted through the night and nobody knew if it was time to push or not but she was going to anyway. Aggie had let out two other women to help and the four of them were inside the trailer, Lorna's grunting and sometimes screaming and the voices of encouragement blending with the beat of the storm. Cohen was inside an empty trailer, only a bare twin mattress on the floor and a rack of empty shelves against one wall, and he slept on his back with his mouth wide open and his hands at his sides as if posing for the portrait of a dead man.

The other women who had seen what was going on were beating on their doors, calling to be let out so they could help, but Aggie ignored them until they stopped. He braved the storm, leaning against the trailer, holding on to one of the ropes, soaking wet, listening to Lorna, and he wanted it to be a boy. He was going to need boys to make this what he wanted it to be.

Cohen jerked up from his sleep as if a grenade had exploded in his dreams, wide-eyed and with quick breaths he looked around frantically. The bullet hole in his leg stung and he grabbed at it and tried to remember where he was and what was going on. He looked around at the empty room, the cabinets and mini-kitchen ripped out, leaving scarred walls, and it smelled like old sweat. He got to his feet and out of the window, through the storm, he saw the man with the revolver leaning against the trailer, and then he saw other faces in the windows of the other trailers and he was reminded that this wasn't a bad dream but the real thing. He licked at his dry lips and rubbed at his throat. The ring of whiskey in his head. He lay back down and calmed himself, recalling what had happened and where he was so he could figure out how to get out of it.

Then the pregnant woman screamed. A twisted, howling scream that split through the storm.

He limped to the door. He unbuttoned his coat and lifted his shirts and he opened the sheath. He took out the bowie knife and he turned it back and forth in his hands, trading it from palm to palm. It was cold and he squeezed it and he felt strong and then the woman screamed again. Cohen slid the knife back in the sheath and put his shirts over it and buttoned his coat. He hobbled out and over to Aggie just as Ava opened the door and yelled out, "Something ain't right." She stood in the doorway with her hands on her hips and the look of the confused. Aggie stepped up to her. Inside, Lorna screamed again. And again and again. They all just looked at one another.

"Something ain't right," Ava said again. "I can see it but it ain't moving. And I ain't sure it's the right way or not."

"You gonna have to cut her, then," Aggie said.

"You cut her. I don't wanna cut her."

"You gonna have to."

"Or you are."

"She's gonna die if you don't," Aggie said with no notion if this was true or not but from the sound of Lorna, it sounded right.

"She might die either way," Ava said. "If I cut her, how am I supposed to fix it up? There ain't nothing in the bag showing me how to do that." She no longer wore the army coat and her sleeves were rolled up to her elbows and there was blood on her hands.

“You gonna have to get that baby,” Aggie said. “He’s the start.”

“I know what he is. Or she is. Or whatever it is,” Ava said. “I been here long as you. Remember?”

“The start of what?” Cohen asked but they ignored him or didn’t hear him.

Lorna screamed out again. And then she stopped. They waited for her to start back but a quiet minute passed and Ava hurried back inside.

Aggie stepped back out and stood on the doorstep. The rain beat on the men and they hunched over and peered at each other from under their hoods.

“Got coffee over there in that one,” Aggie said and nodded toward another trailer but Cohen didn’t answer. He badly wanted some water but he didn’t want to get in the habit of asking this man for anything and before he could decide what to do the screaming started again and this time it didn’t stop. The screaming and the women calling out to her above her screams, above the storm, begging her to hold on, yelling directions to one another, chaotic directions that went around in circles and didn’t help or mean anything but only added to the hysteria of the moment. Cohen closed his eyes. Clenched his jaw. Wished to God he were somewhere else.

Aggie stood without expression.

Cohen opened his eyes and yelled to him, “You proud of this?”

Aggie yelled back, "I probably should have gone ahead and killed you last night. Or right now."

Cohen wasn't sure he'd made it out against the noise of the women, so he asked the man to say it again.

"You heard me," Aggie said.

"No, I didn't," Cohen said defiantly. "Say it again."

"I said I'm going to save you. You were sent here and you know it. Like the rest of us."

"Nobody was sent here."

"You don't understand."

"I understand enough of what I see."

"That's what you see now."

"It won't be no later."

Aggie nodded. He grinned at Cohen from under his hood with the eyes of a man who had been set free. The eyes of a man who understood the power of conviction when there was no one around to judge.

The screaming then became something more than painful. It became torturous. Grotesque. Cohen watched Aggie and he didn't know what he was dealing with here in this place, with this man. Didn't know exactly who Aggie was or what he had done or what he was capable of but he knew it was some bad shit. Women behind locked doors and one man with the keys. The Holy Bible stuck in his back pocket. Wearing the coat he'd taken off a dead man. The power to send out others to ambush and steal. The drop-dead glare of the unrepentant.

The woman's scream was shrill and pleading and there appeared to be no mercy in this land. Cohen stood still, listening to her, watching the man with his brow unchanged while the screaming of the woman splintered the storm around them and he thought of Elisa and what it would have been like with her belly round and the name chosen and the room built and painted yellow or pink or blue. He thought of the tiny nameless thing that died with her and he thought of the small thing fighting for its life inside that trailer where the women stood helplessly around the mother as if they had been ushered back to a time when there was no other choice than to wring your hands and pray. There were the screams and the pleas but there were no answers and the sun was creeping on the edge of the horizon and somewhere people were sleeping in warm beds and somewhere it was going to be a beautiful day.

It was then that Cohen lifted his coat and shirts and he unsnapped the sheath and took out the knife. He held it in his right hand and waved it like a badge. Aggie's eyes widened and he stepped back but Cohen wasn't going for him. He was going for the trailer where the screaming came from and when he got there, he opened up the door and he walked right in and he saw the blood and he saw the anguish and Ava, kneeling between the woman's legs, turned and looked at him and he pushed her out of the way.

19

On the morning of the fourth day in Venice, they awoke to a faint sunshine. Elisa rolled over onto Cohen, kissed him, and said I'm going for a run.

Cohen reached for her as she tried to get up from the bed but she playfully pushed him away and stood at the window.

"I can't believe you brought your running shoes," he said. "Me and you need to discuss what the word 'vacation' means."

She took off the T-shirt that she slept in and she pushed back the white drapes and stood in the open window in only the panties she had bought the day before that had CIAO written across the bottom.

"What are you doing?" he asked.

She stretched her arms and she was beautiful in the morning light. "It's Italy. Nobody cares," she said. "It feels good."

He stared at her freckled back and shoulders and all he wanted to do was snatch her back into the bed and do wild things to her. He was about to go for her when she moved from the window and opened the armoire next to it. She found shorts and a tank top and her running shoes and she began to dress.

"Only a short one," she said. "I gotta sweat out some of this wine we've been putting away." On the nightstand was an empty wine bottle and on the floor by the bed was another.

"You're gonna get lost," he said.

"Probably. But I'll figure it out."

"Well," he said and he rolled over. "I'll be right here when you get back."

She tied her shoes and found her running watch in the suitcase. Then she kissed him again and went out the door and he listened to the sound of her footsteps on the stairway.

He awoke two hours later and heard the tenor voice outside. Elisa hadn't returned. He checked his watch twice to make sure she had been gone that long and he believed she should have been back by now. A short run for Elisa usually meant forty-five minutes. Maybe an hour.

He took a long shower and then shaved and brushed his teeth. When he was done he thought of standing naked in the window like Elisa but realized her curves provided a much more desirable picture. He put on some jeans and a white T-shirt and then he stood in the window and looked out at the courtyard. Healthy vines grew out of terra-cotta pots and up a trellis and red blossoms stuck out from window boxes on the building across the courtyard. The handful of wrought-iron tables were filled this morning with the absence of rain and a young waitress moved between them delivering coffee and plates of bread.

What she has done, he thought, is run until she got lost, then found herself a young Italian stud. They are now on a little boat that will take them to his bigger boat and by this time next year she will be speaking Italian and standing naked in her own bedroom window with her hunky young Italian traded in for a new hunky young Italian.

He smiled but didn't laugh because it didn't seem an impossible scenario with the fairy-tale look that had been in Elisa's eyes since they had arrived.

He sat down on the bed and turned on the television and watched the replay of a soccer match from last night. Milan and Barcelona. He couldn't tell which was which but he listened to the constant chantlike choruses from the crowd and felt almost hypnotized. He watched for half an hour and then he began to worry some, so he turned off the television and put on shoes, socks, and a shirt, and went out to walk around and look for her.

He turned right when he came out of the hotel. A short walk and he arrived at a busy plaza. Tucked in the corners of the plaza were kiosks for newspapers and magazines, cigarettes and postcards, tourist maps and T-shirts. Restaurants and cafés lined the streets and waiters in white shirts and black ties moved from table to table and tourists walked slowly from café to café considering the best place to sit. In the center of the plaza was a small fountain where angels arched their backs and reached toward the heavens and at their feet children tossed in coins and splashed one another playfully. Branching out from the plaza were numerous streets and alleys and Cohen looked around and tried to imagine which one Elisa might have taken, but he realized it didn't matter, as in this labyrinthine city your first turn had little bearing on where you eventually wound up.

He crossed to the other side and bought a pack of Lucky Strikes at a kiosk. He unwrapped the pack, lit a cigarette, and watched the plaza scene for another moment before picking a random alley to follow and try to find his wife.

Cohen moved along the street and crossed a canal and then he crossed another canal and he seemed to have merged into more of a local neighborhood. He passed a grocery store, a Laundromat, an appliance store, and a flower shop. A woman came out of a doorway with a dog on a leash and in another doorway a bicycle leaned against the wall. Cohen walked until he was out of the neighborhood and into a retail shopping district, a series of store-lined streets with sleek, scantily dressed mannequins and shiny jewelry and Venetian-made glass vases in the different windows.

He looked for a running woman. The day was warming and he was sweating some on his face and neck and now he was really worried. He noticed the dead ends where the water was stagnant and the alleys covered in shadows and he realized there were a thousand places to drop and disappear. He kept walking and smoking and looking and he came to a plaza that he recognized from the day before and it seemed he was making some sort of circle back toward the hotel. Maybe she's back, he thought, but the thought only lasted an instant and he decided to call out. He cupped his hands to his mouth and yelled, "Elisa!"

Movement in the plaza paused and people looked at him.

He took advantage of the quiet and again yelled, "Elisa!"

From a window somewhere an unfriendly voice yelled back so he kept walking. As he walked he continued to call out, the echo of his voice sometimes shooting along a passageway and sometimes falling dead in a dead end. He called out and walked more briskly and even looked into the canals as his imagination pictured a floating running shoe or running watch or her beautiful bare back afloat in the still tepid water.

He came to the intersection of five streets and in the middle of the intersection was a statue of a conquered winged lion with a woman in a long, flowing gown, wielding a spear, sitting on top of the lion. Cohen climbed up on the lion, stepped from the lion's head into the woman's lap, and managed to get on her shoulders so he could have a better view. A store owner came out of a gift shop and yelled at Cohen, pointing and waving and clapping his hands. Another Venetian passing by joined with the store owner. Cohen ignored them and from his perch looked down each street, screamed out her name. The store owner came closer to Cohen, waving his arms and shouting and Cohen jumped down from the statue and yelled back at the man and the man backed off. Cohen then turned in a circle, looking at all the streets, trying to decide what to do and sweating more now than before.

He realized he hadn't left a note or word with the front desk and that if she had returned, she would be wondering what had happened to him. So he started running. He ran in what he thought was the general direction of the hotel, hoping to find a familiar street that would take him there. He called her name. Screamed her name. He paused at the ends of streets and looked both ways, he looked down into the canals when he went over a bridge. He hurried but tried not to miss anything.

He ran down a long alley and then cut across a

canal and ran along another long alley and up ahead he saw people passing on the street. He believed that it was the street of his hotel and he was right. He turned onto the street and after several minutes he recognized buildings and the hotel sign came into sight and then he saw, almost to the doorway, Elisa walking with her arm draped around a short woman in a long skirt. Elisa leaned on the woman and they inched along and Cohen raced and he caught them as they made it to the door.

"Elisa," he said, out of breath. He saw that she held a rag on her forehead and it was dabbed in blood and he grabbed and hugged her though she still leaned on the woman.

"She okay. She okay," the short woman said, pushing Cohen away, and then she moved Elisa's arm from around her neck as if to say, Here you go, she's yours. The woman's glasses were held by a silver chain around her neck and she had kind, wrinkled eyes.

"I'm all right," Elisa said, laughing a little and reaching for Cohen. "You look freaked out."

"What the hell happened?"

"Got lost. Like we said I would."

The woman made a fist and bonked her own forehead. "Head hit on ceiling," she said.

"Street," Elisa said and she pointed at the ground. "Head hit on street."

"Okay. Good."

"Head what?" Cohen asked. Her arm was around his neck and she held her hand out to the woman. The woman took her hand and Elisa said, "Thank you so much. *Grazie* so much."

"You okay?" the woman asked, nodding.

Cohen stuck his hand in his pocket and took out some money and tried to give it to her but she wouldn't take it and she backed away, nodding and saying, "Okay, good. Okay, good."

"*Grazie*," Elisa said again and the woman waved and turned and went back her way.

Cohen and Elisa moved inside the hotel and sat down at a table by the bar. She fell into a chair and moved the rag from her head and she was cut and swollen above her eyebrow.

"Goshdammit," Cohen said.

One of the teenagers passing by saw Elisa's eye and Cohen stepped behind the bar. He took a clean rag and wet it with cold water and gave it to her. "Something else?" he asked and she said no and told him thanks.

"I'm stupid," she said.

"You're not stupid, but what happened?"

"Running. Lost. Tripped like I almost had about a hundred times already trying to run on these stones and bricks and hit forehead-first. Knocked me a little loopy. Then that woman walked up and found me. Helped me sit up and I guess she lived right there 'cause she went in a building and came back out with the rag and some water."

Cohen reached over and wiped a trail of blood and water from the side of her face. "You scared the hell out of me."

"I'm sorry."

"I told you that you're not supposed to exercise on vacation."

"I get it now."

He touched her hand that held the rag and moved it from her eye. It was about to stop bleeding. "Does it hurt?" he asked.

"Does it look like it hurts?"

"Yep."

"Then it hurts."

He moved her hand and rag back to the cut and said, "I'll be right back." He went upstairs to the room and found a bottle of Tylenol and went back down to the bar. No one was around so he went behind the bar and got her a bottle of water and himself a beer.

He sat down at the table and handed her three pills. She looked at them. Looked at him. Looked at his beer and her water.

"Are you serious?" she asked.

He got up again and took another beer from the cooler. He grabbed a bottle opener from the bar top and he sat down and opened the beers and slid one to her. She took the pills, stuck them in her mouth, and washed them down with the cold beer.

"Now that makes a girl feel better," she said as she set the bottle down on the table.

Cohen reached into his pocket and took out the Lucky Strikes. He picked up his beer and let out an extended sigh. She winked at him with the eye not covered by the rag. The anxiety of separation fell from them but didn't disappear.

"No more solo excursions," he said.

She shrugged.

"I mean it," he said.

"Should we leash ourselves together?"

"If we have to," he said. He reached over and moved the rag from her face and looked at the cut, swollen and red. He then replaced the rag and said, "Just drink your beer."

20

Mariposa had stood at her window and watched. When she saw Cohen come out of the trailer and walk to where he slept, she waited to see if a light would come on. When it didn't, she figured he must have gone to sleep so she waited. While she waited, she watched the commotion. A couple of the other women and Aggie went in and out of the trailer and when the door opened and there was some light she saw the blood on their hands and arms and shirts and then she finally saw a bloody mess wrapped in Ava's arms and she wondered if it was dead or alive. The door closed for a while and when it opened again Ava held a bundle wrapped in white and she walked out into the rain, Aggie holding her by the arm, and across to his trailer and it seemed as if he or she had made it. For now.

She looked again to where Cohen slept. Still only black inside.

She put on her coat and when she got to the door she remembered that she was locked in. But she turned the handle anyway and found it unlocked and she figured in the madness Aggie must have forgotten the doors. She walked out and the wind slapped the rain against her face and with her head down she moved to his door. She paused, looked around, saw them bustling back and forth in the trailer where Lorna lay.

Then she put her hand on his trailer door handle, turned it slowly, opened the door, and slid inside.

She moved in the dark. Didn't see him. Didn't hear him at first.

Then he snored.

He was facedown on the mattress, his arms and legs spread out as if he were free-falling. He breathed big and heavy, and her eyes adjusted some and she moved over toward him and knelt next to the mattress. He was still wearing his coat and his muddy boots and they hung off the edge of the mattress.

She took a candle and a lighter out of her coat and she lit the candle and set it on the floor. She removed her coat and laid it on the floor, then put her hands on his left boot and felt for the laces and untied and loosened them. She tugged some. He didn't move. She wiggled it and the boot gave and she pulled it off, and then she did the same to the right one. He grunted once and heaved but didn't turn and didn't wake.

She heard voices outside and she stood and looked out. Two others were moving across the compound, going back to where they slept. The light was off in Lorna's trailer.

Mariposa knelt again. She listened to him breathing. Listened to the random snore. Listened to the rain and the wind. Listened to the words in her head that wanted to come out and then she let them out in whispers.

"I know what you came for," she started. "I know you came for her. What's left of her. What's left of it all. I know what you came for."

She paused. Put her hand on the back of his leg.

"Don't let him keep you," she whispered. "Don't be like him. But I know you're not that way. I already know it."

She paused again. Removed her hand.

It was the first time in a long time that she had spoken to someone without angst, without vehemence, without fear.

Her hair was held back with a rubber band and she reached behind and pulled it out. Then she eased herself onto the mattress. Cohen snorted and raised his head for a brief moment. Then it fell and he continued on in his restless sleep. Mariposa leaned first on her elbows, waited on him to settle some, and then she let herself down and lay quietly beside him.

Somewhere else. No countryside. No beach. No pastures or barbed wire or crepe myrtles. A concrete world where he walked down a city street on a normal day with normal people up and down the sidewalks and in and out of the stores. Looking at the street signs but in a language that he didn't understand and there was nothing distinct about this place. He walked on, looking into store windows, stepping into bars and looking around the tables, stopping at a pay phone and dialing and then ringing and ringing and no answer and hanging up and walking on. Newspaper stands and vendors selling hot dogs and a woman in a tight silver dress smoking a cigarette in front of a dress shop. A dog without a collar sniffing at a garbage can. The random honk of a car horn and he walked on, looking in the windows, looking at himself in the reflection. His hands were cold and he blew on them as he walked and then he was lost, stopping and looking back over his shoulder to see if he could recognize which direction he had come, walking on another block or two or three, stopping and spinning and trying to figure where he was or where he was going or how to get back or anything. He tried to ask but no one understood what he was asking and they hurried past or snapped back at him in annoyance or pushed him. He walked on and everything looked the same and he couldn't figure out what or who he was looking for and with each step the anxiety grew until he was calling out for help but none of the strangers responded and then there was a sudden, heavy rush of clouds and they disappeared inside stores and apartment buildings but he had nowhere to go and he stood and watched the black clouds suffocate the daylight and then he felt the body beside him and he turned but no one was there but he felt the body again and then he opened his eyes and there was the darkness of the night and there was the thing beside him that he had felt in his dream.

He was on his back. The low glow of the candle across the room. She was lying next to him and he turned and saw her black hair and he knew. For a reason he didn't understand, he wasn't startled. He lay still and waited to see if she was awake or asleep and he felt her body move in slow breaths and she was sleeping. He picked his head up and her hair was across his arm and then he took his hand and lifted the long black hair and laid it across her back. She breathed a heavy breath and he put his arm down and was still. He was still and he was warm with this body close to him. It was an alien feeling. A natural feeling. And he didn't understand why she had come and he didn't understand why he didn't get up or why he wasn't in a rage and he was relieved that in the dark it didn't have to make any sense. He lay still and warm and felt her breathing and he closed his eyes and let it be.

When he woke several hours later, she wasn't there, and a strange light came in the trailer window. He sat up and felt as if he were moving about in a dream where he couldn't tell the difference between what was real and what wasn't real. He wondered if her body against his had been a part of his imagination but then the truth of her body settled against him and he rubbed his eyes and the back of his neck and felt a complacency in the thought of someone there.

On the floor next to the mattress was his shoe box. On top of the box were Elisa's wedding rings, her earrings, her necklaces. Next to the box was the envelope, the letters and documents inside.

He sat up and leaned to the side. He felt in his back pocket for her picture and it was still there. Then he took her jewelry and he lifted the lid of the shoe box and put the photograph and jewelry with the rest and then he replaced the lid and lay back down and looked out of the window at the sunshine.

The women congregated in the middle of the circle of trailers and talked about the miracles.

"Look at it," one of them said.

"I swear to God it almost looks fake," another said.

The group of women stared admiringly up into the crystal-blue sky as if today were the day of its creation. The storm had moved on and in its wake was a clarity that had been forgotten. No clouds. Only the sun in the afternoon sky. A calm wind.

The other miracle was being passed around between them. He had been cleaned and he slept wrapped in a blanket and none of the women could believe he was alive.

21

Cohen stood out in the field. A low ribbon of pink wrapping the late-afternoon horizon. His hands stuffed in his pockets and the blade wiped clean and back in its sheath and his weight on his good leg. Aggie had not said anything to him as he limped out of the trailer and past the ashes of the fire and out into the field but he could feel the man's eyes on him. Could sense his pleasure in discovering what Cohen was capable of doing. Could feel the strength of the unknown.

He wondered what would happen if he started walking. How far he would get before the rifle rang and a point in his body burned and he lay still like a hunted animal. He was a couple of hundred yards from the tree line and the grass was high and he thought he could drop and crawl but his leg was lame and he didn't want to be hunted down and killed while he was crawling. He'd rather be dead standing up. Birds passed above and there was movement in the tall grass from the small things that needed the break in the weather to find food. He stared south and imagined the water of the calm morning, crawling onto the dilapidated shore quietly, as if careful not to wake it. The emptiness of the ocean and the stretch of the water and the sky, meeting on a seemingly infinite horizon, and he remembered standing on the beach as a boy. His eyes looking out into nothing. Imagining the men, hundreds of years ago, who had stared out across that vast expanse and braved its uncertainty as they loaded ships and said goodbye to their families and hoisted sails and drifted away, the love of land and man overcome by the curiosity of what might be. Drifting away, their homelands becoming smaller and smaller and then disappearing in the distance, the questions out before them like great constellations. Their minds filled with notions of sea dragons rising from the depths, swallowing them whole or burning them with fire or wrapping and squeezing them until the blood ran out. Swirling black whirlpools that could swallow entire fleets, sucking them down into bottomless, twisting graves. Or a world that would simply end. An edge to sail to and then fall off of and fall off into what?

Cohen had played these games in his head as a boy, standing waist-deep in the ocean, and he played them now as a man, looking out toward a limitless sky, curious about those men and what was held in their imaginations and had they been disappointed, at least a little, to find that the wildest creations of their minds could not be true. That there was only rock and sand on the other side that was not much different from the rock and sand they had departed from. That the fountains of life and the mountains of rubies and pearls did not exist any more than the spear-headed, long-necked monsters. Or was the world unknown enough for them no matter what it held? No matter what they found or whom they saw when they got there but simply that it was unknown to them and that was plenty to feed their hunger. Plenty to fill their spirit to the highest plateau. Plenty to reward their risks. The unknown was enough and then some and Cohen thought now as he looked south toward the ribboned horizon that this would have been the perfect place for that kind of man.

He reached down and picked at the dried, crusted blood on his leg. Behind him the women remained, looking at the baby, talking softly to one another as if passing on sensitive information. Ava held him, his pink head poking out of the top of the blanket and his eyes half-open and his mouth stretching in a feeble cry. In between whispers they made soothing sounds to the infant, dirty fingers reaching out to the child and touching his soft head and swelled cheeks. Aggie pulled dry wood out from a storage trailer and he worked to get the fire going while they huddled and embraced the new day. Evan and his small brother gathered wet wood and put it in the storage trailer, leaving the women and child to themselves. Cohen heard them but did not turn and look. He watched the sky and thought of the explorers.

He was still staring when the blond-haired boy walked up behind him and said, "I didn't mean nothing that day."

Cohen turned around and faced him. The boy's hair was slick and flat against his head and he held one hand to his mouth to keep it warm and with the other he held the hand of a young boy.

"I really didn't," he said. "Kinda had to."

"Kinda had to what?"

The boy looked back over his shoulder and Aggie was watching them. He lowered his voice as if the old man had a magical ability to hear all. "Nothing."

Cohen looked down at the small boy and hobbled closer to them. "Who are you?" he asked.

"This here is my little brother. He's why I did

what I did out there." The small boy wore a denim coat buttoned to the top, and a scarf was coiled around his neck and up above his mouth. He held a half-deflated football tucked under his arm.

"You got a name?"

"Which one of us?"

"Either. Both."

"I'm Evan and he's Brisco."

"What's he got to do with you and that girl back there trying to kill me?"

Evan shook his head and said, "I wasn't trying to kill nobody."

"You shot at me."

"Didn't nothing come out."

"That ain't the point."

"The point is I didn't want to. I told you, Aggie keeps Brisco when he sends me and Mariposa out looking around. So he knows I'll come back. And it's best to come back with something."

Cohen looked past the boys. Aggie was smoking a cigarette. His eyes on them. The women passing the baby around behind him. The smoke from the young fire rising and mingling with Aggie's cigarette smoke like a team of serpents stretching up into a watchful perch. Mariposa stood alone, leaning against a trailer, and watched them.

"Cover your ears up, Brisco," Evan said and the boy put his pale hands over his ears. Then Evan said softly, "You kill Joe?"

Cohen paused and tried to figure how to answer. He didn't know if he wanted them to know that he'd never killed a man. Never shot at a man. Never shot at all except to shoot back in the direction of gunfire to let them know to go the other way. He knew they would talk about him and wonder about him, so he said, "Yeah."

Evan reached down and picked the top off a blade of tall grass. "Good," he said. Then he moved Brisco's hands off his ears.

Cohen blew on his hands and rubbed at his face. The small boy moved the football from one arm to the other and then he tossed it to Evan.

"Go long," Evan said and Brisco took off, not looking back and quickly out of range of a deflated football. "Hold up," Evan called and Brisco hit the brakes. Evan let fly of the wobbly, saggy ball and it short-hopped Brisco.

"Practice kicking," Evan told him. Brisco tucked the ball and ran a quick circle. Then he tried to drop it and kick it but it didn't work out and he lost his balance and fell to the ground. But he laughed at himself and got up and started trying again.

With the small boy out of earshot, Cohen asked Evan what the hell was going on out here.

Evan moved his eyes back and forth. Said, "Maybe I shouldn't."

"Go on," Cohen said. "Talk low. It's all right."

Evan's eyes moved across the landscape again,

but then he started talking. Said it began with Aggie and Joe and that woman over there named Ava. Said that from what he could tell, them three had gone around like Good Samaritans, picking up stragglers here and there. Finding people along the road or hid back up in houses or wherever and told them they had food and a safe place if they'd come on. Sometimes it'd be two or three people and they'd bring them out here and give them a trailer to sleep in and feed them a couple of days. Pray with them. Preach to them. All that shit. But they'd only pick up women or women with a man and then when they'd get out here, they'd tell the man they was going hunting and they'd walk out in the woods and shoot him dead. Next thing there'd be a lock on the door and that woman wasn't going nowhere. They got some plan for mankind or something like that. Aggie thinks he's got something to do with Jesus or God or at least that's what he'll tell you. Evan looked out at Brisco as he talked and he had the stare of someone who had seen a lot in a short amount of time, but in his voice remained the charming tone of youth.

Cohen stared at him. Evan's cheeks and eyes thin and hard. "And you. Where'd he find you?" Cohen asked.

"Found me and him the same as the others. We were with my uncle but my uncle disappeared on us and we was walking up Highway 49 when him and Joe pulled up beside us. We didn't know what else to do but to go with them. I couldn't let Brisco starve. They was real nice at first. Then they locked us up like everybody else."

"But he didn't take you hunting?"

Evan shook his head. "No. Not yet."

"And what about the girl?"

"She was here when we got here. She won't tell me nothing else."

Cohen looked across toward the camp. Aggie was drinking coffee now, not looking at them.

"Why ain't I dead?" Cohen asked.

"Guess for the same reason I ain't and Brisco ain't. He's a old man and he can't make all these women have babies by himself. Joe did that. So he don't want to kill us. He wants to convert us."

"For the sake of the human race," Cohen said.

Evan shrugged. "I reckon."

Brisco got the hang of it and kicked the ball a couple of times but grew tired of it. He ran back over to Evan and tossed him the ball again.

"How come y'all don't run off?"

"It ain't that easy," Evan said, tossing the ball back to his little brother.

"No. I guess not." Cohen then nodded in the direction of the women and asked if that was all of them.

Evan looked a minute, then said, "Yeah. That's it. Minus Lorna."

Cohen shook his head some, replayed that

instant with her. The screaming and the swipe of the blade and the moment of disbelief from all of them. Then he told the boys that he wasn't going to be staying around.

"That's what I said, too," Evan said. "But I ain't got nowhere else to go. I'd rather be alive here than dead out there." He reached down and took Brisco by the hand. "There ain't much more of a decision than that," he said, and then he and the boy turned and walked back toward the others.

Cohen let them go a few steps and then he said, "Hey."

They stopped and looked back at him.

"That girl. What's her name?"

"Mariposa."

Evan started to walk off again but Cohen called him again and when he and Brisco stopped, Cohen walked over. He reached into his front pocket and he pulled out the pair of baby socks. He handed them to Evan and told him to take them to whoever had the baby.

The women spent the day with the look of apprehension. Joe had been gone for days now and the women were savvy enough to realize that he wasn't coming back, and even if he were, he wasn't there now, and half of the strength that had held them was missing. They didn't know the man with the gunshot in his leg but he didn't seem to care about what was happening. He had the same formless look on his face that they all had as the blunt finality that awaited each of them came like a siren in Lorna's cries. You can get used to anything. That was something that each of them had come to realize and accept but now as the sun unexpectedly spread out across the land, with Joe disappeared, with the infant fighting to live, and with Lorna dead, the sense of rebellion rose silently in them and they looked at one another as if to say, This can no longer be.

They were careful about what they said around Ava, as she had been working on Aggie's side for as long as any of them had been there. Sometimes they walked around in groups of two or three out in the fields or around the fire and they spoke to one another in the low, serious voices of people who were plotting or gun-shy or both. There was that apprehension in their expressions but also something more. They had heard the screams in the night. They were aware of Lorna's suffering and her fate, and while they had known there would be combat with the pain, none of them was the least bit interested in going through what Lorna had been through. They squinted and their cheeks tightened as they spoke to one another about the moment that was to come for each of them. Caution in their voices and anxiety in their hearts and agreeing with no hesitation that this first episode of deliverance in this place should also be the last. And if we're going to do anything about it, we got to do it now. God knows when there'll be another day like this.

The afternoon wore on and the clear sky disappeared. A soft rain fell and deep gray clouds sat across the Gulf and promised more. The women spoke less but seemed to communicate with their eyes and bends of the mouth and each of them expressed the same thing. He is one man and there can be no more of this. Throughout the day, as they began to help gather wood, stacking the branches and limbs in the storage trailer, or preparing food, or washing out clothes in silver bins, they moved with calculated, robotlike motions, cutting their eyes at one another, as if there were some countdown going on in each of their heads.

Cohen sat on an upright cinder block with his shot leg extended. Twice Mariposa had come over and sat down beside him and twice Aggie had told her to get up and go help the others.

Twilight arrived and the rain was steady and all was gray. They moved around in big coats, hoods over heads, shoulders slumped from the hours, days, weeks spent out in the rain.

Aggie called on Cohen to help him hook up a trailer to the back of a truck. Cohen got up and hobbled out into the field where the trucks and trailers sat.

It was a ten-foot-long flat trailer that wasn't the work of two men and Cohen basically stood there while Aggie dropped the trailer onto the hitch. When he was done, he raised up and wiped the rain from his face and said, "Just so you know, there may be an example set here before this day is done. Don't like the looks of it all. The birth caused a tremor. A tremor when there should be rejoicing."

"Somebody died," Cohen said. "Maybe that's what's wrong."

"Life was given for life and there should be no crying over that. There should be no crying over the beginning. And I see desperation. And desperate people need a message. They need reminding. And if one of them so much as flinches I'm gonna goddamn remind them in a way they won't forget."

Cohen didn't answer. He pulled a broken cigarette and lighter from his shirt pocket.

"Don't you get no bright ideas either or you'll be laying with the dog," Aggie said. He took a step closer to Cohen. "You might start thinking about your place here. About what has been set at your feet. You look around a little more closely and you might see something different from what you think you see."

Cohen snapped off the broken piece of the cigarette, bent over to hide it from the weather, and lit the stump. He looked away from Aggie, and he noticed two shovels in the bed of the truck. "What's all this for?" he asked.

"We going digging. Me and you and that boy. But we gonna wait till it gets dark."

Cohen sucked on the cigarette, then said, "I got some news before we go, you should know."

"Yeah. What?"

"If you think I'm going off to dig my own grave, you might as well go ahead and shoot me dead in this spot."

Aggie shook his head. Laughed. "Jesus, boy. We ain't digging no graves. We going to dig up that money."

Cohen shook his head. "Not you, too."

"Trunkfuls. Ain't no telling how much it is."

Cohen was quickly done with the short cigarette and he tossed it. He'd seen and heard enough about the hunt for the money. The groups of men he'd seen working around the same spot. The shots that had been fired that had caused some of them to drop and the others to scatter.

Aggie stepped back from Cohen. He bent down and yanked on the trailer hitch to make sure it was secure and then he raised up and said, "So see, you put everything together and you might end up a man with all he needs."

"You and everybody else who thinks there's money buried somewhere along the beach are out of your goddamn minds."

"That right there is what the man who won't find it will say."

"Won't nobody find it. 'Cause it ain't there. It's crazy to even be trying."

"Crazy, huh?"

"Yeah. Crazy. Just like the rest of this shit," Cohen said and he turned and waved his arm around the place.

Aggie propped his hands on his hips. Bent his dark eyebrows. "Crazy?" he asked again.

Cohen nodded. "Batshit."

Aggie nodded a little. He took a few steps away from Cohen, turned and took a few steps back to him. "Crazier than living down here in a house with dead people?" he asked in a low, deliberate voice.

Cohen's certainty disappeared. He stared back at the man but didn't know what to say.

"I know you," Aggie continued, speaking slowly. "I know you. I seen everything. Read everything in that envelope. I saw where you were. What you were doing. I put her rings on my pinky finger. Sniffed them little love notes in that sweet little box you kept shoved up under the bed. Saw them baby clothes and them dresses still hanging in the closet. Don't tell me nothing about crazy. You ain't no different from nobody else down here, including me. Crazy comes in lots of different ways. And you got as much in you as anybody else."

He stopped. Waited for Cohen to answer. When he didn't, Aggie walked past him and across the field toward the trailers. Cohen heard him call to the women and he followed, wanting to see what Aggie had to say.

When Aggie was in the middle of the circle, he waved them into their line. Cohen stood back from them, leaning against a trailer.

Aggie told them to close their eyes and then he prayed in his gravelly voice, thanking God that there was a place for them to live and love and breathe and hide themselves from the thunder. Thank you God that we are on the higher ground and that there is food for our bellies and fire to warm our hands and safety in the night from the wolves who patrol these lands for the taste of helpless flesh. Thank you God that this beautiful child has come to us and our family has multiplied and in this child we can see today and tomorrow and forever and this sunshine is your answer to us that you love us and approve of what has come. And this place is our home and your winds are your might and do not let me hesitate to strike down those that rise against you and me. And I will not hesitate to strike.

It was almost dark, an ominous deep gray surrounding them. The rain fell straight and Aggie pushed the hood back from his head and welcomed it on his face and head. As he prayed, he stroked the butt of the revolver that stuck out of his pants. As he prayed, his brow grew tense and he held a fist toward the dripping sky and he reared back his head and closed his eyes and then he was taken away. The hand came off the revolver and then both hands were stretched out before him and in his mind he was back there before them, the pulsing of the chanting and the organ music as he moved his arms around in dancelike motions, the imaginary snake in his hands, its sleek, poisonous body intertwined with his own and the heat of the hot, strip-mall church and the energy of those out in front of him, praising and chanting and speaking in no discernible language, and he moved the imaginary snake from arm to arm, moved it around the back of his neck and down his chest and then back into his hands and the entire time he prayed out to God, You are the power and the glory and this land belongs to You and bring them on, bring them on and deliver us and wash away that which is unclean and may my own strength be like Your strength and we will inhabit this land and keep it pure and we will multiply and be with the beasts and create for You the sons of thunder.

He went on and on, his words filled with conviction and his neck muscles taut and he began to twist his hands and arms, wringing the snake like a wet towel, the feeling that he needed something to kill rising up through him and as he prayed for strength and prayed for vengeance against those who would question the way, my way and Your way, dear God, he became so lost in his own power and might that he never saw the women rush on him and before he could rid himself of the fury of his prayer, he was on his back with his arms pinned and his legs pinned and his own revolver pressed against his lips like the biting kiss of a fierce lover and the snake had crawled away.

22

None of them was sure what to do with him. They hadn't thought that far ahead. Several wanted to kill him with his own gun. Several others wanted to lock him up and let him starve. Still another wanted to cut off his manhood and throw it out in the field for the buzzards and as soon as he bled to death, do the same with the rest of him.

With the help of Cohen and Evan they had tied him to the back end of a cattle trailer in the field. His arms were stretched out wide, and he was sitting on the ground, and he was bound at the wrists, elbows, around his neck, and around his chest. The baby was taken out of Ava's arms and they made clear to her that she had a choice, die with Aggie or live with us. She decided she'd rather keep on living. No sooner had her decision been made than two of the women who weren't pregnant began to dig through the pile of keys they had taken from Aggie. They found the keys to one of the trucks that they knew would run and without another word, without packing a change of clothes or any food or water, they went for the truck and the engine dragged a few times but then it cranked. Before they could get turned around and headed toward the road, three more women had run and gotten into the back of the truck and they were gone.

That left the pregnant woman and two not pregnant and Evan and Mariposa and Brisco. And the less-than-a-day-old child. Cohen rubbed at his beard and looked around and then he knelt on the ground and began looking through the keys for the Jeep key. He picked it out and stood and put it in his pocket and then he walked out to where Aggie was tied and he reached into Aggie's shirt pocket and took his cigarettes and lighter. The rain beat against the rusted iron trailer like some random back-alley drumbeat outside a late-night Royal Street blues bar.

"You could be my brother," Aggie said to him in a humbled voice.

Cohen looked at him and shook his head and covered and lit a cigarette. When he walked back to them, they were standing in a circle, holding hands, and the pregnant woman was crying. They were wet and worn but it didn't seem to matter. Seemed like they had accepted that they were part of what came from the sky. He looked around for Mariposa but didn't see her. Cohen let them be, not wanting to intrude on the things that they had suffered together, and he went into the trailer that had belonged to Joe. Clothes were scattered about and there were empty plastic bottles and empty beer and whiskey bottles on the counter and a bowl filled with cigarette butts on the floor next to the bed. Cohen found a pair of jeans that looked about right and he tossed them over his shoulder and walked out of Joe's trailer and over to the trailer where the woman had given birth to the child.

He opened the door and was greeted with the smell of the sick and the dead and he stepped back. There wasn't much light now but he leaned his head inside and he looked at the woman, covered in crimson, her legs spread and her arms at her side and her head fallen over with an open mouth. He looked at her and then he stepped in and stood at the foot of the bed.

There was dried blood underneath his feet. The sheet across her legs had stuck to her and her naked breasts were smeared dark red. Her bare feet were sticking out of the end of the sheet. Her hands so still against her, never having held her own. The moment replayed in his mind like some memory of a horrific dream and he shook his head to rid himself of it and then he looked around and found the black bag. It was open on a short table next to the bed along with a stack of towels and a gallon of water. He looked inside and found the spray and gauze that Aggie had used on him. He took off his pants, unwrapped the bandage from his leg and washed it with the water. Then he sprayed the wound, front and back, and he wrapped a fresh bandage around his thigh. When he was satisfied with his work, he put on the jeans he had taken from Joe's trailer, then he looked at the woman again. She seemed almost other-worldly, an apparition from the underworld sent to warn them.

He bowed his head and whispered an unfinished sentence. He listened to the rain. And then there came a great boom of thunder that echoed across the night. He wondered if something of his had been lost. Or maybe something had been found.

When he came out they had broken from their circle and begun to plunder through the trailers that Aggie always kept them from. All of them but Mariposa, who stood alone, staring at Cohen, as if waiting for him.

Cohen limped over to her. He held out a cigarette but she shook her head. "You don't look like you'd be much in a fight," he said. "But my neck still hurts some."

Mariposa folded her arms. "You gonna lead us out of here?" she asked.

Cohen smoked. Thought about it. "That sounds kinda biblical. I'm guessing y'all have had enough of that."

"Yeah. I guess."

"I'm about like everybody else here."

She let her arms fall to her sides. "Not really," she said. She looked away from him, at the others plundering through the stockpile of food, water, clothes. Cohen watched her and what he noticed now was her youth. Half my age, he thought. At least.

Aggie hollered out something that Cohen didn't make out. He then called out very clearly for Ava. She was crossing the compound and she stopped and looked in his direction. He called her again. Ava looked around and saw Cohen and Mariposa and she shook her head and moved on to her trailer.

Mariposa said, "Somewhere I got somebody." She looked at Cohen again. What he noticed now wasn't her youth but in her expression, in her deep-set eyes and the bend of her thin lips, he saw something contradicting that youth, far removed from innocence by no fault of her own.

"I got family," she continued. "Somewhere."

Cohen nodded.

"Like you," she said.

He felt like there was something he wanted to say, but he didn't know what it was. He didn't know who she was. Didn't know if he wanted to find out. Didn't want to care. Didn't want to talk to her about her life or his life or anything that mattered. He thought of simply walking away but didn't have to when Brisco came bounding out of a trailer with an armful of Coke cans. He dropped one and kicked it over toward Cohen and Mariposa and then he walked to them and handed them each a can. "There's a whole bunch," he said.

Cohen looked down at Brisco and said, "How old are you?"

The boy set the other cans on the ground, lifted his arm, and slid his jacket sleeve under his nose, and then he only shrugged.

"You don't know how old you are?"

"I know."

"Okay." He waited on the child to continue but he didn't and then Cohen didn't have to worry about walking away from Mariposa because she turned and walked away from him. Brisco headed back toward the trailer. The women had finished their plunder and gone in from the rain.

There was a murmur of thunder and a flash off to the west. Cohen looked down at the ground and watched the rain splatter in the red mud.

Then he walked over to Mariposa's trailer. A low glow of light leaked behind a shirt or sheet or something hung across the window. A concrete block below the door. He stepped up onto the block and stood close to the door, so close that if he leaned forward, his nose would bump it. He heard her moving inside. He lifted his hand and touched his wet fingertips to the wet door and he wondered what she was doing. He wondered why she had come to him like she had, in the middle of the night, no words, no want, only coming to him quietly and almost reverently and lying there with him. He wondered how he had known it was her, how when he woke in the dark and felt the body that he had known it was the girl with the black hair. He wondered why it hadn't startled him and he wondered why he hadn't moved away from her. He wondered why it felt like it had and he wondered what it might feel like again, if it would be the same, tranquil and assuring, or if it would cause disgust and guilt and cause him to run. Inside the trailer, her movement stopped and he wondered what she was doing. He wondered what he was doing. His head tilted forward and he rested his forehead on the door.

"You can come in," he heard her say.

He lifted his head.

"It's okay," she said.

He slid his hand from the door and slowly moved it to the door handle and there was more lightning and for a split second he saw his shadow on the door.

He let go of the handle, stepped down off the block, and backed away.

He turned from her door and walked over to Aggie's truck and took a shovel out of the truck bed. Then he walked down the driveway toward the dog. The rain was coming on and the thunder more frequent. He couldn't see and he tripped over the dog when he came to it. He knelt and scratched its soggy head and its body was cold and stiff. He moved off the gravel and started digging. The earth was soaked and gave easily and when he had a hole big enough, he set the dog's body down into it and he covered it with mud and rocks. He said I'm sorry I got you into this and then he bowed his head and said amen.

He picked up the shovel again and he took ten steps away from the dog's grave and sank the shovel into the ground. He dug and dug, fighting the water running down into the hole, but finally managing to get farther down to where it was easier to dig. He worked for nearly an hour until he was standing down in the hole, almost waist-deep, and he thought it was both deep enough and long enough. He tossed the shovel and climbed out of the big hole and he walked back up the driveway and to the trailers. Lights were off inside all the trailers but hers. His hands were aching and blistered and he wiped them on his wet pants and then he walked over to the trailer where Lorna lay. He opened the door and felt around on the floor and found a blanket and he was glad that it was dark so he didn't have to see her. He spread the blanket beside her and rolled her body over and he wrapped her in it, careful to cover her head and her feet as if to salvage some bit of dignity. She was heavier than he thought she would be but he lifted her underneath her knees and shoulders and they moved out of the trailer and into the rain. He looked across and Mariposa's light was off.

But from the corner of her window, she watched him.

When he had moved back out into the dark, she lit a candle and turned to a plastic bag next to her mattress. In the bag were the dresses she had taken from Elisa's closet. She laid them across the mattress, three of them. A white sundress. A black long-sleeve with a low neckline. Another with pastel blue and pink flowers that looked like it could've been worn with a bonnet on Easter Sunday. She stood back and admired them. Imagined the places they had been. For what occasion each had been worn. Imagined Cohen's hands helping to remove them from her body. Mariposa put her hand to her chin, the pose of decision. After a thoughtful moment, she began to undress, and soon she stood in the candlelight, chill bumps up and down her legs and arms. She picked up the black dress and put it on.

23

In his predicament, the only thing Aggie could do was think. And he did. He thought of the sweaty nights in the sweaty room with the sweaty snakes slithering through his arms and around his neck and waist as the organ played and the people sang and shouted. Thought of how it moved them and how the men wanted to shake his hand and the women wanted to be led by him and how he did lead them all the way and how good it felt when they were only nodding, no matter what he asked them to do. He thought of fists against his face in barrooms and the thrill ride of whiskey and the summer dark and he thought of nights in jail staring out of a square window at a black dotted sky when he felt like he was at the bottom of a well.

He thought of the anarchy of the evacuations and how it filled him to be alive in the midst of the panic and he thought of once when he was a boy and a man who was living with him and his mother had slammed her against the wall and he thought of the knife he had stuck in the back of the man's leg later as he slept on their couch and the sound the man had made as the blade sank in. He thought of the work he had done to gather a community and he thought of the crying of the newborn child and he thought of the purity of the rising sun across the horizon in the morning after a storm. He sat there, tied to the trailer, the rain on him as if he were nothing more than a tree stump, and he imagined that the thunder was calling out to him, a voice from somewhere out there speaking to him in a language that only he could understand. He soaked in the rain and listened to the thunder and his arms ached from being stretched and tied. What more can you give to them? What more can they want? It has always been like this, they did the same thing to Him. He gave them all they could want and all they could need. He showed them the path to glory and they tortured Him, spit on Him, watched Him bleed and bleed and bleed. And now here I am and all I did was protect them, shelter them, feed them. All I did was lead them through the storms, a watchful shepherd and his flock, and now I can scream out in the night and they will hear me and no one will come. Not a one. It has always been like this. And it always will be.

He thought of how this was going to end, realizing the things he had gained and the things he had lost, and it almost seemed to him like these thoughts were the thoughts of another man's life.

Since the moment that Charlie first heard the rumors of the buried money, he had begun to lose interest in his truck and his deliveries below the Line and the small bills he got in exchange for his assortment of small goods. Initially he had figured it was like the other ridiculous news that had been delivered to the Gulf Coast over the years. The prediction that the storms would not stop and would become more harrowing. The prediction that they could go on for years. The prediction that the government was thinking of drawing some bullshit line that you weren't supposed to cross over. All of it had seemed so far-fetched at one time. Yet all of it had been true. And the rumor of this buried money seemed to Charlie exactly like these other bits of fairy-tale information that had come to fruition. So strange that it had to be right. And he wasn't going to be outhustled for it by a bunch of yokels in pickup trucks packed with shovels and picks and coolers of beer.

For two years he had called everyone he knew to call trying to figure out exactly what had been said and who had said it. Most recently, some ex–casino man admitted on television that he had ordered trunks of cash to be buried. And he hadn't thought any further ahead than that because nobody truly believed the storms would last this long or that the Line would last this long. But in the interview, the ex–casino man had his face blacked out, his voice altered, and he didn't identify what casino he had worked for or if that casino was in Bay St. Louis, or Biloxi, or Gulfport, or wherever. Only that it was down there somewhere, buried on casino grounds. Unsure how much but that it was millions, at least ten or fifteen. He had lost count when they were stacking it into the trunks.

Those were the bits and pieces Charlie had put together from his phone calls, the he-saids and she-saids that had spread across the Southeast with jetlike propulsion. The images of buried treasure dancing in the heads of anyone who thought they had the means and ability to get down and search, nearly all of the dreamers unequipped and unprepared for the risks they would encounter below.

But Charlie was not unprepared. He had the means. Knew the roads. Had the muscle. Had the firepower. Had the guts.

He was unlike others who had lost so much. He had been without a wife, without children, and his friends had either passed on or evacuated, and he had taken the government's first pathetic offer for his land to get as much cash in hand as possible to prepare for his role in the new world. The gradual breakdown in order had fed his talents as a hustler, as a trader, and he had found satisfaction in a return to the natural world, where there was no credit. There was no payment plan. There was what do I have that somebody wants and how much are they willing to pay for it. It was a system that he thrived in. A system that gave him a purpose.

He had come into possession of a backhoe, which heightened his expectations and obsession. He explained to his crew that the focus of their responsibilities would be in pursuit of the buried money, which had not been a difficult sell as the job of warding off potential looters of Charlie's truck had become tiring and cumbersome. He told them that things might get a little hairy. He told them that shooting first and asking questions later was acceptable. He told them to be prepared to receive the same treatment. He told them that whoever saw the backhoe would want it. He told them that many a son of a bitch had been put down over a hundred dollars, much less a million. He told them to expect everything. He told them there would be several hundred thousand dollars in it for the finished job. After that, he didn't have to tell them anything else.

Charlie and the crew had begun on the east end of the coast. If it was possible to identify a casino's grounds, and possible to dig on those grounds, they dug. Charlie would drive the back-hoe and the muscle would make a wide circle, keeping watch, fingers on triggers. Charlie would dig a hole and move on. Dig another hole and move on. And over and over until the casino land appeared as if it were home to a brotherhood of giant aggravated gophers. The first few digs had been uneventful and fairly irritating, as the rain didn't stop to let Charlie dig a hole. But as they had moved west across the coast, the digs had become more lively as more treasure seekers appeared, and warning shots had been fired.

The more holes Charlie dug, the more frequent the sound of warning shots, until the warning shots finally hit the side of the truck and pinged off the backhoe and the friendly fire several times turned into straight-up gunfire. In reaction to the increasing danger, Charlie decided to dig at night with a rack of rigged spotlights, but that damn near got them killed the first night out as all it did was shine a bright light to the targets on their backs and blind them from seeing who it was attacking them and from which direction.

But he kept on digging and sliding across the coast. The muscle kept on ducking and firing back. And the influx of interested parties only fueled Charlie's insistence that somewhere out there was the buried money. He believed that it existed. He was certain of it. And like most of the treasure hunters he had seen in movies or read about in books, he decided that he was either going to find what he was after or he was going to die trying.

24

The rain continued all day. Not much stirred around the compound except for trips back and forth to the supply trailer for something to eat or drink. From time to time a high-pitched cry from the baby cut through the sound of the rain. Ava paid most attention to the child. She was the oldest woman there, with wrinkled hands and eyes, but she moved in a straightforward manner, with a stiff back and shoulders high, like a kid at boot camp. She knew where to find the bottles and formula and diapers because she had helped Aggie stash it all away. She moved in and out of the rain, taking things for the baby, delivering something to drink to Brisco, helping open cans and slicing apples for the others when they were hungry. She had been a part of Aggie but now seemed a part of them once the decision of life or death was presented to her. She wore a pair of men's jeans, baggy and rolled to midcalf, and two sweatshirts and the faded blue bandana around her head, with strands of gray-black hair trailing down her neck.

During the day, each time Ava moved from one trailer to the next, Aggie called out to her but she ignored him. Even shouted once for him to shut up.

Around evening the rain let up and Cohen and Evan built a fire. The others came out, stretched, passed around the baby. The woman named Nadine was the first to notice Lorna's grave and she walked out to it. Stood with her arms folded. Stared at the soggy mound and off into the slate-colored horizon. Then she came back to the fire with the others.

In half an hour the fire was going strong and they sat around it in their newfound freedom with their plates full, after taking what they wanted. Baked beans and yams and corn and the empty cans of whatever else appealed to them littered about. Some drinking beer. Some drinking Cokes.

Some smoking cigarettes. All of them thinking about tomorrow. The keys to the vehicles and trailers sat on a table as it had been decided that no one alone was to keep them.

The woman named Kris held the infant and held a bottle to his mouth. But he wouldn't take it and he fussed and wailed.

"What he needs is a good tit," Nadine said. She had a scar on her forehead and her legs were long and she had a sharp chin. She wore a pair of black laced boots with her pants tucked into them. Ava sat with them drinking coffee.

"Well," Kris said and she set the bottle on the ground. Her hands were small and her eyes were close together and she was six months pregnant. "He ain't getting one. Not one that'd do him any good." She took her pinkie finger and held it down to the baby's mouth and he sucked at it and closed his eyes and sucked more until he fell asleep.

"Mine never would do it," Ava said. She ate from a can of green beans.

"Yours? You got kids?" Nadine said.

"Somewhere. Two boys. I ain't seen or heard from either one in probably twenty years."

"Damn," Nadine said. "I thought I hated my momma but I at least knew how to call her." Nadine's long legs were crossed out in front of her. Her dirty-blond hair was cut short and uneven and a small harelip gave her the kind of snarl you might see at a county-fair roller derby.

"I didn't say they hate me," Ava said. "I said I don't know where they are."

"It's all the same," Nadine said.

Ava shrugged. Looked at her wrinkled, spotted hands. "Maybe it is," she said.

Kris hummed a lullaby while she held the sleeping baby, but she paused to say, "Aggie's sure been calling out for you."

"Yep," Nadine said. "You ain't been over there to him, I'm guessing."

Ava shook her head. "I done told y'all."

"You might tell us again."

"Fine. I want to go like everybody else," she said.

"I saw her walk on past him," Kris said to Nadine.

Nadine cut her eyes at Ava but didn't say anything else.

The night went on and the wind began to pick up, pushing at the fire and blowing cups and napkins out across the field. Cohen tried to keep the coffee going on the gas burner but it kept blowing out. Mariposa offered to put the burner in her trailer but Cohen shook his head, said he didn't really want any more. Finally he got up and walked over to Kris and the baby and said, "Can I hold him?"

Kris looked at him, a little surprised. "You ever held one before?"

"He ain't gonna break," Nadine said.

"No," Cohen said. "I never held one."

Kris stood. Cohen folded his arm and Kris set the tiny child in the crook. Cohen adjusted the baby some, couldn't believe how small and light the child felt. He wrapped his other arm around the baby and cradled it.

"It's easy when they're asleep," Ava said.

"Let him be," Mariposa answered.

Cohen looked at the baby's wrinkled eyes and chin. A little sound came from the baby's nose when he breathed. Cohen walked a few feet with him, stepping carefully around the fire, around the others sitting close to the flames. He kept walking, away from the firelight, away from the others, out of the circle of trailers and out into the dark field, where it was easier to pretend that this was a little girl and this was the dark of his own land and the light from the fire was the light of home.

Cohen returned and gave the baby back to Kris and they all sat for a little while longer. Howls and screeches came from the woods surrounding them. Aggie called out every half hour or so for something to drink or something to eat but no one reacted to him any more than they did to the animals in the woods.

Thunder and lightning joined the wind and they knew it was time to go in. But before they dispersed and went to bed it was decided that in the morning they would load whatever they needed and leave out for the Line. Cohen had gone from truck to truck to see what would crank and out of the four sitting in the field, two of them would run. Two trucks and his Jeep. He and Evan searched around for gas cans and they rounded up a handful of containers that still held some gas. They would keep all the supplies in the back of one of the trucks. Cohen would drive the Jeep alone. He told them about Charlie and the supply truck and they decided it would be best to go and see if he were around before heading north. There wasn't enough gas to make it very far otherwise.

The women went to bed, the infant and Brisco going with them, and Cohen and Evan stayed up looking around for what they'd need. In Aggie's trailer, they found plenty of protection. Back in the bathroom, the toilet and sink had been ripped out and the small area was stacked with rifles and shotguns and boxes of ammunition. Cohen spotted his sawed-off shotgun, his own blood smeared across the stock. He picked it up and handed it to Evan and told him to set it in there on the bed. Then he began going through the stack. There were pump-action shotguns and rifles and semi-automatic pistols. As he held each piece he imagined where it had come from. Where it had been found or who it had belonged to and the way it had been taken away. He asked Evan if he could shoot and Evan said all you gotta do is aim and pull the trigger.

"Guess so," Cohen said. "What about Mariposa? Can she shoot?"

Evan shrugged. "All you gotta do is aim and pull the trigger," he said again.

Then Cohen remembered her urging the boy to shoot him, shoot him, and giving her a gun didn't seem so smart. Not until he was certain whose side she was on.

Cohen chose a pump-action 12-gauge for himself and a rifle for Evan. He took two of the pistols and stuck them in his coat pockets. And then he told Evan to go get a bag somewhere and when Evan came back he filled the bag with boxes of ammunition.

When they were done they went into the storage trailers. Several empty boxes were on the floor and they filled the boxes with canned food and bags of coffee and gallon water jugs. There were diapers and a few cans of baby formula and they packed it all and Evan walked the boxes out to one of the trucks while Cohen kept on. Cigarettes and cases of beer and charcoal. Blankets and pillows and toilet paper and towels. Cohen filled up another half-dozen empty boxes and Evan took them out and when the boxes were gone, Cohen sat down next to the fire with a case of beer. Evan sat down with him and he gave the boy a can. The wind pushed the flames down to nothing and a steady stream of orange sparks trailed away.

They sat, drinking the beer, listening to the crack of the fire and the sound of the wind. There seemed to be something in that natural quiet that Cohen didn't want to leave. A humble silence. An honest silence. A silence that seemed so pure, veiled by the dark.

After a little while, Evan said, "You think we'll make it?"

Cohen smiled at the boy. Turned the can in his hands. "Don't see why not."

Evan moved his hand across his smooth face. He had been leaning back in the chair but he sat forward with his elbows on his knees and he stared into the fire. His pupils reflected the red. "The thing is, when we do, what then?"

"Maybe it ain't that bad."

"Maybe not. Think there's even roads to get all the way there?"

"Could be we're gonna hit the highway and be there in two hours. Like the good old days."

Cohen got up and walked circles around the fire, trying to keep his leg from getting too stiff. He sat back down and finished his beer and took another one. Evan continued watching the fire.

"It's gonna be slow going," Cohen said. "No idea what roads are left. What bridges are left. Looks like it's gonna be raining all the damn time. Not to mention we got a full load of not the most agile."

"And a baby."

"Yep. And a baby."

"What'd that feel like holding him?"

Cohen thought, then said, "Felt good. Like you really got something."

Evan blew on his hands then held them out to the fire. "Wouldn't nobody hurt a bunch of women anyways," he said.

Cohen watched him. Tried to figure what to say. He wanted the boy to be certain about getting to the Line, but he also wanted him to be certain about what might have to be done to get there.

"Men down here aren't like the men you think of," he said. "Men down here will probably hurt a bunch of women before they'll hurt anything else. I don't figure nobody ever hurt anything without knowing they could hurt it first. That's the way it is and probably the way it's always been."

"Then that's right," Evan said.

"What's right?"

"The men down here are just like the men I think of."

Cohen set his beer and down and lit a cigarette. "Where's your momma?" he asked.

"Where's yours?"

"Heaven or hell."

"Mine, too," Evan said and then he tossed his empty can into the fire. He sat back down and said, "What we supposed to do when we get there?"

"I don't know." Cohen shook his head. "But this ain't a place for nobody."

"How come you stayed? Your woman?"

Cohen laughed some. "My woman. I guess so. My woman."

"She get killed?"

"Yeah. A while back. Before all this."

Evan looked confused. He thought a second, then said, "So. What'd you stay for?"

"What for," Cohen repeated. "What for." He sat up and looked around. Out across the fields where there was nothing more black. "You can probably understand better one day a long time from now. A long time from now you can probably understand carrying something around with you that can't be real in no way but yet it feels as real as a bag of cement strapped across your shoulders and you walk around with that heavy thing and can't get loose from it. And for whatever reason, that time is now up." He leaned back in his chair again and stretched his legs out in front of him.

Evan got up and took another beer from the case and he stood closer to the fire. "What you gonna do with it when we get there?" he asked.

I don't know, Cohen thought. "Don't know," he said.

"Sounds like it's going with you."

He looked at the boy. So lean and so young and responsible for so much. Cohen said, "You're doing good taking care of that boy."

Evan turned around and went back to the chair and sat. Then he said, "You worry about something that ain't here. At least can't nothing else happen to her. She can't get hurt no worse. But mine walks around and gets hungry and cold. Cries when he's scared. Holds on to my leg."

Cohen sighed. He already understands, he thought. "You ever drink beer before?" Cohen asked him.

"Not more than one."

"So how many is that?"

"Two."

A few minutes later, Evan got up and went off to his trailer, leaving Cohen alone. He kept on drinking. Kept on thinking about what had been and what was to come. Thought about this ragtag band of refugees. Thought about walking over and killing Aggie just to see what it was going to feel like to kill another man. Because he had the feeling that he would have to do it before this was all over.

Later in the night Kris felt a sharp pain in her back and she shifted around, tried to get comfortable, but no matter how she turned the pain remained and she finally woke up Nadine, who slept on the other side with the baby in the middle.

"I'm dying," Kris said.

Nadine sat up on the mattress, rubbed at her face. "What?"

"My back feels like a big cramp and it's moving around my sides," she said and she was breathing big breaths.

Nadine got up off the mattress and walked around and took Kris's hands. She helped her to her feet and she moaned going up. The baby was bundled and didn't wake and Nadine helped Kris to the door and out of the trailer. When they were outside, Kris let out some loud groans and then she doubled over. "At least it's quit raining for a damn second," Nadine said. She got a chair and Kris sat down carefully with her legs straight out and she held both hands on the sides of her stomach.

"Shit," Nadine said. She wanted to do something but didn't know what, so she paced back and forth in front of Kris as if to distract her. She rubbed her hands together and looked around at the defeated fire and she stopped pacing and jumped up and down a little.

"Ooooohhh, God," Kris moaned again and her thick head of hair blew around with the wind.

"What is it? Where is it?" Nadine asked and she knelt at Kris's feet.

"It's all around me like somebody's squeezing a belt. Oh shit."

"Hold my hands."

"Oh shit."

They joined their four cold hands and Kris squeezed like hell, grimacing and grunting. Her round face twisted and she showed her teeth when she moaned. Her short legs lifted slightly off the ground when she squeezed hands and her bushy, matted hair fell around her head like some wild woman's.

"Hold on, honey," Nadine said and she kept talking, kept urging her to hang on but she didn't know what she was telling her to hang on for. Kris squeezed harder and harder and she seemed gripped all over, and she let out a long, extended moan like an animal dying in the woods. Nadine begged her to hold on, held her hands, let go and went behind her and rubbed her shoulders but Kris reached up and took her hands again and squeezed her fingers together tightly. Nadine let her hold on. Several more minutes like this, but then whatever it was began to ease some and the moaning eased, and then whatever it was had gone.

"Oh God," Kris said. Exasperated.

Nadine let go of her hands and pushed Kris's hair back from her face. Her forehead was damp with sweat. "You need to let me cut this wild stuff," she said.

Kris shook her head. Slowed her breathing. "And look like you? You got a worse haircut than Brisco."

Behind them a trailer door opened and Cohen came out. He was pulling on his coat and holding a flashlight and the beam shined on the two women. He walked over and said, “What’s going on?”

Nadine said, “She’s hurtin.”

“How so?”

Nadine shrugged. “Bad.”

Cohen then asked Kris.

“I don’t know,” she said. She was trying to sit up straight in the folded chair and Nadine helped her up. “Got these cramps or something. Started in my back like somebody had elbows all across and then it moved all around.”

Cohen looked back at Nadine, who looked at him, and they both waited for the other to say something that would help. Neither did.

Finally Cohen said, “First time?”

Kris nodded.

“We gotta get the hell outta here,” Nadine said.

“Is it stopped all over?” Cohen asked.

Kris nodded again.

From the trailer, the baby cried.

“I’ll get him,” Nadine said and she left them and went to the infant.

“There’s a bottle in there somewhere,” Kris called.

Cohen took a cigarette out of his coat pocket and lit it and then he walked back to his trailer and came back with a bottle of water. He gave it to Kris and she seemed okay for now. Cohen smoked and she drank the water and they listened to the crying baby and the faint hiss of the few remaining embers.

"You want something else?" Cohen asked.

"Nah. Just to sit still."

Cohen finished and tossed his cigarette and he moved over to the fire pit and tossed a couple of branches on the coals. They watched for several minutes but nothing happened except a little smoke.

"What was her name?" Kris asked.

Cohen looked to her. He cleared his throat and spit. Didn't answer.

"Most people have names," Kris said.

"There were two. Elisa and Rivers."

"Rivers was a little one?"

"Yeah."

"Sounds like a little one. How'd you pick that name?"

Cohen rocked back and forth a little. "We went to Venice one time. Biggest thing we ever did. She loved it there and liked calling it the city of rivers. Took her about nine seconds to name the baby Rivers when we found out it was a girl."

They were silent again. Nadine had found the bottle and the crying had stopped. The fire snapped.

"Mariposa said something about your stuff. That's why I was asking," she said.

"That's all right."

"You was still in your house?"

"Yeah. Was."

"That's a little bit remarkable."

"Not as remarkable as all this shit," he said and he motioned around the circle of trailers strapped to the ground with ropes and spikes.

Kris held out her hand and Cohen took it and helped her to her feet. She was a little round thing in all the bundles of clothes covering her growing stomach. She pushed her hair away from her face, then put her hands on her back and stretched. She edged toward the fire. Cohen lit another cigarette.

Behind them a door opened and Mariposa came out. She tied a scarf around her head to hold back her hair and she stood up a cinder block and sat on it. "You okay?" Mariposa said.

"For this second," Kris answered. She arched her back again. Looked off into the dark. "He killed my husband," she continued. "Right out there somewhere. Just walked him out and killed him after pretending he was gonna take us up to the Line. We got stuck down here trying to come back for some of our stuff. It was so stupid and we knew it was but he had some tractors that was worth something and it seemed like money if we could somehow get a couple up. Soon as we got back down we got caught in a bad one. Him and Joe fished us out and brought us out here. I took one look at it and knew something wasn't right and I told Billy but he shrugged it off. I told him about thirty seconds after we got here, we gotta go. Let's just go. Next day Aggie walked him out there and he killed him. And then he locked me up with the other two or three and then found some more and locked them up and then they stuck this in me." She pointed at her stomach and then she bent over and put her hands over her face and started to cry. She bounced and cried and looked like she might go to her knees but Cohen grabbed the chair and stuck it under her and Mariposa hurried up and helped ease her down. They stepped back from her and she cried and cried and for some reason that Cohen couldn't explain he felt like a fool.

He kept on smoking and Mariposa paced back and forth. Kris cried and then she wiped her eyes. Sniffed. Got it together.

"What about her?" Cohen asked and pointed toward the trailer where Nadine had gone.

"I don't know much. She was here when I got here. You, too?"

Mariposa nodded.

"Think she's been here a long time. She don't say much about it. I know I saw her take a swing at Aggie one day and him and Joe put down that revolution real quick. Think that might've happened a few times."

"At least a few," Mariposa said.

"Did you know them other ones that run off already?" Cohen asked.

Kris shook her head. "Not so much."

"Me neither," Mariposa added.

Cohen flicked away the cigarette. Random raindrops tapped in the red mud.

"It ain't never gonna end," Kris said. She held her hand out toward Mariposa, who took it and pulled her up from the chair. A little more rain came on as Mariposa helped her to her trailer and inside.

Cohen drank one more and then he took one of the pistols out of his pocket and stood. A little drunk. He limped away from the fire and out into the dark where Aggie was tied to the trailer.

"You want to live or die?" Cohen asked him, but he couldn't see his eyes and didn't know if he was asleep or awake. So he asked again but this time he pointed the pistol at him.

Aggie didn't answer. Didn't move. The wind had picked up and lightning cracked to the south. Aggie's body hung limply against the trailer, lifeless and broken. His head forward and heavy. If cut free, it seemed as if he would flop to the earth and never rise again.

Cohen lowered the pistol. Watched for a moment. Then as he turned to walk away, Aggie raised his head and said in a low voice, "I was about to ask you the same thing."

Cohen stopped and looked back at him.

In the dark, Aggie spoke. "Probably ten, fifteen years ago, we was going real strong one night.

Summer night. Hot as hell and then some." His voice was low but strong, like a quiet engine. "I had this rattlesnake burning me up, biggest damn one I think I ever had. Sliding all over me. Organ playing loud and people hollering and jumping and Amen this and God Almighty that and then from the back this man got up. Him and his boy. I hadn't even noticed them there. They got up and come right between the chairs, right up front. Man was carrying the boy. Maybe eight, nine years old. Didn't say a word, neither one. Just stood right in front of me until I noticed and quit, and then the organ quit and all the hollering and dancing quit and everybody just stood there, waiting on them to say something. And then when he finally said something, you know what he said, don't you?"

Cohen said, "Yeah. I know."

"Yeah. I knew. We all knew what was coming. He said fix my boy. Lay your hands on his legs. They ain't never worked right. Doctor says ain't never gonna, but lay your hands on him and let the good Lord fix him. Let the good Lord make him right. Lay your hands on him."

Aggie paused. Coughed some. Cohen waited.

"It got so quiet. I swear I heard sweat hitting the floor. I'd done a lot of shit. A lot. But I'll be goddamned I wasn't claiming to be no healer. Never did mess with it. Didn't want to. And here he was in front of all my people asking me to lay my hands on that boy. Let the power of God come through me and rise him up, fix his legs."

He stopped. His head dropped.

"So?" Cohen said.

Aggie raised his head. "So I set that rattlesnake in its box. I told the organ to play soft. I told everybody to raise their hands to the ceiling and pray for this boy and then I took off my shirt and wiped my face and acted like I was gathering up the Holy Ghost from some deep, dark well and I held that boy's legs and prayed like some lunatic until I didn't have no more gas. And then I let go. Looked at his daddy and looked at the boy and I turned around and ran out the back. Ran out and kept on running till I was at least a couple of miles gone and then I wandered in some shithole bar and drank Jack Daniel's until they laid me out back with the garbage."

When he was done, Aggie let out a heavy sigh. Cohen looked around in the dark. Moved the pistol back and forth in his hands. The wind was against his face and pushed his hair back and the rain washed over his cheeks and eyes.

"I couldn't do nothing. No way around it. No trick. A dead end any way you went," Aggie said. He sighed again, then his voice became sharper. "Like you. Any way you go, dead end. You just think you got plans but you don't got any idea what you're doing. What you think is gonna happen to you? To them? What you think is gonna happen? I know what you're walking around with. Got the rooms boarded up like you can lock the ghosts away but they only seep under the doors. Seep between the cracks in the walls and live right there with you. I saw your place. Saw what you tried boarding up. What you think is gonna happen when you get to the Line?"

He paused, laughed a little. His voice became confident, mocking. The wind whipped around them and Aggie bound to the flatbed seemed to gather himself with the growing storm and rise up. "That is if you get there. If. You see what we got going here and all you see is the locks on the doors. That's all you see and all they see. What you and them don't see is you're alive out here and you're alive 'cause I let you be. You're alive and you eat and sleep and you got protection and I give all that. Every one of them I give all that and I could give it to you too but you'd rather see the locks on the doors and decide that something here is wrong but there ain't nothing here wrong. Every one of them was either alone or damn near alone without no food. No safe place. Every one of them would be dead or worse if I hadn't brought them here and given them everything. All you see is the locks on the doors but you and them are gonna find out what's out there and don't none of you want to find out. I can swear to that. And here you got me crucified. The one who gave and the one who knows how to live out here and the one who created the family that not a goddamn one of them had or ever will have. So you crucify me except you ain't even got the empathy to pierce me so that I can bleed to death. Instead you'll leave me to starve or be devoured by God knows what and all I ever did for every one of them was give, and they'll know it this time tomorrow.

"When it's dark and there's nowhere safe to lay their heads and they'll look at you like you got some answers but you ain't got no goddamn answers. You don't even know how to answer yourself when you ask yourself questions. If you did you wouldn't be living like you were living. You ain't got no answers for yourself or for them and this time tomorrow when it's dark and cold each of you will want for me and want for this place. You'll want to gather and pray and eat but you won't be able to. You'd rather reign in hell than serve in heaven and you'd rather crucify than love. There's no answers between you. None. Tomorrow you and them will set out for the end of your lives and I'll be here. The one who gave and would keep on giving if you'd let me. But you don't want to let me. You and them are going to walk through the valley but you'll have no shepherd. You'll have no answers. And you'll kill the babies. And you'll die. You ain't no healer, no more than I am, but I can give more than you. So I guess if I ask whether you want to live or die, you already answered when you tied me up."

When he was done, he turned his head away from Cohen and fell silent. As if he had been turned off. Cohen stood still and waited. Didn't know why but he waited to see if the older man had anything else to say. And when Aggie didn't speak again, Cohen walked back and sat down. The peaceful night had become something different.

Through the rain and wind, Aggie called out to him. "Maybe you wanna die. Then you'll get to love your ghosts again."

A half-empty beer sat near Cohen's foot and he picked it up and took it all in one swig, got up, and walked over to the trailer that held the guns. Leaned against the wall was the rifle with the infrared scope, the one Aggie had used to shoot him. He picked it up, found the shells and loaded it, and then he walked out of the trailer and away from the compound. He walked until he was only a silhouette.

He looked into the sky. Clouds raced and Cohen knew how quickly it could all come on.

He lowered the rifle and through the scope he found Aggie. Arms wide. Head down. The same pose of death as the crucified man Aggie had used for so many years to feed his wild and insatiable appetite.

Cohen lowered the rifle. Off in the night

something howled, long and draining, as though it might have been a final one.

He raised the rifle and looked again through the scope and this time someone was with Aggie, kneeling and swiping at his arms and wrists and it could only be Ava, cutting at the ropes with a knife. "Son of a bitch," Cohen said and he steadied himself. One arm came free and she moved to the other side and Cohen didn't have time to think about it anymore. He fired and Ava reared and arched her back and then she fell across Aggie's legs. Aggie reached and took the knife from her limp hand, but he didn't go for the rope wrapping his other arm and hand. He simply held the knife, and he looked out toward Cohen, and it was difficult to tell, but Cohen thought he was smiling.

Cohen fired again and Aggie leaped as if receiving a severe shock. Cohen shot him once more, and seconds later, Aggie was still.

The others were out of the trailers and milling around when Cohen came walking in from the dark. With disgust he tossed the rifle on the ground. It didn't take them long to figure out what had happened. The rain fell against their faces and they shielded their eyes and stared at Cohen. Then Nadine told them to come on, let's go see.

"You stay here," Evan told Brisco.

"Why?"

"Just go sit over there a minute."

Evan, Nadine, and Kris went out toward Aggie. Mariposa picked up the rifle and she walked over to Cohen's trailer and set it inside.

"I'm getting wet," Brisco said and he ran back inside the trailer.

Mariposa moved over to Cohen. His head hung down.

"Don't you wanna see?" he said without looking at her.

"Is he dead?" she asked.

"Him and her. She was trying to untie him."

"Ava?"

He nodded.

Then they heard Nadine and Kris screaming at Aggie's dead body. And then at Ava's dead body. You fucking liar, Nadine yelled at the dead woman, her voice savage and vehement. Cohen got up and went over to them and Kris and Nadine were kicking the limp bodies and screaming son of a bitch and go to hell. The bodies absorbed the kicks like old mattresses and lay heavy on the wet ground. The women's voices were filled with hate and celebration and seemed to carry out across the land on the wind. Evan only stood there. Kris kicked little kicks with her round belly and short legs but Nadine reared back and crushed ribs and cheekbones with her heavy boots and winding, skinny legs. Cohen stood back from them in the dark with his arms folded.

Mariposa sneaked up behind Cohen and she wrapped her arm around his and when he turned to her she pulled closer to him and kissed him on the mouth. She held her hand against his wet beard and he let himself go and leaned in to her and felt her wet mouth and wet nose against his own. The women kicked and danced and screamed and cussed and Cohen let himself fall.

Only for a moment. He pulled back from her as quickly as he had gone to her. He stared at her but it was too dark for expressions and she let go of his arm. Wiped at her face. Then she turned around and walked over to the bodies and started kicking with Kris and Nadine.

"Come on, Evan. What you waiting on?" Nadine said. She was bent over with her hands on her knees, getting her second wind.

"He's already dead," Evan said.

"And he deserves a lot worse," Nadine answered. Then she went back to it.

Cohen said, "She was working to get him loose if anybody wants to know."

Kris held her hands on her sides and was out of breath. She backed away and let Nadine and Mariposa have it and Evan took her by the arm and said, "You better calm down before you pop."

She raised up and said, "Ain't nothing wrong with me."

"Hell yeah," Nadine yelled at her. "Get back on it."

Kris moved back to the body and kicked and kicked. Nadine stomped on Aggie's head with the heel of her boot and Mariposa had run out of steam and stood back.

Evan walked quietly to the fire.

Something cracked under Nadine's heel and she screamed I fucking hate you and she stomped and stomped and there was another crack and now Mariposa and Kris kicked at Ava, her body so layered in clothes that it sounded like they were kicking a mattress.

Cohen watched with his arms crossed. He wondered what it would feel like to join them, to let it out, whatever he would be letting out. But he wasn't going to invade and knew he couldn't understand what they had been through or what they owed the two dead bodies.

Kris paused again and bent over. "I can't do no more," she said, huffing.

Nadine and Mariposa stopped and looked at her.

"You all right?" Cohen asked.

"She's all right," Nadine said. "Why don't you let us be for a bit? Go sit down."

"You sure you're okay?" Cohen asked Kris again.

"Cohen," Mariposa said.

Kris dropped down on a knee and Nadine and Mariposa moved to her.

"If you need me I'm over there," Cohen said,

but they didn't hear him, and he left them and went and sat down with Evan. A few minutes later, they were at it again.

Evan had gone inside with Brisco and Cohen was alone when the women walked back into the compound, hands on hips. The rain had lightened and they all sat down. Cohen found bottles of water and passed them out and he stood next to the dying fire.

"I knew it," Kris said. "I knew she was gonna do some shit no matter what she said."

"Yep," Nadine said. "I damn well knew it, too. And we ain't burying nobody just so you know."

Cohen lit a cigarette and blew warm air on his hands. He looked at Mariposa and she was looking at him. When their eyes caught, he stared at her a moment. Then he blew on his hands again. Nadine turned up her bottle and finished it and tossed it onto the red coals. The bottle twisted and melted.

"I been thinking I'm gonna give it away," Kris said. "That's the first thing I thought today when I realized we were getting out of here. Don't even wanna see it. Just take, I'm gonna tell them. Don't show it to me only take it on. But when it started hurting before I started changing my mind. Right in the middle of them cramps, I started wanting it to be all right and wanting to see it. Even when I was hollering it hurt so bad I was wanting to be able to hold on to it and hoping I get to. Now I'm hoping I get to."

Cohen said, "You'll get to."

"If we make it," Nadine said.

Now he was tired of smoking and he wanted to drink again. He went over to his trailer and came back with a whiskey pint. He handed it to Kris and she shook her head.

"One sip ain't gonna hurt," Nadine said.

She took the bottle and a sip and her shoulders raised and fell. "I never did like that shit," she said as she passed it to Nadine.

Cohen said, "You'll be fine."

"Maybe."

Nadine drank and then she said she was sick of being wet and Aggie was dead and gone and no offense but there was nothing else worth sitting out there for. She took another drink and passed the bottle to Mariposa and went inside.

Mariposa held the bottle to her nose and sniffed. Then she took a little drink and winced. Cohen shook his head and took the bottle from her.

"What'd she look like?" Kris asked.

Cohen switched the bottle from hand to hand. He thought of the picture in his back pocket and started to pull it out. But instead he said, "She looked like a runner 'cause that's what she was. Kinda tall. Ate whatever 'cause she burnt it all up. Ran cross-country in high school. Ran whatever after that. Used to run on the beach. I'd lay there and drink beer and she'd run up and back a few miles. Then she'd go out into the water and cool off and call me names for being so damn lazy."

"You shoulda got up," Kris said.

"Nah. I shouldn't have. That was her thing. I liked it being her thing. Said it kept her sane and I woulda screwed that up huffing and puffing trying to keep up."

"That was probably smart."

"Yeah. One of the smart things I've done, I guess."

Cohen drank some more. Knelt next to the ashen fire. "Not that long until light," he said. "You know it's gonna rain hard again soon. You should probably go lay back down."

"Probably," Kris said. "Lemme have one more sip."

"It ain't no good, you said."

She held out her hand. "I know it ain't. But it's a sleeping pill."

He handed her the bottle. She took a sip, shook her head, then took another. She gave it back and said ugh. Then Mariposa helped her out of the chair and walked with her as Kris moved gingerly toward the trailer. Cohen asked if they needed any help but Kris said no. "Save all your help for getting me to the Line, 'cause I told you I decided I want to hold on to it. If God'll let me."

Mariposa closed the door behind Kris and she walked back. Cohen drank again. She wiped at her face and said, "I don't wanna sit in the rain. Do you?"

He looked up at the night sky. "It's not raining much."

"It will be. You said."

He nodded.

She stepped over to him and held out her hand. He looked at it. It was wet and frail-looking. She seemed the same way. He looked around the compound, out into the dark acreage, out toward the place where Aggie and Ava lay. Then he looked back to her and down at her extended hand and it seemed to shake from cold or fear or something.

He reached out and took it and she led them to her trailer.

25

It seemed as though her entire life had been driven by her imagination. From an early age, her head filled with ghost stories and listening from behind the curtain to the spiritual confessions of those who paid for her grandmother's otherworld connections and the French Quarter spirits that gathered in the glow of the lampposts and her own childlike manifestations of the space between the imagined and the real. The tarot card readers in Jackson Square who let her sit and listen and the friendly vampire who stood outside

Lafitte's in the winter and led the cemetery tours and the Mardi Gras masks and the fabulous costumes of the parades. The stories she created for the Quarter regulars who came in and out of her father's store and the stories she spun while she looked into the windows of empty buildings as she and her mother walked back and forth from home to school and the boats up and down the river and the beautiful women and handsome men she imagined sitting on the decks and drifting in and out of her city.

And then the storms. From bad to worse and more frequent and sometimes evacuations and then regular evacuations and then bold predictions of a weather pattern that would go on for years and years and continue to destroy and many scoffed and many refused to believe but her mind processed it easily. She would lie awake nights, on the eve of another storm, and dream of the catastrophe in vivid colors, see the shingles ripping from rooftops and hear the cracking of tree limbs and feel the flooding waters around her neck. She saw the skeletons of buildings and wrecked ships and heard the crashing of waves and heard the great roar of thunder before it ever arrived. And when the storm did arrive and perhaps it hadn't been quite what she had imagined, melancholy came over her that lasted until the next warning and then her mind would create havoc all over again and eventually the reality of the storms caught up with the projections of her imagined landscape. Even as the storms worsened and morphed into one long stream of destruction, even after the insanity arrived with the proclama-tion of the Line, it all seemed to be something that she had seen before, as if when she closed her eyes she had always been off in some other world where Mother Nature was a vengeful authority. There was not a sky darker than the skies behind her eyes, there was not a wind more powerful than the winds of her mind.

Then she had found herself alone and she had discovered that there were plenty of things in this world that were unimaginable. She had never been able to understand this place with these men and their roped-down trailers. Never been able to conjure anything more horrific than this as she lay down at night. Instead of creating new worlds, her dreams were filled with fascinations of escape. Filled with fascinations of revenge. Filled with the faces of those she had loved and now missed. And in the waking hours, she could only wonder where they were. Wonder if someone was looking for her. Wonder if anyone was still alive who cared. She was certain she had family. Somewhere. But this new world was so vast and shifting and unanswerable that she hadn't been able to create anything but an unhappy ending for herself and the others. The little girl whose mind once was a carnival of ghost tales and spirit worlds and the romance of hurricanes was now a young woman whose insatiable imagination had been replaced with the sharp edges of the real thing.

Then she and Evan had gone out, and she had choked the man in the Jeep, and she had gone to his house and she had seen where he slept and whom he slept with and what his life had been like and what he was holding on to. And she had taken his shoe box that held the contents of his life and she had held the letters and worn the jewelry and her mind had come alive again. It was as if she had walked through a secret door and taken the hand of someone she once created and had led him out of the dream into reality. It was as if she had become again that little girl. Since she had been alone, since she had been brought to this place, since she had been forced to endure what all the women there had been forced to endure, she had in some ways forgotten that she was alive, that her life belonged to her.

She held Cohen's hand and led him into the trailer and on a shelf on the wall she lit the candles. He stood holding the whiskey bottle and she took it from him and set it on the shelf. She stepped back from him and removed her coat. He reached out and took a strand of her black hair and let it trail through his fingers.

She whispered to him, "I can be who you want me to be."

She wore a flannel shirt and she began to unbutton it as he held her hair, rubbed it between his fingers as if it were a fabric that he had never touched before. She unbuttoned the shirt to the end and she pushed it back from her chest, and then her shoulders, and it fell and the wind pushed the trailer and the candlelight waved.

He let go of her hair and looked at her.

Her hair was around her neck and down her chest and he moved it back and exposed her neckline. The V of the dress reached between her breasts.

Cohen stepped back. The long black sleeves. The tie around the waist that he had tied for her each time she wore it. Mariposa tugged at her waist and lifted the rest of the dress, which she was wearing tucked into her pants, and it fell over her hips and reached her knees.

He began to shake his head. She took a step toward him and he took another step back. "Stop," he said.

"It's all right," she said and she reached out for him, but he grabbed her by the wrist and lowered her hand.

"I said stop," he said and his voice had changed. "That's not yours."

"I know. I didn't mean it to be. I meant it to be hers."

He reached to the shelf and grabbed the bottle. He turned it up and drank hard. Then he looked at her again. "I don't wanna pretend," he said. "I don't know why you'd think I would. I don't know why the hell anybody would want to do something like that."

The expectation left her face. Her shoulders slumped and she seemed to shrink.

"Whatever else you got, don't let me see it," he said and he turned and walked out the door.

Mariposa stood still. Watched her shadows. She realized now that this would be her last night here. That tomorrow night, they would be somewhere else. She lifted the dress over her head and dropped it on the floor. Put the flannel shirt on again. Put on her coat. He is not a dream, she thought. He is not a story. No matter how hard you try. She stood still and wondered if maybe he was just outside the door. Maybe he was coming back. Maybe there would be a long pause and then a knock.

She waited but there was nothing. You can't put a spell on him, she thought. Not down here. You can't put a spell on nobody and you can't make the dead come to life.

26

Cohen changed his bandage, put on his coat and put the pistols in the coat pockets, tucked the shoe box under his arm and came outside and found them ready to go. Evan was holding the shotgun and he handed it to him. They gathered in the early morning in the middle of the compound, around the smoldering, wasted fire. It rained and the wind had become steady and out across the Gulf the sky was a deep, threatening gray.

Cohen walked over and they told him that these were the rules that had been agreed upon—whatever vehicle you get into belongs to you and the others in it. At the Line, the baby and Kris go to a doctor immediately. After that, no one owes anybody anything. Cohen nodded.

"Yeah, but what about when we get up there?" Kris asked.

"That's what we're talking about," Cohen said.

"Not all that. I mean like, are we still alive or wrote off?"

Nadine said, "Guess we'll find out. Might be some resurrections."

They looked around for the last time at this place where some of them had spent weeks, some of them months, some of them almost two years. The rain fell on the drab, lifeless compound. The bodies of Aggie and Ava lay off to the side at the back end of the trailer. It was now a place for restless spirits, a grave site.

They loaded garbage bags filled with clothes and other possessions into the beds of the pickups. Kris held the baby and he was sucking on a bottle and the rare air of optimism appeared on their faces as they prepared for what was next. Cohen stood at the back of the truck they had filled with supplies and checked to see if there was anything that he had missed. In the last act of preparation, Evan began to put the gas cans into the truck bed. Kris and Nadine walked over together to the trucks. Mariposa went with them. Kris handed the baby to Cohen and they began to take the gas cans and he asked them what the hell they were doing.

"Don't worry about it," Nadine said.

The three of them went from trailer to trailer, opening the doors and stepping inside and pouring gasoline onto the beds and floors and then out again and along the ropes that held the trailers strapped into the ground. Cohen cradled the child and held the bottle to his mouth and shook his head as he watched them, knew that their journey was becoming more troublesome with each drop spilled into the trailers. He also knew that his voice would not be enough to stop this cleansing. He talked to the baby as the women continued their work. Be a good little man, he said. Got a pretty good trip coming up. Hope you ride well. We'll get you somewhere if you can stick with it.

When they were done, the women returned the gas cans to the truck bed and then without being asked, Cohen produced a cigarette lighter from his pocket. Nadine took it from him and Kris and Mariposa filled their arms with rolls of toilet paper. They splashed back and forth across the compound, ducking into a trailer, lighting a toilet paper roll and tossing it in, and moving on to the next until they were all done. Then they gathered again in the middle and within minutes there were heavy coils of smoke curling out of the open doors of the trailers, and then there were yellow flames burning through the roofs and out of the windows. Pops and hisses and low roars of the growing flames fought against the rain. They stood and watched until all of the trailers were burning like giant campfires and then they walked out of this ring of fire and they all moved over toward the trucks. Nobody said a word as Kris took the infant from Cohen.

Evan cranked one truck. Nadine cranked the other. And then Cohen cranked the Jeep and Mariposa got in with him. He had cut a piece of tarp and roped it across the top of the Jeep and the rain slapped against it. He looked at her and said, "The last time you rode with me I almost died."

She held up her hands and showed him both sides, as if she were a magician proving there were no strings. "You should know that story by now."

"Yeah. I know it." He pulled off his sock hat and shook the rain from it and then put it back on.

"I see why you did it," she said.

"See why what?"

"I see why you came looking for it."

Cohen shook his head in disagreement. “You didn’t see nothing last night.”

She nodded. “I know, but I see now,” she said. “I can see that she really loved you. And you really loved her. I can see that in all those little things. I get it.”

Cohen stopped looking at her. He looked over his shoulder at the shoe box behind the seat as if Elisa might be there in its place and then he looked out toward the burning trailers, across the flooded lowlands. He squeezed his hands together as if they belonged to two different people who missed each other. Behind him one of the trucks blew the horn but he didn’t pay attention. Didn’t move.

She said quietly, “I’m not gonna hurt you.”

He unclenched his hands. Moved his head around in a circle as if stretching his neck. Then he opened his coat and took out a cigarette. He lit it and put the Jeep in first gear, and he told her that it didn’t matter what she said she was gonna do or not do. Nobody really knows what they’re going to do until the moment they decide to do it.

The three vehicles moved across the field, driving slowly across the rough, weather-beaten terrain. As they turned onto Himmel Road, the fires were beginning to lose against the rain.

27

It was a spectacle and difficult not to watch. Out across the Gulf the lightning storm snapped and delivered steady strikes against the darkening backdrop. A circus of lightning that seemed like it might be shooting straight from the fingertips of God. Those who weren't driving watched. Those who were driving watched out of one eye and spied the road with the other.

Once they stopped to change the baby's diaper and once more for the pregnant woman to pee and soon they arrived at the ocean. The sights were almost new for Nadine and Kris as neither had been away from the compound since their capture. The washed-away chunks of beach. The water sitting where houses used to be. The buckled storefronts and uprooted ancient trees. They had almost forgotten.

But not Mariposa. The sights and lightning strikes only triggered her memories of the old world and as she surveyed the landscape, she heard the voice of her grandmother warning anyone who would listen. Pack it up and go she had said from the start. We need to pack it up and forget all this. This is only the beginning. The crazy will go crazier and the wind will blow harder and the rain won't stop. But none of them listened. Her father didn't listen. Her mother didn't listen and neither did her aunts or cousins or anyone in the neighborhood. No one listened until the men in uniforms with automatic weapons slung over their shoulders started making them get on the buses and even then it had been too much to believe. Too crazy. So much insanity with the National Guardsmen lined around Jackson Square, the last evacuation, herding people onto buses where locals once climbed into horse- drawn carriages, women and children and the young and the old in a fury of pushing and shoving, while maniacs shot at them from alleys and from behind cars and from rooftops under a gray lightning-infested sky. A war against itself. Something beyond hysteria. The buses finally filled and they drove away, the Guardsmen shooting from the windows, the buses escorted by tanks, bodies left behind to be cleansed by the coming storm.

That had been the last time she had seen anybody from her family, the buses driving in different directions, and she had been pushed onto one, separated from anyone that she knew. The woman at the high school gym where they were delivered five hours later told her that it'd take some time but we'll find them but Mariposa could tell by the sound of her voice that there were too many people asking the same question.

She felt it again now. Heard the screams and

the gunfire and the roar of a confused, desperate crowd.

Cohen leaned on the steering wheel and interrupted her thoughts.

"What?" she asked.

"I ain't real enthusiastic about Charlie with the rain and the sky looking the way they look."

They drove carefully, passing the fallen neighborhoods, navigating the telephone poles and roofs and debris scattered across the four-lane running parallel to the water. They moved on until they came to the Grand Casino parking lot, and when Cohen saw what was there, he stopped. He told Mariposa to get out and go and tell them to back up.

"You see something?" she asked.

"We're not turning in here. Just go tell them."

She got out and did as he'd asked and returned to the Jeep. The vehicles backed up until Cohen waved and then he stopped. He got out and called for Evan.

"What is it?" Evan asked.

"Something your little brother doesn't need to see. Something nobody needs to see. Keep everybody back here."

"But what is it?"

"A bunch of bodies."

"Dammit. New ones?"

"It looks like it from here. Keep everybody where they are."

Evan walked back to the trucks. Cohen took one of the pistols out of his coat pocket and he started walking toward the parking lot and Mariposa came up beside him.

"Go on back there with them," he said.

"I don't want to," she answered.

"You don't want to come up here, either."

"I wanna see."

He stopped arguing and walked on and they crossed the front lawn of the Grand Casino. There were giant holes here and there in the lawn with big piles of dirt next to them. One palm tree stood though several had fallen and a thick black electrical wire weaved across the lawn like a sleeping snake. They walked to the circular driveway where limousines once delivered well-dressed patrons and then they came to the parking lot where the bodies lay in awkward positions like castaway dolls.

It had been a massacre. Bodies scattered across asphalt. Mariposa gasped and Cohen said stand here and he moved out among them. He had seen some of them before at Charlie's truck. There was the fat man with the poker chips. Next to him lay the old man with the sign, now splattered in dark red. Twenty or so bodies in all, some of them with closed eyes, others with open eyes staring at the sky and taking in the rain. The blood had washed from them and out into wide circles on the pavement, thin rain-mixed blood that spread in abstract, almost artful shapes. He noticed the holes in their chests and arms and heads. The bewildered looks on some of their faces as if they had posed for a sudden, brutal death. Then separated from these men were two of Charlie's muscle, barrel-chested men in their black shirts and black pants, their strong arms and thick thighs no longer the sign of strength. Their weapons were gone and their laced black boots taken from their feet. Cohen stepped over them. Around them.

He stopped and looked up and down the road. All gray and getting darker and the rain kept anything from appearing clearly.

Thunder roared across the choppy Gulf waters and the lightning remained as the wind was beginning to push the waves. He looked again at the parking lot where the bodies lay and he realized that there were very willing and capable men out there. Probably not far away. Maybe even watching. Men who would take whatever they found from whoever had it and it seemed that everyone had already had enough of that.

"You know any of them?" Mariposa asked.

"I've seen most. Those two in the black over there are Charlie's. Some of these others were Charlie's customers."

"Rain makes it look like they're still bleeding. Are they?"

Cohen shook his head. "Nah. That part's over."

"We better go," she said and her eyes seemed nervous. "I don't like this."

"I know."

There wasn't enough gasoline to get to the Line. Maybe not enough gasoline to get halfway to the Line, depending on what roads and bridges were available. He looked across the street and counted one, two skeletons of gas stations. He looked back in the direction they had come from and he wondered how many miles had been lost in the gasoline used to burn the trailers.

Nadine and Evan walked up and Nadine said, "I told Kris to stay in the truck with the baby and Brisco. She's a little freaked out over this shit."

"So am I," Evan said.

"How many is it?"

"A lot," Mariposa said. "I wouldn't walk over there."

"I ain't walking over there. I can see it from right here. Aggie and Ava are the only dead people I ever laid eyes on up close and that's how I plan to keep it."

There was more thunder and more lightning and they were hunched underneath their hoods, looking at one another with bent necks. A truck door slammed and Kris came toward them.

"Where's the baby?" Nadine asked.

"Asleep on the seat," she said. "So I'm guessing no gas."

"No gas. No nothing. I'd siphon the gas for the

trucks together if I had something to siphon with, but I don't."

"Well, I don't like standing here. It's a gosh-damn graveyard," Kris said.

"We better hide out," Nadine said. "We got food and stuff. We can wait."

"Hide out and wait for what?" Evan asked.

"Hell I don't know but there's plenty of vacancy. All we need is half a hotel. Not even half. A quarter."

"I ain't waiting down here no longer," said Kris. "My stomach hurts. My back hurts. My legs hurt."

"Hiding out doesn't get us gasoline," Cohen said and then he motioned toward the sky. "And you all know what's coming."

"Hiding don't get us gas but it don't get us killed by whoever did that. And there ain't been a storm yet to lift and carry this bunch."

"We didn't leave out there to go hide somewhere else," Kris said. "We left to get back to the world."

"Won't do no good if we ain't alive when we get there," Nadine answered.

"You don't know we won't be."

"You don't, neither."

"Don't nobody know," said Evan. "But I got the keys to one truck and I ain't hiding out and waiting on a miracle."

"Me neither," said Kris.

"You ain't got the keys," Nadine said and she

reached into her pocket and pulled out the keys to the truck she and Kris were riding in.

"That ain't yours," Kris said. "It's ours."

"I know whose it is. But my half says we hole up for a little while."

"My half don't want to have a baby in the middle of goddamn nowhere." The two women had inched closer to one another as they spoke, Nadine a head taller than Kris and the fingers cut off from her gloves and she looked like something that might hide in an alley and jump on you. But Kris, in all her roundness, bellied up to the taller woman and she squeezed her hands in tight, hard fists.

"I guess you forgot about the baby," Mariposa said.

"I ain't forgot about nothing."

"It's gotta see a doctor or somebody."

"I know what it needs."

"Not this," Evan said.

The thunder came again and momentarily silenced them. They all looked at one another. Looked around at the trucks. Looked around at the weather.

"I ain't staying here," Evan said to everyone. "Simple as that."

"Me neither," said Kris.

"Fine."

"Thank God," Cohen said as the thunder gave a long, bellowing roar.

"There ain't nothing to thank Him for yet,"

Nadine said with a cautious air. "But we'd all better hope there is before it's over with."

"Look down there," Mariposa said and she pointed east along the highway. Far off in the distance, there was a white dot.

"What is it?" Evan said.

"A headlight. Gotta be," said Kris. "Can we please get the hell outta here?"

"Go get in," Cohen said and the women hurried back to the vehicles, but Cohen grabbed Evan by the coat and said, "Come with me." Across the highway were two gas stations and though there was likely no chance, Cohen didn't want to leave without finding out.

"Run over to that one and try every pump," he said to Evan. Evan hurried across the road. The only things left standing at the stations were the pumps, as the buildings that once sold cold beer and lotto tickets and wooden-tipped cigars were long gone. Cohen had eight pumps to check and there was nothing. Evan had six and there was nothing. They ran back to the vehicles. Cohen looked east and the white dot remained. He told Evan to keep his headlights off. No way they can see us if we don't show ourselves. Then he told Nadine the same thing and he hurried to the Jeep. Mariposa had it cranked and he put it into first gear.

It was several miles east to Highway 49 and impossible to do anything but drive methodically against the weather and around the debris. The makeshift cover did little to protect Cohen and Mariposa and they were both drenched. She had brought her knees up to her chest and made herself a ball that her big coat could cover and Cohen leaned forward as if the slight difference in his posture might make things more visible. It'd be nice to have the damn windshield, he almost said to Mariposa but he'd already made one comment about their last ride together and decided to let that be. He had told her to keep watch on the white dot ahead, and sometimes it was there and sometimes not, and she reported when it came and went.

At Highway 49 the entire intersection was underwater. The harbor, once home to a battleship that crawled with elementary school children and sightseers, had pushed inland, and a small lake covered the intersection and the highway had become a canal. They had to backtrack through the crumbled remains of downtown Gulfport, the fallen historical buildings and the landmarks and the bumpy stone-paved streets. They finally made their way back around to 49 and turned north.

Away from the beachfront and old downtown were miles and miles of concrete. Vast, empty parking lots in front of superstores without their glass doors, busted by bricks or tire irons or crowbars. Strip malls and bank branches. Restaurants and gas stations. An abundance of pawnshops and liquor stores and video stores for adults only, the only kinds of stores that had prospered in the months leading up to the declaration of the Line. Here and there metal frames were exposed through roofs and telephone and electrical poles had crashed across storefronts and across the six lanes. Trash everywhere. Graffiti everywhere. Abandoned cars on the roadsides and in the parking lots. Giant steel poles that supported billboards stood straight without the advertisements. An abandoned National Guard outpost was situated in the parking lot between two strip malls, cinderblock painted black, thick glass riddled with bullet holes, a head-high chain-link fence with barbed wire wrapping the top. One of many like it that had been erected across the coastal region in the year before the declaration of the Line.

It was vigilant driving. As if some elaborate obstacle course had been set up for a school of stunt drivers. Cohen led, weaving around bigger traps, bouncing over smaller ones, one eye on what was in the road and one eye everywhere else. He was expecting to see Charlie's truck or the men who had apparently ambushed it, though he had no idea what to do if either appeared.

It took over half an hour to reach the north side of Gulfport and the thunderstorm was heavy. Six lanes became four. Corporate concrete gave way to locally owned concrete. Fewer stores and more apartment buildings that stood like very old men with their third and fourth floors missing. Up ahead Cohen saw something broad and white blocking the road and it was two trailers of eighteen-wheelers, end to end, turned on their sides. Cohen pulled up to them. There was room to get around on either side but he noticed one of the back doors lying open. The trucks pulled up behind him and stopped.

"What are you doing?" Mariposa yelled, no other way to communicate now.

He couldn't help but think of her, her splintered head in his lap, underneath a rig much like this one.

"Cohen?" she said and she reached over and grabbed his arm.

He shook his head and looked at her and said, "I gotta see what's in there."

He climbed out and waved to the others to wait and he bent over and walked through the storm. He held his hand on the pistol inside his coat as he moved toward the back end of the trailer, where the open door was a rectangle of dark. But he didn't go any farther. Even through the driving rain and wind, he could smell whatever was inside so he hurried back to the Jeep and they drove around. A half mile up the road, Mariposa pointed and said, "Look right there."

It was a truck on the roadside. The truck that the other women had driven away in as soon as

Aggie had been tied up. The back window had been busted out and both doors were open and it sat on cinder blocks, the four tires gone. Cohen paused but didn't fully stop and Mariposa said, "What do you think that smell was?"

"Something that's been in there a while," he said.

Evan honked and waved and Cohen stopped. Evan pulled up beside him and said, "We gotta get out of this storm. The damn truck is wobbling and I don't wanna be sitting in it no more."

"All right," Cohen answered. "We'll find a spot to pull over. Backside of one of these buildings somewhere. Follow close."

Most of the superstores were behind them and there wasn't room to hide behind the smaller buildings and gas stations leading out of town, but when they reached the outer limits of Gulfport, there remained, mostly intact, a larger than usual strip mall that had housed a supermarket on one end and a furniture outlet on the other end. In between was what looked like a kid's store, with the faded face of a giraffe on the facade. Cohen pulled into the parking lot and they followed him. He told Evan and Nadine to wait a minute and then he drove up close to the storefronts, looking in the windows and doors. Then he moved behind and there were no other vehicles there. The metal door of a loading bay was raised at the back end of the grocery store and he stopped and climbed the steps and he looked in and around. Wooden pallets and animal droppings scattered across the concrete floor and little else. No sign of people. He came back out and drove the Jeep to the front and told them it was all right. They followed him to the back of the grocery store and parked close to the building.

The women and the baby and Brisco got out of the weather and Evan and Cohen unloaded the gas stove and pots and cans of food. Cohen grabbed a bag of clothes as he and Mariposa were soaked through.

"Why don't you leave that Jeep and get in with us?" Evan asked as they stood in the stockroom of the grocery store. Their voices echoed some in the big empty space.

"Because me and that Jeep been through it and wherever I go, it goes."

"You're gonna drown driving it."

"Not so far."

"She might," Evan said, pointing at Mariposa. Her wet clothes hung on her and her hair was limp and dripping.

"She can ride where she wants," Cohen said.

Mariposa shook her head like a wet dog and then she took off the heavy coat and dropped it on the concrete. She grabbed the bag of clothes and went off looking for a quiet corner, dragging the bag behind.

They found boxes to sit on and in half an hour

they were eating. The wind sprayed the rain through the open bay and whistled through the random wind tunnels of the beat-up building. They were silent as they ate, worn out from the anxiety of what already seemed like a long trip.

Cohen had found some dry jeans and a shirt and he had changed in the manager's office. Kris mixed a bottle and she carried the baby over to Cohen and asked if he wanted to give it to him.

"I don't know how," he said.

"That's the point," she said. "You might need to one day." She held the baby out to him. Cohen looked at her sideways, but then he held out his arms and she gave him the child. He was fussing from being hungry and Kris showed Cohen how to tilt him so the milk would go down.

"Is that it?" he asked.

She shrugged and handed him the bottle. "If you figure out something different, let me know."

He stuck the nipple in the baby's mouth and the child fought it at first but then took the nipple and went quiet and started sucking. Cohen moved over to a stack of pallets and sat down. He watched the busy cheeks, the tightly closed eyes. Felt the rhythm of the tiny body as it sucked and breathed. He leaned close to the child and whispered, "I buried your momma. I just want you to know she's not laying out there for the animals."

"Gotta burp when he's done," Kris said to Cohen.

"Him, not you," Nadine said. She lay stretched across the concrete, her elbow on the floor and her head propped in her hand, picking at her food lackadaisically like someone who had never been without. Evan and Brisco counted Vienna sausages, adding one and counting again or subtracting two and counting again.

Mariposa ate from a can of sweet potatoes and she came over and sat down next to Cohen. She reached over and touched the baby's hands, pink and shriveled.

"My dad used to have a store," she said. "Not big, like this one."

"Where at?"

"The Quarter. Ursuline and Dauphine."

"Sounds like a good enough spot."

"It was. I guess."

"Get flooded?"

She paused. Tossed the can on the ground and it rolled with the wind. "Eventually. Like everything else. But he got shot before that happened. When everything started going crazy. When people started running around taking whatever they wanted to take. But he didn't want to let them so he and my uncle locked the doors and stood there with shotguns until they busted out the doors and came on in anyway and that was it."

Cohen adjusted the baby and the bottle. "Reach in my shirt pocket," he said. She did and she took out a pack of cigarettes and he asked if she wanted one. She shook her head and held the pack and then he asked how she had ended up down here.

"Hitched some rides," she said and shrugged. "Don't really know where I thought I was going."

"It's hard to know what to do."

She nodded. "Like you," she said, looking up at him.

He nodded slightly, as if surprised by what she had said. "Like everybody," he answered.

Evan came over to them and said that maybe they should look around. See if there was anything worth having.

Cohen got up and gave the baby and bottle to Kris. "How was it?" she asked.

"Different."

Mariposa looked at him like she wasn't done talking, but she sat down with Kris and Nadine. Brisco walked over and took hold of Evan's hand and said, "I wanna go."

"You want these?" Mariposa asked and she held out the cigarette pack. When Cohen grabbed it, she squeezed tight, kept his hand there an instant. Then she let go. Cohen took out a cigarette and lit it and he and the boys walked away.

Nadine said, "I can't stop thinking about all them dead people. How many you think it was?"

"At least fifteen or so," Kris said.

Nadine sat up, shook her head. "I'm beginning to wonder if this was such a good idea."

"We don't have a choice," Mariposa said.

Nadine stood, suddenly unable to be still. She marched around them, rubbed her hands together. "We ain't had a choice for a long time and now we got one and there don't seem to be any good ones."

"We left," Kris said. "That was a good one."

"We got to get somewhere," Mariposa said.

"I know, but damn."

"We got Cohen to help," Mariposa said. "We got rides."

"We ain't got gas. And Cohen ain't bullet-proof."

"We'll find some," Kris said.

"Where?" Nadine asked.

"I don't know. Somewhere. Sit down."

The baby had fallen asleep sucking on the bottle.

"Lay something down over there," Kris said, nodding toward an empty corner of the storage room. Mariposa got up and pulled a few shirts from the garbage bag. In the shadowy corner she folded them and then she came back and took the baby from Kris. She walked over to the corner but she didn't put the baby down right away. She held him. Admired him.

Nadine leaned over to Kris and said quietly, "She's in trouble."

Kris nodded.

"She better watch it. About twelve seconds

after we get over the Line, he's gonna drop us all like a bag of dirt."

Kris looked at Nadine and grinned. "You and me both know it ain't nothing you can help."

Nadine sat up again. Made a frown.

The rain beat against the building. Against everything.

Mariposa stood in the corner and held the baby, swaying gently.

"You got somewhere to go when we get there?" Nadine asked Kris.

"The hospital. If there is one."

"Not that. You know what I mean."

Kris folded her arms. Looked at the floor. "Not really."

Nadine lay down again and propped her hand under her head. "Me, neither. I used to have some cousins around Aberdeen but probably not no more. I got brothers somewhere."

"I figured you had some brothers."

"Why's that?"

" 'Cause you're sitting on go with them hands of yours. You act like you'd fight a wildcat."

"Shit. You don't know the half of it. Three brothers, all older. Cousins all boys. And me the youngest. Brought up on a damn chicken farm. And on top of that my momma was the toughest son of a bitch you ever met."

Kris laughed. Stretched her legs out and leaned back on her elbows. "I don't know nothing about all that. Only child right here."

"That's about what I'd call paradise."

Nadine's last word hung in the air between them. Paradise. They were so far removed from anything of the sort that it was difficult to put an image with the word.

"I wanted to tell you I'm sorry," Nadine said.

"About what?"

Nadine pointed at her stomach. "I'm sorry that happened."

Kris put her hand on her stomach. Rubbed her hand around in a circle. "I'm more sorry for Lorna than me," she said.

Nadine nodded. Then she turned on her stomach and lay her head on her folded arms with her face toward Kris.

"Maybe I'm wrong about all these bad feelings I got," Nadine said. "Maybe we're gonna get somewhere. Maybe it's gonna be okay. But I swear to God, I'm almost as scared of getting to the Line as not getting to it. Don't none of us have nothing."

Kris lay flat on the concrete and stared at the exposed metal beams of the ceiling. Nadine turned over and put her head facedown in her arms.

"Where's your brothers?" Kris asked.

"Wherever Aggie left them," Nadine said, her voice muffled. "We hunkered down to guard what was left of our place and equipment and

Aggie and Joe came wandering up like they was about to starve to death or something. Played us real good. I went to sleep one night in the cab of Eddie's truck. Woke up the next morning and they was all gone. Aggie was sitting on the tail-gate, smoking a cigarette." Nadine then rolled over on her back. "I don't have nowhere to go. And if I did, I wouldn't have nobody when I got there."

Kris pushed herself up. Scooted over to Nadine and touched her elbow. "Listen to me. All I want is somewhere to have this baby. That's it. If God don't give me but one thing the rest of my life, that's all I want. And when it comes and when I'm laying there and they give it to me, I'm gonna need somebody."

Nadine sat up and looked at Kris. "Then I'm gonna be there," she said.

"And then we'll figure it all out."

Nadine nodded. "Okay."

They touched hands, and then they each lay back down. They didn't talk anymore. They rested and listened to the rain. Mariposa sang softly to the sleeping baby, but when the thunder roared they were reminded that no matter what kind of tomorrow they dreamed of, they were all very lost.

28

There was nothing left in the storage area of the grocery and Cohen didn't expect to find anything in the front of the store and he was right. The aisles remained and there were shopping carts up and down but the shelves and coolers had been cleared. At the checkout, the cash registers had been removed.

"Looks like somebody planned ahead," Cohen said.

"Looks like it," said Evan.

"Come on. Let's see what's next door."

They walked back through the grocery and out into the rain and they hurried along the alley until they came to the kids' store and the lock was busted and the door was open. Cohen opened it wide to let in some light and the storage room was much different here. Boxes opened and pilfered and shelves turned over and the office door off its hinges and lying on the floor. In the small office the desk drawers were pulled out and several file cabinets were open and their papers and files strewn across the floor. They moved on through the mess and went into the store area and it was much the same. Some clothes racks standing and some knocked over. Plundered shelves. But scattered about were kids' clothes, baby clothes. Toys in unopened boxes. Evan picked up a toy truck and said, "Look here." Brisco took it excitedly and ripped it from its box and started making truck sounds as he ran it up and down the length of the shelf.

"Go get the others," Cohen said and Evan went back to the grocery store and called for them. In a minute they were all in the kids' store, sorting through the leftovers. Mariposa laid the baby down on a pile of blankets and he woke and started to cry. They ignored him as she and Nadine took a box and went around filling it up with baby shirts and pants and rattles. They found random pieces of clothing for boys or girls, for kids and infants, and they put it all in the box, taking the time to hold up each piece and show it to one another and oooh and aaah when something was particularly sweet. When one box was filled they found another and Kris said this one is for the baby to keep. They filled it with only boy things. And when the baby's box was just about full, and with his crying at its highest pitch, Nadine shrieked and raised her hand in the air and she was clutching a pack of pacifiers.

"Thank you, dear Jesus," she said and she opened up the package and walked over to the baby. She knelt down and said, "Here you go, little madman." She touched the pacifier to the edge of his open mouth and he took it in and his eyes opened wide. He sucked on it and the tension left his face and the tears slowed and soon he was sucking and quiet and in another minute he had returned to sleep.

"Do not lose these," Nadine said and she handed the remaining pacifiers to Kris and picked up the two boxes and walked out back.

On the other side of the store, Mariposa was helping Evan with his own box of toys for Brisco. A couple more trucks and a Frisbee and some coloring books. A dinosaur and a robot and a checkerboard and checkers. Brisco circled them with the first truck he had found, treating it as an airplane now, his arm extended and moving the truck in a rising and falling motion, landing it and lifting it again and lost in his own world.

Cohen sat in a chair next to the cash register. He smoked a cigarette and watched. He looked out the storefront where windows used to be, and the wind came in and the thunder was on them and the lightning flashed around them now, brilliant shards of white interrupting the gray. The rain seemed to have eased some but remained constant. He finished the cigarette and stomped it out on the carpeted floor and then he slumped a little in the chair. Leaned his head back against the wall. Closed his eyes.

As he drifted, he found himself thinking about Mariposa. Thinking of her in Elisa's black dress, believing she was doing something that he wanted her to do.

He opened his eyes and saw her sitting on the floor, trying to piece together an arm onto the body of something shiny and blue. She had pushed up the sleeves of her shirt. Her forearms were girlish but she seemed more of a woman in her shoulders and chest and she bit her lip as she worked the arm into place. Her hair was blacker than a clear night and he noticed how soft her eyes could be when her mind was taken off this thing surrounding her. He wondered if she was even twenty but he didn't think so. He wondered if she might lie against him again tonight, wherever it was that they would lie down to sleep. The arm popped into place and she held the toy out in front of her and she caught Cohen looking at her. Her eyes went down in embarrassment, then back up with satisfaction.

He stood up and walked to the storefront and tried to light a cigarette but couldn't in the gust. He stepped through the doorway and he walked along the covered sidewalk to the furniture store. Like the grocery store, it had been cleared out by the people who were supposed to clear it out, not looters and animals. The front windows remained and he stepped back and looked at his reflection. It was the first time he had seen his full figure in a long time. He noticed that he was thin. His beard was uneven. He leaned to one side because he kept his weight on his good leg. He noticed that the hand that wasn't holding the unlit cigarette was in his coat pocket and he was unconsciously grasping the pistol.

He let go of the pistol and took his hand out of his pocket and he made a peace sign. Then he shot the bird. Then he turned his hand sideways and made a dog. When he was out of tricks, he posed as if holding the baby, imagined what he looked like with a child in his arms. He thought of that baby boy and how out of place he seemed down here, this child of thunder. How out of place they all seemed. For so long, staying below had made sense to him but no more. He was sick of the rain and had been sick of the rain for months and he was sick of the cold and sick of the wind and sick of trying to build that goddamn room that he swore to God that he would build. He knew that whenever he was above the Line, a day from now or a week from now or a year or five years from now, that he would feel a guilt in having left. He knew that some part of him would want to come back. Want to return to the place and want to imagine her there and want to go and sit out by their tombstones and talk to them. He didn't expect that there would ever be a time when he would be free of his desire to be there, with them. But he realized that he had started something new and he wanted to finish it.

He let his hands fall to his sides and stared at his reflection. He looked at himself as if he had seen someone from across a room and knew that he knew the person from somewhere but couldn't remember exactly who it was. And the stranger stared back with the same curious expression.

They looked at each other, but their curiosity was interrupted when he heard a strange thunder. When he turned to look out, it wasn't thunder but the murmur of an engine and along the four-lane, a camouflage-colored lifted truck with tires as big as small people was rolling in their direction, a spotlight above the truck cab slicing through the storm.

"Shit," he said and he ran back to the kids' store and ducked inside and he told them to get to the back, get to the back. They're coming this way.

Kris scooped up the baby and Nadine helped her along and Evan grabbed Brisco by the arm and lifted and carried him. Mariposa followed and Cohen was behind them all. They ran into the storage room and Cohen ran outside and to the back of the grocery store. He jumped off the loading bay into the back of the truck that held the guns and ammo. He reached under the tarp and grabbed three rifles and ammo and hurried back up and he shoved one in Evan's chest as the boy put Brisco down and he told Evan to come with him and everybody else to find a dark corner to hide in. And keep that damn pacifier in that kid's mouth.

"Get down," Cohen said in a whisper as he and Evan crept back into the storefront. They made their way behind the counter and knelt. He set one rifle on the floor with the boxes of shells and then he propped the other rifle on the countertop and told Evan to do the same. Steady yourself. Use the counter. Don't jerk. Keep your head down as far as you can but still see. Don't move.

They listened and the hum of the big truck grew a little louder as the seconds ticked away. "They're going slow," Cohen whispered.

"Did they see you?" Evan asked.

"Don't know."

From where they were back inside the store, they wouldn't be able to see the truck until it was almost directly in front of the strip mall and it was not visible yet but almost there. Cohen took his hand from the trigger and flexed his fingers and hand. Evan saw him and did the same thing.

"Don't be scared," Cohen said.

"Too late."

And then the truck stopped, not yet in their sights. The engine was turned off. Then the sound of doors opening and closing and the voices of loud-talking men.

"What'd he say?" Evan asked.

Cohen shook his head. "Couldn't tell."

There was a banging on the side of the truck and the back door sliding up and more voices back and forth in a brief dialogue and then silence.

"Listen," Cohen whispered. "If they come walking this way and we have to shoot, you start on the far left and I'll start on the far right. Don't matter how many it is. You start left and I start right. Got it?"

Evan nodded. He was breathing heavy but his eyes were steady.

"Show me your left hand," Cohen said.

"What?"

"Your left hand. Show it to me."

Evan took his left hand off the rifle barrel and waved it.

"Just making sure you knew which was which," Cohen said.

In the back room the women and Brisco scurried around looking for a place to hide as Cohen and Evan waited on the men to show themselves.

29

The men walked into sight, moving cautiously into the parking lot, sticking close together. Four of them. They all wore thick black raincoats. Cohen recognized the automatic weapons that had belonged to Charlie's muscle slung over the shoulders of two of them. The one who walked in front didn't wear his hood but instead a cowboy hat and he had a long goatee that touched the middle of his chest. He raised his hand and they stopped. They looked around. Then the man made other hand motions and they split, two of them walking to the right toward the grocery store, two to the left toward the furniture store. Cohen and Evan knelt in the middle, in the shadows.

The man in the hat whistled and they stopped. Maybe thirty yards away from the storefront. Evan took his hand from the rifle and wiped his sweaty palm on his pants. And then the lead man called out.

"Pretty day out here," he yelled out above the rain. "Don't get no better. Might as well come on out and enjoy it." He paused and waited for a response but the only reply was from the thunder. He waited until it died and then went on. "Come on out and get something to eat. I know y'all are hungry. Get you something to eat. Something to drink. Sandwich cart don't come around often anymore." He waited again. Lightning cracked and the men in the black coats jumped but then steadied. "I saw you and I know you're back in there somewhere. Turns out it's your lucky day. We always looking for a good man. If you are one. Good man can come on out and get something to eat. Maybe get himself a job and a title. Every-body out here's got a title. But we can't divulge until we get a look at you."

A couple of them laughed. Cohen noticed that none of them held their rifles ready to fire but instead hanging at their waists. One man had his hands in his coat pockets. The man doing the talking had folded his arms and was enjoying listening to himself talk and it was then that Cohen realized their mistake. Their miscalculation in assuming that a single person was somewhere back in there and that he had no way to defend himself against a posse. These same men who had earlier ambushed and slaughtered men who were ready and prepared and armed were now making the most crucial mistake of all in this land and that is you can never be sure. But they seemed sure and unconcerned as they waited on what they thought was a defenseless straggler and Cohen knew that there would not be another opportunity like this one.

"Evan," he whispered.

The boy looked at him.

"Don't talk. Listen. You see the one on the left. Put your sight on him and when I count three shoot him. Don't miss. You got it. Don't goddamn miss."

Evan nodded.

"Shoot him and as soon as you do, run to the back and get everybody in the trucks and get ready to drive like a son of a bitch. I got the rest here. You just shoot and hit and then run back and get everybody in the trucks and get cranked and then I'll come running and hop in the back and we'll get the hell out of here. You got it?"

"Yeah."

"All right. On three. You got left and then go and I got the rest."

"All right."

"Be cool."

"Just count."

"Okay." They each propped and resteadied themselves. From behind the counter they were undetected and each had a clear shot.

The man with the hat said, "Fine. Have it your way. Never heard of nobody who didn't want food and a title. But if we have to come in there the offer is revoked. Won't be nothing but—"

Cohen said three and the man on the left went down with the crack and Evan was up and gone. Cohen took down the man on the right and turned to the other one on the left who had raised his rifle and was firing wildly and Cohen hit him once and he went down and then Cohen hit him again. He turned next to the leader, who had taken off running and gotten behind the concrete base of a parking lot light. But he couldn't get all the way behind and Cohen hit him in the leg and the man aimed the automatic rifle over his shoulder and sprayed the strip mall. Cohen ducked down on the floor as the bullets shattered through the walls and windows and concrete. He crawled around the side of the counter but couldn't get a shot from down low. When the man turned to get to his knees Cohen raised and fired and hit the pole and the man fell back, thinking he was dead. But he wasn't dead and he raised up and sprayed fire again and Cohen went down and from behind the building he heard Evan yelling for him to come on, come on. The firing stopped and Cohen raised and shot and hit the man in the chest and he dropped. Cohen fired once more into the concrete post and then he stopped and waited.

Nothing moved in the parking lot.

"Come on!" Evan yelled.

Cohen waited, counted to five, and still nothing moved. So he turned and ran out the back of the kids' store and jumped from the loading bay into the back of the truck. Evan was in front of Nadine and the truck leaped and Nadine was close behind as they sped out from behind the stores and the trucks leaned at the left turn into the parking lot and at the right turn onto the highway. Then Cohen slapped on the back glass and yelled, "Stop it! Stop it!"

Evan hit the brakes and Nadine nearly rear-ended them but she swerved to the side. Cohen told her to wait and told Evan to turn around and go back to the big truck and hurry your ass up. Evan spun around in the four-lane and drove hard back to the truck and he slammed on the brakes and Cohen crashed into the back window. He dropped his rifle and grabbed a pistol out of his pocket and told Evan to get turned back around. Cohen ran around to the back of the men's truck and dropped the tailgate and saw what he was after. He jumped in the truck bed and the first two gas containers he grabbed were empty and he tossed them aside, but the next two were full five-gallon containers.

He lifted the gas containers and set them on the tailgate and he jumped out. He waved Evan to back up and Cohen set the containers in the back of the pickup and as he was climbing in, Mariposa pointed and yelled, “Look back there!”

Coming for them were the headlights of an army utility truck and standing in the back was a handful of men pointing in their direction. The truck was coming fast and Cohen took out the pistol and fired it over and over to make the sound of men with guns instead of man with gun and Evan hit the gas pedal. When the pistol was empty Cohen tossed it over the side and took out the other but didn’t fire. They shot back and the side-view mirror shattered and then a rim shot off the back fender. Evan laid on the horn as he got to Nadine, the shots skipping around them and Cohen lying flat in the back and Mariposa screaming come on, come on. Evan and Nadine together drove off like hell, swerving and splashing through the big stuff and busting through the little stuff and when the army truck got to the U-Haul, they kept firing, but they stopped to see about the others, and within minutes, the two trucks were out of town and out of sight, and the rain came on as if it had something to prove.

When it felt safe, they pulled the trucks off the

highway underneath the cover of a half-standing auto shop and they all got out and walked around and the wind and rain relieved their anxiety-ridden faces. Some thanked God and some were still breathing heavy from the excitement and some did both. The baby had to be fed so Nadine climbed in the back and found the formula and a bottle of water and gave it to Kris, who sat in the truck cab with the baby. Brisco and Evan walked behind the building to pee. Cohen, after taking the gas cans and pouring gas into the trucks, walked away from them all and stood alone, looking back south from where they had come. It was charcoal gray and the rain fell in big drops and swirled with the twisting winds.

He managed to get a cigarette lit this time and he couldn't believe it. Couldn't believe he had panicked and left the Jeep. Made the decision to hop in the back of the truck without thinking about the Jeep. Son of a bitch son of a bitch son of a bitch, he kept saying to himself.

"What?" Nadine said.

"Nothing," he snapped.

"Bullshit."

"My Jeep. I left the Jeep and I got to have it."

"It's a Jeep. It ain't a gold brick."

"I know what it is and I got to get back to it."

"Like hell," she said.

30

Cohen got away from her and he smoked and cussed himself. By the end of the cigarette he had calmed some and he went to each of them to make sure no one was hurt or hit.

"That was like a movie," Nadine said. "And I like watching a lot better than being in one." She rubbed her wet head with her hands and her short hair stuck up in different directions. "I'm going to sit with Kris," she said.

Brisco hopped around with his hands made into pistols and he shot imaginary bullets at imaginary bad guys. Evan told him to stop it but he kept on. Cohen asked Evan if he was all right and Evan nodded.

"That was a good job," Cohen said and he patted the boy on the shoulder, but Evan still didn't answer.

Mariposa told Cohen she'd like that cigarette now. He lit one from his and gave it to her.

"You're not hit, are you?" she asked.

"No."

"You think that was them that got all the others down in the parking lot?"

Cohen nodded.

"You think that's all?"

"It's never all, Mariposa."

She smoked and squinted. Seemed to get used to it. She looked scared. They all looked scared but for Brisco. Evan walked away from them, his hands in his pockets. Cohen wanted to say something to him but he didn't know what.

Mariposa's hand shook as she moved the cigarette to and from her mouth. Her head was wet and she shivered from the cold or from what had just happened or from both or from something else altogether. She dropped the cigarette and looked at Cohen and she was about to cry and she said, "I didn't mean nothing in her dress. I swear it."

"I know."

"I swear," she said and she was in a full shiver and Cohen stepped to her and wrapped his arms around her. He couldn't tell if she was crying or only shaking but it didn't matter to him. His chin sat on top of her head and he felt her shivering against him and he saw Evan standing alone staring out into the storm and he looked out at the truck where the women sat with the baby. He held Mariposa and it crossed his mind that it had been years since he had held on to anyone like this. He thought to let go once, twice, but he didn't. He let her cry or whatever it was she was doing. He held on to her until she stopped shaking. He let her move away from him.

And she finally did. She wiped her eyes. Wiped her face.

"We better go," he said and she nodded and sniffed.

Brisco raced by and shot Cohen with each hand. Pow, pow, pow, he cried with each shot. Evan had turned to see what he was doing and he stomped over to Brisco and yanked him up and yelled, "Don't you do that shit!"

Brisco yelled ouch and Cohen said, "Calm down. He don't mean nothing."

"You let me be. He ain't yours."

"I know he ain't but he's playing."

"That ain't no way to play," Evan said and he shoved Brisco away. "I mean it, Brisco. Quit that shit."

"Jesus," Cohen said. "Settle your ass down. We got enough shit going on."

"You settle down," Evan said and he told Brisco to come on and get in the truck. He took the boy by the coat arm and dragged him out into the rain.

Mariposa called out to Evan but Cohen said let him go. Let him be for a while.

"What's wrong with him?" Mariposa asked.

The storm roared now and it was damn near dark. They had to get somewhere. Cohen tugged at his beard, looked out at the weather and looked back at Mariposa. "What's wrong with him?" he said. "Only the same thing that's wrong with all of us down here. Come on."

They got back into the truck cabs. Mariposa

wiped her face again with her hands. She noticed Cohen's anxious look and she asked him if he was all right.

"I got to go back," he said.

"No you don't."

"Yeah. I damn sure do," he said. Son of a bitch. He was sick for not thinking about the Jeep when it mattered.

Mariposa said, "You don't need anything down there. We're almost there."

"We might be almost there."

"We are."

"If you were to look at a map, we are. But it doesn't matter where we are or what's between here and there, I got to go back."

She moved closer to him on the seat and said, "You don't. Really, you don't."

"Really," he said. "I do."

She moved closer. "I don't understand."

He fidgeted in the seat. "I just have to go back. It's my Jeep." He wrapped his hands tightly around the steering wheel and stared out at the weather. She touched his arm, pulled at him some. He let go of his grip on the steering wheel and she pulled his arm to her.

"You don't have to, Cohen," she said. "I know you want to but you don't have to." She leaned over and kissed his cheek delicately, almost undetected.

Cohen didn't move. Didn't look at her. He

cranked the truck and started out and said, "Let me think."

Despite the rain and wind, they had luck the first ten or so miles, moving up Highway 49 with nothing more to navigate than the occasional fallen tree or light pole. Kudzu had overlapped the highway here and there like a green rug meant to beautify the rough asphalt. They passed through the tiny communities of Saucier, McHenry, Perkinston. The road signs were bent and twisted and they saw random cars but little else.

The first trouble came somewhere between Maxie and Dixie. A bridge had been washed out by what was once a creek but was now more like a flowing marsh. They had to backtrack six miles to try and detour around it but found another washed-out bridge along the cut-through and they had to backtrack again. No one was familiar with the roads in this part of the country but they knew north from south and they kept trying to get themselves north on nameless back roads or strips of forgotten highway. It was all but dark and the storm was gaining strength and even with headlights it was almost impossible to see. Cohen was in front and when it was too much, he stopped and ran back to Evan and the others and said, "Let's find shelter for now and try again in the morning. I know it's hard but if you see something flash or honk or something."

In another slow mile, the other truck honked and

Cohen stopped. He looked around but didn't see what there was to honk about. Evan ran up and hit on the door and Cohen cracked it open.

"Back across there, did you see it?" Evan yelled against the rain.

"Where?"

"Right back over. That gravel lot. Looked like an old store or something back some. Looked like it had a roof."

"All right," Cohen yelled back. "Get in and back up and we'll see."

He shut the door and Evan ran to the truck. Both vehicles moved in reverse for twenty or so yards, then stopped. Like Evan described, to the right was a gravel parking lot and back from the road was a small brick building. Cohen turned and shined the headlights on the building. Crossbars covered the empty windows and there was no door. A rusted ice machine stood guard and a sign had been ripped from the front awning, but it looked like the roof was intact and it showed no sign of living things.

Mariposa leaned forward with her hands on the dash. Cohen flashed his lights on bright but it didn't change anything. "Might as well go see," he said.

He took a flashlight and made sure the pistol was in his coat pocket and he got out. The four headlights shined on Cohen and the old store and the rain fell sideways through the yellow beams.

He stepped into the door and momentarily disappeared from sight, but then he waved for them to come on. Mariposa killed the ignition and Evan killed the other truck. Brisco hopped from the seat into Evan's arms. Kris held the baby and Nadine held Kris by the arm and they stepped carefully to the doorway.

"Careful, it's slick," Cohen told them as they came in one by one. He shined the flashlight out across the linoleum floor that was wet and black with dirt and scattered with overturned stock shelves. Along the back wall of the room glass coolers once held beer and Cokes for the workingmen who had spent the day in the field or on the job site. The doors were open and the racks still there as if waiting optimistically for the day when the bottles and cans would once again sit inside and be greeted by thirsty eyes. It was a small store and the weather came through the windows but it seemed like it would do.

They congregated in the middle of the room, the fallen shelves around them. Evan kicked at one and it slid and banged into another. Nadine jumped and said, "What the hell."

Brisco hugged Kris around her leg.

"It's gonna be a long night," Nadine said.

Cohen continued to move the light around and they watched, standing closely together, a tension binding them, as if only waiting for the moment they would be shocked by what the light revealed.

In the back corner of the store was another door and it was closed and locked with a padlock. The cream-colored walls were spotted with mold and the ceiling sagged from water leaks and there were drips here and there but no holes.

Evan looked around and found a couple of folding chairs and a short bench behind the counter. The women and Brisco went and sat down. Evan and Cohen moved over toward the locked door. Cohen held the light on the padlock.

"That door don't look like much," Evan said. "Not if you really wanted to get in." He shined the light up and down the metal door and there were footprints about waist-high and indentions up and down it.

"Maybe it's tougher than it looks," Cohen said.

"Probably ain't nothing," Evan said.

"Probably not."

"You gonna get it open?"

Cohen shrugged. He turned and walked to the counter and Evan followed. They both hopped up and sat on it. Cohen shined the flashlight around again and then turned it off. Nadine said let me take a turn and Kris handed her the baby. Then each of them sat still and quiet. It rained and the wind came in gusts.

As they sat there in the dark, the weight of it all began to collapse around them in the confined space. The storm muted all and left them suspended in the absence of sound. A steady, heavy drone. Mariposa slumped in her chair and Brisco lay across her lap. Nadine held the baby, her head bowed and resting on top of the tiny bundled body. Kris stretched out her legs and rested her hands across her stomach. Evan stared at Brisco. Cohen stared at his hands. Quiet, fatigued silhouettes.

They were small things against this big thing. Against this enormous thing. Against this relentless thing. Small, exhausted things whose lives had become something so strange and extraordinary that it didn't seem possible that they could be anywhere but sitting in this abandoned building in this abandoned land in this storm-filled night in this storm-filled world. They sat still and exuded exhaustion. Maybe even hopelessness. Maybe even helplessness. The day had begun with the idea of a finish line, but that idea was being washed away in this torrent of despair.

Cohen stood up from the counter and folded his arms. He walked away from them and stood in the center of the floor between fallen shelves. He listened. Looked around in the dark. Water dripped all around him. He thought about the baby and what would become of his life. Or would he have a life? Would he live to see another place? A normal place where lights shined and refrigerators kept food cold and beds were soft and sometimes the sun came out and people rode in cars and had jobs and if you needed something you went to a store to get it and the sound of thunder didn't sound an alarm but only meant nourishment for rosebushes and the front yard. Would he live to another place? And if they managed to get him somewhere, who would change his diapers and teach him his colors and ABCs and would he have friends and would he go to school and would he ever call anyone Momma and would he ever call anyone Daddy? Would he ever play T-ball or learn to ride a bike or not have to worry about being hungry? Would he ever know the story of how he was born and where he was born and who his father was and what a miracle it was that he was alive at all and would he ever know the story of the group of misfits who somehow managed to get him across the Line? He was a long shot. They were all long shots. In every direction, a long shot.

Cohen uncrossed his arms and looked at his hands and he thought of the knife in his hands and the baby's mother and her screaming and her pleading and her blood. In this blackest night, her blood flowed across his mind and turned his thoughts crimson, and he saw crimson on the walls and on the floor and dripping from the ceiling and puddled on the floor and blowing in from the windows and he felt it dripping from his beard. He saw crimson and he heard her begging for somebody to do something and then her voice became his voice and he heard himself cry out as he sat on the road with Elisa's head in his hands, crying out for somebody to do something but there was no one who could do anything as it had already been done. The choice for her to die and for the baby to die had already been made and there wasn't a goddamn thing he could do about it. He heard his own voice and now the blood that flowed in his mind was Elisa's blood and he felt it on his hands and he felt it across his legs and he cupped his hands and felt her head resting in them and he begged for help but there was none and he felt her heartbeat disappear and then he felt the heartbeat of his little girl disappear.

He brought his hands to his face and he touched his fingertips to his cheeks as if to make sure that he was real. He held them there. Closed his eyes and the spirit of renewal that had filled him earlier in the day was buried under all else.

She sat in the seat with her legs crossed while they drove on Highway 90. Summer sun and the windows down and they went to Ocean Springs and parked downtown and walked to a patio bar and sat down and drank draft beer and ate crab claws and then they got up and walked to another patio bar and drank more beer and ate boiled shrimp. A white-bearded man sat on a stool in the corner and played his guitar and the day faded and when they were done they got up and walked again, underneath the moss trees and past the two-story houses and once or twice they exchanged waves with people sitting on an upstairs balcony.

They walked on, pushing and pulling at each other, laughing at stupid jokes and stopping now and then to kiss and then slapping and grabbing at one another as they walked on and then they came to the beach and it was getting dark. They left their flip-flops at the sidewalk and stepped into the white sand, holding hands and smiling devilish smiles at one another. A mother was corralling the kids and packing up towels and plastic buckets and shovels and some teenage girls sat in a circle and passed around a cigarette. The two of them walked on until there was no one around and then they sat down in the sand and watched the last of the light drift away. The stars appeared and he lay on his back and she lay her head on his stomach and stretched out and they made the letter T. The water washed gently onto the shore. Down the beach somewhere a dog barked. Elisa hummed a song he didn't quite recognize. He slipped his hand into his pocket and eased out the ring box. He reached over and lifted her shirt and ran his hand across her tan stomach, and then he set the ring box on her bare skin. She stopped humming. Sat up and looked at him and smiled and he smiled back and she didn't open it but squeezed it in her hand and fell back on top of him and they rolled in the sand, laughing and kissing and crying a little.

Cohen moved his fingertips from his face and opened his eyes. He opened his coat, reached inside, and took out the pistol. It was cold in his damp hand. Everything was cold and damp in his hand. Everything was cold and damp. Or cold and wet. Or cold and soaked. Or cold and underwater. Or cold and wet and knocked over. Or cold and wet and shattered or cracked or busted or gone. Or just gone. Everything was gone. Everything was gone but for his very real Jeep and it was his very real chance if they ever got the hell out of here but none of that mattered because he had panicked and left it behind. He had to go and get it, wanted to go and get it, but the chance of getting back down there and out with it didn't warm him with confidence. It was his and he didn't have to share it. He had his chance and missed it and now here he was, with them, stuck in the middle of this, and somewhere was his life, but he didn't know where.

He lifted the pistol and touched its nose to the bottom of his chin. He held in a breath. The water was all around them and the wind was all around them and hell seemed to be closing in and if there was a darker place on the face of the earth he didn't know where it could be.

"Jesus Christ," Kris said with a start and then she let out a quick shout of pain.

Cohen jerked at the sound of her voice and he lowered the pistol and put it back inside his coat. She yelled out again and Evan hopped down off the counter and moved to her and she was grabbing at her sides again. Cohen stepped around the shelves and came to her and said, "Same shit?"

"Oh yeah. Oh yeah," she said. Her breaths were quick and had little moans in between.

The others sat up and they all formed a circle around her. Oh God, oh God, she kept saying. She rocked back and forth, took deep breaths. Oh God, oh God.

Mariposa stood behind her and put her hands on Kris's shoulders. She rocked and moaned, rocked and moaned. They stood there and watched because there was nothing else they could do. And then the baby woke up and started crying.

"Shit," Cohen said.

Nadine talked to the infant and put her lips on his forehead. "Damn, he's hot as fire," she said.

"Ooooooh, hell," Kris said and Mariposa told her to hold on. Hold on.

Cohen reached over and touched the baby's face. "Goshdamn," he said.

"Yeah," Nadine said. "Goshdamn. He's smoking."

The baby wailed and Kris grunted and said Oh God and squeezed Mariposa's hands. Brisco made a sound like he might start crying and Cohen went to reach over and touch his shoulder but they all jumped at the loud thwack from the back of the store.

"What the fuck!" Cohen yelled.

Evan stood at the metal door with part of a busted shelf. “I wanna see what’s in here,” he yelled back.

“Leave it alone,” Cohen said.

“Quit messing around, Evan,” Mariposa said.

He drew back the shelf and whacked the door again.

“Oh God, oh God,” Kris said.

“Quit that shit!” Nadine yelled over the crying baby.

Evan drew back and whacked the door again and this time Cohen walked over to him, kicking at whatever was in his way, and he tried to yank the piece of shelf from Evan but Evan didn’t let go.

“I wanna see what’s in there,” he said defiantly.

“Why the hell you gotta see what’s in there right this damn second?”

“I just wanna see.”

“You might not.”

Kris yelled out and Cohen let go of the shelf piece and turned to look in her direction.

Thwack!

Cohen grabbed Evan by the collar of his coat and yanked him back. He shined the flashlight on the padlock and pulled out the pistol and fired. The lock busted and he fired again and the doorframe exploded.

“There,” he told Evan and the gunshots sent Brisco crying and Nadine and Mariposa were both yelling something and the baby screamed and Kris gripped her sides and said Oh God oh God.

"Here," Cohen said and he shoved the flashlight into Evan. "Go see for yourself, you little shit."

Evan took the light and told Brisco to calm down but the boy didn't listen. Cohen stood there and waited to see if he would open the door. Evan shined the light on the busted lock and frame, then he stepped over to the door. He pushed, but it wouldn't open. He pushed a little harder, and the top of the door opened but the bottom was stuck.

"Listen," Cohen said.

"What?" Evan asked.

They stood still a moment.

"You hear something?"

Evan waited. Shook his head.

"Nothing," Cohen said.

Evan put his foot on the bottom of the door and pushed and when he did, whatever was on the other side gave way and the door fell open. Almost instantly, Evan started hopping up and down and then Cohen did the same and Evan shined the light down into the room and hundreds of rats came pouring out of the storage room that had been filled with boxes of pasta and peanuts and bags of potatoes and whatever else might be good in a bind. The rats quickly filled the store and Evan and Cohen were jumping around and slipping and sliding and the rats skidded across the wet floor and went up and over the shelves and along the walls and everywhere. The women were up and screaming, even Kris whose pain had been momentarily overwhelmed by rat terror. Mariposa helped her up and then she lifted Brisco onto the counter and it was screams and leaps and rats rats rats. Evan busted his ass and went down and the rats climbed up and down his body. He came up swinging and twisting and shook them off and Cohen slapped at the rats up and down his legs and then he screamed for everybody to get the hell outta there. Nadine and the baby were the first ones out and Mariposa held Kris and helped her out. Brisco was jumping up and down on the counter and screaming and Cohen snatched him and went for the door and Evan nearly knocked them both down as he flailed like a runaway scarecrow toward the exit.

Outside, Nadine held the baby tucked like a football in one arm and she held Kris with the other and she was fighting the wind to get into the truck. The last of the aluminum awning on the storefront snapped free and crashed across the windshield as they were ducking in the door. Mariposa stepped in a deep puddle and went down with a yell. She rolled in the water and grabbed at her ankle and Evan ran to her and helped her up and over to the other truck. The rain beat and beat and Cohen carried Brisco on his hip and managed to get the driver's door open and he tossed Brisco in.

When the four were inside, Cohen said, "I got to go see about her. Evan, drive this one." Mariposa moaned and held her ankle and Evan climbed across her and Brisco to get to the steering wheel. Cohen was out and over to the other truck and when he got in, Kris was leaned over grasping at her sides and the baby screamed and Nadine had the look of the bewildered.

Cohen cranked the truck and turned on the lights and the rats were wild in the doorway and across the storefront but none of them went out the doorway and into the rain.

"Can you sit up?" Cohen asked Kris but she said oh shit and the baby screamed.

The storm beat like a thousand drums and the truck moved with the wind.

"Fucking-ass rats!" Nadine yelled.

"Oh shit," Kris groaned.

"Where the hell's a pacifier?" Cohen said.

Nadine reached around on the seat and floor-board but couldn't find one and then Kris said, "My pocket." Nadine felt in Kris's coat pocket and pulled one out and touched it to the baby's lips. He took it in his mouth and sucked and Nadine thanked God. But Kris didn't as she was too consumed with the feeling that something was going to pop out of her from somewhere. One of the doors of the ice machine whipped open and broke off and disappeared across the gravel lot that was quickly becoming a gravel pond.

"Goshdamn," Nadine said in a high, anxious voice. She was touching the baby's face and head. "He's hellfire hot. We gotta do something."

"Yeah, no shit," Cohen said, but he didn't know what.

The other truck honked and Mariposa was waving to them. The truck then moved in reverse and Cohen backed up and followed Evan out of the parking lot and back onto the road.

"He don't know where he's going," Nadine said.

"I can't help it," Cohen said. "You want me to let them ride off?"

"Son of a bitch," Kris said with her teeth clenched. She huffed and puffed and then said help me up. Nadine held out her arm and Kris grabbed on to it and got upright. She slumped down in the seat and squeezed her stomach. "Oh hell no," she said.

"Cross your legs," Nadine said.

"What the hell?"

"Hell, I don't know," Nadine yelled.

They were back out on the skinny back road and it was almost impossible to see. Evan drove out front at a crawl and moved on until the road declined and at the bottom was a wash. Flooded as far as the headlights could show. Cohen saw the red taillights and stopped, then began to back up. Water and dirt and mud rushed along the road and the tires spun some but caught enough to make it in reverse to the store.

They turned around, and Cohen got out in front this time. So dark and so much rain everywhere. In the next few slow miles, Kris's pain subsided and the baby sucked the pacifier and fell asleep and Nadine was oddly quiet as they crept along the back roads. The houses were separated by miles of countryside and Cohen several times went up a long driveway only to find that there wasn't a house anymore. Or there was half a house and he couldn't trust it to ride out a storm. After several more tries and another hour, they were all surprised when they followed a winding driveway and came upon a two-story farmhouse still standing.

31

Evan pulled up beside Cohen and they sat for several minutes with the four headlights on it. It had once been white but was weathered and the paint was peeling and half its shutters had blown away and some windows were gone. They watched for some minutes more to see if there was any light or any movement but it sat quiet, its tall rectangular windows like big black eyes staring back at them. Cohen waved at Evan and they drove up closer to the house and parked around on the backside where a porch stretched the house length. The right side of the porch had sagged to the ground and parts of its roof were missing and water dripped or poured all through the porch. The back door was closed and a refrigerator lay on its side next to the door.

Cohen waved at Evan to hold on, and then he backed up the truck and shined his headlights on the house and they watched again. Looked for shadows or anything. Still nothing.

Cohen killed the truck, got out, and hurried around to the passenger door to help Nadine and the baby out first and then Kris. They went carefully up the porch steps and opened the back door. Cohen called out, "Anybody in here? Anybody? We're just looking for somewhere for the night. That's all."

"Ain't nobody here," Nadine said and pushed through. She walked in the house as if it were hers and Kris followed her. Mariposa and Evan and Brisco trailed Cohen through the doorway.

Cohen pulled a flashlight from his coat pocket and he shined it around the room. They stood in a big kitchen with tall cabinets and wide-plank hardwood floors that were bowed from the wet and humidity.

Together they moved through the bottom floor of the house. Four great big empty rooms with the same wooden floors throughout. Two fireplaces surrounded by handcrafted mantels that had to be a hundred years old. Water stains down the walls and on the ceilings, and branches and leaves scattered across the floor that had blown in the missing windows. The stairway separated the bottom rooms and thcy wcnt up carefully, wary of rotted steps. Upstairs were four more rooms and more water stains and drip spots on the floors and only one room with its windows remaining. The wind and rain pushed in all the windows not covered with plywood and with a big gust the house moved some and they collectively held their breath. There was no furniture anywhere. A bathroom separated the rooms on the east side and there was a claw-foot tub and two pedestal sinks. Cohen shined the flashlight on the tub and he stopped. Held the light on the curved neck of the faucet.

"What is it?" Evan whispered.

"Why are you whispering? It ain't more rats, is it?" Nadine asked.

"Hold on," Cohen said. He held the light on the tub and walked over to it. When he got there, he reached down and touched his fingertips to the end of the faucet and it was wet. Then he shined the light down to the drain and he touched it and it was also wet. He then turned the handle for the cold water and there was a delay, and a groan, and then water sputtered out of the faucet, copper-colored and filled with little specks of something. It kept on sputtering and spitting but Cohen left it running and soon the line had cleared and a stream of water ran from the faucet.

Cohen stood back and smiled and said, "I'll be damned."

"I got it. I got it first," Nadine was yelling as she turned and gave the baby to Kris. She ran out of the room and back down the stairs and then they heard her running through the house, yelling, "We got a tub and water. We got a tub and water, a tub and water." Kris and the baby and Mariposa and Brisco followed her back down the stairs.

"Hadn't seen one of those in a while," Evan said. "Gotta say I wouldn't mind a bath myself."

"Gonna be a cold one," Cohen said.

"No colder than these birdbaths we been taking since forever."

"That's true."

Evan walked around the tub, moved around the dark room. "Sorry about that back there," he said.

Cohen shook his head. "Don't worry about it."

"I was curious."

"No shit."

"I didn't think it'd be a thousand rats."

Cohen moved across the room and shined the flashlight out of the window. He thought about the look on the boy's face after they had gotten away from the men in the parking lot. He turned back to Evan and said, "I hate I had to ask you to shoot."

Evan didn't answer.

"You all right?"

He nodded. "I'm all right."

"Just so you know, Evan, there is one thing in this world I won't worry about," Cohen said. "And that one thing is you."

Evan was about to speak again but the footsteps of the others were on the stairs and into the upstairs hallway and they came in the bathroom with lanterns and bars of soap and towels and clothes. Mariposa came in behind them, holding the baby.

"Get out, get on out," Nadine said and she and Kris ushered the men out of the room.

"Come on, Mariposa," Kris said. "Let's get the baby first."

"Where's Brisco?" Evan asked.

"He said he didn't want a bath," Mariposa said.

Cohen said, "Go ahead and run the water but don't get undressed. I got an idea."

He and Evan headed downstairs and outside to the trucks. Evan held the flashlight while Cohen raised the tarp covering the truck bed and stuck his head under. He found the propane burner for the stove and he went back into the house and up to the bathroom. He took the legs off the stove and the tub sat just high enough to slide the stovetop underneath. Cohen took a lighter from his pocket and lit the stove and the blue flames wrapped the bottom of the tub. "That'll help knock off the chill," he said.

"That's plumb genius," Nadine said. "Now get on."

Cohen and Evan went back to the trucks and worked against the storm but were able to get out what they needed for the night. Food and drink and some blankets. They took it all into the kitchen. Then Cohen went out one more time and he came back with a shotgun and shells.

Cohen and Evan and Brisco had taken off their coats and they sat on the floor in the kitchen. Cohen drinking a beer. Evan and Brisco sharing a bottle of water and eating from a can of green beans. The voices of the women upstairs and the rain coming down and the wind shoving at the house and Brisco trying to explain why he did not need to take a bath and Evan trying to explain why he did.

And then Evan said, "You know that girl likes you."

Cohen didn't answer.

"I said you know that girl likes you."

"I heard you."

"Don't you know it?"

Cohen shook his head. He started to make some crack about he-said-she-said up and down the high school hallway, but then he realized Evan wouldn't know anything about that. That he had never been up and down a high school hallway, had never passed notes, been to ball practice, skipped out on class in the afternoon, climbed into the backseat with the girl from history class and felt around for things. Never been to a movie with a girl or gone riding with the windows down and the music loud on a spring afternoon. That he was the perfect age for such things but he would not know them and he seemed to be so far beyond them anyway. And it was then that Cohen began to feel the weight of the others in this house on this dot on the map below the Line. He had always been aware that he wasn't the only one who had lost, but the losses for others seemed different to him, more true and exact, now that the losses of others had eyes and faces and arms and legs.

"I think she's just lonely. Like everybody else," Cohen said.

"Nah. I think it's more than that."

"You remember she wanted to kill me. You remember that?"

Evan laughed. "I remember. She didn't mean it, though. I told you we didn't mean nothing. We had to."

"You told me *you* didn't mean nothing. You didn't say *we*."

"Yeah, but you know it. Anyway, you're probably twice as old as her."

"I wouldn't go that far."

"You might be."

"How old is she?"

Evan shrugged. "Eighteen? Nineteen?"

"But you don't know."

"I never asked."

"How old you think I am?"

"About twice whatever she is."

Cohen shook his head. "Got me there."

Brisco got up from the floor and started playing with his shadow on the wall, his arms out and gliding like a hawk.

"You like her?" Evan asked.

"No. Not really."

"Why not?"

"Because."

"That ain't no answer." Evan huffed. Wiped his mouth on his sleeve and set the can of green beans on the floor. "Just seems like—" he started, then stopped.

"Seems like what?"

"Nothing."

"What is it?"

"Seems like a miracle that anybody down here would find anybody else. Especially you."

Cohen drank his beer. Tried to figure out how to answer. "Nobody's found nobody. Nobody's looking for nobody. I'm guessing about forty more miles and the road splits us all."

"You think?" Evan asked.

"Which part?"

"That we'll all split up."

On the floor next to Cohen were two more beers and he took one and handed it to Evan. "Here," he said.

Evan took it. Nodded. "What'd you used to do?"

"Do?"

"Yeah. Like work or whatever."

"I framed houses. Built a bunch of these houses that are nothing but litter now."

"How'd you learn all that?"

"My dad did the same. Started working with him in the summers when I was, I guess about your age. Kept on from there."

Evan thought a minute. Sipped from the beer. "I think I'd like that. Be outside and stuff. See something happening every day. You like it?"

"Yeah," Cohen said. "I liked it. Even kept on for a while after all this mess started."

"You mean that thing on the back of your house."

Cohen nodded. "That thing." He felt so stupid now, thinking he could finish that room. "Let's talk about the weather instead."

"Okay. I think it's gonna rain."

"It's already raining," Brisco said, making an alligator chomp with his shadow.

"Then it's a good thing we own a farmhouse," Cohen said. "Complete with a tub and running water and a kitchen."

"Too bad it didn't come with firewood," Evan said.

"That's true," Cohen said. Then he thought a minute and he set down his beer and said maybe it did, to come on and bring the lantern. They walked into one of the other rooms where the floor was warped and bowed. Evan held the light and Cohen set down his beer and got his fingers up under one of the boards and he pulled. It came right up. And when one was up, it was easier to get the others, and in minutes they had the floorboards of half the room pulled up and in a pile. Evan gave Brisco the lantern and he and Cohen gathered the boards in their arms and they walked into the front room of the house where there was the fireplace. They dropped the boards on the floor next to the fireplace.

"Think it'll burn down the house if we light it up?" Evan asked.

Cohen knelt and said come here with that light, Brisco. Brisco stood over him and shined and Cohen ran his hand across the brick bottom of the fireplace, feeling for bits of crumbling mortar. When he didn't find any, he said we might as well give it a try. And they did, and the floorboards were made of oak and they burned easily, and by the time the women came downstairs with their wet hair and shiny faces, the room was aglow and warm, and no one cared that the house that protected them was also the house they were burning up.

32

Mariposa slipped away. She found a candle on the kitchen counter and lit it and she went upstairs to look into the other rooms. More warped wooden floors. More crumbling plaster and peeling wall-paper. Shredded bird nests and molded fireplaces. The rooms were great and wide and she imagined a large family living there, the children upstairs and the steady rumble of their running and playing while the mother and father sat downstairs and read the newspaper and drank coffee and felt the cool autumn breeze through the open windows.

She stayed away from the windows as the rain and wind bullied the house and she held her hand across the flame to protect it. She came into a room where the wallpaper flapped in the wind and the closet door hung by its top hinge. The candlelight led her to the fireplace mantel and it was decorated with hand-carved rose vines. She touched the vine and then the rose petals, running her fingers along the grooves that were still smooth. She set the candle down on the mantel and listened to the storm, listened to the voices and movement of the others about the house. The flame danced and Mariposa put her hands on the mantel, stretching them wide, letting her head drop as her hair fell around her neck and head and nearly reached her knees.

"There's no such thing," she whispered. She waited for her grandmother to answer. "There's just no such thing," she said again and she raised her head. Looked at the twisting, delicately carved vine.

It was all disappearing. The French Quarter ghosts that she had chased as a child, hiding with her friends as they trailed the horse and buggy and listened to the man in the overcoat and floppy black hat regale his passengers with the wraithlike tales of the pirates and the hanged criminals and the brokenhearted debutantes who still roamed the dark and murky streets. The smell of incense wafting from her grandmother's reading room as she delivered the messages from the grave beyond to the hopeful soul sitting across from her at the table. The notions of spirits and gods and angels that hovered in the realm between life and death and helped us along, or drove us into a corner, or waited and watched until it was necessary to intervene and save us from catastrophe. It was all disappearing as the very real world beat at her, beat at them, beat at all things from every direction.

She waited for the voice of her grandmother to come in through the window or exude in a slow smoke from the flue of the fireplace. That voice that had created that childlike hopefulness in wondrous things. She waited for that voice to appear gently, like the candle flame, and assure her that such things would always exist. No matter how hard the world strikes, no matter what men do to one another, no matter what men do to you, no matter what is lost, and no matter how badly you may want something that you cannot have, there are such things that stand in the shadows and drift with the clouds and rise with the sunshine and wait for you. Watch for you.

Mariposa waited but couldn't hear her grandmother's voice. She looked at her wrinkled, wet fingertips. Touched them to her mouth.

The ghosts will kill you, she thought, and then there was the image of Cohen living alone in that house, with his memories overwhelming him when he thought they were protecting him. The power of what he had loved and what he had lost so incompetent against the careless strength of the living.

She picked up the candle and crossed the room. The rain blew against her as she passed the window and she walked into the corner and stopped. She nudged her back into the crevice of the walls and slid down and sat with her knees up against her chest. With both hands she held the candle. She let her faith in other things, in other worlds, fall way down inside her.

Right now, she thought. And she waited for Cohen.

33

Evan and Brisco went up next and got clean despite Brisco's pleas against it. The women sat with the baby next to the fire. Cohen had laid the blankets across the floor, where they could all sleep in the same room with the fire and now he sat with his back against the wall. No one knew where Mariposa had gone.

"She didn't take no bath," Nadine said.

"Can't understand that," said Kris. "I coulda sat in that thing for a month."

"You know some people have babies like that. Sitting in a big ol' tub. Baby and everything else comes out floating."

"Jesus Christ," Kris said. "That makes me want to vomit. I want the drugs and tell me when it's over."

"Amen to that. Why the hell would anybody want to be in the same tub with all that mess."

Kris held the baby but he began to cry and she handed him to Nadine. Nadine rocked him in her arms and got up and walked around the room with him but he kept on.

"Gotta be hungry," she said.

"I tried already. Didn't want nothing."

"Give it here," Nadine said and held out her hand and Kris held the full bottle up to her.

Nadine tried to give it to him but he fought it and kept on crying. "You think getting his ass clean would make him happy. Not the other way around," she said. "He's still hot."

Cohen stood and looked out of the window. Outside was as black as a hole. He thought about the Jeep again. Thought about the shoe box that had gotten him into all this, sitting on the back-seat of the Jeep, being pelted by the rain. Being ruined by the rain. He put his hand in his pocket and felt the key to the Jeep. Mumbled to himself and shook his head.

"What?" Kris asked.

"Nothing," he said.

Another half hour passed and the baby kept crying. Evan and Brisco came down from the tub and told Cohen it was his turn.

"I left you a shirt of mine up there if you want it," Evan said. Cohen nodded to him and took the lantern and he headed upstairs. Evan and Brisco went into the kitchen to look for something to drink.

Nadine paced with the child. Bouncing and singing and talking to him and trying the pacifier and trying the bottle and nothing. But she kept on. She told him about the smell of a chicken farm and told him about the time her stupid brother pushed her in the creek before she knew how to swim and she told him about the time her other stupid brother took their daddy's truck before he had a license and drank a quart of beer and ran the truck into the back end of a parked cattle trailer. During the stories the baby paused, but when she had finished he'd start crying again. So she'd walk and bounce and sing and talk some more and he finally slowed down enough to take a bottle. Nadine sat down with him in front of the fire.

"You think they'd let me keep him?" Nadine asked.

Kris smiled. "Who you talking about?"

"Whoever is where we take him. Doctor, I guess. First thing they ask is who's the momma."

Little sucking sounds came from the infant. She was a rough woman who had lived a rough life, but there was something tender in the way she looked at the baby boy.

"I think so. I think that's a good idea. He can be a big brother," Kris said.

Nadine grinned, her harelip snarl disappearing some in the rise of her cheeks. "Don't be none of my brothers," she told the baby.

The fire was warm and the room dry.

"It sounds kinda weird, don't it?" Nadine said.

"What's that?"

"Making plans."

Kris folded her arms across her stomach. Rocked back and forth. She nodded and stared at the fire. When the baby finished with the bottle, Nadine propped him on her shoulder and patted his back and he burped and threw up down her back.

"Aw, hell," Nadine said and the baby began to wail.

Kris took the baby from her and Nadine found a shirt on the floor and wiped herself. The baby screamed and Kris got up and walked with him and tried the bottle again but he wouldn't have it.

Nadine tossed the dirty shirt aside and got up and took the baby from Kris. "Sit down," she said. "You don't need to be walking around no more than you got to." She cradled the baby and marched around the firelit room, bouncing him and half-singing, and the crying eased some.

"He just don't look right to me," Nadine said.

"Babies puke," Kris answered.

"I know they puke but he won't quit hollering. He's so damn miserable."

"Just keep bouncing around. At least that slows him up."

Nadine walked him and talked to him. He cried, paused and listened, and cried again. Kris lay down and closed her eyes. Nadine touched his red head and tried to get him to suck on her fingertip but he didn't want it. Didn't want anything but to scream. She paced the house, walked in and out of the dark of the other rooms, and felt the child against her. As she rocked him in her arms in rhythm with her steps, she allowed herself to imagine somewhere new, without the crying, the boy learning to walk, the babble of his voice, his tiny hands reaching out for her.

34

The trip was halfway along and they decided it was time to do what tourists are supposed to do. They armed themselves with the guidebook and maps and the camera and spent the next three days going to the major and minor museums, the plethora of cathedrals, the war memorials, the Venetian landmarks. They shopped for souvenirs, buying key chains and art prints and T-shirts. They found local markets and Elisa bought a handmade scarf and tablecloth and Cohen got himself a leather belt and he bought Elisa a silver ring that he planned to give her on the plane ride home. They rode the water taxis across the channel and through the major canals to save themselves time and to keep on track. The overcast skies remained and they were chased into a café now and then by a rain shower but the showers were brief.

At the end of the three days, after having seen all they felt like they needed to see, after having bought keepsakes and taken hundreds of pictures, they returned to the earlier pace of sleeping late and perusing the city looking for a good place to sit. A good coffee. A good bottle of wine. A good meal. These were the priorities.

They sat outside at a table in Palazzi Soranzo. Elisa had her feet propped in an empty chair and she wore a Band-Aid on the cut over her eye. Cohen leaned back with his hands behind his head. A carafe of red wine and a carafe of water sat on the table. It was a busy plaza and across the way they watched members of an orchestra take instruments from black cases and sheet music from black folders and begin to get comfortable in their seats. On the stage were several levels of stairs meant for a choir, and milling around the stage and around the center of the plaza were dozens of children in white robes.

"They'd better hurry," Cohen said, looking up at the cloud-covered sky.

"I hope it holds off. I wanna hear them," Elisa said. He took the wine carafe and refilled their glasses.

The orchestra began to warm up. The violins and the deep throbbing of the kettle drums, the higher-pitched clarinets and the strumming of harp strings, the tremble of the oboes. As if the instruments had sounded an alarm, the children in robes began to migrate toward the back of the stage. A woman in a sleeveless red dress ushered them and then a man in a gray suit passed by the orchestra and made sure each musician saw the three fingers he was showing.

"That's weird," Elisa said. "I just thought about something I haven't thought about in a long time."

Cohen reached for his wineglass and asked her what she remembered.

"Something I read back in college. *Death in Venice.* You ever have to read it?"

"If I did, I don't remember it."

"Well, then you didn't. Because if you read it, you wouldn't forget it. Especially now that we're here. I can't believe I just now thought about it."

"So. What was it about? A double murder?" Cohen asked.

She stared across the plaza toward the children. "No," she said flatly. "It's about this man, an old man. He was an artist or maybe a writer. Anyway, he decides to come to Venice for a vacation and he ends up seeing this boy, this beautiful young boy and he falls in love with him. Crazy love. He becomes completely obsessed by this boy."

Cohen sipped from his glass of wine. "Old pervert," he said.

"But that's it," Elisa said, turning from the children and looking at Cohen. "He wasn't an old pervert. It seemed that way at first but if you really looked at it, when he thought about the boy, it's like he was thinking about a work of art or a sculpture or something. I think I remember something about him comparing the boy to a Greek statue. That's how it started out. He was an artist and he saw the boy as art. But then when he started following the boy around was when he began to lose it some. He watched the boy all the time. Followed him in and out of the hotel, around the city, to the beach. Wherever. I think he even went to try and leave but couldn't."

The sounds of the tuning orchestra began to lessen and the children, who earlier stood in a huddled mass, had broken into lines and were waiting behind the stage with their hands at their sides. The woman in the red dress had come onstage. Across the front of the stage were four microphone stands and she went to each one to make sure that they were on and ready.

"What'd the boy do?" Cohen asked.

Elisa shrugged. "Nothing, really. He noticed the man but didn't seem concerned. He had a governess or servant and they noticed him following them around but nobody ever said or did anything. The whole thing was strange. He loved the boy, it seemed like to me. But not in some weird sexual way. He just loved him. At least that's what I thought."

Elisa took her wineglass but didn't drink. She held it up and watched the wine move around in it. Then she set it back on the table.

"The end?" Cohen said.

She shook her head. "The strangest part to me was that the old man found out there was a plague in Venice but that everybody was keeping it quiet so the tourists wouldn't get out of town. The boy and his family were staying at the same hotel he stayed at, and I said he loved the boy, but when he found out about the plague, he didn't warn the family. He didn't do anything to try and protect the boy, though he knew that the plague was already killing people."

"Did the old man leave?"

"No. He waited it out. Finally the family was getting ready to go and the old man kept on watching the boy and then he died sitting in a chair on the beach. I guess he got the plague, but you're never really sure."

Cohen emptied his glass and poured himself more. Across the way, the orchestra was silent for a moment and then began to play.

"I don't know if he loved him," Cohen said. "If he did I think he would have told them."

Elisa raised her glass and drank, trying to decide.

"And he killed himself, basically," Cohen said. "Right?"

Elisa set the glass down and emptied what was left of the wine carafe. The orchestral song echoed across the Palazzi Soranzo, echoed through the streets and alleyways, echoed against the thousand-year-old stone buildings and underneath the arched walkways.

"I think he was willing to die for the boy and he forgot everything else," she said. She turned her head and looked across the plaza, up into the sky, as if trying to see the music. "I don't think he knew the difference between right and wrong. Not because he didn't care. He just lost touch with it."

Cohen watched her. Could see her head and heart working together. He had always loved her this way and had seen this look on her face many times before as they sat on the beach and stared out across the ocean.

"It sounds like a good story," he told her.

The orchestra played and the white-robed children began to file onto the stage and fill the rows of stairs. The woman in the red dress stood at the front of the stage with her back to the orchestra, her hands folded in front. People from across the plaza and from the extending streets began to drift toward the stage as if pulled by invisible strings. When the children were in place, the woman raised her hands, held them there. She brought them down gently and the angelic voices of children spread softly across the day.

35

It was cold at first but he got used to it and the propane burner helped in time. The first thing he did was clean the gunshot wound in his thigh, turning the water pink. When it was clean, he stood and let the dirty water run out and then he ran a new bath. Then he sat down in the tub and he stared at the wall and tried to figure out the best way to get back to the Jeep.

He figured they couldn't have come more than twenty miles or so. He closed his eyes and slumped down beneath the water. Felt it cold and refreshing on his head like the spring's first dive into the Gulf. Twenty miles didn't seem like such a long way, not if the weather gave a little. He held his breath and stayed down as long as he could and then he came up with a gasp, wiping the water from his face and when he opened his eyes she was there, holding the candle in front of her as if keeping a vigil for the lost. Her overcoat was gone and her flannel shirt was gone and she was in a too-big T-shirt and jeans and barefoot. Her shadow rose behind her against the wall and up onto the ceiling.

They were right, he thought as he looked at her. She had not taken a bath. She stood still and stared at Cohen. He sat up straight and looked away from her, down into the bathwater. Then she walked across the room to the lantern and she turned it off.

He slipped under again, floating some, the images of the Jeep and the storm and the hole in his leg disappeared and his mind wandered off into a vast, empty place, and this time when he came up, her clothes and the candle were at her feet and she held her arms close against her body.

Wild patches of hair at her armpits and between her legs. Her wavy black hair fell down across her breasts and reached her belly, like black silk cords of a velvet curtain that could be pulled back and allow you into a secret room. The beating of the rain against the roof and across the land and the light from the candle dim but pure as she came to him. He sat up with his arms on the side and she stopped at the edge of the tub and traced her fingers across the top of his hand. He didn't look up at her but stared at her hips as she stepped over into the tub and nestled herself between his legs and she lay flat against him and held her mouth close and he smelled her and she waited to see if he would come to her.

He didn't move. There was betrayal and hope and fear and love and hurt and yesterday and today and tomorrow twisting around in his head like a bed of snakes striking against one another for supremacy.

She moved her head down and leaned her face against his chest and her arms slid down into the water and wrapped around his back and she lay there. This black night and this nowhere and this rain that wouldn't cease and downstairs the endless crying of the baby who seemed to have taken time to acclimate to this world and had now decided to rage against it with his angry but feeble voice that was as helpless against the grasp of nature as everyone and everything else.

In the corner of the room, water began to drip from the ceiling and it tapped the floor rhythmically as if readying for the strings to join in. One two three, tap. One two three, tap. The rain and the thunder and the crying infant and the one two three tap and the dull yellow light and the shadows long and this woman or maybe this girl but this person across him. Close to him. As close as she could be. Her head against his chest and her arms around him and their bodies together in the cool water and he moved his hands from the side of the tub and he moved them to the curve in the small of her back. She then lifted her head and he felt her tongue across the nape of his neck and he slowly exhaled, as if allowing the years of solitude to escape from him, if only for a little while.

36

The baby cried through the night, never wanting to eat and randomly spitting up something thick and sticky. He slept only in half-hour intervals, his forehead and arms and belly hot like a rock in the sun. The floorboards were plentiful and kept the fire going and with the vague light of dawn they had all risen and were standing together in the kitchen, looking out of the windows at the storm. It had gained strength through the night and several times caused the old house to crack and bend in ways that a house shouldn't. And now, as they stood together in the early morning, the wind came hard and there was the sound of wood splintering and a lengthy groan.

"It's never gonna let up," Evan said.

"Something ain't right with him," Nadine said. She had held him most of the night. His head was wet with sweat. "I say damn it all and let's go. We try to sit this one out, we could be here for two weeks."

"We can't go out in this," Cohen said. The house cracked again somewhere. "But we might not have a choice."

"We got to get the baby to a doctor," Kris said. "We can't let him die out here."

"Look at him," Nadine said and she showed him to the others as if they had never seen him. His strained face and damp head and dry lips and gasping cries.

Mariposa moved over to Nadine and touched the child's forehead. She looked at Cohen and nodded.

"So. What the hell?" Evan asked Cohen.

"Nadine's right. God knows how long it'll go on."

"The screaming or the storm?"

"All of it."

"You think this is the worst?" Evan said.

"I can't tell anymore."

"Shit," Nadine said. "It ain't safe nowhere in this fucking world."

"Hey," Evan said sharply, pointing at Brisco.

"Hell, I can't help it."

"Not the F-word. Damn."

Mariposa moved from the baby and over to Cohen and she said, "Have you figured out which way to go?"

"Kinda. About like yesterday," Cohen said. "I do know that somehow Charlie used to make it down here and back all the time in that big truck so there's gotta be a good road somewhere. We just got to find it."

"It's probably out there at the highway," Evan said. "If we could loop back around to it."

"We can loop back around to it," Cohen said. "Just depends on what everybody wants to do."

"We got to go," Nadine said. "I ain't letting him die after all the shit Lorna went through to get him here."

"I say go, too," Kris said. "I ain't a baby professional but God knows how high his fever is and he keeps throwing up when there ain't nothing in him. It was something pink last time."

Evan said, "With it like this, there's probably less chance of running into anybody else."

"That's a good point," Cohen said.

"I'm with them," Mariposa said. "We could sit here for days but I don't think the baby would make it. Nobody thinks it."

"Let's go then," Nadine said.

"All right," Cohen said. "Come on, Evan. Let's try and load what we can."

"And hurry up," Nadine ordered and then she walked around in circles with the child.

Cohen and Evan began to gather canned food and lamps and plastic bags of blankets and clothes. Mariposa helped them get it all to the door and Cohen and Evan ran in and out of the storm, loading the truck. When they were done, Mariposa went out and helped them get the tarp tied.

They ran back inside and the wind slammed the door behind them. The baby screamed and Nadine danced around with him and tried to get him to take the bottle but he wouldn't.

Cohen picked up the shotgun and the box of shells and handed them to Evan. "Let Nadine drive and put Kris in the middle with the baby and Brisco," he said to Evan. "You ride against the window. We see anybody, you make sure they see what you're holding."

It rained so hard and the wind was so stiff that they had to pull over on the side of the road and wait. In lulls, they had gone east and then been able to maneuver north on Highway 29. But they moved at a walker's pace, through decimated communities, houses and stores huddled around four-way stops and town squares. It took nearly an hour to manipulate several miles. They finally came to Highway 98, a four-lane running east and west. Fifteen miles to the east was Hattiesburg, a once slick university town that had sprawled with subdivisions and shopping malls and movie theaters. The interstate ran through Hattiesburg, which would get them to the Line most efficiently, but it was also likely that with the abundance of places to hide there would be more risks. This was the debate that they were having through rolled-down windows as they sat at a stop sign.

"I say we keep on this way," Evan said.

"Which way?" asked Nadine. Evan pointed straight ahead, continuing north on 29.

"Might run out of road that way," Cohen said.

"Better than getting shot."

"I agree with that," Nadine said.

"How's he feeling?" Cohen asked.

"You hear him, don't you?" Kris said about the wailing baby in her arms. "And hot. Don't seem like that's gonna change."

"I ain't interested in the interstate and what might be on it," Evan said.

"I bet Charlie came that way," Cohen said.

"Charlie had some help," Evan said.

"Yep."

"Let's just keep on," Nadine said and she pointed forward.

Cohen looked ahead. "All right," he said.

But before they went any farther, he got out of

the truck and took a gas can and put a couple of gallons in each truck, the wind pushing him off balance, his clothes stuck to him and his eyes fighting to stay focused on the job. He spilled a little but most went into the tanks and when he got back in the truck cab he was out of breath. Mariposa gave him a towel from the floorboard and he wiped his face and head. Then they crossed over Highway 98 and continued on north.

After another hour and twenty careful miles, the rain constant and the roads flooded in some places but able to be crossed, they came upon a sign as big as a billboard, sitting solitary in the countryside, that read: U.S. GOVERNMENT–LEGISLATED TERRITORY 10 MILES.

"That's it," Mariposa said and she sat up straight.

The next ten miles were a drowning landscape that, as they drove closer to the Line, became littered with the waste of man—shells of vehicles, abandoned government trailers, burned houses, beer bottles and shredded tires and trash like the remains from a crowd that had made a run for it. All of it soggy and stuck to the earth. It was difficult to see that far ahead and they came upon another sign, as large as the first, that said the Line was two miles away. Two more filthy miles along the desolate highway and then they came upon a station, a square brick thing with a metal roof, the illumination of the electric light from inside a patch of yellow in a portrait of gray. A ten-foot-high fence stretched out from either side of the station and reached out of sight, with three black Hummers parked on the other side. A group of men in black coats, the same black coats they had encountered before in the parking lot, looked out at them from behind the thick glass of the station, like some powerful assembly of storm gods who had taken refuge from the work of their own hands.

Cohen stopped the truck. The other truck stopped behind him.

"What?" Mariposa said.

"I don't know. What does it look like to you?"

They sat and stared ahead at the station. The rain beating and the windshield wipers thumping and the irritation of it all.

"They'd be coming this way if it was bad. Right?" she asked.

Cohen wasn't sure. But it was time to decide. He put the truck in drive and they moved on toward the station.

There were five men inside behind bulletproof windows, and two of them put up the hoods on their black coats and walked outside. They both had rifles hanging from their shoulders and across the back of their coats in white were the letters USLP. One of them slid back the gate that crossed the road and the other stood at the entrance and motioned for Cohen to drive forward. Cohen moved ahead and the man held up his hand and Cohen stopped. He motioned for Cohen to roll down the window. He held his rifle like he was ready and he moved toward the window while the other guard moved to the passenger side of the truck. The three on the inside watched closely.

The man stayed two steps back and held his head tucked back in his hood as the rain slapped on the bulky black coat. Cohen leaned toward him to hear through the storm.

"You American?" the man called out.

Cohen nodded.

"I said you American?"

"Yeah. American."

"What business you got up here?"

"Business?"

"Yeah," the man said and he pointed his rifle at the ragged tarp and rain-soaked supplies in the back of the truck. "Business. Looks like you got business. Who you got up under there?"

"Nobody. Look for yourself."

"Then what business you got?"

"I ain't got no business. We're trying to get the hell outta this mess."

The guard moved closer and looked in at Mariposa. "She American?"

"Yeah. American."

"She don't look it."

Cohen looked at Mariposa and back at the guard. "How so?"

"How about them back there? They with you?"

"Yeah, with me and her. All Americans. God bless America."

The guard looked at the truck behind Cohen. He motioned the other guard to walk back to it. "You sit still," he told Cohen.

Cohen rolled up the window and he turned and watched the guards as they walked to the other truck. It seemed like he was having the same conversation with Nadine as she was nodding and pointing at the others and then they stepped to the back of the truck and untied the tarp and looked underneath. They moved to Cohen's truck and did the same thing. The guard tapped on Cohen's window and he cracked it and the guard told him to cross through and pull over on the side of the road. He did and Nadine did the same.

Two more guards came out of the station. The four of them stood together and talked for a minute.

"What's wrong?" Mariposa asked.

"Take a look. Just about all this," Cohen said.

The guards split up. One went back inside the station and picked up a telephone. Another went to one of the black SUVs parked next to the station and he cranked it and pulled around alongside the vehicles. One guard walked to Cohen's truck and the other to Nadine's. Cohen let the window down again.

"Women back there say they got to get to a hospital. That right?"

"That's right."

"How long y'all been down there?"

Cohen shook his head. "Some longer than others."

"Who the hell had the bright idea to get knocked up and have a baby down there?"

"I know it. Don't make sense. But it's a long story, I can promise that."

"You got relations with them back there?"

Cohen said no.

"Then we're gonna take that woman and that baby ourselves. Make sure they get where they need to go. You got anything up here that belongs to them?"

Cohen thought a minute. Looked over his shoulder and Kris and the baby were being helped into the SUV and Nadine was taking Kris's plastic bag of clothes and whatever else out of the back of the truck. She handed it to the guard, who put it into the back of the SUV, then she hurried up to Cohen and said, "I got to follow them seeing as how that truck belongs to both me and Kris. We got to go." She reached in the window and hugged Cohen around the neck and he said to hold on. He leaned back and took some money out of his front pocket and he gave it to her. "Be a good momma," he said.

She took the money and smiled and she was

getting soaked so she ran back to the truck. Evan and Brisco got out and came and got in next to Mariposa and they all watched the SUV and the truck drive away.

"Where they going?" Cohen asked.

"Depends," said the guard. "About a hundred miles northeast to a decent spot for that baby and pregnant woman."

"A hundred miles?"

"At least."

"But ain't this the Line?"

The guard laughed. "Officially, hell yeah. Unofficially, hell no. The Line ain't nothing more than a line in the sand these days. Where you going, anyhow?"

Cohen shook his head. "I don't guess we know. I can't make it another hundred miles or whatever. Not in this thing."

"Ellisville is straight on up this highway."

"What's there?"

"Mostly nothing. But maybe gas and food if you're lucky."

"Lucky? They got that stuff or not?"

"You'll see when you get there."

"All right," Cohen said.

"And you got quite the arsenal in the back of that truck. You got plans?"

"Only plans we got is to get somewhere dry and warm and eat something cooked."

"You can't go riding around with all those guns

in the back. Wrong people get back there, it'd be ugly."

"What's the gun law?"

"Gun law? I guess it's if you got one, you'd better not let nobody take it from you. You're still a long ways from law."

"I got it."

"Then go on. Ellisville is another dozen miles. Better find somewhere soon, 'cause there's another storm right behind this one and it looks like a monster."

"I haven't seen one that isn't."

The guard shook his head.

"Ask him about Charlie," one of the other guards called out.

"Yeah. Any chance you might've seen this old guy named Charlie down there somewhere? He runs a truck back and forth. Left out a while back but didn't come back through this way."

Cohen nodded. "We saw a couple of his boys. And about twenty others laid out."

"Damn. Where at?"

"Down at the water. Casino parking lot."

The guard shook his head again.

"You know," Cohen said, "there's some of you running roughshod down there. Even wearing the same coats."

"I know it. They drive by here about once a week and fire over our heads just to see if we'll do anything."

"Do you?"

"I'm not getting paid to do anything. Don't nobody sent down here know what the hell is going on, but some of us took it different than others."

Cohen rolled up the window. The guard backed off and walked over to the others. Cohen put the truck in drive, but then he stopped and said wait a second and he got out of the truck and called out to the guards who were walking back into the station. They stopped and Cohen hurried over and asked if there was anything in particular they needed to be looking out for.

The guards smiled. Looked at each other. "Yeah," one of them said. "If I was you I'd be on the lookout for whatever's got two arms and two legs and sense enough to make them work."

IV

37

The gas gauge was right at the E as they drove into Ellisville. The highway led them into downtown, a decrepit town square with a fractured awning running the length of the buildings, and underneath the awning stood groups of men sheltering from the rain, watching the truck as Cohen drove around the square looking for a place to park.

"What they all waiting for?" Evan asked.

"Nothing, it looks like," Cohen answered.

Lights shined from the square buildings. A café stood in one corner and its door was open and a big man with an apron loomed in the doorway. Cohen lapped the square twice, watching them, some with the look of menace, others with the look of the defeated, but all seemingly interested in the unfamiliar truck and the unfamiliar refugees.

Cohen turned off the square and drove around to the backside of a row of buildings. He parked in between two dumpsters. A metal staircase rose up the back of one building, and at the top of the staircase, standing with an umbrella, was a square-shaped woman in only her panties and bra and she was waving at them to come on up, calling out in a singsong voice muted by the rain.

"Let's go to that café and eat. Maybe find out about a place to stay," Cohen said.

"You sure?" Evan asked.

"Not much other choice. Just stay close. Hold on to Brisco."

"What about all that stuff in the back?" Mariposa asked.

Cohen reached into his coat where he still held two pistols and he took them out, made sure they were loaded. The bowie knife was still on his belt. The rifle leaned against the truck door next to Evan and Cohen told him to lay it down across the floorboard. They raised their legs and Evan set it down and pushed it under the seat.

"We won't be long," Cohen said. "Nobody saw us park back here."

"Except her," Evan said and he pointed up at the woman, who waved again.

"She ain't going nowhere. Come on."

They got out of the truck and hurried through an alley that took them to the square. The water rapped against the awning and it was mostly rotted and let in almost as much as it kept out. The café was on the other side so they started walking. Along the sidewalk, nobody moved to let them by and they wove carefully through and around the faces of men ready to take what didn't belong to them. Some of them whistled at Mariposa, called out the things they'd do to her. Evan held Brisco tight and Mariposa held Cohen tighter. It smelled like cigarettes and old beer and here and there were bodies curled against building fronts, sleeping or passed out or dead. At the first corner a group of women huddled around a doorway of a building that had iron bars across the windows. The women were dressed like thrift-store mannequins with strangely matching low-cut shirts and hiked skirts that ignored the rain and cold. A woman wearing a baseball hat and a boa promised them anything they wanted for twenty dollars.

"I'll do all that twice for fifteen," another one said and they all laughed and called out after Cohen as he crossed the street and made a left and continued along the square. Cohen saw the big man with the apron protecting the doorway of the café and they walked a little faster and halfway there, a man threw his shoulder into Cohen as they passed, knocking him off balance. He staggered against Mariposa but kept his feet. Several of them stood together, all of them with beards and wild red eyes and they each held a bottle and together they smelled like hell. Cohen stood up straight and looked at the one who had shoved him. Tattoos circled his neck and his nose was a little crooked.

"Good day, sir," the man sang out and a couple of them laughed. Up and down the sidewalk, everybody stopped and watched and waited.

Cohen nodded and he took Mariposa by the

arm and started to walk again but the man moved in front of him.

"I said good day. You got manners, you say the same." He stood close to Cohen and glared, then he looked at Mariposa, up and down. A couple of his buddies moved in behind him.

"Go on, Evan," Cohen said. "Take Brisco and go get something to eat."

Evan and Brisco started to move and Cohen was surprised the men let them but they did and the boys walked on toward the café, Evan watching over his shoulder.

"What you want here?" the man asked.

Cohen nodded at the café. "Something to eat."

"Who you got with you? Sister? Cousin? Daughter, maybe."

"We're just walking over there."

"You might have to hold on. We here are the welcome-to-town committee. I'm president and them behind me is vice presidents."

Cohen looked past him and counted. "You got four vice presidents."

"That's right."

"What for?"

"It don't matter. Does it?"

"Not to me. But I wouldn't split the vice presidency with three others."

The man reached out to touch a strand of Mariposa's hair and Cohen swatted his hand away.

"You better be careful," Cohen said.

"I was thinking the same thing about you," the man answered, loudly, over the rattle of the rain. The others moved in closer.

"We just want food and gas," Cohen said.

"I done heard that one. Seems like it unites us all."

"We're not looking to be united."

"That right?"

"That's right."

"You might get a whole lot more than that. Might get united and anointed and invited and provided and God knows what else. 'Specially her."

"Got that right," one of the others said.

"How old are you, darling?"

"Don't talk to her," Cohen said.

She squeezed his arm.

"Well, then," the man said and he grinned. He stepped back and waved his arm as if showing them to their table. "Cowboy gets to get on his way. Pardon the interruption. Y'all go and enjoy yourselves and we'll be right here watching. Right across there we'll have us a drink or two tonight, maybe." He pointed at a storefront on the other side of the square where JOINT was spray-painted across the glass in a childlike script.

"Come on," Cohen said to Mariposa and they moved ahead. Cohen watched the men as he walked past, uncertain.

"We gonna make you feel right at home," the man called out. "Know why? 'Cause there ain't nothing else to do. Ain't nothing else to do but take care of the visitors to this fair city. God knows we about to be wiped away anyhow. Might as well enjoy it."

38

It was as if they were a quartet of unrehearsed actors who had been cast into an ongoing production and directed to play the role of silent, exhausted, and bewildered. They sat in a booth at the front of the café next to the window. Brisco and Evan on one side, Cohen and Mariposa on the other. Along one wall were more booths and nearly every seat was filled. Women with children, old people sitting six in a booth, a table of Mexican boys talking quickly with nervous looks. More people and more normalcy than any of them had seen in years. More normalcy than Brisco had seen in his life.

Opposite the booths there was a long counter with ten stools occupied by men with coffee mugs and cigarettes. Behind the counter stood a black woman wearing a sweatshirt and a red bandana tied around her neck that she used to wipe the sweat from her upper lip as she worked the grill. A black girl hurried from table to table with a small notebook in one hand and a towel tossed over her shoulder.

"What's she doing?" Brisco asked.

Evan leaned down to him. "She goes around and asks people what they want, then she writes it down and takes it over there to the cook. The cook fixes it, then when it's done, she goes back and gets it and takes it to the person who asked for it."

Brisco's eyes followed her as she moved between tables, pausing to write down an order or lift plates from a table. "Oh," he said.

The girl stepped carefully across the slick linoleum floor. Crooked cracks ran from the ceiling to the floor in the plaster walls and in some places the plaster had fallen away, exposing the original brick walls. The big man with the apron stood in the doorway like a roadhouse bouncer and in his right hand he held the heavy end of a pool stick, a foot long, and he tapped it on his leg to the rhythm of the song that he was humming.

Mariposa put her head down on the table and Cohen watched the square through the window. The rain still falling and the people lining the sidewalks and the water rising and spilling over the curb about halfway around. The men drank. They smoked. Some whispered to one another. Every now and then a push and a shove. A ragged blend of the young and the old. Across the square, Cohen noticed two police cars parked in an alley and he figured that was why things hadn't escalated before when the men confronted them.

The big man, tall and barrel-chested with his hair in buzz cut, walked over and tapped the end of the pool stick on the table and they turned their attention to him. His sleeves were rolled up past his elbows and a scar ran the length of one forearm as if it were an extension of the pool stick.

"Y'all hungry?" he asked.

"I am," Brisco said.

"I bet you're always hungry."

"Mostly," Evan said.

"We got burgers and breakfast, and that's about it as far as eating," he said. "Coffee, Coke. Milk, juice."

They all looked at one another. Seemingly unsure how to answer being asked what they wanted to eat or even how to think about it.

"We don't have anything else so don't try and dream something up."

"Gimme some scrambled eggs. Bacon. Sausage. Toast. Better yet, everything you got with breakfast on it," Cohen said.

"Me, too," said Mariposa.

"Me, too," said Brisco.

"You don't even know what half that stuff is," Evan said to his small brother.

"Yes, I do."

"No, you don't," Evan said. "Maybe we'll just get some toast or something."

"Hell you will," Cohen said. "Bring it all for everybody."

Thc man turned and shouted to the black woman behind the grill. "Four breakfasts. All of it on all of them." Then he asked what they were drinking and he shouted that out too and then resumed his place in the doorway along with the humming and the tapping.

"God knows you've earned a breakfast," Cohen said to Evan and the boy nodded.

Cohen stood up, took off his coat, and set it on the seat next to Mariposa. Then he reached into his pocket and took out the folded money. "Might as well see what we got." He unfolded the money and began to count the hundred-dollar bills. When he was done, he said, "Thirteen hundred."

"Damn," said Evan.

"Damn like good or damn like bad?" asked Cohen.

"Damn like good. Right?"

Cohen shook his head. "Damn like bad. We got this and we got the truck and everything in it, though. But we're back in the real world now where it costs money to breathe."

"Not me. Watch this," Brisco said and he huffed and puffed as if trying to put out a fire.

"It's enough," Mariposa said.

"Not really. It's more than nothing. But less than something," Cohen said. I could fix that, he started to add, but he stopped.

At the doorway, two men holding bottles in brown paper bags tried to come in but the man told them to go on and he poked at them with the stick. They backed off and walked on by, looking longingly into the café as if the mere sight of food might ease their hunger.

It wasn't long before the food arrived. Plates of eggs and grits and bacon and sausage. Toast with butter and jelly and biscuits with gravy and sliced tomatoes. There was no more talking for some time.

When Cohen was done, he stood up and walked to the doorway and lit a cigarette. He asked the man if he wanted one but he said no and then Cohen asked if there was such a thing as a hotel around here.

"Where you coming here from, anyway?" the man asked.

"Down there. Kinda expected something different at the Line."

"The Line?" the man said and huffed. "That's turning into an old wives' tale."

"That's what I keep hearing."

"You better keep on going then," the man said. "That Line is bullshit. See those cop cars over there?" He pointed the pool stick. "Been sitting there for about a year. Go look at 'em. Windows busted out. Gutted. Same way with anything else that was supposed to mean something. Been more than a year since we had anything to hold on to."

“How much farther to where it all starts?”

The man shrugged. “I got no idea. Everywhere I know about is like this. Probably as far up as Tennessee, I guess. On the east side. West side is washed out.”

“What you mean, washed out?”

“Damn, man. You need to get educated if you plan on getting anywhere with that crew. Go look over there at the end of the counter. There’s a newspaper about two months old but it’ll do.”

Cohen crossed the café and sat down on a bar stool at the end of the counter. He picked up the newspaper and unfolded it. It was a national newspaper, and the front-page articles spoke to the weather, boundary issues, relief issues, banking issues. The legend at the bottom said WEATHER 16A. It also said BOUNDARIES 16A.

Cohen found 16A to be the back page. Across the top half of the page was a map of the United States that provided regional weather information. Across the bottom half of the page was another United States map, the boundary map. “Good Lord,” he said.

A blue-shaded area split the country and covered all the states bordering the east and west sides of the Mississippi River. Across the blue-shaded area was written THE FLOODLANDS. Texas and the southeast region, above the Line, were red, up to Tennessee and North Carolina. SERVICES AND SECURITY LIMITED covered the red region. The Line was a thick black line that appeared to be in its original place ninety miles inland. Maroon covered the region below the Line and read ACCESS FORBIDDEN. On either side of THE FLOODLANDS, the northeast and the west, the map was green, and across both of these regions was written SERVICES AND SECURITY UNLIMITED.

Cohen laid the newspaper on the counter. His mouth was open some as he turned and looked blankly at the man in the doorway, at the riffraff milling about on the sidewalk.

He had no idea what to do.

"Don't look too spiffy, does it," said the black woman working the grill.

He didn't register her.

"Hey," she said loudly.

Cohen shook his head some and turned to her.

"I said it don't look too spiffy," she said again and she pointed her spatula at the newspaper.

Cohen closed his mouth. Shook his head.

Then he got up and walked back over to the big man in the doorway.

A woman with a blanket draped over her head and shoulders came along. She held out a shaking hand and said, "Got dollar? Got dollar?"

"No dollar. Go on," the man said. "Can't buy a damn stick of gum with a dollar."

She went on. There was a clap of thunder and a snap of lightning and some of them out on the sidewalk applauded and cheered. The man turned and saw Cohen behind him and said, "You educated now?"

"Yeah. More than I'd like."

The thunder roared again and again they cheered.

"They do this all day, I'm guessing," Cohen said.

"All day and all night. Sidewalks never get still. They crawl in and out of these building like goddamn rats. Starting to grow little rats now. It's a crying damn shame. Used to sit right here in this spot every morning and read the paper. Drink my coffee. Say hey to whoever. By the way, I'm Big Jim."

The two men shook hands and Cohen lit a cigarette. They stood there watching the rain, watching the others. When Cohen was done, he tossed the butt out on the sidewalk. A bent-over old man reached down and picked it up and tried to smoke it.

"Get the hell out of here," Big Jim yelled and the old man looked at him without care but shuffled away.

Big Jim folded his arms and looked at Cohen. Then he looked over at their table. "I got two rooms upstairs. Second floor. I live up on the third so you probably don't have nothing to worry about. Best you're gonna get."

"How much?"

“Hundred.”
“A hundred what?”
“Dollars.”
“For both?”
“For one.”
“Jesus.”
“Fine. Both. How long you planning on being here?”
Cohen looked out at the rain. Imagined someplace where the sun was shining on the sidewalk. “At a hundred dollars a night not very damn long.”
Cohen walked back to the table and sat down. The plates were empty and they sat slumped in the booth. The three of them seemed to have changed color with their full bellies as if they had ingested some magical potion for happiness.
“We’re gonna stay upstairs tonight,” Cohen said. “Got two rooms. The café man lives up on top so everything will be fine.”
“And we go tomorrow?” Mariposa asked.
Cohen heard her but didn’t answer. He repeated the question in his head with the emphasis on the word “we.” And *we* go tomorrow? Yes, he thought. We.
“Won’t be going nowhere tomorrow, by the looks of it,” Evan said.
“We’ll see what the storms do first.”
The woman came over and refilled their coffee mugs.

Evan said, “You think the others made it to the hospital?”

“They will. Eventually. Gonna take a while,” Cohen said. “They seemed serious about getting them there.” He thought about Kris getting into the black vehicle, about the guard telling him it was a hundred miles to a safe place. He wondered what that meant for the Line. Or if there was such a thing anymore.

“Think that baby is okay?” Evan asked.

“I bet he’s fine,” Cohen said. “I hope so.”

Evan sat up straight. Put his elbows on the table. “Only seems fair that he would be,” he said.

The others nodded. And then they sat quietly for a while. Brisco laid his head in his brother’s lap, his feet hanging out of the end of the booth. Mariposa leaned against Cohen’s shoulder and closed her eyes.

Outside they moved along the sidewalks, looking in at those lucky enough to have a seat in a dry café and money to spend once they were inside. Big Jim shooed them away like flies. The man with the tattooed neck walked by, stopped when he noticed Cohen in the window. He grinned and pointed at him and he pointed at Mariposa and then he clapped his hands softly and nodded. Cohen, trying not to wake the girl, slowly stuck his hand into his coat that lay on the seat, took hold of a pistol, and he raised it and showed it to the man. The man threw back his head and laughed, and then he grabbed at his crotch and walked on.

Then Charlie walked into the café.

39

"Damn. I figured you were dead," Cohen said as he met him inside the doorway. He shook hands with his old friend.

Charlie's face and eyes looked tired and he smelled like a wet dog. "Pretty damn close. Looks like you finally wised up," he answered. "Where you sitting?"

Cohen pointed at the booth where Mariposa and Evan and Brisco napped.

"Where'd you find them?" Charlie asked.

"You wouldn't believe me if I told you. I wouldn't believe it neither if I didn't see it all myself."

"That's a lot of mouths to feed."

"Come on," Cohen said. "Let's sit down."

Charlie took a chair and slid it to the end of the table and sat down. Cohen touched shoulders and woke the others and introduced everybody. Charlie shook Evan's hand. He looked curiously at Mariposa, and then at Cohen, and then at Mariposa again.

"What the hell happened?" Cohen said.

Charlie waved to the girl waiting tables and told her to bring him some coffee. His hands were dirty and there was a scrape across his cheek and mud on the elbows of his coat. "I tell you what happened. Ever since that backhoe got spotted, every time I rode it out of the back of the U-Haul, the damn Indians started popping out from everywhere. Especially them crazy-ass army boys or Line patrol or whatever they are. They came from everywhere but me and another boy somehow managed to drive that backhoe back up in the truck and haul ass while they were busy killing each other. Shot my U-Haul full of holes."

"I still can't believe you're running around digging blind on a ten-mile stretch of beach."

"I ain't no more. Lost damn near all my boys. All but one laying up there waiting to die."

"Up where?"

"Across the square over there. I got a top floor where I come and go."

The girl brought Charlie's coffee and set it on the table.

"Looks like y'all are trying to get fat," Charlie said as he took in the empty plates and cups on the table.

"It's been a while," Cohen said. "You want something?"

Charlie sipped his coffee, then he stood up. "Come over here, Cohen. Let's me and you talk." Cohen got up from the booth and Charlie nodded to the others. Cohen followed Charlie over to the counter and they sat on bar stools.

"What you got going on?" Charlie asked.

"I got nothing going on. We had to haul ass out of there, too. Think the same boys that got after you got after us. We hit a couple of them and then ran out of Gulfport. Ended up here just a little while ago but it wasn't easy."

"It never is. You staying?"

"No longer than we have to."

The girl passed with the coffeepot and refilled Charlie's cup.

"We?"

Cohen nodded.

"You know about this storm coming, huh?" Charlie asked.

"Like I know about all the rest."

"Nah. Not like the rest. That's what the word is."

"We've been down here too long to get worried."

"Maybe. But I was listening to the radio and they kept on like this one is bigger than hell. A real monster." Charlie took another sip of coffee, then said, "You're right. I ain't worried. I gotta go see about that boy up there. Where you gonna be?"

"Staying here. Man said he's got rooms upstairs."

"That's good. Don't run off. I might need some help."

"I might, too."

Charlie set down the cup and he reached into his coat pocket and pulled out a wad of cash. "Here.

Let me pay for that food." He held the money out, but Cohen pushed his hand away.

"Save your favors for helping me out with supplies and gas. I don't plan on being here but for a day or two."

Charlie put the money back into his coat and he stood up. "I'm right across there," he said, pointing out of the café door. "Top floor, middle building. Stairway is in back. But don't sneak up on me." He took out a cigarette and turned up the collar of his coat, then he walked out of the café and onto the crowded sidewalk. Cohen watched him walk, thought he had a limp. Thought he looked old and worn. More than usual.

He moved from the counter back over to the booth and asked if they were ready to go upstairs. Outside there was thunder and then more thunder. More lightning. More applause from the crowds on the sidewalk in their satisfaction of the storm. As if it gave them what they desired.

The two rooms were much the same. Off-white walls with mismatched furniture, end tables and dressers and headboards that looked as if they had been gathered at yard sales. Scratched hardwood floors, discolored here and there, and windows that looked across the square. In each room, a chair and small table sat next to the windows, and on each table was a short stack of several-year-old magazines. A small glass chandelier hung from each ceiling. The bathroom separated the rooms, with its claw-foot tub and its sink that had streaked orange from the years of the dripping faucet and its diamond-shaped ceramic tile. A bookshelf next to the sink, with candles and matches on the top shelf and toilet paper and towels on the bottom.

Brisco ran to a bed and jumped up and down and Mariposa headed into the bathroom and turned on the faucet. The water came out copper-colored but after a minute ran clear and she washed her face. She walked into the other bedroom, took off her coat, and fell back on the bed.

Cohen and Evan went out to the truck and they took what was important and returned to the rooms, staying off the square and sneaking around and behind buildings and knocking on the back door of the café until the big man let them in. They brought the guns and ammunition and bags of clothes and the big man only nodded at the rifles and shotgun when Cohen said I gotta keep them somewhere. Once they were all upstairs again, Cohen slid the rifles and shotgun underneath the bed in the room that he and Mariposa would share. He stashed the boxes of shells in the bottom drawer of the dresser and then he handed one of the two pistols to Evan.

"I don't want it," Evan said.

"You need to keep it. Hide it somewhere."

"What for?"

"Jesus, Evan. You know what for. For whatever thc hcll comcs along."

"Unload it," Evan said.

"It don't work if it's not loaded. You don't have to sleep with it, just hide it in there somewhere. Take it," Cohen said and he pushed it on the boy. Evan took it and went into the other room where Brisco had discovered the television.

"Go hide it for him," Mariposa said when Evan was gone.

"If I hide it for him, he won't know where it is." Cohen put the other pistol in the top drawer of the dresser. "You see where this is?" he asked her. She nodded.

He walked to the window and pushed back the curtain. He looked out at the rain, at the people across the square. He thought about the guard at the Line warning about the monster that was coming, thought about Charlie's mention of the same thing. Maybe we haven't seen it all.

"What do you think?" Mariposa said.

Cohen closed the curtain. Sat down in the chair next to the window. "I think we're dry. We're safe. I think we won't be here long."

Mariposa walked into the bathroom and closed the door to the adjoining room. Then she came back into their room and began to undress.

"What do you think?" he asked.

She let the dirty, damp clothes fall in a pile and

said, “I think I’m going to be clean. And then I think I’m going to sleep in a bed.”

The first night he dreamed of children. He dreamed of babies on their backs, their mouths open and bodies relaxed in innocent slumber. He dreamed of early walkers, wobbly and unsure, knocking against coffee tables and doorways and dropping flat on their bottoms and then getting up and going again. He dreamed of big kids riding horses and playing freeze tag and fishing from the bank and he dreamed of teaching a girl to ride a bicycle without the training wheels and the trust she put in him to make sure that she didn’t fall. The children of his dreams were both girls and boys, sometimes blond and sometimes dark-haired, sometimes loud and rambunctious and sometimes tender and mild. The children of his dreams were never wet and never cold and they had shadows because they had sunshine. He woke several times in the night and each time he hurried back to sleep, trying to catch up with the little bodies and voices running through his mind.

His restlessness kept her awake and then her mind began to spin and she couldn’t sleep. She got out of bed and put on her jeans and sweat-shirt and walked to the window. She was unsure of the time, though it was still the middle of the night. The rain fell hard and she saw only blurry images of bodies out under the awning. Some standing, some sprawled out, orange tips of cigarettes dots in the dark. She closed the curtain and walked quietly to the door, eased it open and slipped through, and went downstairs to the café.

The café was dark. Chairs were upturned on tables and the lights were off in the seating area, but the storage room light glowed through the square window of the swinging door. Along the counter, coffee mugs and hard plastic glasses were lined in rows and spatulas and tongs sat in a silver bowl on the grill top. Condensation fogged the windows and the café was thick with humidity.

Mariposa walked to a booth along the wall in the darkest corner, and she sat down facing the café windows.

She was unprepared for the uncertainty that came with this place. She had thought that tonight would be a night of heavy sleep, of rest for the body and rest for the mind. A night of satisfaction in survival. A night that would be a bridge into the land of new beginnings. But it was none of those things. It was a night of four walls and a bed and a warm meal eaten on a real plate with a real fork but it was not a night that signified the end of anything. It was not the night she had expected and she felt a tinge of defeat as she stared at the back of the empty booth on the other side of the table.

I have people somewhere. And she wondered

now if she did. How far do we have to go before the world doesn't look like this?

The rain and the rain and the rain. The awning leaked everywhere and those who stayed out in the night moved around like waterlogged, mindless drones. Why didn't they go inside? Why didn't they crawl under something? But she knew the answers to those questions and she knew what it felt like to have no one and nothing and she knew that there was a fine line between standing inside the café and standing outside the café and she thought of Cohen tossing and turning in the bed upstairs.

She thought of the day that she and Evan got into the Jeep and she thought of wrapping the cord around Cohen's neck because she had to and trying to pull the air from him and she thought of Evan with the shotgun on Cohen as he struggled in the water and how she had urged Evan to shoot him. *Shoot him now.* She thought of Evan pulling the trigger once, and then twice, and how the shotgun didn't fire and she wondered about the God who had decided that the last shell already would have been fired and wondered what her life would be like right this minute if that last shell would have remained. She wondered if it was the same God who decided everything else.

She got up and walked to the counter. At the end of the counter, next to the coffee mugs and plastic cups, lay the newspaper that Cohen had looked at earlier. The light from the storage room filtered down the counter and she picked up the news-paper and lay it out, back page facing her. She stared at the map and the different shades of the different parts of the country and she read the headings and she realized they were a long way from anywhere.

Outside a woman screamed above the pounding rain.

Mariposa folded the newspaper and put it back in place.

She crossed her arms on the counter and put her head down and thought of her father and his belief that he could defend his livelihood and his life against the violence of either man or nature and how foolish it seemed then and how foolish it seemed now. But there was no second-guessing because it had been impossible to make decisions then. Nothing seemed right. Nothing seemed logical. Nothing seemed safe. And nothing had changed. She thought of the stubbornness of her father and his dedication to protect and defend what belonged to him and then she thought again of Cohen in his house, on that land, with those memories and the box of keepsakes and the closets that still held her clothes and the baby's room with the dusty stuffed animals.

She wondered if he would remember her part in separating him from those things he had tried so hard to protect. She wondered when he would leave her. She wondered where he would leave her.

There was another scream and this time it sounded like a man and Mariposa lifted her head. She looked toward the window but there was nothing clear, only vague rain-covered images. More screaming and yelling and now the images moved in a shuffle along the sidewalk, pushing and grabbing and going for one another. A loud crack cut through the storm and she thought she heard breaking glass but the voices gained strength and she couldn't tell what was going on. Part of her wanted to go to the window and wipe it clean and take a closer look. Part of her didn't.

Behind her, the door to the staircase opened and she turned and saw Cohen. There was another scream and Mariposa looked from him and back to the window. As she watched anxiously the scene on the street, Cohen came across the café to her. He touched her elbow and she looked at him. "Come on," he whispered. "You don't want to see what's out there."

40

A week ago the decision would have been simple. Go get the Jeep. Much like the decision had been made to go and get the shoe box of memories. Just go get it. There was no one else to think about, no one else to ask, nothing else that needed any consideration. What do you want to do and do it and that's the end of it, like every other decision he had made in the last four years, including the one to bury Elisa under the tree in the back field and stay there with her. But that was a week ago and walking away and going back down there was not a simple decision now.

He wanted to tell Mariposa that he was leaving and give her enough money to eat for the next couple of days and go find a ride with somebody crazy enough to take him back down there. By now it had to be sixty-five, seventy miles to the Jeep on the north side of Gulfport. But he figured that he knew the way, and if he went alone he could make it down in three or so hours, make it back in less time when he was sure of the way, do the whole thing in a night. He wanted to extend his arm when she came near him. He wanted to tell her to be quiet when she started talking. He wanted to slide out of bed in the middle of the night and go and do what he needed to do.

Instead of making the move, he had spent the next two days and nights with her in the hotel room, the rain strong and the room warm. They had made love carefully, awkwardly, and sometimes clumsily, like two kids learning their way, unsure of their movements, their sounds, their reactions, this thing different in a real room with electric light and pillows and sheets than it was in an abandoned, candlelit farmhouse. They would fall asleep naked and he would wake with her talking and he would lie there, pretending to be sleeping, and listen to her, her voice low and patient like a mother speaking to an infant. I will listen to you when you want to talk about her. Or about anything. I will listen to you. If we go together we might be able to believe in each other and I will believe if you will believe. I don't want to be left alone and I don't think that you do and there is nothing that makes sense and I think that is okay. I don't think we should try to make any sense. I will listen to you if you ever want to talk about her. And I will stay with you as long as you want me to.

He would wake in the middle of the night and she would be talking, her head against him and her black hair across him like some type of protection. He noticed her hands, her fingers long and begin-ning to get into him, to sink below his skin and through the blood and into the places that mattered. He smelled her and listened to her and sometimes he wanted to answer her and sometimes he wanted to stop her and sometimes he was disappointed when she had nothing else to say.

She fell asleep quickly then, as if what she had to say emptied her, and afterward he would lie there and listen to the music and the voices coming from the square below, the yelling and the breaking bottles and the wild laughter, and he wondered if this was what we would all become if given the opportunity. If what they had seen below would ultimately win when it was all broken down. He imagined a world where there was nothing to rule but man's own instinct and desire and wondered would that make us better or worse. Cohen had seen the worst and it seemed to be standing at attention, ready to strike, but then he would remember Evan and his almost inexplicable goodness and the image of Evan and Brisco walking together, holding hands, would be enough to ease his mind and allow him to sleep.

Each time he woke she was talking and later, when they were both awake, he did not mention it and neither did she. He didn't say anything about the Jeep for two days, as the monster in the Gulf crept closer, grew stronger, prepared itself to teach them all a lesson in true power.

During other moments in the night, when he wasn't listening to her whispers, he thought of Nadine and Kris and the baby and the other baby that was to come. He regretted the haste with which they had all been separated. He regretted the quick ending because he had suffered his share of quick endings. Elisa and his unborn child. The ambush and the house being ransacked. Habana disappearing in the storm. The dog being shot by Aggie. It seemed as if each ending came and went like a pulse of lightning and he wished now that he had told the men at the station to hold on, I need to talk to them a second. And he wished he had gotten out in the storm and gone back to them and climbed in the truck and held the baby once more and he wished that he had told Kris and Nadine that he thought they were braver than hell and he wished that he could have been with them for a moment. To see them before they were gone. He believed they were safe. He believed they were going to be taken to a place that would help them all. But he knew that though there was a quick ending, it also meant that there was a quick beginning. And this time their beginning seemed hopeful.

For two days, he had been clean. He had been dry. He had thoughts of others. He had touched and been touched. Sometime during the second night, as he lay still next to her, as he thought of the others, as he replayed his dreams filled with voices and sunshine, he decided that the Jeep and the shoe box could stay right where they were. The road was out in front.

Mariposa stood in the window looking down across the square. It was the evening and the lights had gone out in most of the buildings but the lights had now come on in the few places that stayed open until whenever. The music had started, the clunky sound of an electric guitar accompanied by clunky drums, sounding out into the early night, through the rain that had not stopped. Cohen sat on the bed watching television, trying to figure out when the lull would come, those handful of hours when the rain stopped and the wind fell still, before the next storm poured onto the coast. The sound of another television came from the other room, as Evan and Brisco had been for days hypnotized by the bluish glow from the nineteen-inch screen that picked up two random channels from somewhere, one of them in Spanish.

The bedsheet was wrapped around Mariposa and it had been this way for most of the two days, as they only got fully dressed to go down to the café to eat. She turned from the window and slid herself down onto the bed and leaned against him, her hand across his bare stomach.

He raised the remote and turned off the television. "It's coming. Tonight. The lull is after midnight. Before dawn," he said. "And that's our best chance to make a move."

She raised up from his chest and sat with her back against the headboard. He stood and put on his shirt and jeans. She crossed her legs Indian-style and pressed her fingertips on her knees. "What about the Jeep?" she said.

"I don't care about the Jeep," he said.

"What about the other stuff?" she asked.

"What other stuff?"

"Her stuff. And your stuff. The box." She uncrossed her legs. Held her hands together.

He sat down on the edge of the bed. "It's gone."

"It might not be."

"No. It's gone," he said.

"It's okay if you want it."

"I know it is. And I do want it. But I don't want to die because of it. Not now."

He stood from the bed and walked across the room. Looked out of the window. It was almost dark, gray turning black. A neon light glowed from the corner building down to the right. He shoved his hands in his pockets, thinking about Elisa. He wondered if there was such a thing as rising and living in another world where there was only light and no rain and no pain.

He turned and looked at Mariposa. "There's more than one reason I wanted to go back to the Jeep. And one day I'm gonna tell you what that reason is, but not tonight."

"I've been dreaming about you," she said quickly, almost interrupting him. "You leave and you don't come back." It seemed to leap out of her mouth as if it were something she'd had to fight to hold in.

He sat down on the bed next to her. Outside the voices howled. The music howled. The storm howled. He could see that she had resigned her fate to him. And he thought that maybe he was doing the same.

She crawled off the bed and began to get dressed. He moved across the room and stopped her. "I'm not leaving," he said.

She wouldn't look up at him.

"Mariposa," he said and he waited on her to look at his face. He held her shoulders and waited and then she turned to him. "I'm not leaving. Not without you. Not without Evan and Brisco. Tonight when it calms, we're all getting in that truck and we're all driving out of here and we'll go as far as we can. And whenever we get to where we're going, I'm not leaving you there. But you gotta promise me something."

Her anxious expression relented. "What?"

"I said you gotta promise."

"Okay, okay. Promise what?"

He moved his hands from her shoulders down to her arms and held them carefully. "You won't leave me."

She moved her hands to his. "I won't."

It seemed as if a window had been opened in the room. He moved back from her and she continued to dress. She pulled on her jeans and buttoned up the shirt and pulled a hooded sweatshirt over her head. She sat down on the edge of the bed.

He put on his socks and boots and said that he was going to go out and try and find Charlie and if he couldn't find Charlie then find some gas from somewhere else. Maybe the man in the café can help us out. He put on another shirt and a coat. He stepped through the bathroom and knocked on Evan's door. Evan said come in and he and Brisco were in the bed, the covers over them, watching a cartoon cat chase a cartoon mouse.

"I'm going out for a minute," Cohen said. Neither Evan nor Brisco acknowledged him. So he walked over and stood in front of the television. "I said I'm going out," he repeated. "I gotta find some gas. See if I can find Charlie. After we get back, I need you to help me take some stuff to the truck."

"What for?" Evan asked.

" 'Cause we're leaving tonight. Should be a lull sometime and we're gonna get going."

"You want me to go out with you?"

Cohen shook his head. "No. You stay with him."

"You sure?"

"I'm sure. Relax. Mariposa is in the other room. If y'all want something to eat, go get it. I'd hate for you to miss five seconds of television, though."

But Evan didn't hear the last part as he stared at the light. Cohen shook his head, then closed the door and went out of the room and down the stairs, imagining how good it was going to feel to be somewhere else.

41

The café owner wasn't there, so Cohen went out across the square. He made his way around to the back of Charlie's building but he found the door locked. He beat on it but there was no response and he didn't figure Charlie could hear from upstairs even if he was there. So Cohen set out to find somebody to tell him where he could get gasoline.

Charlie was sitting in the top-floor window and he had watched Cohen come out of the café and over to his building. But then Cohen had disappeared into the alleyway alongside and Charlie decided he didn't want to talk to him right now. He didn't want Cohen to come in there and see what he would see.

The building had been a checkpoint for him and his men for as long as he'd been tracking back and forth with the U-Haul. A handful of folding chairs and a couple of cots and empty beer and liquor bottles littered an otherwise empty space. The hardwood floors bowed and a bathroom in the back sometimes worked.

Charlie got up and looked at the man lying on the cot. He had been lying there for two days, slowly bleeding to death, slower than Charlie wanted. He'd been shot in the low back and through his shoulder and he was lying there dying.

Charlie had promised to find him some help but they both knew there was none to be had. The first day Charlie had tried to talk him through it with the promise of that money-filled trunk at their fingertips. How there were fewer people to split it with now. I can't help they came from all sides like a bunch of goddamn fleas. You know they all been sitting and waiting for us anyhow. That backhoe is the key to the promised land. Another five minutes and we'd have been gone. One more shot is all.

Otherwise, Charlie had sat in the window and watched the storm, trying to figure out how he was going to get back and dig again with no men. He thought about Cohen but knew it was a lost cause. He thought about recruiting from the crowd below but he figured he might as well go ahead and cut his own throat now and save them the trouble. He had worked too hard already, dug too many holes. He wouldn't let the scavengers beat him to it.

He sat in the window and Cohen reappeared along the sidewalk, stopping here and there and talking to someone. Then moving on again. Charlie had always wondered about Cohen and he wondered about him now. Why did somebody like him who didn't have to stay down here stay down here? Didn't make sense to someone like Charlie. He'd tried every time he'd seen Cohen to get him to come and work for him. If you're gonna be down here, at least make a damn dollar, he'd tell him. At least be the king. No sense in living life with your head tucked between your legs, waiting for your own ass to get blown off. Hell, even your daddy knew how to turn a quarter into a dollar.

He was initially surprised that Cohen would turn him down, but then he came to accept it as routine. It was part of the trips below, part of Cohen driving to the spot, part of Cohen picking out what he needed, part of Cohen paying Charlie for what he took. And Cohen had been a nice tipper and that usually ended the conversation with Charlie happy and unconcerned about Cohen's well-being. Cohen handed him a hundred-dollar bill, said keep the change, Charlie would quit bugging him about why he did what he did, and see you next time.

He always handed me a hundred-dollar bill, Charlie thought. Never wanted nothing back.

He stood from the chair and Cohen had moved out of sight, along the sidewalk underneath the window.

He always handed me a hundred-dollar bill. And then he heard Cohen making fun of the backhoe. He heard Cohen joking about the fool's gold and treasure maps and the insanity of digging random holes in random spots underneath hurricane skies. He heard Cohen say you'd have to be insane to get your ass shot over something that ain't there. I don't care what nobody says, there's no buried money along that beach or next to those casinos. And you'd be better off sticking to the day trade than ducking bullets on a backhoe. I'm telling you.

Over and over and over, Charlie thought, he said the same things and he always handed me a hundred-dollar bill. Always.

Charlie hurried down the thin staircase and out into the street. He spotted Cohen on the opposite side of the square from the café and he cut across the square to get to the café before Cohen. He went in the door and asked the cook if Big Jim was around and she said he just walked in the door.

"Where?" Charlie asked.

She pointed to the swinging door that led into the storeroom in the back. Charlie moved quickly around the tables and he went through the swinging door and Big Jim was sitting in a chair opening a wide rectangular box with a box cutter. The cut-off pool cue was on the floor next to the chair.

Big Jim looked up and said, "Where you been, Charlie?"

"I ain't got time for that. That boy Cohen. What'd he pay you with?"

"Money," Big Jim answered and he opened the box flaps and began to take out sleeves of plastic cups.

"Hundred-dollar bills?"

Big Jim nodded.

"Let me see them," Charlie said.

"I ain't letting you see them. I already spent them, anyway."

"You ain't spent it. I know you got them stuck somewhere and I need to see them."

"I ain't showing you that money or where I put it."

"I bet you will," Charlie said. "You will or I'm done ever running anything down here for you, making any delivery, taking anybody or anything anywhere. You show it to me or the Charlie train don't stop here no more."

Big Jim huffed. Tossed down the plastic cups and got up. "I don't know what damn difference it makes, but come on."

Charlie followed Big Jim around boxes and short shelves to the back of the storeroom. Big Jim slid a stack of boxes to the side and knelt down and pulled up a square piece of floor. Underneath was a small rectangular safe. Big Jim spun the knob a couple of times and opened the door. He reached in and pulled out a ragged envelope, and from the envelope he took out a stack of fifties and hundreds. He handed two from the top of the stack to Charlie.

Charlie smoothed them out flat in his hand. The two bills were wavy from having been wet, but otherwise they were awfully straight and clean.

"That son of a bitch," Charlie said.

42

Charlie stood on the sidewalk and looked around and saw Cohen walking in his direction. Charlie took out a cigarette and lit it. Cohen waved and walked on to him.

"You're just the man I need to see," Cohen said.

"Yeah? I was about to say the same thing," Charlie said. "Let's go in there." He pointed at the café. They walked in the door and Mariposa had come down and she sat at a booth alone. They walked over and Cohen sat down next to her. Charlie stood.

"She with you now?" Charlie asked.

Cohen nodded.

"You sure?" Charlie asked.

"Would you sit down?"

Charlie slid into the other side of the booth.

"I need some gas," Cohen said. "You got some?"

Charlie looked around the café and put the cigarette in his mouth.

"Charlie?"

He took a long drag and then stared at Cohen with an expression of knowing. "I got news," he said.

Cohen looked at Mariposa, then back at Charlie. "About what?"

"About this witch hunt I been on since forever."

"You mean treasure hunt?"

"Whatever you wanna call it."

"Let me take a guess," Cohen said and he grinned. "You know a guy who knows a guy who knows a guy."

"Better than that," Charlie said. He smoked again and then he smirked at Cohen. "I know *the* guy."

Cohen asked Charlie for a cigarette. He lit it and he looked out of the window and then back to Charlie.

"I think you know him, too," Charlie said.

"How would I know him?"

"You know him. I've known him since he was a boy. Used to be buds with his daddy. Watched him ride horses. Watched him play ball. Even gave him a few Santa Claus toys way back when. You'd think knowing somebody like that would make you friends with him. But evidently it don't."

Cohen laughed a little. "That's some theory."

"It ain't a theory. Are we gonna play the game or get to it 'cause I'm all outta patience."

"What makes you think I know where the pretend money is buried?"

"I don't think you know where it's buried, 'cause it ain't buried no more. I think you know where to touch it."

"What I think is this rain is making you crazy."

Charlie finished his cigarette and dropped it in the metal ashtray next to the ketchup bottle. He then leaned to the side and pulled out his pistol and showed it to Cohen and Mariposa. "Put your hands on the table," he said.

"Charlie."

"Put. Your hands. On the table."

Cohen did as asked.

"You too, honey."

Mariposa set her hands on the table.

"I told you I ain't playing around, Cohen," Charlie said and he moved the pistol beneath the table. His eyes were scattered and wild. "I want you to look around. See where you are. There ain't nobody in this café or outside this café that don't need something from me. There ain't nobody around here who wants my truck to stop showing up. There's no law worth mentioning. You're sitting in one of Charlie's towns. I can buy anybody out there for a pint of tequila. So what I'm gonna do is count to five. When I hit five, she's gonna catch a bullet where she don't wanna catch it. In between one and five, you decide if there's something you want to say to me."

"Charlie, come on," Cohen said.

"One."

"Me and you can talk, just put it away."

"Two."

"Cohen," Mariposa said in a shaky voice.

"Three."

"I have it," Cohen said.

Charlie opened up his coat and took out a flask

and handed it to Cohen. Cohen unscrewed the cap and drank and handed it back. Charlie drank and set it on the table. Outside the rain drummed against the awning and more people filed onto the sidewalks. Cohen looked around the café as if there were an answer to his predicament written across the wall.

"How long you had it?" Charlie asked.

"Had what?" Mariposa said.

Charlie laughed. "Hell, you ain't even told your girlfriend? I don't feel so bad now."

Cohen sat still and stared.

"How long you had it?" Charlie asked again.

"Pretty long."

"You little shit. All those goddamn times you knew I was out there and you knew all these crazy assholes were down there digging and shooting and sometimes just shooting and you let me keep on. I oughta blow your kneecaps off right now and make you crawl to it." His jaw was clenched as he spoke and it seemed the pistol might fire at any second.

Mariposa said, "Cohen?"

"Don't say nothing else," Charlie ordered her. He then licked his lips, scratched at his cheek. "You're a curious son of a bitch, Cohen. I'll give you that. Besides being a fucking liar, you're sitting on Fort Knox and living out there all alone like the rest of all those waterlogged weirdos when you could be any damn place you wanted.

All because of what? ’Cause of Elisa? Gimme a goddamn break. I wish your daddy was here right now so he could slap your dumb ass for being so stupid.”

“Don’t say her name again,” Cohen said.

“Don’t start crying.”

“And I didn’t lie to you.”

“Call it what you want but we both know what it is and that shit don’t matter right now anyway because we got real business to get into. The long and short of the real business is that you’re about to get up and take me to it. You and her both.”

“She don’t have nothing to do with this.”

“We’ll call it collateral.”

Cohen shook his head. “I can’t go right to it ’cause I don’t have it.”

Charlie leaned his head back and shook it in disbelief. “Oh God,” he said. “We really gonna keep on like this. Really?”

“I know where it is.”

“Hell yes, you do. And we’re going.”

“It’s down there.”

“That’s bullshit. Ain’t no way you’re up here and it’s down there.”

“It ain’t bullshit. I already told you the other day we had to run out of there when them others showed up and that’s where it is. In the Jeep where I left it when we took out.”

Despite what he felt about Cohen now, Charlie

thought that he was telling the truth. He was too smart to keep lying with a pistol aimed between his legs.

"How much is it?" Charlie asked.

"I never counted it."

"Holy shit. More money than you can count. Always hear people say that but I never heard anybody say it that meant it."

Cohen leaned back. He looked at Mariposa. She stared at him as if unsure who he was.

"What you driving?" Charlie asked.

"Truck. Still need gas."

"I got that."

"But we need to wait, Charlie. It's brutal out there right now."

"It's been brutal."

"Hasn't stopped for weeks. We barely figured out how to get up here."

"I know it's bad and it's getting badder with every drop that hits the ground. Won't be no better time than this minute."

Charlie drank from the flask again. Paused and thought. "She's gonna ride with me in the U-Haul and you'll follow."

"No, hell no," Cohen said.

"Hell yes. If you think I'm piling you two up next to me and driving through this mess then you're the crazy one. First time I look off you'll be on me. She rides with me and you follow. U-Haul's heavy anyhow and we're gonna need that."

"I wanna know what's going on," Mariposa said.

Charlie picked up his cigarettes and took one from the pack and said, "You tell her."

Cohen rubbed his hand at the back of his neck and then looked at her. "In the Jeep I have a lot of money. Money Charlie and everybody else has been looking for. We're going to get it."

"I don't wanna go get it," she said.

"Me, neither."

"I didn't want all my men shot dead, neither," Charlie said. "And I didn't wanna spend the last two years of my life dodging shotguns and hurricanes digging for a pot of gold when your boy here knew where it was. But at this juncture you are both sitting in the world of have to. Hell, I wouldn't worry about it. The way I see it, Momma Nature knows us. She'll take care of it."

He lit the cigarette and stuck the flask back in his pocket, then knocked the pistol three times underneath the tabletop and told Cohen to stand up. When Cohen stood, Charlie checked his coat and pants for a gun. He found the bowie knife and he took if off Cohen's belt and stuck it on his own.

"You can have this back when you deliver," Charlie said and then he waved the pistol at Mariposa. "Now move your ass. I'm ready to go."

"Not yet," Cohen said. "You gotta let me do something first."

"I know that one, son."

"No, I mean it. We got two others with us. You saw them yesterday in here. A boy and his little brother and they're upstairs. I can't run off on them without saying something."

"They'll be all right."

"They'll be all right if we're all right, but what if we're not? It won't take but a second, Charlie. They're boys."

Charlie looked around. Told Cohen to stand still right next to this table. Then he walked to the doorway of the café and looked out along the sidewalk, his head turning back and forth and on his tiptoes some. He saw familiar men standing half a block to the left and he put his fingers to his mouth and whistled and then waved. A moment later two men approached and Charlie talked to them, the pistol in his hand waving in the direction of Cohen and Mariposa. The two men listened carefully and Charlie reached in his front pocket and handed them some money. Then he turned and came inside and the men followed him over to Cohen.

"What are they for?" Cohen asked. The men were young but worn, one a head taller than the other. They were dressed in layers of mismatched coats and smelled and looked like wet dogs. One of them had a nervous shake in his hand and the other had a brown birthmark the size of a dime above his right eye.

“They’re gonna keep watch,” Charlie said.

“Hell no,” Cohen said. “You’re already making Mariposa go.”

“They ain’t gonna do nothing but sit outside the door and wait for us to get back. When we do everybody is free and clear. But I ain’t taking no chances.”

“And what if we don’t get back?” Mariposa asked.

“Then I guess they’ll work it out amongst themselves. You ain’t making the rules anyhow. Now show me where your boys are, ’cause we got business to get on with.”

Cohen and Mariposa went up the staircase first, followed by Charlie and then the two men. Cohen opened the room door slowly and looked in at Evan and Brisco, who hadn’t moved from the bed. Brisco slept with a blanket pulled to his chin and Evan remained locked on the television.

“Evan,” Cohen said.

“Open the damn door and go on in,” Charlie ordered and he pushed him a little.

Cohen and Mariposa entered the room and Cohen walked to the television and turned it off. He told Evan to sit up and when Evan saw the old man come in behind them and the pistol in his hand, he sat up quick and swung his legs off the bed and to the floor.

“Don’t get up,” Charlie told him. The watchmen

moved into the room behind Charlie. "Say what you gotta say, Cohen."

Cohen moved toward Evan and in the dim light of the room, Evan saw the concern on his face. Mariposa moved next to Cohen.

"You got ten seconds," Charlie said.

"We gotta go back down tonight," Cohen said. "Me and Mariposa are going with Charlie to get the Jeep and then we'll be back." He reached into his coat pocket and held what was left of the money. He turned around to Charlie and the men and said, "He better have every damn thing he's got right now when I get back."

"He's gonna," Charlie said.

"Tell them."

Charlie turned to the men and said, "Everything stays as is or you don't get another dime." They nodded. As Charlie spoke to them, Cohen leaned over to Evan, tucked the money under his leg, and whispered, "Twenty-four hours and then do what you gotta do." Evan nodded.

Mariposa walked around the edge of the bed and brushed Brisco's hair away from his face. She tucked his blanket around his small body and then she and Evan looked at one another. An uncertain, concerned, wordless exchange and she thought of telling him goodbye but didn't like what it suggested.

"Time's up," Charlie said.

Cohen mouthed twenty-four hours to Evan and

then he and Mariposa walked out the door, where Charlie stood waving the pistol like an usher escorting guests to their seats. Cohen and Mariposa started down the stairs and Charlie pulled the door shut, told the men to stay put and that the boys don't leave unless the building catches on fire which ain't gonna happen. When the three of them were downstairs, Charlie stuck the pistol in Cohen's back and led him and Mariposa out of the café door and into the night, telling Cohen, "Don't get fancy. It'll be my way or it'll be a bad way."

43

The Line had been official for six months and the two-year mark for Elisa's death was approaching. Cohen had been trying to keep busy. Trying to fend off thinking of her death as an anniversary. One morning he had been outside looking under the hood of the Jeep when he saw the horse standing in the back field. She was brown and her wet coat shined and she wore a saddle but no rider. He put down the socket wrench and wiped his hands. Stood still as the horse looked unsure and he didn't want her to bolt. She lowered her head and grazed, then she looked around, looked in the direction of Cohen, and she made a few steps in the direction of the house.

He walked across the backyard, moving patiently. He stepped over a barbed-wire fence and out into the field. The horse moved again, stopping along a fallen oak tree, her coat the same color as the mound of dirt wrapping the massive roots of the old tree. Cohen stopped. She remained unsure but curious. He whistled and she looked at him. Moved several steps in his direction. He whistled again and held his hands out by his sides, showing his palms. He moved a little closer and so did she and in another careful minute he was an arm's length from her.

He looked her over without touching her. He spoke in a calm voice as he moved around her backside, making sure she wasn't wounded in some way. Water dripped from her tail and mane and she was muddy but didn't appear injured. She wore a saddlebag along with the saddle and her name was engraved on each of them. Habana.

She snorted. Shook her wet mane. He held out his hand to her nostrils and she craned her neck forward. He held his hand there and talked to her and then he reached out and touched her and she accepted it. He rubbed her nose. Ran his hand along her neck. Patted her some. He turned and began to walk back toward the house and he told her to come on but she didn't follow.

"Come on," he said again and whistled. "Let's get your saddle off. Come on. I'm safe."

She turned and looked back in the direction

she had come from, to the jagged tree line along the back field.

"Come on, girl."

She didn't follow. Instead she started walking back the other way.

Now Cohen was the curious one. He wasn't wearing his coat and he didn't have the sawed-off shotgun nearby and he felt like if he went back for either, she would be gone. He wore his rain boots and he thought that was good enough, so he followed her.

She took him back into the trees, moving over or under or around what was left of the cottonwoods and oaks and pines. He stayed seven or eight steps behind her, and she frequently turned to look and see if he was still there. For half an hour they walked and Cohen thought several times of trying to turn her back but she seemed to know where she was going.

It wasn't five minutes when they came upon the body. Habana stopped and leaned over and nudged it with her nose but the body didn't move. On his back were three dark red blotches and three small holes in his shirt. He was laying facedown in the leaves and mud. One arm under him and the other stretched out and his legs crossed. Cohen knelt and felt the man's back pockets but there was nothing in them. He then rolled the man to his side and felt the front pockets and he pulled out a set of keys and a silver

Zippo. He stood up and looked around on the ground for a pistol or shotgun or anything that might come in handy but there was nothing. Habana nudged the man again and Cohen patted her and apologized. He thought that was it, that she would go with him now, but she nudged the man a final time and only then did she continue on.

The day was overcast and windy and there were probably three hours of light remaining. His instincts told him not to, but he followed her anyway.

Eventually the trees thinned and they came to a clearing and he figured they were at least four or five miles from his place. The land was marshlike and Habana stopped to drink the muddy water, then she looked around for him and kept walking. She didn't walk out into the clearing but kept to the tree line, sloshing through the mud and rainwater and in no hurry. He had no idea how long this would continue and he was beginning to regret letting it go this far, but then the tree line extended around to the east and when they moved around the bend, Cohen saw a far-reaching white wooden fence. Some of it stood and some of it didn't but it stretched on and he didn't see the end of it right away. Habana walked toward it and when they were closer, Cohen saw the house.

He wanted her to stop and called for her to stop but she didn't stop. He moved from out in the open and back into the tree line. But she walked casually and Cohen was able to get a good look at the place. It was a two-story Spanish-style house, terra-cotta-colored with arched windows and doorways. A balcony reached around the entire second floor and the ceramic roof tiles seemed intact but for one missing here and there like a lost tooth. A patio stretched out of the back of the house and there was a pool. The house appeared to sit in the middle of the fenced-off property as the white fence lined all sides but was at least a hundred yards away from the house in all directions. A horse trailer and truck were parked in the field to the west side of the house. Cohen wondered why he had never seen this place but he didn't think about it long as two SUVs drove around the side of the house. He grabbed Habana's reins and held her. He whispered to her and she let him lead her back into the trees.

The SUVs drove out toward the horse trailer and truck but continued past and didn't stop until they came to the fence. At the fence line, five men piled out of each vehicle. The back doors of the SUVs were opened and each man took a shovel from the back. Each man put on a pair of gloves, each man went to a fence post, and each man started to dig.

Cohen stroked Habana's neck and watched. He watched for an hour as the men dug in a spot, then moved on and dug in another, working their way from fence post to fence post in an orderly fashion. There wasn't much light remaining in the day and Habana was getting restless. Cohen saw the men were occupied and he and the horse were far off and in the trees, so he felt safe moving. He held Habana's reins and led her and she went with him this time without hesitation.

After walking for a mile back along the tree line and into the woods, as the last of the day disappeared, he stopped and told Habana that this might go a little better if we do it the old-fashioned way. She seemed calm, so he put his foot in the saddle and mounted her and led her home.

The next morning, at first light, they returned.

This time Cohen had the shotgun and a shovel and gloves. When they came to the house, the SUVs and truck were not there. The horse trailer sat in the field.

Cohen waited against the tree line and when he felt certain that no one was there, they rode out to the part of the fence where he had last seen the men digging. What he discovered as he rode along the fence were holes at every post along almost the entire south section of the fence. The holes were a yard wide and a yard deep.

He got down from Habana, tied her to a standing piece of the wooden fence, and then he didn't know why, but he started digging. He added five holes to the long line and then he stopped. His back ached and his hands were sore and it was midmorning. The feeling that the men in the SUVs would be back told him to quit, so he quit.

The next morning he came back before daylight. At the fence line, he noticed that the holes now made the entire length of the south side and there were another ten stretching up the west portion of the fence.

He got off, tied Habana, and went to work. He dug through dawn and then it started to rain and he quit. Riding back to his place, he explained to Habana that he didn't know what the hell was going on but that he was done. My damn back is killing me.

The next morning he was back again. A light rain fell and made him nervous as he dug because he couldn't hear as well if the SUVs returned. Habana seemed unhappy standing in the rain, moving around more than usual and picking up her feet and smacking them down in the wet ground. An hour past dawn, he was wet and hurting and felt a little stupid.

And then the shovel hit something. He was about two feet down and whatever he hit was strong and solid, and as if he had been plugged in, he began to dig at double speed, his imagination and adrenaline both racing, and in a matter of minutes he had uncovered all sides of the trunk. It was wide and broad, larger than any of the holes that had been dug. He didn't bother trying to dig it out but instead he removed the dirt from the top and from around its sides. When he was done, he lay down on top and it was as long as he was, and he stretched out and grabbed the sides with his arms straight. He got up and stood on top, thought quickly about what to do. The trunk latch was padlocked and he didn't want to fire the shotgun and risk making a big noise, but he had to. He fired and the lock and latch busted and Habana reared and whinnied. Cohen tossed the shotgun aside, stepped off the top of the trunk, and knelt at the edge of the hole. He reached down and tugged at the top and pulled it open.

He was unsure what to think. He looked around as if it were a joke on one of those hidden-camera shows where the jokesters were waiting to leap out and point at him and cackle hysterically. There were stacks and stacks and stacks. Pretty and clean. Crisp and straight. So perfect, they seemed fake.

He took Habana's saddlebag and stuffed in as much as he could. Then he shoved stacks into his coat pockets and down into his pants and into his boots and anywhere else he could shove them. He mounted Habana and ran her across the field, hurried her through the jigsaw of the fallen trees and limbs, and ran her to the house. He hopped off, took the saddlebag inside and unloaded, then hurried back out, mounted, and ran. He was able to make two more trips and it took until midday. The rain fell steady and Habana seemed to be getting tired but he didn't have half of what was in the trunk.

"One more trip," he told her and they took off again.

This time when they came around the bend of the tree line, the SUVs were there. And the men were there. They were pointing and yelling at one another and he didn't wait to see what they were going to do.

He turned Habana and disappeared.

44

Evan realized that no matter what the old man had said, no matter what had been agreed upon, and no matter what had exchanged hands to make the agreement, it wouldn't be long before the two men outside the door decided to come in and see what they could find. It was a simple message that was delivered by both common sense and by Cohen's twenty-four-hour whisper.

In less than a minute, the world had changed again. One moment he was lying on the bed watching television, with Brisco safe and dreaming next to him. The next moment a man with a gun had pushed Cohen and Mariposa into the room and Cohen had told him they had to go back down and those two will stand outside your door and make sure you don't leave until we get back. Brisco never woke through the exchange and Evan was glad he didn't. But Evan paced the room now, looking at his little brother, looking out of the window, walking in and out of the bathroom, replaying Cohen's words in his head, wondering what the hell.

Twenty-four hours and then do what you gotta do.

A lamp on the bedside table provided low light in the room and the wind had picked up outside and drove the rain into the windows and walls of the buildings on the square. Evan heard the men talking outside the bedroom door but couldn't make out anything they said. Only muffled words in a muffled night but he didn't need the details to know what they were talking about. They were talking about the same thing that damn near every other human being he'd ever known talked about—how much can I get and what's the best way to get it.

He reached between the mattress and took out the pistol that Cohen had given him. He tucked it into the back of his pants and knew he needed to find the other one. He walked through the bathroom into the other bedroom and went to the dresser. The top drawer was the last place he had seen Cohen put it and he opened the drawer but it wasn't there. He wondered if Cohen had somehow managed to have it with him but didn't figure

Charlie was the kind of man to make that sort of mistake. The room was a mess, with clothes on the floor and laid across chairs and the bedsheets and blanket twisted and half hanging off the bed. Evan lifted sheets and picked up and tossed aside clothes, opened the nightstand drawer and the other dresser drawers, looked on the closet shelf and looked between the mattresses, but he couldn't find it. He knelt and looked under the bed at the rifles and shotgun and thought it would take the men about fourteen seconds to find them, and then what would happen?

He went to the window and looked down. They were on the second floor and the awning was not ten feet below the window but Evan was almost certain it wouldn't hold and if it splintered or collapsed then the fall could be much worse. He tried to open the window to get a better look but it was nailed shut. The window would have to be broken and with the sound of the storm it might be possible to get away with that. But then he would have to handle Brisco out of a jagged window onto a rickety awning in a driving storm. The entire scenario kept getting worse and worse.

He walked back into the room where Brisco slept and he looked at the small digital clock on the bedside table. An hour had passed and he didn't believe it would be much longer before they came in. He walked gently over to the door and put his ear against it. They had stopped talking. Evan waited for them to start again.

Nothing. Only the beating of the rain and force of the wind.

He moved his ear from the door and looked down at the doorknob. Above the doorknob he noticed that the latch on the door was unlocked. He turned the lock and it clicked shut.

And then from the other side of the door, a voice said, "That ain't gonna do you no good."

Evan eased back from the door and over to the bed. He took out his pistol and then he sat on the bed, his back against the wooden headboard. Brisco turned in his sleep and grunted some but didn't wake. Evan held the pistol in his lap and watched the door.

45

Cohen couldn't stand being alone. After burying himself, after becoming what he wanted to be—alone with his memories and ghosts of a life—after everything he had done to be alone and remain alone, he couldn't stand being alone now as he drove the truck behind the U-Haul. For two hours they had been moving back toward the coast, the hurricane forceful and gathering strength and the endless black night and the pounding of the rain and the wind and the twisting and turning across the beaten land and all he could think about was how alone he felt and it hurt like a broken bone.

During this solitary time he thought of everything. His life with Elisa and the early days when they were new and how he would quit work early and pick her up and they would drive up and down the coast, drinking beer and talking about all the things they were going to do, and at twilight they would find a pier to sit on where they could eat and drink some more beer and then at dark, before taking her back home, find a quiet strip of beach and lay out towels and lie naked under the empty sky, and when it was all done, kiss good night, anxious for tomorrow and the chance to do it all again.

He thought of the positive pregnancy test he danced around the living room with, holding high like a trophy, and her laughing and saying I peed on that, I peed on that, but him only dancing and twisting and turning like a madman. He thought of the many times he should have cut loose and taken her and gotten out of there, sold the house, sold the land, started over somewhere else and if he would have done that, how she would be alive now and he would be lying in bed with his daughter reading a bedtime story instead of caught in the middle of this impossible night in this impossible land.

He thought of the man he had left to bleed to death when the man was begging him to end his misery and he thought of slitting the stomach of the pregnant woman with the knife his grandfather had passed on to him and he thought of the two he had shot and killed back at the compound and he knew all those things made him something different now. He thought of Aggie and his twisted ideology and he thought of standing in the rain and trying to frame a child's room and he thought of Habana and where she might be and he thought about the shoe box and how the things in it were probably scattered all across Gulfport. He thought of Mariposa and what must be going through her mind and how he hadn't gotten to assure her of anything and did it matter anyway. Would any of it matter and would they even survive the night. He drove closely behind the U-Haul and being alone in the truck chewed at his heart and his mind and he seemed to relive his entire life in those hours and he wondered how in the hell the roads of his life could have led him to this moment. It seemed impossible.

Charlie was taking him places he had never been and if set free Cohen wondered if he could even find his way out of this hurricane. In almost every direction the ditches overflowed the road and the creeks ran the heights of bridges and there were great spaces of water everywhere but Charlie seemed to somehow find a way around. Cohen smoked without cease and the truck headlights and windshield wipers were ill-prepared for such intense combat. The winds rocked the back of the U-Haul and several times Charlie stopped and waited and then went on again but it never seemed to make sense to Cohen because there was only the fierce velocity of the wind and rain and never any ease.

He didn't have a damn clue where they were. He wasn't even certain whether they were driving north or south. Or east or west. In his angst he knocked his head against the steering wheel, against the door window. He pulled at his beard, at his hair. He squeezed at his chest and he smoked and he smoked and he felt so alone. Once when Charlie momentarily stopped, Cohen let his head fall down on the steering wheel and he began to cry and he wished that he had lived a better life so that he could call out for the hand of providence to guide him and half expect a response. He had expected sometime in the night for the lull to come and ease their journey but there wasn't going to be a lull. There was no such thing anymore.

Mariposa had told him that in her dreams he left and didn't come back. He had scoffed at the notion in the dry room but now he felt the possibility of not being there. And he thought of Evan and Brisco and the predicament he had left them in and he wondered how soon it would be before the boys were doing things out of desperation or if they were already. He thought that he should have sent them off with the black Hummer and the women and the baby. But hell no, he couldn't have thought of that then.

He wanted to know anything. What time it was. Where they were. How much strength was left in the storm. Would the Jeep still be there or had someone found it and for some reason found the latches underneath the backseat and opened them and lifted the seat and hit jackpot. Would the night ever end. Would they be blown away. Would they drown. Would they be shot. All he had were questions.

He smoked his last cigarette. The night raged on. They continued like patient water beasts migrating toward their violent ocean home. Another hour of Charlie making turn after turn. Another hour of going nowhere. All around was black and floating countryside and they were on a road that was not much wider than the U-Haul. The brake lights of the U-Haul shined and it came to a stop and Cohen knew it was another dead end. The hazard lights began to blink and this was the sign for Cohen to come get in the U-Haul so they could figure out what to do next.

Cohen fought his way to the U-Haul cab, fought the door open, and Mariposa grabbed and pulled him in and he fell across her lap. He sat up and she slid into the middle of the bench seat between the men.

"Told you we'd make it," Charlie said.

"You okay?" Mariposa asked and she held on to his arm.

"There's no way in hell to do this, Charlie," Cohen said, catching his breath and sitting up straight. "You can't hardly stand out there."

"It'll be all right," Charlie said. He held the pistol in one hand and the flask with the other.

"Shit. You been drinking all this time?"

"All this time," Mariposa said.

"This is all so damn insane."

"Not yet it ain't," Charlie said. "We got a little ways to go."

There was a gust and the U-Haul swayed and Mariposa squeezed Cohen's arm with both hands.

"We're gonna have to wait on this wind," Cohen said.

The rain pelted the windshield and the headlights gave little notice and something big smacked against the side of the U-Haul and they all jumped.

"All we gotta do is get right over there and it's home free," Charlie said. "About a mile up is one left turn and then another two or three miles to 49." He pointed out in front with the flask. At the end of the headlight beams there was a bridge that was being washed over by an overflowing creek. The water rushed across the bridge and tree limbs and mounds of leaves and chunks of earth moved along with the strong current. The bridge rails were low and they leaned and wobbled with the flow, beaten nearly to death.

"No way," Cohen said. "That thing's about to go. You can't even see it."

"You can't see it but it's there. I been over this one before."

"Then why'd it take so long to get to it?"

" 'Cause it ain't my first choice."

"We can't go over that," Mariposa said.

"Can and are."

Cohen put his hand on hers. Squeezed a little. "You just remember, Charlie, if we get washed away, you don't get the money."

Charlie drank from the flask. Thought about it.

The U-Haul rocked constantly in the wind. The creek seemed to rise even farther as they watched and no one could see the bridge or the other side of it.

"We got to wait," Cohen said. "It's a goddamn river."

"Please," Mariposa said.

"Just hold on," Charlie answered.

"Hold on, hell," Cohen said. "Back the hell up and let's either sit or go another way."

"It's fine."

"Goddamn it ain't fine," Cohen yelled and reached across Mariposa and shoved the old man. Charlie dropped the flask and shoved back and they began to wrestle with Mariposa in the middle and she yelled at them to stop and she yelled at the fierce night. They grabbed and pulled at one another and then Charlie stuck the pistol against Cohen's ear.

"Don't do it again, Cohen. I swear to God," Charlie said.

Cohen didn't move. Mariposa went quiet.

"Now settle down. Everything's fine."

"It's not fine," Mariposa said.

"Shut the hell up."

She wrapped her arms and rocked back and forth and watched the water run across the bridge and the road.

"Put it down," Cohen said, the tip of the pistol touching his earlobe.

"I'm gonna put it down," Charlie said. "And no more shit. You got it? We're gonna sit. Watch. And then we're going across that bridge."

He removed the pistol from Cohen's ear and Cohen sat back. Mariposa leaned over on Cohen and dropped her head in his chest. She began to talk, "God get us out God get us out God get us out."

"Don't do it," Cohen said with a tight jaw and Charlie ignored him.

Cohen lowered his head and leaned on her. His forehead resting on the back of hers. His teeth clenched in frustration. Another swoon and the U-Haul seemed to want to give way and Cohen realized he had done it again. He was going to lose another one in a place where she shouldn't be.

One side of the bridge railing bent way back, then broke free and disappeared into the current. Charlie turned to him and in the dim glow of the dash light his drunk, crooked grin seemed like something out of the underworld. He raised his pistol to remind Cohen that he hadn't put it down.

Cohen shook his head slowly.

Charlie said, "Hang on." He shifted the U-Haul into drive and stomped on the gas.

The truck plunged into the current and they felt the surge immediately. "Goddamn," Charlie said, surprised by its strength and he dropped the flask and gripped the steering wheel tightly and the truck pushed to the left and toward the missing rail. Charlie stayed on the gas and the engine made a gurgling noise and then the bridge buckled underneath them and the back of the U-Haul dropped and the three passengers were suddenly reclined and looking up, as if someone had pulled a chair out from under them. Mariposa screamed and Charlie kept turning the steering wheel as if that somehow mattered. The back end swung around but the front end was caught on something and kept the truck from taking off downstream. Water poured into the floorboard and the head-lights looked up into the vicious sky and Cohen shoved Mariposa back and leaned across and shattered Charlie's nose with his right fist. Charlie roared like a wounded bear and he dropped the pistol onto the floorboard. Cohen went for it but then the U-Haul bed broke loose from the cab and flipped on its side and was gone with the current.

The cab fell to the driver's side and Mariposa and Cohen were on top of Charlie, their bodies frantic and tangled and fighting at one another and Charlie's nose bleeding freely. The pistol was there somewhere but Cohen went for Charlie instead and in the frantic mass he got his hands around the old man's throat and he squeezed and Charlie's arms were pinned by Mariposa's body on top of him and Cohen's body on top of hers. Cohen squeezed and tried to hold on as the cab dislodged and floated downstream and then it crashed into something and they all banged against the windshield and dashboard. Cohen's hands came off Charlie's neck but Charlie was hurt and spitting and coughing. The rushing water rocked the U-Haul and Mariposa and Cohen fought to get their bodies turned and their heads up and Charlie stayed pinned against the door. Mariposa got her feet on Charlie and stood on him and was down and grabbing at him again when the pistol fired. Cohen reared and expected to feel a burn somewhere but he didn't and then he grabbed at Mariposa and expected her to tumble but she didn't. Cohen got on his knees and he reached for Charlie but Charlie's body had gone limp and he wasn't fighting anymore. Cohen grabbed Charlie's wrist and found the pistol in his hand and a bleeding hole underneath his chin. He took the pistol from Charlie's dead hand and the water rushed into the cab and by the time he and Mariposa pulled themselves together and realized what was going on, the cab was half filled with water.

Cohen set his feet on the steering wheel and he held Mariposa around the waist. She was panicked and crying and he said be quiet, be quiet, just be quiet. Their heads were at the passenger door and the water was to their waists and rising and Cohen pushed at the door but it wouldn't open. He said help me and they pushed together, grunting and crying out, but they couldn't get it open and the water was at their chests now.

He told her to stop and put her head down and he fired the pistol twice and shattered the window and glass exploded and fell around them and so did the rain.

"Get out," he told her and he lifted her by the legs and she climbed up and out of the window. The wind nearly pushed her off and into the surge but she held on. Cohen dropped the pistol and reached down in the water for Charlie. He felt around and pushed open his coat and got his hands on Charlie's belt and he found the bowie knife. He jerked it from Charlie's belt and raised up and stuck it into his coat and then he pulled himself up and out. They lay flat across the door, and Cohen realized that the cab was stuck against a fallen tree. Somehow the headlights still shined and he saw that the tree might stretch across to the bank. The water rose around the U-Haul and the rain came like bullets. Mariposa slipped and screamed and was nearly gone and he reached out and grabbed her by her long, beautiful black hair. He held on to the truck door through the broken window and pulled her hair and her legs were in the current and he fought to hold on and she got her hands up and grabbed his wrist and they managed to get her back up onto the cab door. They put their heads down and hooked their arms inside the door and held on like hell.

Cohen screamed, "Get on the tree! Crawl across!"

The truck swayed and seemed like it might be ready to go again and he helped Mariposa get to her feet and she fell forward and onto the broad tree trunk. Cohen got to his knees and got up and did the same. That way, he screamed and she turned and wrapped her arms and legs around the tree trunk and began to nudge along. Cohen was right behind her and they kept on, little by little, until they saw the tree roots and the ground out behind them. Jump! Cohen yelled and Mariposa went as far as she could along the trunk and then she got on her knees, on her feet, and dove over the edge of the clump of roots and disappeared. Cohen followed her over and they were not out of the water but they were out of the flood and they helped each other to their feet and they trudged through the knee-deep water. When they came to the end of it, they collapsed, lying on their stomachs, their faces buried in folded arms, waiting for someone or something to show them mercy.

46

Underneath Evan's window was where the awning first came loose and with a loud crack and then a metal groan it ripped from the brick building facade and twisted away in the night. The stragglers outside had run for cover and the wind howled through the square and piece by piece the awning was torn away and it slammed against buildings or flew through windows or shot off into the dark. As if signaled by the rise in the storm, Charlie's men kicked the door and splintered the frame and came into the bedroom.

In the passing hours, Evan had sensed the storm gaining strength and he had awakened Brisco. Brisco whined and moaned about it but Evan told him he had to get dressed. Get your shoes and your coat and hat. Don't argue with me just do it. When the men came into the room, Evan and Brisco sat on the bed, Brisco crouched close to his brother, scared of the storm and scared that Evan had told him they might have to get out of here and scared that Evan couldn't say where they would go if they had to get out of here. Evan wore his coat and he held his hand inside, gripping the pistol.

"You ain't got to get up," said the man with the birthmark. The other one came in behind him and went looking in the closets and dressers, digging into the pile of clothes in the corner and disgusted to find nothing. He checked the other room while the man with the birthmark stood at the foot of the bed and stared at Evan. He had the stare of the sleepless and his upper lip quivered.

"Holy hell," the other man yelled from Cohen's room. "Hit the damn jackpot."

"What you got?"

"Got rifles and lo and behold a sawed-off shotgun. Holy hell."

"Bring them on in here."

"Hell, just found a pistol, too."

The short man came into Evan's room holding the rifles and shotgun and several boxes of ammunition across his arms. Cohen's pistol was stuck in the front of his pants.

"I damn well knew you had some shit in here," the man said as he took a Remington and a handful of cartridges and loaded it. Then he held it on Evan.

Evan hugged at Brisco and said, "Don't point that thing at him or me. You got what you want now go on."

"We ain't got it all," said the man with the

birthmark. Outside a piece of the awning smacked against the building and busted out a window in Cohen's room. Brisco shouted and they all jumped.

Evan sat up and yelled, "Hell you don't. Go on."

"He's right. Let's get on," said the short man and he moved toward the door. The other man grabbed him and said, "We ain't going nowhere."

"You ain't staying here," Evan said.

The rain and wind rushed through the broken window and the man said, "Not going out there for damn sure. Besides you got something else. I saw your boy slide a little something to you. Where's it at?"

"I don't have nothing."

Brisco yelled, "He don't have nothing."

"Shut up."

"Let's just get," said the short man.

"Where is it? A few dollar bills?" the man said and he shoved the rifle toward Evan. The wind howled through the broken window.

"You damn coward," Evan said.

The man with the birthmark looked at Evan surprised, then looked at his partner and laughed. He turned back to Evan and said, "What'd you say?"

"You ain't shit without that gun."

"Don't matter what I am without it, 'cause I got it."

"Come on, dammit," the short man said.

"I ain't coming on. You got any money?"

"Charlie's gonna give us some more."

"You and me ain't never gonna see Charlie again. This boy's got a wad and I'm getting it," he said and he aimed the rifle above Evan's head and fired, a spattering of plaster raining down on Evan as he ducked across Brisco. "Where is it?" the man said.

Evan stayed across Brisco. Didn't move or answer.

The man lowered the rifle closer to Evan and fired again and this time the shot pierced the wall not a foot above Evan's head. "Jesus Christ," the short man yelled.

"Shut up," the man said. "I don't wanna shoot your ass with your boy here but I ain't asking but one more time then I'll find it on your dead body. Where's it at?"

"Okay. Okay," Evan said. "Just don't shoot no more." He lifted his head off Brisco, who was crying now with his face down in the pillow and his hands pressed over his ears. Evan looked at the short man with his arms out like a rack, holding the other guns. The man with the birthmark lowered the rifle a little and the wind howled through the square. Evan sat up and looked down inside his coat and said, "Here, you can have it all." He then pulled out the pistol and shot the man with the rifle in the shoulder and he fell back out of the doorway, and then he fired on the other man, who was dropping his armload and reaching for Cohen's pistol. Evan hit him in the rib cage and he went down. Evan was out of the bed and on his feet and the man with the birthmark was trying to get back up and fire again but Evan hit him again in the chest and he went back flat and motionless. Brisco screamed with each shot and tried to burrow into the mattress and the short man got to his knees and was pulling the pistol when Evan shot him again and he fell back with flailing arms.

Brisco screamed and the storm raged. Evan's hands shook as he held the pistol on the men. He moved closer and nudged the short man with his foot. He didn't move. Cohen's pistol was on the floor next to him and Evan nervously bent down and picked it up. Then he stepped out of the doorway and nudged the man with the birthmark and he was dead, too. Evan put both pistols in his coat pocket and he was shaking and light-headed. He knelt down to pick up the other rifles but he couldn't calm down, so he tucked his hands under his arms as if to force them to be still. He squeezed his eyes shut and took heavy breaths and hurried to gather himself so he could get to Brisco.

He only gave himself seconds, and then he pulled out his hands and for some reason blew on them. Then he grabbed the Remington and the other rifles and Cohen's shotgun and took them into the other room. He set them on the bed and the rain was blowing in the window and glass was scattered across the floor. He went back to Brisco and he sat down on the bed and pulled the boy to him and held on. It's all right. It's over. It's over. It's all right.

Then he heard footsteps above. Big, pounding footsteps. Then he heard a door open and the footsteps move to the top of the staircase. A voice yelled, "I don't give a damn who's down there but I'm coming and shooting first and asking second!"

"Don't shoot!" Evan yelled back. "It's over!"

"I'll decide it," Big Jim called. He came down the staircase, careful seconds between each step. When he was down on the second floor, he stepped across the men and the slow spread of blood in the doorway and then he looked at Evan and Brisco. Big Jim wore overalls with no shirt underneath and only one shoulder strapped. He held a shotgun pointed from his hip, but he let it down when he saw the boys. He shook his head.

Brisco sat up. His face was red and he wiped at it with the bedsheet. Evan started to speak but an explosion-like crash sounded below as the storm hurled something through the large café windows. Big Jim jerked with the big noise and disappeared down the staircase.

"Stay here, Brisco," Evan said as he went to get up to go with Big Jim. But Brisco held on to his coat and was pulled across the bed. “Don’t leave me!” he yelled.

Evan grabbed his little brother, lifted him to his feet, and stood him on the bed. “You got to stop crying. Okay? I ain’t going nowhere I swear it. You got to stop crying and yelling. It ain’t easy but we got to.” He wiped the boy’s face with his hands as Brisco huffed and tried to suck it in. “Don’t look at nothing, Brisco. Just look at me. Look at me.”

Brisco put his eyes on his brother and Evan told him to count. Start counting and see how high you can go and look at me. Brisco nodded and said, “One.” Then he stopped.

“Keep going. How high can you get? Count and calm down. Come on.”

The boy started over with one, then moved to two, three, and he continued. Evan held him by the arms, waited until Brisco had reached seventeen, eighteen, and then let go of him and backed away, over to the dead men.

“Look up,” Evan said. “Watch the ceiling and keep going. I bet you can’t go to fifty.”

As Brisco looked up and counted, Evan grabbed the man with the birthmark by the ankles and dragged him through the bathroom and into the other bedroom, leaving a trail of red as if the room had been crossed by a bloody mop.

“Keep going. Eyes up,” he called out to Brisco as he returned to the doorway. Brisco was somewhere in the thirties and back to the twenties, confused but trying to make it work. The other man was heavier and Evan had to wrestle him around to get turned where he could drag the body, but he managed and laid him next to the other one in a sloppy, bloody mess. He took a blanket from the bed and covered them and then gunshots sounded out across the square.

In the other room, Brisco lost count and screamed, “I can’t do it no more.”

47

They lay in the mud, still and submissive. Mariposa moved underneath Cohen and he lay mostly on top of her, their faces down, their heads rested on folded arms. The headlights from the U-Haul had gone out and all was black. The rain beat them, the wind swooshed through the remaining trees along the creek bank, and they could only hope that nothing came crashing down on them. It was as if they were being returned to the earth, driven into the ground by the force of the storm, their stiff bodies less skin and bone and more mud and root with each passing moment. Mariposa tried to think of colors, of reds and oranges and yellows and greens or anything that would strike against the black canvas of the world that she saw when she closed her eyes or opened them. The colors came and went and she tried to imagine brilliant stars and a crescent moon but nothing would stay.

In a couple of hours, the black world weakened. Cohen got off her, got to his knees, and helped her do the same. They climbed to their feet holding on to one another.

In the morning gray, they headed back toward the collapsed bridge. The flooded creek raged on and the truck cab had become dislodged from the tree sometime during the night. The trees thinned and disappeared and the wind blew at their backs and they walked methodically with hunched, depleted bodies and rain-soaked souls. Sometimes they stopped and knelt and then encouraged one another and then rose and walked again. They had been washed along in the cab much farther than it seemed and once or twice they wondered if they were going the right way. They had been flipped and tossed and turned and spun and it would have been easy to lose sense of direction. Cohen said, "Let's give it another minute or two and if we don't see the road and the other truck, we'll turn around."

The storm had not passed on but had relented some. The rain had eased with the dawn and the winds had also given way and no longer threatened to push them to the ground. They helped one another along another quarter mile and then Cohen said, "There it is." At first sight, Mariposa buckled and dropped to her knees. Cohen went down with her, telling her, “It’s right there. It’s right there.” She nodded and knew it was right there but it seemed to her that the sight of the truck was simply a prolonging of the end of things.

“I can’t,” she said.

He understood but it didn’t slow him. He stood and moved behind her and lifted her underneath her arms. Her rag-doll legs wouldn’t take her weight and Cohen yelled, “Come on, goddammit. We ain’t doing this shit right here.”

He shook her and she planted her feet and twisted from his grasp.

Cohen pointed and said, “Let’s go. You can cry in the truck.”

“I ain’t crying in the truck.”

“You’re not crying here, either.”

“I know it,” she said and she stood taller and moved again, walking faster. Cohen followed and her energy rose as they splashed across the flooded fields with high knees, fueled by the disgust of having to keep on.

When they made it to the truck, Cohen helped Mariposa in the passenger side and then he went around and got behind the wheel. They sat and slumped. The adrenaline gone. The hunger and thirst and weariness and disgust still there.

Cohen looked at his hands. The skin was tender from so much water. Hers were the same. Mariposa stared blankly at the windshield, her arms dropped at her sides. Trails of water from their clothes and bodies ran across the bench seat of the truck, down their legs, and across the floorboard. It was as if they were melting. They sat and the water ran from them and their bodies seemed incapable of movement. Their minds incapable of thinking about anything other than rain and thunder and wind.

They sat with the earliest, dullest light of day. Cohen moved first. He opened the truck door and stood outside and peeled off his jacket. He tossed it in the back of the truck and got in. Mariposa sat up and leaned forward and he helped her get her coat off and he dropped it on the floorboard. She fell over then and lay across the bench seat with her hands folded in prayer and her head resting on them. Cohen leaned on the door with his head against the window. They were both out within seconds.

The storm had ravaged what was left of the town. Storefronts were blown out and the awning had been torn from the square buildings and landed in trees and in upstairs windows. Water had stopped draining and was pooling shin-deep across the square and across the sidewalks, and trash and tree limbs and liquor bottles and clothes and dead animals and God knows what floated in the water. The water had crept into the buildings and covered floors and was slowly rising as the rain kept on.

Evan and Brisco had spent the storm in the storage room of the café, sitting underneath a stainless-steel table with thick legs. Big Jim had sat along the back wall of the café, shotgun pointed where the windows used to be, waiting on them to come as soon as there was the slightest break.

The slightest break came with daylight. A stiff wind and the heavy rain continued but it wasn't the part of the storm that scared anyone. Heads began to poke out of windows and out from behind doorways and around the edges of alleys and what they discovered was access. Soon there were packs of them going into buildings and coming out with whatever they could carry. Furniture and picture frames and toilet seats and boxes they hadn't even opened to see what was inside. The looting came with howls of victory, as if the discoveries were of priceless treasure that could dictate fate and not worthless remnants of a once normal life.

Some of them carried ax handles or bedposts and those who were armed finished off the shards of windows or busted out the windows that remained. Doors were knocked open and the crowds filed into the buildings and up onto the second and third floors and they threw chairs and tables out of the upper windows and they smashed and they took what they wanted and they fought one another and everyone seemed to have given up except Big Jim, who sat with his shotgun and fired over their heads if they took as much as a step toward the café.

But then he changed his mind. He called for Evan, and Evan and Brisco came out of the storage room. "Get on over here," Big Jim said and waved them to stand behind him.

A man with a bleeding forehead peeked around the café door and Big Jim fired and the man splashed down onto the sidewalk and scurried away.

"I'm done," Big Jim said. "They can have it. I got a safe back there in the storage room and I'm going to it then I'm the hell outta here. You two can come along if you ain't got nothing better."

Evan looked out of the windows at the craziness. He looked down at Brisco. "I'm supposed to be waiting on them to get back," he said.

"Get back from where?"

"Down there. They went back down late last night."

"Holy shit," Big Jim said. "If they ain't floating somewhere they might get back but how long you supposed to wait?"

"Twenty-four hours."

Big Jim huffed. "I ain't waiting that long. I don't have enough shells."

"I got some upstairs," Evan said. "Some rifles, too."

"I don't plan on being here at dark. I've had it. This place has been waiting to sink into the ground for a while and it just might before night. It'd be God's own grace if it did."

Evan sat in a chair and put his head down. Brisco sat beside him. Evan rubbed at his eyes and tried to believe that Cohen was alive and coming back for them. He lifted his head and said, "Where you going?"

Big Jim shrugged. "I'll know when I get there."

"What if we leave and they come back looking for me and him?"

"It won't take but about a minute to look around and figure you made a run for it."

Evan dropped his head again. "Shit," he said.

"Shit," Brisco said.

"Your call," said Big Jim and he fired again out the window just for the hell of it. "I'm running upstairs and getting shoes and then I'm in and out of the safe and then I'm gone. You got a minute to think on it."

He handed the shotgun to Evan and Evan took it by the barrel and then Big Jim lumbered up the stairs. Brisco reached out for the shotgun but Evan moved it away and said, "I told you not to touch these things."

"You're touching it."

"It's different, Brisco."

"It ain't fair," Brisco said and he folded his arms.

Evan leaned back in the chair. Stared at the yellowed ceiling. You're right, he thought. It ain't fair.

He was hungry. He knew that Brisco was hungry. At least there was food in the café and that was the beginning and end of his pros-and-cons list. There was no way to know anything but he had to decide. Out in the middle of the square, out in the rain and the wind, three men chased another man who had a bag of some sort tucked under his arm. They surrounded him and he wouldn't give it up and then they were on him, splashing and yelling and hitting and kicking and the man went down. The bag was jerked away from him but the hitting and kicking didn't stop until he was motionless in the water. All around the square they swarmed in and out of buildings like starving rodents.

Evan leaned the shotgun against the wall and then he looked at Brisco, wishing that his little brother could tell him what to do.

Cohen woke first to a roll of thunder. He wiped his face and looked out at the drowning land. He figured they had been out for an hour, maybe two. But he didn't know for sure. He touched Mariposa's shoulder and shook her some. She woke and pushed herself up on the seat. She looked around like she was confused, but then it seemed to come back to her and she rubbed her eyes and moved her hair away from her face.

"We have to go," Cohen said.

He cranked the truck. He carefully backed up and went forward several times to get turned around without moving off the narrow road. As he put the truck in drive and moved along the road, Mariposa said, "What about the money?"

He tapped the brakes and stopped. "What do you mean?"

She sniffed. Ran her shirtsleeve across her nose. Without looking at him, she said, "You know what I mean."

He put the truck in park and took his foot from the brake. They stared out in front.

"Is it far?" she asked.

"I don't think. But I don't know how to get to it any other way than what we already did all last night."

"You think Evan and Brisco are okay?"

Cohen shrugged. "Don't see how they could be."

Mariposa shifted in the seat. Pressed her hands on her knees. "Maybe we give it one try and then go," she said. "The wind and rain let up some."

"I don't know which way to go. I ain't even sure I know which way to get out of here and back to them."

Mariposa looked at him. "I know. I don't know what I'm talking about but it sounded like there's a whole lot of it. Is there?"

Cohen nodded. Smacked his lips. “Yep. A whole lot. It’d go a long way.”

“So?”

“So what if we get to looking around down here and something happens? What about the boys?”

“I know,” she said.

“It was a bad, bad one. Bad like they warned it was gonna be. Didn’t think it could get worse but it damn sure felt like it and I’d bet them two Charlie put at the door weren’t real good company.”

“I know.”

“So we can’t take any more chances. Right?”

She wiped at her face again and said, “I know. You’re right.”

They sat for a moment, waited for the other to say something that would kill the thoughts of the money. The thoughts of how far the money could take them. The thoughts of the absence of worry that the money could provide. Mariposa lay her head back on the seat and wanted to say, All I want is an end to this, some kind of promise that we won’t keep spinning around in the storms and the filth and the chaos. She hadn’t thought of money hardly ever in her life but now it seemed to stand in front of her and scream, You need me, drowning out the voices of Evan and Brisco.

Cohen put the truck in drive and said, “One loop back around. I got one idea and that’s it.”

“Cohen,” she said.

"What?"

She shook her head. "Nothing. Just hurry."

He backtracked several miles to a crossroads. Half an oak blocked the road to the east and water blew across the asphalt. He turned left and the road seemed to shrink, the wild growth bunched along the roadside and trees pushed over but not uprooted, and the truck was able to slide underneath them, the branches screeching across the hood and top and doors. He manipulated the clustered road for ten slow miles and then he arrived at the left turn he had been anticipating.

"I think there's another bridge down this way. Bigger than that other one."

"Where was it last night?" she asked.

"I don't know. Didn't he say anything when we were right about here?"

"He said crazy shit all night. I quit listening."

Cohen turned left and the road was lined by pastures. In several low places the water had risen across the road but nothing to keep them from continuing. In a few miles, there was a four-way stop, the signs all twisted and leaning in different directions. Cohen continued straight. They passed through a small community. A gas station and a few hollow houses and a one-room brick building that had VOLUNTEER FIRE DEPARTMENT stenciled on the side in white paint. Another couple of miles and they came to the bridge that Cohen was looking for.

The bridge was there. But so was the flood that had washed them away last night. The push of the water had not broken the bridge or its rails but it was at least two feet over the road. Cohen drove the truck right up to the edge of the muddy, rushing water and stopped. On the other side of the bridge was a sign that read 49 JUNCTION AHEAD.

"That's it," Mariposa said.

"That's it," Cohen answered. He killed the ignition. He got out of the truck and took a gas can from the truck bed and emptied it into the truck. Then he walked around to the front and out into the water. Up on the land, the current wasn't as strong so he tested it, walked closer to the bridge until the water rose knee-deep and pushed him and caused him to stretch out his arms to catch his balance. He was another six or seven steps from the bridge and the water surged confidently. Cohen backed out of the water and stood in the rain at the front of the truck. He stood with his hands on his hips and he looked up and down the small, strong river.

He turned and walked back to the truck and got in and he found Mariposa bent over and crying. He reached for her but she shoved his hand away and rose and cried out, "Evan. Evan and Brisco. Jesus, Cohen."

They had both been wrong but she was right now and he hoped to God it wasn't too late, that they hadn't wasted too much time and that the boys weren't being hurt. He hoped to God that the extra minutes and the extra miles wouldn't cost them and he felt like one of them, like one of those who only searched for a moment's weakness and took what mattered right then without the thought of another man. He felt like one of those he had been fighting against. Like one of those he hated. He hoped to God this didn't cost them.

He put the truck in reverse and spun around, then shifted into drive and they were moving as fast as they could move through the infinite storm. Mariposa kept calling out for Evan, telling him they were sorry. Telling him that they didn't mean it. Telling him they were coming. Please hold on.

48

The power of the storm was evident as they tried to get back to Ellisville. Newly fallen trees and freshly flooded roads kept them backtracking and twisting and winding. With each blocked pathway and wasted mile, their anxiety grew stronger. And so did the storm. What little relenting there had been was gone and now the back end came on with a recognizable power.

They had been in the truck for almost three hours as they approached and drove toward the town square and the bedlam showed itself. Somehow black smoke wafted in the air amid the rain and wind. Road signs and big branches and other debris were scattered across the water-covered streets. Cohen drove the truck to the back of the café and the back door was open and through the doorway he and Mariposa saw people inside, fighting over boxes of hamburger buns and bags of potato chips and hitting at one another with giant spoons.

"Oh my God," Mariposa said.

Cohen didn't stop but stomped on the gas, splashing through the standing water, and at the end of the buildings he turned onto the square. They saw the missing awning and the broken windows and the busted doorways and the people running about without regard for the storm and the black smoke coming out of the top floor of a corner building. Cohen drove to the front of the café and slammed on the brakes and the café was filled with scavengers. The square was filled with scavengers. Several bodies lay in the water up and down the sidewalk.

Cohen grabbed the door handle and Mariposa grabbed him and said, "Don't, Cohen."

"Hell, I have to. What the hell else are we gonna do?"

"I don't know," she said and she was scared and he was scared and worse, he didn't have a gun or a bat or even a big stick.

"He can't be up there. Can he?" Cohen said. He looked all around. Slammed his fists on the steering wheel and said goddammit goddammit. The rain beat like a thousand drums and amplified the desperation.

From the sidewalk a cluster of men stopped what they were doing and stared at the truck. Then one of them pointed.

"Cohen," Mariposa said and the men began to run toward them and Cohen put the truck in reverse and spun around, hitting the curb he couldn't see under the water on the opposite side of the street. The truck bounced and Mariposa and Cohen bounced. Her head smacked against the window and Cohen fumbled to get it into drive as they came quick and surrounded the vehicle. They realized Cohen didn't have a gun or he would have used it by now. Ragged, limp clothes and ragged, limp faces and arms held out as if the truck were a crazed animal that needed to be calmed before being caged. Cohen reached over and opened the glove box though he knew nothing was there and then he did the same underneath the seat and Mariposa locked her door as if that would matter. Cohen got hold of a tire iron and he waved it at them ineffectually. But then a series of shots were fired from somewhere and one of the men grabbed the back of his leg and went down and the others turned and scattered.

"Get down," Cohen yelled but Mariposa was looking and spotted the gunman in the second-floor window above the café.

"It's Evan," she yelled and pointed. Evan sat in the window with the barrel of the rifle aimed down at the street. The glass was gone from the window and he knelt on the floor with his elbows on the window ledge. Evan waved them toward the building as Brisco stood behind him with his hands on his brother's shoulders.

Evan leaned out and fired several more shots to ward off any others and Cohen put the truck in drive and jetted across the street. The crowd split as it bounced onto the sidewalk and its front end hit the storefront as it slid to a stop.

"Get Brisco," Cohen told Mariposa as they grabbed at the door handles and hurried out.

Cohen pumped the tire iron at the café as he moved underneath the window and someone called out, "That ain't shit!" There were maybe twenty of them bunched in the café and twice that many along the sidewalk and they immediately began to creep toward the truck.

"Throw me something!" Cohen said and flung away the tire iron. Evan dropped the sawed-off shotgun out of the window just as Mariposa screamed as two women had come up behind her and snatched the back of her coat. Cohen turned and fired into a piece of twisted metal awning that was lodged in the café window. The women let go and dove back into the café. He waved the shotgun at the rest of them and they held still.

"I got the doors jammed up with everything up here and we can't get out," Evan yelled down.

"Jump on the top of the truck," Cohen yelled back.

Mariposa climbed onto the hood and then on top of the cab and held out her arms for Brisco. No no no, he called out, but his feet appeared out the window and then there he came and he fell right into Mariposa. She lost her balance and they slid down the windshield and landed on the hood. She grabbed Brisco around the waist and got them down off the hood and into the truck and then there came the thwack thwack of bullet holes into the tailgate of the truck.

"Back there," Evan yelled and Cohen turned to see a handful of men coming at him around the truck bed. Evan fired three quick shots and one of the men went down and another grabbed his arm and the rest covered their heads and ran. But it seemed like in every direction the crowd was gathering to rush Cohen and in the roar of the rain it was damn near impossible to see who was coming from where. Another thwack and Cohen ducked in front of the truck.

"Corner building," Evan called and he fired across the square at the building where he had seen the white flashes. Cohen's back pressed against the truck grille and he pointed the shotgun at the café.

From inside the truck, Mariposa and Brisco yelled for them to come on, come on. The rain came hard and the others crept closer and the gunshots sprayed.

"Right now, Evan," Cohen screamed. "We gotta go now."

"He's gonna get us," Evan yelled back.

"No, he ain't. Right now."

Evan fired several more quick shots and then he jumped out of the window, rifle in hand, and he crashed on top of the truck cab. He fumbled the rifle into the bed and scrambled after it as shots from across the square pelted around him. He lay flat in the bed and counted to three and he jumped out and raced into the cab with Mariposa and Brisco.

Cohen rose and fired his last shot into the café ceiling and they shrank away. Mariposa pushed open the truck door and he sneaked around the front end and then darted to the door and one more shot sliced through the storm and it caught Cohen and he buckled and fell against the side of the truck.

"Cohen!" Mariposa screamed. Evan climbed out and ran around and tried to get Cohen to his feet. More shots missed them and smacked the truck and dropped people coming out of the café toward the truck. Evan got Cohen's arm around his neck and raised him and Cohen held his hand to his side and half-crawled, half-walked with the boy. The shotgun was left behind and Cohen called for it but Evan didn't stop. He dragged Cohen to the passenger side and Mariposa pulled him in the cab. Evan slammed the door and ran around and got behind the wheel. The crowd waited no more and came running at them out of the café and from up and down the sidewalk, several more being dropped by the hidden gunman but the crowd without fear now and intent on getting that truck.

Evan shifted into drive as they pounded on the hood and sides, savage rain-drenched faces and bony fists and mouths open and screaming. He went hard on the gas and some of them fell away but others clung to door handles and the tailgate and another had managed to get one leg into the truck bed and was dragged along as the truck cut through the flooded street.

"Evan!" Mariposa yelled as she turned and saw the man trying to claw his way into the truck bed and the other hands and heads at the tailgate. At the end of the street, Evan cut hard left and slammed the gas again and the man was thrown from the bed and the heads disappeared from the back, but four clinging hands remained on the edge of the tailgate. When the others saw Evan turn, they began to splash across the square, trying to catch up and hopeful the truck would turn again. Evan did turn again, another hard left, and now the hands were gone and the bodies rolled.

Mariposa said, "That's it, don't stop. Don't stop, Evan, keep straight and don't stop."

He stayed straight and got away from the square, away from the chasing crowd and the scattered bullets. Brisco had curled himself on the floorboard and though they had shaken free, Mariposa looked around frantically to make sure there was no one else attached. Cohen had collapsed against the door, his cheek against the window. They drove on and left the square and the crowd behind and now there was only the rain and they needed much more than that.

Cohen leaned forward and doubled over and Mariposa pulled at his coat and said, "Where is it? Where is it?"

"Holy goddamn," he said and he couldn't catch his breath and he moved his hands from his side. She pulled Brisco up from the floorboard and put him next to Evan and she helped Cohen off with his coat and the bullet hole was just above his stomach. He lifted his shirt and the blood ran from the nickel-sized hole like water.

"Oh Jesus," Mariposa said and in a panic she looked around for what to do but she didn't find any answers.

"What?" Evan asked and he started to pull over.

"You can't stop," Mariposa screamed.

"Goddamn," Cohen said again.

"What!" Evan yelled.

"What do you think?" Mariposa yelled back. "His stomach. Gimme something."

"Give you what?"

"Drive," Cohen said and he bent over and vomited a little on the floorboard. He held his hands over the hole and his fingers and hands and stomach and everything was turning red. Mariposa got out of her jacket and took off her top shirt. She wadded it and helped him back against the seat and she pressed the shirt against the hole.

"What the hell?" Evan yelled.

"Drive," Cohen said again. "And don't stop."

"Where? I don't know where."

"Jesus, Jesus," Mariposa said.

"Tell me something," Evan said.

"Just go as fast as you can," Mariposa said and she was pressing the shirt on the wound.

"Fucking where?" Evan said and Brisco repeated his brother and the child reached his small hand around Mariposa and put his hand on Cohen's leg. Evan drove as fast as he could, which wasn't fast in the strength of the rain and wind and the water-covered road.

"God," Cohen said and sweat gathered on his lip.

Mariposa smacked his cheek and said, "Come on! Come on!" She pressed the shirt and her hands were bloody. Cohen's head fell back against the seat and he smacked his lips. She began to plead with him to sit up, look at me, hold my hand, think about the sunshine, don't be a quitter, look at me Cohen I said look at me, we'll get somewhere, don't think about it, I know it hurts but it won't forever we'll get somewhere so hold on.

He lifted his head and stared at her blankly.

Evan cussed and drove and beat at the steering wheel and the storm wouldn't stop. Mariposa moved one hand away from the shirt and wiped the rain and sweat from Cohen's face with the back of her hand.

He stared at her and they drove the impossible highway. Blood filled his pants and his strength began to leak away. A half hour passed and they kept north and Cohen tried not to slump, tried not to show what he was feeling, but he knew he was slipping. His forehead against the door window and his eyes wide open and his hands on top of Mariposa's hands which pressed the shirt against the bleeding hole. He stared out the window and he heard Mariposa pleading and he heard Evan and he heard the rain and the thunder and the rush of the water under the tires. He heard it all, felt it all. He stared out at the suffering land and then there she was.

She walked along the stone street on the clearest day in Venice. The men turned and watched her long stride. The women outside the shops noticed her as she passed. She walked toward him and sat down at the table for two outside the café. The sun cut across the alley and she moved from the light into the shadow and looked at him and said I don't want to go. On the table was a mask he had bought for her at a kiosk on the Rialto Bridge, purple and black around the eyes and a teardrop on its left cheek and burgundy around the mouth and trailing up in a devilish smile. She picked up the mask and covered her face and her eyes danced and she said I'm getting used to this place. Like I belong here. And he could see that she might belong somewhere like this but he didn't care where she was or where she belonged as long as he was there.

I don't want to leave, she said again and she removed the mask and her face fell, the insinuation of something going away.

"Cohen," Mariposa said and she touched his cheek. "Head up. Come on. Head up. Jesus Christ, come on."

His eyelids were heavy but open and he saw the waiter come out of the café and he brought them espresso. Elisa watched the people along the street and he watched her, the Venice air filled with the chatter of another language and the tink of espresso cups and saucers and somewhere an old man singing. It's weird, she said without looking at him. Me and you have been at the water our whole lives but it feels different here. You are surrounded by the water. She pressed her lips together and he asked her if that was good or bad and she said good. You'd get used to it, he said. And she shook her head and turned to him and smiled and he felt the peace in her.

I will bring you back one day, he told her and he reached for her hand.

"Stay here," Mariposa screamed and she had his face in her hands and was shaking his head back and forth. He looked at her but didn't look at her. "Stay here, Cohen. Stay here, come on and stay here. Come on!"

"What is it?" Evan yelled. "What's happening?"

"Look at me. Look at us. We're getting there. It's all behind now, Cohen. It's all behind," Mariposa said, her voice wavering and his face in her hands and the rain and sweat and blood in tiny rivers down her fingers and wrists and she could see that he was somewhere else. "Cohen. Look at me. Please come on. It's all behind I swear it."

Maybe next time we'll have a stroller with us for you-know-who, Elisa said and he smiled and asked her who she was talking about. It's coming and you know it's coming. We can wait a little while longer but you know that, right? And you might as well get ready but you'll be good at it. Her eyes changed again, from peaceful to confident and excited for the years before them. She grinned and said don't be scared.

I'm not scared. Those things are little and I'm pretty sure I could win in a fight.

A young girl in sandals and a long white skirt came along the street holding an armful of roses. She stopped and held them toward Cohen, said something, nodded at Elisa. He held up two fingers and the girl pulled two from the bundle and gave them to Cohen. He paid her and she nodded and moved on and Cohen held the two roses out to Elisa.

One for the Venice water, he said. And one for the Mississippi water.

She took them, smelled them. Touched her fingertips to the petals.

From a distance, he heard someone calling him but he wasn't sure who it was or where it was coming from and he didn't try to answer.

The sun moved and their shadow had disappeared. The Venetian sunlight brushed the side of Elisa's face, her arm, her leg. She seemed to him like something made of marble, her beauty perfectly sculpted and preserved.

49

Mariposa sat in a bus station in Asheville, North Carolina. The bus station was a twenty-minute walk from the shelter that they had called home for months and she sat in the same spot where she sat each time she waited. Her legs were folded and her bag was next to her on the wooden bench and the ceiling fans clicked as they circled overhead. She thumbed through the pages of a newsmagazine, fanning the pages, enjoying the fluttering sound that they made. A woman with glasses sat behind the ticket counter and talked on the telephone and two men who looked like brothers sat on the other side of the small waiting room. One of them flipped a coin until the other guessed heads or tails correctly and then they swapped and the record was four misses in a row. Outside Evan and Brisco picked up rocks and tried to hit a garbage can they had moved out into the empty parking lot.

A denim jacket lay across the bag and Mariposa wore a sleeveless shirt with ruffles around the neck. The late spring was muggy and windy and there was little need for a jacket during the day but the nights remained cool. She uncrossed her legs and set the magazine on the bench. The magazine cover was a photograph of a man in a suit standing on a sun-soaked podium, red, white, and blue flags flapping in the wind behind him. He made a fist with his right hand, seemed to speak with indignation. She picked up the magazine and turned it over and slid it to the end of the bench.

She looked at the round clock on the wall behind the counter and there was another ten minutes to wait if the bus was on time but no one was certain of the chances of that happening.

She moved her jacket from the bag and opened it. She took out a folded sheet of paper and counted the places she had been. Huntsville, Birmingham, Roswell, Augusta, Athens. The names of thirteen more towns and the addresses of thirteen more shelters remained on the list and she was making her way east for the first time, heading for Winston-Salem. The shelters on her list held thousands of people and stretched from Alabama across to North Carolina, up into Kentucky and Virginia. There were more across on the other side of the Floodlands, over into Texas and Arkansas, but that would have to wait and hopefully she wouldn't need to get across. The shelters functioned out of high school gymnasiums or National Guard armories and served as a way of living for most. Children went to school at these shelters, job training was provided at these shelters, mail was delivered to these shelters. And she was going to go to each one on her list until she found someone that she knew. Somewhere she had a mother and cousins and aunts and she was ready to find them.

She looked out of the glass doors at Evan and Brisco. Thought of the place where they had buried Cohen, somewhere off the road in northeast Mississippi, after they had driven almost three hours with him dead against the door, nobody in the truck wanting to let him go. The rain had eased the farther north they had gone, and they turned off the highway and drove along a side road where there were no lights and they went out into a field.

In the truck bed, Evan found a shovel and he used it to dig a grave while Mariposa sat on the ground with Cohen lying across her lap. Brisco stood strangely quiet and watched his brother dig. When Evan was done, with the truck lights shining on them, they lifted and carried Cohen to the grave and set him down gently. Then they stood there in silence until Mariposa turned and walked away and Evan and Brisco covered him with the dirt. After Cohen was buried, Evan turned to look for Mariposa but she had walked out into the dark and he let her be. He sat with Brisco on the tailgate and they were chilled by the wind but it felt different than the chilled wind of down below. He and Brisco talked and Evan heard her crying out there in the dark but when Brisco asked is that Mariposa, Evan said no. It's only the wind.

After an hour she returned from the dark and they began again.

They had driven east until noon and wound up in Asheville at a shelter that occupied an old department store. A group of women were standing outside the front doors smoking when the three of them got out of the truck. Filthy, exhausted, hungry, skinny. Bullet holes and dents in the truck. Bloodstained clothes. The fragile gait of the weary. One woman had dropped her cigarette at the sight of them. Another said what in God's name is this.

Mariposa folded the paper with the list of towns and stuck it back in her bag.

She rested her hands on her stomach and hoped for a kick. The little kicks helped the day go by and kept her spirit alive and she pushed some to see if that would get them going and it did. A handful of kicks and she talked to him as they came and went, and then he settled again.

The woman at the counter hung up the telephone and she announced to Mariposa and the two men that, believe it or not, the bus would arrive any second.

Mariposa got up from the wooden bench and as she rose the baby kicked again and made her oooh. Her eyes got big and she put her hands on the sides of her stomach and said, "Easy, little man." She took a deep breath and walked to the glass doors and went outside. Brisco and Evan were arguing over the score of whatever game it was they were playing.

There was another kick and she thought of Cohen and the dream that she had in Ellisville about him leaving and not coming back. Thought of the way that he assured her that it wasn't going to happen. *I'm not going to leave you, and you have to promise not to leave me.*

It was the only dream left to focus on as she

had stopped having them altogether, her subconscious nights replaced by sleeplessness, lying on her back, staring at the exposed metal beams of the shelter ceiling, trying to figure out what had been real. She had conjured up his life based on the remnants of it—the trinkets and tokens and letters and his expressions when he was forced to talk about it. But then the illusion she had created succumbed to the intensity of the real man. She had talked with the real man and slept with him and bled with him and she wondered how far he had come toward her. All the way?

She couldn't decide.

Mariposa arched her back and felt the breeze. She was ready for the bus. Ready to go and look again. She folded her arms across her stomach and looked into the passive sky, tangled between all that had been lost and all that had been found.

Acknowledgments

I would like to thank my good friends Andrew Kelly and Steven Woods for their feedback and encouragement through the early stages of this manuscript. Thanks to Kendall Dunkelberg and Bridget Smith Pieschel for supporting me in the neighborhood. The Mississippi Arts Commission and Alabama Arts Council have been instrumental in supporting my artistic endeavors and I am very grateful to both organizations. Thanks to Nicki Kennedy, Sam Edenborough, and everyone at the Intercontinental Literary Agency for their enthusiasm, and to Stefanie Broesigke at Heyne Publishing for getting on board so early. I'd like to say thank you to Matthew Snyder at Creative Artists Agency for his vision and hard work. Thanks to Edward Graham of the Steinberg Agency, whose sharp eye was instrumental in the revision stages. Peter Steinberg, my literary agent, possesses creative vision and the ability to inspire, among many other immeasurable qualities. Thanks, Peter. I want to thank Sarah Knight, my editor at Simon & Schuster, who helped drive this manuscript to its highest level, and then held it up proudly for all to see. Thanks also to Molly Lindley, Michael Accordino, and the team at

Simon & Schuster. To my blue-eyed Mississippi girls, thank you for every day. And, finally, my gracious thank you to Sabrea, who has come to my rescue more times than I can count.

About the Author

Michael Farris Smith is a native Mississippian who has spent considerable time living abroad in France and Switzerland. He has been awarded the Mississippi Arts Commission Literary Arts Fellowship, the *Transatlantic Review* Award for Fiction, the Alabama Arts Council Fellowship Award for Literature, and the Brick Streets Press Short Story Award. His short fiction has twice been nominated for a Pushcart Prize and his fiction and nonfiction have appeared in numerous literary reviews and anthologies. He attended Mississippi State University and later the Center for Writers at Southern Miss, and he now lives in Columbus, Mississippi, with his wife and two daughters.

Center Point Large Print
600 Brooks Road / PO Box 1
Thorndike ME 04986-0001 USA

(207) 568-3717

US & Canada:
1 800 929-9108
www.centerpointlargeprint.com